A TEAM OF FOUR

THE UNSANCTIONED ASSET SERIES BOOK 4

BRAD LEE

PART 1

SATURDAY NIGHT

1

A RELAXING DINNER

Haley sat in the restaurant with her parents, nervously looking around. She couldn't shake the feeling that something bad was about to happen.

For once, the country seemed to face no obvious threats. She should be able to enjoy an evening with her parents. They worried about her. But she couldn't relax.

I have to calm down, she thought. *There's no danger.*

Acting jumpy wouldn't soothe the minds of her family, so throughout dinner, she had pretended she was fine... while keeping her eyes open.

The popular restaurant was filled with well-dressed diners enjoying themselves. It was early February, people were sick of winter, and going out to eat with friends made the cold, dark evenings easier to deal with.

Three weeks earlier, she had returned from her Florida vacation after the team's latest mission and dove right back into work at the Central Analysis Group. Tonight was a chance to break free from searching for threats and spend time with her family.

Her mom and dad sat across from her at a four-top table along the far wall. The crisp white linen tablecloth was splashed with soy sauce that had dripped from one of her sushi rolls.

Haley tried to focus on her father's latest fishing tale and ignore the sense of impending danger.

When did Dad start getting old? He's only fifty-five.

His hair had gone full gray and his face was fleshier than the last time she'd seen him—he'd put on weight.

"I swear it was this big," he said, spreading his hands three feet apart to finish his story. His eyes danced, but Haley believed him. There were no micro-expressions of lying.

I have to let it go. I can't be on duty all the time, looking for lies in the faces of my family.

"But when I removed the hook, it flew out of my hands and back into the lake. Honest to God!" He pantomimed a fish leaping from his hand as he struggled to grab it before it got away.

Haley laughed at her dad's animated telling of the story for a second until a server dropped a wine glass behind the bar across the room, causing Haley to jump. She held herself back from pulling the 9mm from the holster at her hip, carefully hidden from view—and her parents' worrying eyes—by her black fleece jacket.

But both of them caught the movement of her arm before she stopped herself. Between that and her hyper-vigilance, they looked worried.

"How are you doing, kiddo?" her dad asked, concerned and suddenly serious.

Here it comes. The twenty questions about my life—none of which I can answer.

"Doing fine, Dad. Really," she said, pulling her long blond hair back into a ponytail and adding a plain black scrunchie to hold it in place. A middle-aged man at a nearby table checked her out, his eyes lingering, but she ignored him. She was used to strangers staring or asking if she was a supermodel.

"How's work?" Mom asked.

She's desperate to know about the note I asked her to give to the First Lady.

Several weeks earlier, Haley had sent her mother a text via a secure communication app, asking her to write out a message for her best friend —the First Lady of the United States—and pass it to her covertly. The note was then given to the President of the United States, who had done what Haley asked. When he staged the photo op—sledding in the snow on the South Lawn of the White House—it set up a sequence of events that led to Haley and Axe, her retired Navy SEAL asset, assassinating the president of Russia.

We're not talking about that. Ever.

Haley checked the small restaurant's entrances as she debated how best to answer the question.

I have to reassure them without lying... too much.

Just inside the front door, a Secret Service agent—Boyd, she remembered—stood alert and watchful in a dress shirt, slacks, and sport coat. At the back, near the hallway to the restrooms, kitchen, and alley, a dark-haired agent named Claire guarded the room in a nondescript black pantsuit.

Given her mom's close friendship with the First Lady, her parents were provided a protective detail upon request. Not 24/7 security, but Haley had begged them to take advantage of it whenever they were out in public. With what she knew of the country's threats and enemies, the protection couldn't hurt.

"Work is good," she said with a reassuring smile. "Nothing exciting."

Her stomach tightened. She still sensed a threat.

It's my imagination. Stop worrying.

"Honey?" her mom said. Haley had missed a follow-up question.

The noise of the restaurant seemed to fade away as Haley scanned the room again. Neither Secret Service agent looked concerned.

It's nothing. I'm not going to make a fool of myself by jumping at shadows.

Time seemed to slow down as Axe's voice filled her head. "Always trust your instincts," he said, as if he stood next to her.

She made up her mind, snapping back to the full sounds and speed of the restaurant around her. "Do exactly as I say," she said to her parents, looking them each in the eye. She was running on instinct, not conscious thought.

If it's a mistake, so be it.

Another Axe expression, "Better safe than dead," came to mind.

"In a second, I want you to stand up and follow me behind the bar, where you're going to get down on the floor and hide."

Her mom looked scared. Her dad opened his mouth to protest, but she cut him off. "No arguing, no discussion. Ready?" Looking around the room, she saw no enemy, no danger, but she was committed. Taking action felt right. "Stand up now!"

She pushed her chair back too hard, and it fell over. Her parents stood quickly, confused and worried. She guided her mom, then her dad, toward the bar across the room. On the far left, an opening led behind it.

Haley smoothly drew her weapon as she made eye contact with Boyd at the front door. His eyes went wide.

Her mom reached the end of the bar as the front door banged open. A man with a ski mask over his face brought his pistol up, aiming at Boyd.

Haley shot the would-be assailant, putting two bullets into his heavy black parka. White puffs of down feather insulation flew out.

Her bullets pushed the man back, causing his shot to miss Boyd despite the nearly point-blank range.

She didn't have time for a shot to the head. Another man in a ski mask loomed at the door, letting the first man fall to the ground instead of catching and helping him. She shot him as Boyd got his weapon out and put a round in the head of the first man.

Haley shoved her father in the back, propelling him the rest of the way through the bar opening.

Gunshots came from the front door as Boyd shot another masked person coming in.

Claire, the agent at the back door, fired down the hallway, then cried out.

"Stay back there. Stay on the ground!" Haley yelled at her parents as they cowered on the black rubber floor mats behind the bar. The bartender lay near them, his hands over his head.

As Boyd fired at the front, Haley shot down the hallway at two masked figures rushing forward.

They fell, but the door to the kitchen opened and gunfire poured through the gap, forcing her to take cover. She returned fire and risked rushing across the hallway opening to Claire.

"How bad is it?" Haley asked the agent.

"Hurts like hell, but I think I'm okay." Claire switched her gun to her left hand and grimaced from the pain, but she was still in the fight. Her shoulder had been hit, just missing the ballistic vest under her blouse.

More gunfire came from the doorway to the kitchen.

That's covering fire.

Haley didn't even glance down the hallway. Instead, she stuck her gun around the corner, aimed low, and fired until her magazine emptied.

Cries of pain came from the floor where, she guessed, at least one man had been crawling below his buddies' covering fire.

As she reloaded, the restaurant's huge front window shattered.

Claire shot at the man outside, in front of where the window had been, as he racked another shell into his shotgun.

Haley joined in, putting rounds into the man's body and one to his face.

The man fell, dead.

Pistol fire came from the front door and Boyd dropped, landing hard on his back near the hostess podium, unmoving.

Shit.

She had to get him to safety. Whoever shot him would finish him off in a second.

If he's not already dead.

"Cover me!" she cried to Claire.

Haley fired at the latest assailant opening the front door.

She killed him before he could finish Boyd. Gun up, waiting for more men to appear, she grabbed the back of Boyd's suit coat and dragged him to the bar opening, depositing his body next to her father, who looked up at her, his face white with fear.

"Dad—check him out. See if you can help."

Another shotgun blast came from where the window had been. Near the back wall, Claire cried out and her return fire stopped.

That's bad.

Haley popped up from behind the bar. A man kicked the jagged glass at the bottom of the window as he stepped over the knee-high threshold into the restaurant, avoiding the patrons curled into the fetal position on the floor.

His gun swung toward Haley, but she was faster. She killed him with two bullets to his chest and another to his head—easy at this range.

For a moment, there was calm.

Claire was slumped against the wall, struggling to raise her left hand to aim her gun. She had been hit by the shotgun. The only reason she wasn't dead was because of the range—the buckshot had spread, leaving her a bloody mess but without big holes in her body.

I hope her vest protected her from the worst of it.

A head poked around the corner where the window had been but was gone again an instant later. Haley didn't have a shot.

She heard movement from the hallway to the back. When a man in a ski mask looked around the corner, she was ready.

He dropped dead instantly when she shot him in the head.

The restaurant was a disaster. Sobbing diners lay on the ground, hiding under their tables. Glass from the front window was everywhere.

There's one guy out front and one in back—at least.

How many had been sent for her?

She had one full magazine left, plus the backup gun on her ankle. And both Claire and Boyd were out of the fight.

I might not have enough bullets.

2

A QUIET EVENING AT HOME

The Nalen Farm
Rural Virginia

Admiral William "Hammer" Nalen's old farmhouse sat on a small hill in the middle of sixty-five acres of farmland and woods. His nearest neighbors were half a mile away. He had nothing but the crackle of the fireplace and the occasional hoot of an owl to keep him company.

The farm wasn't fancy. The house was over one hundred years old, though he had extensively renovated it, improving its security and energy efficiency. A long, winding gravel driveway led past hayfields, rented to and handled by a local dairy farmer. The home and land were perfect for him. Quiet, peaceful… and secure.

It was his first time alone in a while—ever since saving Senator Woodran's life five weeks earlier. He'd been with her constantly since, first as her security guard and protective detail, then as a friend and confidant, and eventually as more than friends. After a month of rest and healing from her near-fatal gunshot, she'd gone to Washington, D.C. to get back to work in the Senate and he'd come home.

A documentary streamed on the large-screen TV in his den, the sound on low, but he mostly ignored it. His mind was elsewhere, considering the pros and cons of dating—and falling in love with—Senator Woodran. But as occupied as he was, trying to talk himself out of his growing feelings for her, nothing could distract him from the chime of the motion sensor monitoring the driveway. It *dinged* quietly.

Probably the damn deer again, he thought.

The sensors detected movement when an object broke the invisible beam between them. In the fall, a large buck had been wandering the area, looking to mate, frequently tripping the alarm as he walked up and down the driveway. William had raised the sensors higher on the trees lining the path to avoid them being set off so often.

He took a sip of his beer, waiting. Ten seconds later, the chime sounded again. And again after another ten seconds.

It's not the buck.

Deer don't travel in a carefully spaced column.

The chime sounded five more times as William hurried to the gun safe in the corner of the room.

Eight men coming. Two four-man fire teams.

Would there be more?

I would split my men as they approached and ideally have at least one sniper on overwatch.

The men were probably not professional soldiers, who would not have waltzed straight up the driveway or missed the motion detector. Still, facing eight men who knew enough to walk in a well-spaced column was nothing to laugh at.

The safe opened to his code, revealing an assortment of choices.

I have plenty of weapons... but not enough men.

He first slipped on a black sweatshirt over his white t-shirt, then the plate carrier with extra magazines. It felt familiar and comfortable. A 6-inch knife was attached and ready, clipped to the front.

Next, his M4's tactical sling slipped on easily and the weapon dangled exactly where he liked it.

The 9mm pistol holster clipped on the right. The extra magazines matched it on his left waistband.

Finally, the shotgun completed the ensemble. At least, from a weapons standpoint. He slipped the best civilian night-vision goggles money could buy onto his head as he turned off the TV and the lights in the room.

Outfitted and ready to defend himself, he had a crucial decision to make. Should he slip outside and ambush the men coming for him?

There were pros and cons to staying inside. He knew his house and they—hopefully—didn't. He would have the advantage... except for bullets ripping through the walls and killing him once he gave away his location by firing on the attackers.

Or they might just set fire to the house and wait.

Flash-bangs—grenades that emitted a crushing light and sound to incapacitate—would also make quick work of him and would be hard to defend against once he gave away his position.

On the other hand, being outside would provide less cover.

Either way, he faced bad odds and was at a distinct disadvantage.

One of the old sayings came to mind.

'You win every fight you avoid.'

Hiding would be best, but if the enemy was halfway competent, they'd already have men in position to watch the front and back doors. They would have come earlier, through the fields, before the main force of eight men. At least, that's how he would have done it. Two men already set up on the house, two others in reserve or guarding the vehicles, plus the eight coming up the driveway.

He hoped the attackers didn't know about the old, narrow crawlspace connecting his root cellar in the basement to the barn twenty-five yards away.

If I can make it to the barn unseen, I have many more options.

He smiled in the darkness, his hallway clear as day in the green glow of the NVGs as he made his way quickly to the basement. His grin was feral, dangerous—the look of a tiger when it is assured of its next meal.

They should have brought more men.

3

A CABIN IN THE WOODS

Alex "Axe" Southmark's Cabin
Rural Virginia

Axe had been awake a few hours after getting back to his normal sleep schedule: in bed around eight in the morning, up at four in the afternoon.

The recent vacation was wonderful... but sleeping during the day still feels natural after all my years in combat, he thought.

Predators hunt after dark. As a retired Navy SEAL, it's what he was. What he'd always be. Enjoying a relaxing few days along the beach or by the pool was one thing, but he was conditioned to prefer the night.

He sat in his small office, which did double duty as the guest bedroom. He had a nice view of the cabin's backyard—or would have if the sun hadn't set an hour before. Only the large computer monitor lit the room as he clicked through pictures from the Florida vacation.

Blurry—delete.

Decent—keep for consideration later.

Excellent—mark it five stars.

He'd been at it since going for a six-mile run as the sun set, then lifting weights once he returned. Haley and her team were still working on why the Mexican drug cartels were going broke, but so far had nothing to go on. Which meant no mission for him. He clicked to the next picture.

There—that might work.

The photo was of Haley's new boyfriend, Derek, taken from behind as he stood on the stern of the fishing boat in the Gulf of Mexico, off the coast of Key Largo. He was silhouetted against the sun. His fishing line shimmered as he reeled in an Atlantic sailfish.

The image wasn't magical enough to sell in Axe's next art show, but he could frame it and give it to Derek.

Suddenly, his senses tingled. Something was wrong.

He shut off the bright monitor, plunging the room into darkness, and hurried out of sight of the window.

Axe sensed danger, but it was... off. He couldn't put his finger on it.

What's going on?

With his back pressed against the wall next to the window, he extended his senses, probing the darkness around the cabin.

Nothing.

He heard only the normal evening sounds of the woods. A light breeze made the trees move. Far in the distance, a jet passed overhead, but there were no other manmade noises. Nothing crunched the dusting of snow in his yard.

What could he have sensed?

A deer?

No, he might be aware of them if they approached the house, but his intuition wouldn't interpret the local fauna as a danger.

It felt like the time he'd missed a mission because of a horrible flu bug he'd picked up. While he lay in bed, too sick to move, his Team had run into trouble. Through his fever and delirium, he'd known they were in danger—and he wasn't there to help.

That has to be it. Haley—or maybe Nalen—is in danger.

As soon as the thought hit him, he knew it to be true. And as strongly as he felt it, he suspected it wasn't one or the other of his partners—his friends.

I bet anything it's both of them.

He moved to his gun safe and started gearing up. Plate carrier with lots of ammo. Pistol at his side. M4 slung across his muscular chest. Night vision goggles on his head, his dark hair—with more and more gray strands each month, it seemed—short enough to not get in the way.

Ready for battle.

I'm too far from them to help... but if they're in trouble, I probably am, too.

4

TIME TO FIGHT

Ryuji's Asian Fusion Bistro
Alexandria, Virginia

The assailants had learned from their dead comrades whose bodies were going cold at the front door of the restaurant and in the back hallway leading to the kitchen. They were careful not to give Haley a clear shot.

She looked over the top of the bar, pistol in both hands, ready to shoot. She counted eight dead tangos but knew there were at least two more. One guy moved in the hallway, by the kitchen. It sounded like he was pulling a wounded—or dead—buddy to safety.

I bet they're coordinating. As soon as I leave cover to deal with the one in the hall, the tango hiding in front will take me out.

A masked enemy poked his head around where the window used to be in front, checking for movement, confirming her hunch.

Should I try to take one of them out or stay here behind the bar, protecting Mom and Dad?

It felt like hours, but the firefight had taken less than a minute so far, she guessed.

The police will be coming. This much gunfire won't go unnoticed, especially in an upscale neighborhood.

But would she really put the police in danger when all the enemy wanted was her?

If I don't finish this before the police come, I risk putting them in jeopardy—over me.

She couldn't live with that.

"Dad, how's Boyd?" she asked her father, who crouched near her behind the bar.

Boyd groaned and spoke before her dad could answer. "Broken ribs for sure and I think I caught one in the stomach, but I'll live," he said. Haley glanced down and saw his white dress shirt sopping wet with blood from a bullet that must have hit below his ballistic vest. His eyes were closed and his face was white from shock and blood loss.

He's not going to make it without help.

Across the room, the other Secret Service agent, Claire, slumped against the wall, eyes closed. She clung to her pistol but didn't look like she had the strength to raise it. Her black suit coat hid the blood, but Haley could see at least two darker spots where she bled enough to soak the material.

In the distance, sirens wailed.

The decision was easy.

Without taking her eyes from the room, she pulled her small backup pistol from her ankle holster and held it out.

"Dad—take this. If anyone besides me comes back here, you point and pull the trigger until they go away or die. Understand?"

Her father was no stranger to guns—he'd taught her to hunt when she was young. But shooting a deer once a year was quite different from killing a human—even in self-defense.

"Be careful, kiddo," her dad whispered as he took the gun from her hand.

"Honey, no!" her mom cried as Haley started past them. "Wait for the police!"

They hadn't spoken of it, but surely her parents had noticed the change in her over the past year. They were smart people. They could put two and two together and guess their daughter had transitioned from a gifted intelligence analyst sitting safely in an office to an occasional field agent who had killed—repeatedly.

"There's no time, Mom. Trust me, I know what I'm doing."

First, the guy out front. It's where the police and ambulances will come. Then I take out the guy in back.

5

EVEN THE ODDS

William Nalen had only a narrow view of the driveway and house from inside the barn. The little-used tunnel from his basement opened up into a horse stall—still filled with riding tack from years before when he'd briefly owned a horse. The stall had a window, but he'd be too exposed if he used it. Instead, he lay in the dirt near the huge sliding front barn door, peeking under it. Groundhog after groundhog had burrowed under the door over the years to use the barn to nest, creating an opening large enough to see out.

At least the damage the damn things have done is coming in handy now.

Two men stood in front of his garage. They were dressed in dark tactical clothing, had cheap night-vision goggles, and held rifles.

The rest of the men must have spread out to cover the backdoor and windows, William figured. The two he could see would likely enter the front door and go room to room looking for him with the others ready in case he tried to escape.

They're in for a surprise.

Unfortunately, he was trapped for the moment. The assaulters wouldn't have reason to look in the barn, but at the same time, he couldn't leave it without giving away his position. The fifteen-foot-tall front and back sliding doors, big enough for a hay wagon, would make noise if he tried to open them. The doors to the horse stalls—one on each side of the main door—could be opened quietly, but they faced the house. He would be exposed if he tried to slip out now.

The two men moved from his garage and onto his porch, weapons up and ready.

They've had training... but not much. Probably not mercenaries, then. So who are they?

The second man let his rifle dangle from a sling and used a lock pick gun on his front door.

As good as the locks are, this proves I need some sort of bar to secure the doors.

The lock opened and the men entered his home.

This is my chance.

Everyone's attention would be focused on the house.

Time to take the fight to them and even the odds.

6

GAMBLE

Ryuji's Asian Fusion Bistro
Alexandria, Virginia

There was no cover in the restaurant once Haley left the relative safety of the bar. Slipping through the opening near the wall, she left her mom crouching on the floor next to her dad, who held the pistol at the ready.

Come on, make this easy. Poke your head around the wall again so I can blow it off.

Haley waited another second, hoping the attacker outside would be compelled by her silent directive, but he didn't move.

Has he bugged out after seeing his friends die and hearing the sirens? Or is he waiting for reinforcements?

As she walked forward in a crouch, avoiding the whimpering patrons scattered under their tables, she had a dangerous thought.

Could I take one of the bad guys alive?

The police would be here too quickly for her to ask many questions, but a living assailant might be compelled to roll over on his employer or whoever sent him to attack her.

No. I can't risk it.

Not with her parents, two wounded Secret Service agents, and a few dozen diners relying on her to end this.

At the far wall, she passed the table where a few minutes before she had enjoyed a delicious dinner.

The middle-aged man who had checked her out minutes before looked up at her, his eyes wide with fear. Haley brought a finger to her lips as the man started to speak. Then she patted the air, telling him to stay down, which he did, letting out a whimper of fear as he covered his head with his arms.

A little closer...

Haley took another step and froze. Her left foot, which she was about to place on the ground, would have stepped on a small piece of broken white plate, making a noise and giving away her position.

She moved the foot two inches to the side and stepped forward, avoiding the plate.

A few more steps brought her to the front corner of the restaurant, where she had seen the assailant disappear seconds earlier. The cold January air poured in through the opening, empty of glass except for a few jagged pieces poking up from the bottom.

If he's out there, will he still be around the corner? Can I just jump out and shoot?

Any halfway competent attacker would be ready for a counterattack and shoot her as she looked around the corner, exactly as she had hoped to do to him earlier.

No. He vanished. He's either gone or...

Her mind flashed back to the soccer stadium in St. John, United States Virgin Islands. While she had been distracted fighting for her life, two guards had dropped to the ground behind her and crawled up the rows of seats, hidden from view, planning on catching her by surprise.

The windows in front of the restaurant didn't extend all the way to the ground. A small wall, knee-high, ran the length of the restaurant.

He saw me behind the bar, where I had a great angle to shoot him the next time he poked his head out. Would he risk going low to get a better angle of attack?

She had to gamble. Instead of looking right, prepared to fire, she had to look left, along the ground where she guessed he was crawling toward the front door for one last assault.

He's already seen his buddies die. If he didn't run, he's committed—but doesn't want to go the same way. He'll try to be sneaky.

As she leaned outside, avoiding the jagged glass, a scared diner near her moved, making noise.

Time seemed to slow down as she took in the scene of the tango, dressed like the others in a black parka and ski mask, crawling on the ground near the front door of the restaurant, ten feet in front of her.

Haley's gun sight found him as he rolled onto his side, bringing his shotgun to bear on her. His eyes widened as his face filled her vision.

She squeezed the trigger, killing him before he could fire.

One down, one to go.

7

YARDWORK

The Nalen Farm
Rural Virginia

William reluctantly left the shotgun behind in the horse stall. The weapon would be perfect inside the tight confines of the house, but he needed the firepower and range of the M4 outside.

Besides, he'd need his hands free for the first part of his plan, and the shotgun didn't hang on a sling like the M4 did.

He slipped silently through the smaller horse stall door into his front yard, the familiar landscape lit up in the NVGs. The evening remained quiet and still. If he hadn't seen the men, he would have trouble guessing a hit squad moved through his house, trying to kill him.

The side of the barn was six feet to his right. Though he'd moved quietly through the door, he expected any attacker stationed at the corner to either sense or hear him.

With his combat knife in hand and the M4 still dangling from its harness, William hustled forward. There is a time and a place for stealth, but he had ground to cover before...

There.

The head of an assaulter peered around the corner, moving more with curiosity than suspicion.

He thinks I'm one of his buddies changing positions.

William slammed his knife into the man's throat, silencing him before he could cry out. Yanking back on the knife, he next sliced the enemy's carotid artery. The man clutched his neck, trying to stop the surge of blood. William caught him as he died and lowered the body silently to the ground.

One down. A bunch more to go.

8

COVER UP

Ryuji's Asian Fusion Bistro
Alexandria, Virginia

The sirens were getting closer to the restaurant—police and at least one ambulance, Haley figured.

The ambulance will hold back until the scene is safe.

Haley quickly checked the attackers lying near the front door, ensuring they were dead. There were pools of blood everywhere. After confirming no wounded bad guys would shoot her in the back when she went to the kitchen, she moved to the rear of the restaurant and prepared for the most dangerous part of mopping up.

The hallway to the kitchen is a kill zone.

It had worked to Claire's advantage a minute before, but now the long hall would leave Haley with nowhere to hide if the man—or men—left in the kitchen heard her approach.

Is there time to go around and attack from the rear?

No. The upscale strip mall the restaurant occupied was too long to run around, and she couldn't leave her parents, the two injured Secret Service agents, and the rest of the patrons unguarded should the killers choose that time to attack. She'd have to risk the frontal approach.

Slow and silent, or fast and furious?

She peeked around the corner. Two black-clad men lay dead halfway down the hall, one shot by her and one by Claire. A smeared trail of blood showed where another attacker had been dragged through the swinging doors to the kitchen.

Might have been a leader or a buddy—injured but not dead. Alive enough, at least, to risk exposure to get him to cover.

Haley considered the situation and rehearsed the steps she would have to take.

No shots from back there. No attempt at another assault. Are they all dead? Have they bugged out? Or are they waiting patiently, suspecting I'll come for them sooner or later?

She ejected her mostly spent magazine, switching it out for her last full one.

As long as there aren't more tangos on the way, I should be fine.

She gave a silent thanks to Axe for insisting she always carry extra ammo.

I wouldn't be here now without the spare mags.

Haley had choices, but she decided on surprise and violence of action.

She moved down the hallway as fast as she could without making noise, the rubber soles of her practical, unfeminine shoes—which always got her a few looks at the office—making it easier than if she wore the typical low heels of an office worker.

As she passed the restrooms, she didn't clear them, knowing it was a tactical risk. The tangos could have moved down the hall and ducked into one of the bathrooms, but she considered the probability low.

At the door to the kitchen, she didn't stop. Her approach had been silent—she would take them by surprise.

The man in the black facemask waited, his body partly concealed behind metal shelves in front of her, less than ten feet away. His eyes locked on hers as she burst through the door. Her aggression must have surprised him. She fired first, putting a double tap of bullets into his torso, driving him back a step as he fired at her.

The bullet went wide, thrown off target by her own quick shots.

Her next bullet missed where she aimed by a few inches as the tango went down, either from the first shots or out of a self-preservation instinct to duck. Instead of hitting right between his eyes, it nailed the top of his head, sending a chunk of skull and blood against the stacked stainless-steel bowls on a shelf against the wall. The hours of training Haley spent at the range paid off.

As he collapsed onto the floor, Haley shot him again to be sure, then ducked behind a shelf for partial cover, expecting more gunfire.

After a few seconds, she stepped out again, gun sweeping the area as she stalked through the kitchen. Aside from her latest kill, only one other tango was in the kitchen—and he had bled out where he lay next to the door.

"There were only those two," a middle-aged man in black and white pants and a crisp white jacket by the stove called to her in a Japanese accent, his hands raised as he looked up at her. "They spoke Russian, I think."

Russian? Well, shit.

Could she and Axe have been caught on surveillance in Russia, killing President Pavel Zimalev? Had they tracked her down and sent a hit squad?

I'll have to deal with that later, back at the office.

"Are you the chef?" she asked the man.

"*Hai,*" he said. "Yes." He ducked his head in a small bow.

The sirens were close now—the police were here. She had to be out front when they arrived.

"Delicious dinner. Sorry for the mess," she said. Lowering her weapon, Haley returned to the front to make sure Boyd and Claire got the urgent medical treatment they needed... and begin a long night of questions.

There would be no getting out of this one without her name attached to reports—she couldn't just vanish out the back door, leaving her parents behind. But if she hurried, she could alert Gregory to the situation, warn Axe and Admiral Nalen, and get her story straight with everyone. She wasn't Haley Albright, intelligence analyst at the Central Analysis Group. Her fake ID—one of several she carried—would prove she was Holly Schoharie from the Drug Enforcement Administration.

The attack tonight needed to be considered an attempted hit on a DEA agent, not an attack against her personally as revenge for her role in assassinating the President of Russia more than a month ago.

9

BACK IN THE GAME

The attacker on the other side of the barn died the same way as the first—sticking his head around the corner to find William with a knife instead of his buddy.

Two.

The more tangos William could kill silently before bringing out the guns, the better. He couldn't get into a firefight against such a superior force. They would pin him down with fire while the others flanked him. He'd be dead in minutes.

Now, where are the others?

Two tangos were dead, lying with their throats cut on either side of the barn. Two were in the house looking for him.

I have a few more minutes until they come up empty and wonder where I am.

If they only had the eight men he'd heard walking up the driveway, there would be one man held back, probably to his right, where the gravel drive curved before heading downhill.

That makes a natural defensive position going either direction.

He would have to be dealt with next.

Then there would be one on the far side of the garage, one on the south side of the house, and one to the east.

Killing them before the two in the house realize I'm not there will be challenging.

He fought back a smile. It felt great to be back in the game again.

Circling into the north hayfield behind the barn, he approached the small patch of woods at the top of the driveway.

Yep—right there.

The man, wearing the same low-end, single tube night-vision goggles as his two dead buddies, knelt with one knee down, body facing south, swinging his head to cover the garage to his left and the driveway to his right, likely trusting the two men who had been at the barn to guard his rear.

William crept through the edge of the field and across the driveway, stepping lightly and carefully, the knife ready for more action. He could switch to the M4 in an instant if necessary.

'Slow is smooth and smooth is fast.'

In seconds, he slowed further, stalking his prey. Three feet. Two feet. One.

He plunged the knife into the base of the man's skull, levering it to be sure he severed the spinal cord. The guard collapsed without a sound, incapacitated and dead in moments.

Three.

William stalked the next enemy at the south corner of the garage. This one had better instincts than his dead buddy near the driveway. The tango spun from his position near the bushes when William was two feet away. But the man's sense of danger couldn't save him. William killed him with two fast but deep slashes to the sides of his neck, followed by a stab to his throat.

Four—but numbers five and six are going to be tough.

He wiped the gory blade off on the man's jacket before sliding it back into its hanging sheath. Switching to the M4, he considered his options.

The yard extended thirty feet south from the house. At the edge of the yard, a hayfield started. A third cutting had been taken in the fall, so there was no cover from the house to the hedgerow of trees one thousand feet further south.

It made picking out the sentry laying fifty feet into the hayfield easy to detect in the NVGs, but the lack of cover would also make it next to impossible to stealthily approach the killer.

Unless…

The older, cheaper NVGs worn by the enemy had a narrower field of view. Could William circle and approach from the rear, over the open terrain, without being caught? How focused was the man on the house versus checking his sides and rear?

Moving slowly, William crawled south a few feet, then froze. He could see enemy number six's head and rifle a hundred yards to the east, where he lay in the winter hayfield that wrapped around the yard.

If I can see him…

In a flash, William aimed and fired, killing the man with a headshot.

An instant later, he put a bullet into the skull of the enemy closer to him, in the south field.

Two left, but my element of surprise is gone.

The big question—how would the two tangos in the house react to the gunfire outside?

10

ALONE

Alex "Axe" Southmark's Cabin
Rural Virginia

Axe lay on the floor in the hallway with the perfect angle to shoot anyone coming through the front or back doors. His night-vision goggles bathed the house in a green glow, triggering the warrior in him.

How many hours have I looked at the world through NVGs?

The next time he had to stay awake on overwatch, he'd add up the missions over his fifteen years of active duty.

I bet I've spent as much time viewing the green world as the real world.

He breathed out slowly, trying without success to release his frustration.

Why haven't they attacked?

After ten minutes geared up and ready for a fight, he had to admit the truth to himself.

No one's coming for me. The danger is elsewhere. But why?

Axe had his phone entirely silenced, not wanting even the gentle vibration of a message to potentially give away his position as he waited for an attack that apparently wasn't coming. He slid the device out of his cargo pants pocket, flipped up his NVGs, and checked the screen. A message had arrived moments before from Haley via their secure communication app, addressed to both him and Admiral William Nalen.

Attacked by hit squad at restaurant w my parents. Safe. 13 EKIA. 2 Secret Service down-critical condition. Report tangos spoke Russian. Stay safe.

Thirteen enemy killed? Nice shooting, Haley. And Russians? That's not good.

The attack on her would explain his intuition, but not why no one was shooting at him.

If they know about Haley, they have to know about me, too, right? Especially if involves the assassination of Russian President Zimalev.

He typed a terse reply, knowing she had a lot to deal with in the aftermath of the assault. *Copy. Safe here. No attack. Able to travel if you need backup.*

Axe hit send and waited a second, expecting a quick check-in from Nalen... but there was nothing.

I know the old guy goes to bed early, but not at 19:00 hours.

He waited longer, trying to convince himself his friend and fellow warrior was in the shower or on a call with Senator Woodran, his new girlfriend.

No. He's in contact—or dead.

SEVEN, EIGHT

The Nalen Farm
Rural Virginia

William took a risk and stayed in place.

Normally, he would shoot and move to make himself harder to hit. But from here, on the south side a few feet from the garage, the tangos in the house wouldn't be able to see him. He had a good angle and could take a few seconds to decide—wait for the enemy to emerge or take the fight to them.

The earlier situation had reversed, and the shoe was now on the other foot. Would the men inside make the same decision he had and sneak out? They didn't know about the cramped old tunnel from the root cellar to the barn, and he doubted they would find its hidden entrance.

Would they risk climbing out a window, betting he could only cover two sides of the house? Or did they dare wait for him to enter, wondering if the police were on the way?

William hesitated, torn. Going into the house made sense. He knew which old floorboards creaked and which didn't. He'd be able to pinpoint the source of movement and could hide behind some of the larger pieces of sturdy wood furniture once the gunfire started.

But his shotgun was still in the barn, and he couldn't risk exposure to get back to it. Maybe waiting outside made more sense.

Besides, I'd hate to clean up blood from the walls and floors.

If he ducked low, below the windows, he could get to the east side of the house unseen. Then, if he continued far enough into the hayfield, he'd have an angle to view the east, north, and south sides of the house—but not the west side, where the front door was.

I'm overthinking this. They aren't top-tier operators. They're grunts doing something they're not good at.

They wouldn't risk going out a window. So he was in a perfect position right where he was—he'd see the men leave through either the back door to the south or the front door on the west. Lying on the frozen ground, he aimed the M4 at the front door, predicting they'd come out the way they went in.

Thirty seconds later, the front door handle turned, then stopped.

Gotcha.

Still, caution dictated a glance at the back door.

Damn—these two are smarter than I thought.

The handle on the back door was vertical instead of horizontal, indicating someone was holding it and preparing to come out.

They're coordinating now...

A moment later, both doors flew open. A man emerged from each, guns up, heads swiveling, searching for danger.

William easily put a round through the first man's nose as soon as he left the house, splattering his brains against the worn wooden board and batten siding of the house.

Seven.

An instant later, the tango exiting the back door looked toward him. William put a bullet in that man's head, too.

Eight.

Ducking behind the corner, William jumped to his feet and rushed to a new position, hiding in the bushes along the west side of the garage, near the fourth intruder's body. They wouldn't protect him from bullets but would prevent him from being seen by other enemy still in the area. He didn't think there were any—they would have fired on him by now. But better safe than dead.

Now I wait to see what happens. If there are other tangos, they have to come out of hiding.

He hoped they'd hurry up.

I'd love to clean up the blood on the walls of the house before it freezes.

12

PLAY IT OUT

Axe sat at his kitchen table in the dark, night-vision goggles off, pondering the puzzle and reassuring himself.

They didn't attack me for a reason.

He stewed, one of his worst fears simmering. He faced death easily and wasn't scared of dying. But getting old? That terrified him.

No one would consider him washed up.

I'm not a has-been... right?

His phone buzzed with an incoming call on the secure communication app.

Nalen. Finally.

He answered with a tap on the small wireless receiver in one ear. "You okay?" Axe asked, trying to mask his concern.

"Not a scratch," Hammer replied. " I told you in Las Vegas—I've still got it."

He sounds happy.

"Never a doubt," Axe said.

I'm worried about getting old? He has at least twenty years on me and is still kicking ass! When I grow up, I want to be just like him.

Axe smiled in the dark, buoyed by the older man's abilities. "What happened?"

"Kill squad," Nalen said. "Eight guys, military trained but not very experienced. Definitely not operators. But their tactics were decent."

"Didn't they know who they were up against? I would have expected them to send more than eight men."

"Yes, especially considering Haley's situation. You saw her message?"

Is he annoyed they sent thirteen guys after Haley and only eight for him?

"Yes. Though she also had two Secret Service agents with her, so..." Axe reminded him, trying to soften the blow of being seen as the lesser threat. "And hey, at least they attacked you, right? I'm sitting here in the dark with no action!"

Axe slipped the NVGs back on and checked the yard, carefully going from window to window without exposing his body to a potential sniper shot.

Still nothing. Maybe they got lost?

"Seems like we pissed off the wrong people, Hammer," Axe said, seeing nothing in his front yard and moving to the back.

"Or the right ones—it depends on how you look at it. Some would say we're doing a great job if we have people coming after us."

"You think it's about..." Axe almost said "Russia" but held back.

You never know who could be listening, even with a secure app.

"Our most recent op?" he asked instead.

Hammer will know I'm referring to assassinating the Russian president and not the three of us saving Senator Woodran's life, or the work he and I did in Las Vegas.

Nalen hesitated a moment, then spoke, contemplating the options. "Could be, though I don't know how they'd get the intel and act so quickly. I was thinking it could also be a dead man's switch from Todd 'The Assistant' Burkley."

"Him again?" Axe said, his voice filled with annoyance.

I thought we were done with him.

The idea of a dead man's switch—a final bit of revenge planned for after a person's death—made sense. Burkely could have used a small part of his millions to pay for hit teams to come after Haley, Axe, and Nalen in the event Burkley didn't check in every few months or at certain times. The bad guys would assume the worst—the person hiring them was dead —and do the job they were hired for.

Axe shook his head as he looked through the main bedroom windows at the side yard, still seeing no one. "It doesn't explain why I'm not targeted, too. Yes, the house is in the name of a shell company now, but when I inherited it from my dad, it was in his name. It wouldn't take a genius to track me here."

He saw nothing in the back yard either and returned to the front to wait a few minutes before starting again. "And nothing against you, but when we tracked down Burkley, you were behind the scenes. He likely wouldn't have known about you. Our most recent enemy, on the other hand..." Axe let the implication hang there.

The Russians would have easily found out about Nalen—his actions in Las Vegas and at Senator Woodran's ranch.

"True," the admiral agreed. "Which brings us back to you. Are you sure you're all set?"

Axe checked the front windows again.

Nothing.

"I'm not feeling any danger. They could be planning an ambush when I go out next, or waiting until daytime when I'm usually asleep, but hitting the three of us all at once makes the most sense."

"What if they got lost?"

Axe laughed. "I thought the same thing. But I'm off a state road—gravel, sure, but I have an address. Mail gets delivered. It's a cabin in the woods, not off the grid."

If it was the Russia operation, they would figure out I took the shot that resulted in Zimalev's death and send a team after me.

"Okay, here's what we do," Nalen said, taking charge. "Stay frosty, but we play it out. I'm sure all will be revealed. Absent an enemy, or a lead, we sit tight until we can go on offense."

"Works for me. But offense against who?"

"That's Blondie's department. She'll figure it out," Nalen said, no doubt in his voice. "But I have to say—this time it feels personal."

13

NEED TO KNOW

Central Analysis Group Headquarters
Conference Room C
Alexandria, Virginia
1:05 AM

"Here's what we know so far," Haley said, capturing loose strands and re-wrapping her long blond hair into a new ponytail. She stood in front of the big monitor along the far wall of the conference room. Dave and Nancy had just arrived and took frequent sips of coffee as she spoke, trying to wake up.

Gregory looked haggard. His normally perfect longish gray hair wasn't slicked into place. His fashionable tortoise-rimmed round glasses had a smudge on the right lens. Haley had to wonder if his worn look was from tiredness or personally coming to the sushi restaurant crime scene to see firsthand the blood and death—and knowing much of it was her doing.

"The restaurant I was eating at with my parents was attacked at six-thirty last night by thirteen armed men. Two Secret Service agents were shot and badly wounded, but it looks like they'll pull through. None of the diners were injured, thank God."

"Wait," Nancy jumped in, her shoulder-length gray hair frizzy after removing her hand-knit beanie. "What were the Secret Service agents doing there?"

Does she really not know my mom's connection to President Heringten?

Haley glanced at Gregory, who just raised his eyebrow.

I guess it's up to me how I handle it. But if I can't trust these two after all they've seen and done, I'm in trouble.

Haley tried to gloss over it. "A couple dining there has a connection to the White House and warrants Secret Service protection, but it seems unlikely they were the target. Anyway, at the same time—"

"How can you say that?" Dave asked. He rubbed his hand over his close-cropped salt-and-pepper beard. "What makes you sure they weren't the target from the start?"

Thinking back, Haley saw the scene unfold in slow motion.

I hustled Mom and Dad to the bar and saw the front door open... The first tango with the face mask brought his gun up... Aiming at Boyd, not me.

She hesitated, suddenly unsure. Speaking slowly, staring into the distance, she remembered as she thought out loud. "They might have known ahead of time about the Secret Service," she admitted. "The first shooter was focused on the agent by the door when I shot him."

Nancy choked on her sip of coffee and looked up in surprise.

"Sorry," Haley said, "I was going to get to that. Between the Secret Service agents and I, we took out all thirteen bad guys."

"Took out..." Nancy started, then continued softly. "You mean you killed them."

"Yes," Haley said with a short, matter-of-fact nod.

They know I'm a killer, but I guess it's a surprise to hear it straight from me—especially when it happened so close to all of our homes.

"We need to do a deep dive on those two people under protection," Dave announced, reaching for a pad of paper and a pen from the neat stack in the center of the table. "Names?"

Haley again looked at Gregory for relief, a plan, anything, but he shook his head.

He has nothing. It's all going to come out now.

Not everything, though. She couldn't talk about the Russia connection —and hoped Dave and Nancy wouldn't put the pieces together about her role in assassinating the President of Russia shortly after she had resigned from the Central Intelligence Agency last month.

Haley hesitated long enough for Nancy and Dave to share a confused look.

Haley finally spoke up. "They're my parents," she admitted. Knowing there would be more questions, she continued. "My mother is best friends —since they were kids—with the First Lady of the United States." Nancy's eyes widened and Dave fought to cover his shock. "When I was a kid, long before James Heringten was the president, he was my Uncle Jimmy."

The admission hung in the air as the two senior analysts processed the information and thought through the ramifications.

Are they wondering how much of my getting this job was because of my qualifications and how much is from my connection to the president?

Nancy either read her mind, her face, or had the same thought process. "You got this job because of your abilities, Haley. I'm positive—I've seen your work. Never let anyone say otherwise." The words came out forcefully.

As another woman, she knows all too well what I've gone through to get this far.

"That answers one question," Dave said, "but you're assuming you were the target. The men could have been criminals robbing an upscale restaurant. Or they could have been after your parents. Certainly, you may have been the target," he admitted, "but I think it's too early to conclude that."

"You may be right," Haley said, trying to make her tone match her words and likely failing.

I had to be the target. Going after my parents makes no sense.

"But let me continue. At the same time—to the minute—Admiral William Nalen, whom you've interacted with but haven't met in person, was hit. Eight men—likely former military—attacked his house in rural Virginia."

"Is he okay?" Nancy asked with a hand to her mouth. She and Nalen had spoken a few times on Haley's previous operation to save the United States.

The question caught Haley by surprise. "Of course he's okay. He's Hammer," she said, using the man's call sign. "A former SEAL and all-around badass. He's got a stack of eight dead guys and the FBI is trying to make sense of it right now." She'd had a nice chat with the admiral, who was fine except for being pissed about having to scrub frozen blood off the sides of his house.

"No longer the FBI," Gregory said quietly from the other end of the table. "We have some other people on it now. They'll handle it much more quietly than the FBI would have. The same at the restaurant," he explained to Nancy and Dave. "Compartmentalized and left for us to manage."

There's that, at least. We can keep it quiet.

"What about Axe?" Dave asked. They knew about her unsanctioned asset from the previous operation when his involvement had come to light, changing from an open secret no one discussed to common knowledge.

"He wasn't attacked," Haley admitted.

This is the part that doesn't make sense.

Dave and Nancy both looked confused again, perfectly matching Haley's feeling.

"Sorry, Haley, I don't get it," Dave said after a few seconds. "If your team of three was the target, why didn't Axe also get attacked? If they could find out where Admiral Nalen's home is, track you to a suburban restaurant, and coordinate the attacks to happen at the same time, why not go after Axe, too?"

Haley frowned and nodded slowly, her tiredness hitting as the last of the evening's adrenaline faded from her system. "Excellent question," she said, "and one we'll have to figure out."

"Where do you want us to start?" Nancy asked. "Do we know the identity of the assailants at either the restaurant or the farm?"

Gregory spoke up. "Fingerprints show the men at the restaurant are mid-level Russian criminals based in New York. At the farm, they were Americans from a small town in Kentucky who were all former military. Honorably discharged. Best guess is they were a loose-knit group of political extremists. Why they would target Admiral Nalen, a decorated American hero who has never expressed political views on one side or the other, is unknown."

Dave was making notes. "So we need to find out whether these two groups were connected, which they must have been. The timing of the attacks can't be coincidental. Who was in charge? How was it funded?"

"I'll handle that," Nancy said.

"And what is the connection between Haley and the admiral that doesn't involve Axe?" Dave added, then hesitated, looking unsure about asking the next question. He lowered his voice to a whisper and brought up the elephant in the room for the past month. "What exactly happened when you were away from the office, Haley?"

This is dangerous territory.

Gregory saved her. "She was on sabbatical. Personal time."

Nancy and Dave looked at him skeptically, then at Haley, but she kept her face neutral.

No one spoke, and the silence grew uncomfortable.

After several seconds, Gregory sighed. "Anything else is 'need to know,'" he said, directing his words to Haley, not Dave and Nancy. "And none of us need to know. Right?" It was more of a directive than a question.

"Right," Haley said, her tone making it clear the discussion was over.

They already know I abducted Victor Baranov from the airport. They saw the news and later intelligence reports of retired veterans saving the city of Las Vegas from destruction. It's not hard to guess Axe, Admiral Nalen, and I were behind it. I also called for Senator Woodran's plans and location, so they can guess I was involved in saving her, too.

Haley could let all that slide—and even admit it if she had to.

Let them believe what they want. But Russia is off-limits. They can think I was on the hunt for the Russian sleeper spies in the government and American industries, instead of flying to Georgia, driving to Russia, and killing President Zimalev.

How much did Nancy and Dave guess, she wondered. When Dave spoke to her about Russia's plans to invade Ukraine, Latvia, and Lithuania, she had taken it in stride, not acting surprised. Then, less than forty-eight hours later, the President of Russia was dead. The invasion never happened.

This is stupid. How can they not guess? Should I just tell them?

Gregory stood up, his brow furrowed. "Time to get to work. Do any of you have pressing intel you're working that I need to reassign?"

Nancy and Haley nodded, but Dave shook his head and moved from the small conference room table to his workstation near the door.

"We've been looking into why the Mexico drug cartels are out of money," Haley said.

"What do you have so far?" Gregory asked.

"Not enough," Nancy admitted. "There's a chance the War on Drugs is working. Lately, we've had more border patrols, more inspections of vehicles coming through the checkpoints, and drug-sniffing dogs. Drug prices are way up because supply is down. We may finally be interrupting their smuggling operations enough to make an impact. It could be hurting them in the pocketbook."

Gregory looked skeptical. "After all these years, suddenly we're winning?"

"I agree," Haley said. "It seems odd, but it would explain the facts. The DEA and other organizations have an operation set up for tomorrow night—an ambush, really. They have intel that a large shipment of drugs is coming over the border near Nogales. We think the cartels are using a migrant wave approaching Texas as cover. Earlier this month, small groups of migrants from El Salvador and Guatemala slipped through the authorities' checkpoints along Mexico's southern border."

"Those groups have joined Mexican migrants south of Laredo, Texas," Nancy continued. "They're about a day away from the border. Initial estimates put the numbers between three and five thousand people. Most are single men or women, but there are some families and unaccompanied kids, too."

"Is there a concern they're going to rush the border?" Gregory asked.

"Exactly. It has the Border Patrol stretched pretty thin."

"Who do you want to give it to?" Gregory asked Nancy, but Haley jumped in.

"I need an hour with it. Maybe two. I'll pass it to Marcus in the morning if I'm not finished."

Gregory frowned. "You think this is more pressing than you, your parents, and Nalen being targeted and attacked?"

Haley nodded. "Nancy and Dave can handle that for now."

She and Gregory shared a long look while Nancy pretended not to notice.

Gregory has guessed Axe and I were behind the assassination and doesn't want Nancy and Dave digging there. But I need to finish this cartel puzzle.

"Two hours. I can get it done," she repeated. "There's more there than meets the eye—I feel it."

He's learned to trust my intuition… right?

"Since you put it that way, Haley, you better take all the time you need," Gregory said. "I'll get my laptop and pitch in with Nancy and Dave. Let's get to work."

Haley left the conference room and moved to her desk with the huge dual monitors. The work she had to do was well within her CAG mandate, so there was no need to hide in the conference room with the others. Besides, she worked better when she could block out all distractions. She tilted her head from side to side, cracking her neck, and settled in.

It's time to hunt.

Two hours and a bottle of diet cola later, Haley pushed back from her desk. She had found what she was looking for. Or rather, she had found not a hint of evidence to support her theory but knew in her gut she was right. Now she had to convince Gregory... while not second-guessing herself.

I hate this part.

Scooting back to the keyboard, her fingers flew, putting together a quick presentation. Nothing fancy—just the facts, figures, a few maps, and the outline of her plan to prove she was right... or that it at least made sense to cover all the bases—which included her wild hunch.

The real danger wasn't the thousands of migrants approaching the border near Laredo or the drugs being smuggled into the country tomorrow night—or rather, later today—near Nogales.

If I'm right, it means we're facing an actual invasion from a much deadlier force. We're about to get hit again.

UNOFFICIALLY OFFICIAL

The White House
The President's Exercise Room
Washington, D.C.

Four Weeks Earlier

Gregory's arms felt like overcooked spaghetti. He pushed as hard as he could, but the barbell rose only an inch.

Come on! he thought, pushing himself. *Last one. Get it to the top and you're done.*

It didn't help that the President of the United States was the man spotting him at the weight bench.

Why don't we hit the treadmill? I can run much better than lift.

Retired Admiral Nalen stood to the side in gray gym shorts and a crisp white t-shirt, arms crossed, watching with an amused expression.

Gregory gave it all he had in one last, desperate attempt. The bar came within an inch of where he needed to place it. The president grabbed it and guided it to the holders.

"Don't worry, you'll get a lot stronger," President Heringten said. His thick hair showed more gray as he was about to start his second term in office, but his muscular physique proved he took plenty of time to stay in shape.

What does he mean by that?

His look must have given him away because the president added, "You're going to be spending time here regularly. The three of us are now workout buddies. Unofficial, on my personal time."

Gregory sat up and looked from one to the other, confused.

"Congratulations. You're the new director of the NHAA."

Nalen, Haley, Axe, and...

Addison—me?

"Thank you?" He didn't mean for it to come out as a wishy-washy question, but it did. "Officially?"

Is this the real deal? They're making the NHA legitimate?

"Officially unofficial," the president said with a wry grin. "All the responsibilities, none of the backing. If things go well, great, you get very quiet credit."

The president handed Gregory a small towel to wipe off the sweat, which he could barely accept with his dead-tired arms.

"Meaning?"

"Meaning you tell no one. Only your team and you know the good work you're doing."

"And if it goes bad, Mr. President?"

"Don't let it." His voice and face were stern.

"Not a reasonable order, sir."

The president shrugged and looked at Nalen, who did the same. They looked like an old-time comedy duo playing off each other. "Life isn't fair," the president said matter-of-factly.

"Seriously, sir." Gregory couldn't let it go so easily.

This is worth pressing.

"Situations go sideways, Mr. President," he said. "It's inevitable. We do our best to get them back on track, but... what if?"

"You take one for the team," the president answered in a low, quiet voice. "You're technically legal, but if the shit hits the fan, whatever you did was unsanctioned."

Gregory stared at the two men standing with their muscular arms crossed, looking down at him sitting on the bench. He stood. He had to be at their level. "Are we being frank here, Mr. President?"

"Yes. If this is going to work, we have to be."

"Then I have to say it sounds like a shitty deal for me, sir. No offense."

Nalen and the president both fought back smiles before the president got serious again. "None taken. You can always pin it on the people below you if it comes to it. Axe in particular; use the excuse that he's an unfortunate veteran with PTSD acting on his own. He'd understand."

Gregory frowned.

Not my style. Or theirs.

Nalen leaned closer to the president but spoke loudly enough for Gregory to hear. "I told you to sell it better," the admiral said in a lighthearted way, which reinforced Gregory's feeling they had planned and rehearsed this whole pitch. "Tell him what he gets out of it."

President Heringten nodded, but waited a few seconds, his eyes boring into Gregory's. Then he spoke. "A few weeks ago, you told me you'd become what you always hated. A bureaucrat worried about protecting his ass instead of following your instincts."

Damn it! I should have never confessed those feelings to the Commander in Chief.

The president continued. "If you accept this position, you get to go back in time, to be who you were when you first started out. A maverick. You'd have the freedom to do what's right, follow your instincts, with limited oversight."

"From Admiral Nalen?"

"No," the admiral said with a slight smile. "I work for you."

"Light supervision from me only," the president said. "As needed, here, during our workout sessions. Advice—and consent for the larger, riskier operations."

It's a tempting offer. No more picking through the dregs of the other agencies. No more writing big-picture reports which often get ignored or shuffled aside. A chance to get back to my roots.

"You also get to manage Haley Albright," the president said, his face serious.

There was a long pause. Gregory was sure they were all thinking the same thing.

Can anyone manage her? And is it a perk to do so, or a burden?

He waited for the two men to crack smiles or break into knowing chuckles, but they looked serious.

Gregory hesitated. "Is Haley a deal-breaker?"

Am I actually playing hardball with the President of the United States —who is also Haley's Uncle Jimmy?

The man eyed him coldly but didn't answer.

"It's only—I'm not sure I can promise to manage her, sir," Gregory continued. "She's her own woman. As you know," he added under his breath.

"I'll have a talk with her," Admiral Nalen said. He turned to the president. "How about domestic operations only for Haley?"

President Heringten considered it, then nodded. "I can live with it. And I understand if she can't be completely controlled. But if she goes into the field, she does so with a larger team—and I'm informed immediately, understood?"

"Yes, sir," Gregory said. "If I can get her back on board." He changed directions. "What about overall operational parameters for the organization?"

"Worldwide operations, in the office and the field, as you see fit. You'll have working control of many domestic and international resources. Basically, the people in charge will know you speak for me… as long as things don't go bad."

Gregory felt torn, and the president picked up on it.

"You'll also have my gratitude, and the thanks of the entire United States of America."

"Unofficially."

"Yes." The President gestured to the weight bench. "You can think it over while you spot me." Gregory moved out of his way while he and the admiral added several large weights to each end of the bar. "But if you say yes, I suggest you hire Haley back aboard the CAG immediately and recruit a few more people to your team."

"And the name," Admiral Nalen said as the president took his position under the huge stack of weights.

"Yes. Change the name of the team from NHAA in case anyone ever asks. Maybe…" he thought for a second. "What about the World Intelligence Agency—the WIA?"

Not bad.

Gregory moved to the head of the bench to spot the president as ordered. He stared at the weights, doubting he could be of much assistance if the president needed it.

"Don't worry," Nalen said from next to him. "I'll be right nearby to help."

Does he mean spotting the weights, or for the new team?

15

RECON

5:30 AM—Present Day

Gregory's arms shook as he forced the bar upward. With a final grunt, he raised it the rest of the way and seated it in place.

The President of the United States stood to the side in the cramped room, wearing black gym shorts and a black t-shirt with a small presidential seal, watching. Retired Admiral Nalen stood over him as his spotter.

Nalen's been up all night, too. He's older by a few years but still looks fresher than me.

"You're getting stronger," the admiral said.

"Definitely," the president agreed, handing Gregory a towel.

That's what comes from working out one-on-one with the president... but I still feel like hell.

For the past month, Gregory had woken early every few days, left his wife sleeping peacefully in bed, and made the trek to the president's small workout room in the basement of the White House.

With Gregory's last set finished, it was time to get down to business. Admiral Nalen had been in the room when Gregory arrived at 4:30 and had brought the Commander in Chief up to speed with the evening's activities.

"How's Haley doing?" President Heringten asked. "I imagine she's been in the office all night tracking down who did this?"

"She's fine. But actually, Mr. President, she will be getting to that about now," Gregory admitted. "She is focused on the drug cartel puzzle and requested permission to finish with it or prepare the data for hand-off to another analyst."

The president tried to hold back a smile but couldn't. "Requested permission?" he asked, amused and skeptical.

"Well... no, not in so many words."

"More like told you what she was doing, I bet," Admiral Nalen said with a chuckle. "She probably ordered you to jump in yourself, I bet!"

Gregory allowed a tired smile to appear on his face to cover for how close to home the admiral's guess was.

"Maybe we should have made her the director of your newly formed World Intelligence Agency," the president told Nalen, his face serious.

They're yanking my chain, right?

The two men cracked up at the look on his face.

I'm too tired for this.

"We're just trying to lighten the mood," Nalen admitted with a kind look. "We know you've had a long night. Haley's a handful, but without her instincts last night, two Secret Service agents would be dead, along with her, her parents, and who knows how many people at the restaurant."

"Agreed," the president said, back to being all business as he removed the weights from Gregory's barbell and placed them in their holder. "I have a full day but run it down for me. What do I need to know?"

"Sir," Gregory said. "Haley is... being Haley. She believes there may be a threat at the Mexico border."

"Yes, the migrant wave. I'm confident the Border Patrol is on it, but the governor of Texas and I have spoken. He may call up the National Guard today if necessary."

"No, sir. She has a hunch."

The mood in the room changed the instant the word left his mouth.

"Hell," Nalen muttered.

"Shit," the president agreed.

"It's backed by one intel hit. A human intelligence report of a small group of 'dangerous' men holing up in Chihuahua, Mexico, two-hundred-thirty miles due south of El Paso."

"And we have no DEA or other assets in the area, I presume?" the president asked.

"Correct, sir. Haley wants to send Axe to Texas. She used some type of Haley magic to come up with a location. She thinks the reported dangerous men are going to enter the United States for an unknown reason. Axe would have a view of the area she has determined is the most likely crossing point." Gregory hesitated.

Why not go all-in? These two know all about Haley and her abilities.

"Also, admittedly without evidence, she believes the migrants have been infiltrated by the cartels—or another, as-yet-unknown group—and are being directed as a distraction."

The president and admiral contemplated the news.

It doesn't matter to any of us that she has only a feeling—we believe in her.

"What about the DEA ambush tonight?"

"Mr. President, Haley believes..." Gregory hesitated again.

"Just say it," Admiral Nalen said. "She's been right every time so far."

"She suspects that's also a misdirection for the real incursion southeast of El Paso."

"What might happen there? Who are the men and what are they up to?"

"She doesn't know, sir." Gregory left unsaid how frustrated that made Haley, but he could see on the faces of the other men that they understood.

"You want to send only one man? Just Axe?" the president asked, skeptical.

"No," Admiral Nalen corrected. "One SEAL."

The president frowned. "Certainly, one capable SEAL—but who is retired and slightly past his prime." He thought it through. "But better to have a very low profile. We don't know who is in the area keeping watch."

"Yes," Nalen agreed. "If we go in force, we'll scare them off. We'll lose the recon-ambush opportunity when they sneak in another way. And we don't know who might be on the cartel's payroll, even on our side of the border. Best to keep this compartmentalized."

"Fine," the president said, tossing his workout towel in the hamper by the door. "Make it happen," he told Gregory. "But don't mess it up. Tensions are high enough with the migrant wave. I don't want an international incident at the border." He offered fist bumps to Gregory and Admiral Nalen. "Good workout, gentlemen. See you in a few days, though it sounds like you're going to be busy. Keep me as much in the loop as necessary."

The president left to shower and change for another day running the country, leaving Gregory and Admiral Nalen alone.

Nalen turned to him. "You ready for this?"

He knows I'm not a hands-on, operational leader. I'm an analyst. Or I was before I turned into a manager.

"I'd love your assistance," he admitted. The all-nighter had caught up to him.

I'll need to sleep or drink a lot more coffee to get through the day.

"I'm going with Axe," Nalen said. "We can't stage a vehicle—it might be noticed. I'll drop him off and be his backup. I'll be on comms with you and him."

Gregory felt relieved at Nalen taking an active role. "Just remember what the president said," Gregory said. "No international incident." He hesitated, but the question had to be asked. "Is Axe manageable? Or is he more like Haley?"

In other words, will he listen to what we tell him, or is he just going to do whatever the hell he wants?

Nalen barked a laugh and shook his head. "He does what he's told… within reason. But I don't micromanage. Axe will understand the mission and do what needs to be done. It's how we work."

Gregory nodded his understanding.

"I'll get us moving if you can approve transportation for us?" Nalen said.

Gregory nodded again. He now had the authority to do so, as long as he didn't go overboard… or let things go wrong.

"Then we should both get some rest," the admiral said. "I'll pick up Axe at his cabin in Virginia and we'll be ready to fly out when you have a plane for us. I don't want to tempt fate and go home in case they try again." He shook his head ruefully. "Cleaning up blood makes me grumpy."

At least I don't have that problem. Seeing Haley's handiwork at the restaurant last night was bad enough.

Following the admiral out, Gregory thought sleep sounded like a great plan. It would be a long day and a longer night. Despite his team comprising Nalen, Haley, and Axe, he worried about managing his first field operation.

I hope I'm ready for this.

16

THE WAR

The White House
Oval Office
Washington, D.C.
6:15 AM

"Finally, my fellow Americans," the president said, standing behind the podium and ignoring his notes. "I need to bring up the War on Drugs. Some say it has been a success. Without it, the reach of the drug cartels would be greater. Additional people around the world, including more Americans, would be victims of addiction. We would have more violence, more fear, more loss."

He paused, his face hard as his dark eyes swept the room.

"I agree completely."

He waited a moment, then continued. "Others say the War on Drugs has been a failure. Our beloved country still has more than one hundred thousand drug overdose deaths per year. Addicts are desperate for a variety of drugs. They have insufficient access to treatment and other programs many of them desire. The billions we have spent on the war over these many years haven't produced the results we need."

He waited a few seconds, preparing to drop the bombshell.

"I agree with them as well."

He continued quickly. "How can I reconcile these two opposing beliefs? Easy. I'm a politician." He offered a charming, self-deprecating smile.

"Mr. President," Chad David, the president's chief of staff, interrupted the rehearsal. Even sitting, his muscular physique and strong jawline made him look formidable. "I know you love the joke, and it's sure to get a chuckle, but it takes away from the message. The laugh line will be the lead of every news report after the State of the Union speech—not the announcement of your visionary plan. And the other side will have a field day with it. 'The president makes a mockery of both our brave police fighting crime and the plight of poor drug addicts.'"

"But I'm poking fun at myself—at all politicians," James argued.

I sound like a pouty child, James thought, chiding himself.

"I understand, sir, really. But most people don't watch the State of the Union speech. They watch or read the commentary the next day. People will only hear about it from the viewpoint of the reporters. Using the line is a losing proposition."

James sighed.

He's right and we both know it. But I wish I could keep it in.

"I get it. Consider it cut, Chad," he said, using a red ink pen to cross out the section on his written notes. "Let me pick it up from there." The president put down the pen and readied himself.

"How can I reconcile these two opposing beliefs? Easy. They are both true. Without the War on Drugs, the world, and the United States of America, would be worse off. But we have yet to get to the root of the problem. Which is why I am proposing a bold plan. This administration, with the help of Congress, and state and city governments, will solve once and for all our national nightmare of addiction, violence, and despair caused by drugs. First, we will assist our men and women on the front lines of the war to eliminate the importation of drugs into the country. Second, we will do what we have not focused on enough before, but has had great success in other countries: we will address the problem on the user end."

This is the part they'll all be talking about.

"I have planned three experimental substance abuse programs. With the backing of several members of Congress, on both sides of the aisle, we will implement a plan for attacking the War on Drugs on another front— the demand side. With both diminishing supply and demand, the problem will quickly be eliminated."

President Heringten narrowed his eyes and looked around the room, imagining himself standing in the Capitol building, giving his latest State of the Union address.

"We're not winning the war, but we've set the enemy back on their heels. Now is the time to counterattack."

He straightened and let fly his bold plan.

"I have already begun working with cities around the country to enact the programs. Two cities will experiment with a zero-tolerance stance. No drugs allowed in the area. Period. Those caught with drugs—users or suppliers—will face immediate imprisonment, from the lowest courier or street dealer to the largest distributor.

"In two other cities, there will be another approach. Safe, secure, monitored locations will be set up. Any drug user will be supplied with high-quality drugs at an affordable price—to be used on-site only. This is aimed at drug addicts, not recreational drug users. Aside from these sites, the cities will have similar policies to the first two towns: no tolerance for the sale, distribution, and use of drugs.

"Finally, two other cities will fully legalize most drugs. However, like several states' current marijuana policies, the drugs will be carefully produced, controlled, monitored, and taxed. Any driving under the influence or other behaviors contrary to the safety of non-drug users will be dealt with harshly."

I can't wait to hear the sounds of the Congress after I say that. It's going to be a madhouse.

He held for several seconds, planning for the murmur, discussions, and uproar at his announcement. "We as a country will try these three approaches, let the programs gather data for a year, then look at the results. We will then determine—as a country and each locality—what is the best approach. Now, there will be those who protest—especially at the legalization experiment. They will say we are being soft on crime." Another pause.

"That's bullshit." He raised his hand to Chad before the man could speak. "I know, I know. How about just 'bull?'"

"We'll come up with a good word or phrase for you, Mr. President," Chad said, making a note on his legal pad.

I wish I could say what I want, but then that would be the lead of all the stories.

"There are others who will say we have our priorities backward, that we should reduce money to the police and fund trial legalization programs in every city in the country, not only the ones we have planned. That too is…" He glanced at Chad.

"On it, sir," Chad said, making another note.

"The truth is, my fellow Americans, that this is a complex problem with many nuances. Even the experts don't agree on what the perfect approach is. Instead of assuring you I have the answer, I'm asking for your help and patience. This administration is committed to solving the problem of drug addiction, along with the crime and violence often accompanying it. We will try several ways to take back our streets, protect our neighborhoods, and help those who are stuck in a cycle of addiction."

James leaned forward and spoke softly. "Some of these approaches may miss the mark." He raised his voice, building as he finished. "But others will show great promise. We will throw our country's incredible resources behind those successful methods. We will help our fellow Americans. We will put an end to drug violence. We will win the war." He pounded his fist on the podium as he said the final words of the speech. "We. Will. Not. Fail."

Once again, James swept his gaze across the imaginary audience, remembering where his key allies would be sitting, pretending to catch their eyes one by one and nod in recognition.

If we do this right, if I can keep the coalition together, we might change the course of our country.

Big 'ifs' with no guarantee of success. Spending billions on police made sense—there was a lot to show for it. More officers on the street, better equipment.

More Border Patrol agents were helpful, too. It made for good optics. And it worked. The new scanning technology put into place caught so many bulk shipments, the cartels had been forced to scale back transporting the drugs in trucks across the border. And a drug-sniffing dog program cost little overall—but had taken time to implement. It too had a profound effect, reducing drugs smuggled by car.

Spending millions on addicts—who might not vote and didn't have political action committees or lobbyists, was a much tougher sell. Showing drug addicts lined up for a morning hit didn't look as good as showing long rows of recent police academy graduates ready to defend the liberties of the average Joe.

"Mr. President," Chad began slowly.

"Let me stop you right there. I know what you're going to say and yes, this is the direction I want to go. If we can take this on and win, imagine what it will do for our country. Our streets safer. Our kids and adults no longer hooked on drugs. If we have to completely seal off the borders, we'll do it, and damn the costs. If it goes the other way and we have to push for full legalization, fine. I truly don't care which approach works best. I just want to see our country in better shape."

He took a breath, calming down. He'd seen fine men and women—in the military and out, including a few SEALS—succumb to drug addiction. "This is my last go-round. I have a year, maybe two, of political currency before the next candidates from both parties start taking a whack at me in the press. I'm not worried about the next election. I want to make sure I leave this country in a better place—safer, more secure, and more prosperous, for whoever comes after me. This will be my legacy." He stood before his long-time friend. "We've never run from a hard fight before, and we're not going to start now."

Chad nodded slowly and glanced at his notes.

He's not convinced, but he'll charge into battle with me, regardless. And with a little luck, we can win this thing.

"Having said that, what do you think?"

Chad looked up and broke into a wry grin. "Mr. President, I think you're going to get clobbered from all sides."

James barked out a laugh. "Yep. I'm going to stir up a hornet's nest worth of trouble. And I love it. Bring the fight. Maybe we can put a dent in this problem and do some good in the world."

It might work, as long as there were no serious threats to the status quo over the next three days before the State of the Union address, when his carefully crafted plan became public. He shook his head as a common SEAL mantra sprang to mind.

'No plan survives first contact with the enemy.'

17

THE FIVE

The huge airplane hangar easily held the five fast executive jets, their engines still running as they faced the wide-open doors on either end—three jets at the front and two at the back.

Ready to escape at the first hint of danger.

Arturo Ruiz, the head of one of Mexico's drug cartels, smoothed his thick dark hair and stepped out of his small jet. Ten of his most trusted men surrounded it, fully armored, rifles at the ready. He walked briskly to what looked like a brand-new, tan shipping container on the back of a flatbed tractor-trailer centered in the hangar. A large swinging door on one end stood open, revealing an inner, normal-sized door, which he opened to check inside.

Empty and ready, Arturo thought.

He nodded at his right-hand man, Hugo, who stood next to the door. Hugo's salt-and-pepper goatee was freshly trimmed but shaved lopsided, making him look less like the stocky, dangerous second-in-command of one of Mexico's most notorious drug cartels, and more like a cartoon character who couldn't groom himself well.

"It is ready?" Arturo asked.

"Yes, *Jefe*. It has been swept twice by our man," Hugo said, nodding at the nearby semi driver guarding the truck, "and no one has approached it."

"Fine. Alert the others. And make sure our men make no sudden movements," he reminded Hugo.

As jumpy as everyone is, I don't want this to turn into a bloodbath.

Arturo guarded the door of the portable SCIF—the Sensitive Compartmented Information Facility. A shipping container had been professionally outfitted as a secure facility to conduct ultra-sensitive meetings. Plush and comfortable, it was bulletproof, safe from forced entry, soundproof, and guaranteed to keep conversations within from being overheard or monitored by any of the USA's incredible electronic wizardry. It took endless discussions to get an agreement to use it and cost him a fortune to buy and move around, but he and the four other cartel leaders could use it to meet safely when their planning required it.

Or as safe as possible when the five most wanted criminals in the Northern Hemisphere meet in person.

Time was always of the essence. Every moment on the ground—away from the safety of their regions and home compounds—was a risk. A tip of their whereabouts would bring the authorities sweeping in for the biggest arrests of the century.

Assuming they could get here quickly and fight their way past our forces.

The police wouldn't be able to keep secret an attempt to apprehend them. In the event of an attack, the room would be uncomfortable for the five of them for any length of time but would protect them long enough for their forces to mount a counterattack and rescue them.

The chances of an attack are slim... but none of us got where we are today by being cavalier about our security.

He checked his watch.

Three minutes.

Aside from landing and taxiing to the hangar, they needed to be on the ground for less than twenty minutes. He estimated the authorities—even the DEA working with Mexico's national police—could not get a tip, travel to the airport, and mount an assault within that time period.

At Hugo's signal, the doors of the other four planes opened and well-armed, dangerous-looking men emerged. They eyed each other warily, rifles at the ready, pointed downward only enough to not directly threaten Arturo's guards or the other men deplaning.

With the presence of heavily armed bodyguards from all five drug cartel leaders, there was a greater threat of a takeover attempt than a national police raid.

The guards formed perimeters around their respective planes, while several others surrounded their bosses as the VIPs hurried to the SCIF.

The four most wanted men in Mexico—in all of North America— glared at Arturo Ruiz as they stalked past him to enter the narrow, secure room. The anger and annoyance were palpable as he closed the door behind him and made his way to the chair left open at the round table.

"None of us enjoys the risk of being here, Arturo," Guzman said in his unusually high-pitched voice. His thin frame, narrow face, and messy black hair, along with the falsetto voice, disguised a brutal and ruthless man who had done unspeakable things to rise to power—and stay there.

"My apologies. We have much to discuss. Traveling and meeting in person is less risky than any electronic means," Arturo said.

"So you always say," said Duarte, the youngest and most tech-savvy member of their select group. He ran the business for his father, who was jailed in America. At thirty-five, his face was unlined, his teeth white and perfect. He chafed at how careful his elders were and their reluctance to use technology. "Yet somehow the governments of the world meet via secure videoconference. I believe we could—"

"Yes," interrupted Salazar, the eldest and grumpiest. He had a large head and fleshy face, but the squinting hard eyes of a ruthless killer. The comb-over of what few strands of dark hair remained—obviously dyed— fooled no one. He was mostly bald, but everyone knew his vanity refused to allow him to accept it. "We all know what you think and the rest of us reluctantly disagree. Let us please move on and not waste time having the same argument again." He nodded grimly to Arturo. "My sources confirmed what you discovered, Arturo. America's President Heringten will not only propose the legalization of drugs in certain cities—the plan is already in motion. And, of course, the legal drugs will not be supplied by us."

In another setting, with lesser men, there would be murmurs and side discussions around the table. With this group, there was merely a shifting of weight in the seats from the three others who hadn't believed Arturo's initial report delivered via courier.

"Yes," Arturo said. "And I have new details. In all areas, including the legalized cities, there will be stepped-up enforcement and policing of illegal drugs—our drugs."

"This is a disaster," Duarte, the youngest, mumbled.

Without his father's steadying hand, he's been prone to drama from the start... but in this case, he is not wrong.

"This could be the end of our business," Guzman said in his high voice.

As usual, the tall, thin Cortez, overdressed in his customary three-piece suit while the others wore slacks and perfectly pressed dress shirts, sat silently, watching and waiting.

"You are being alarmist," Salazar said, his voice deep and reassuring, though Arturo caught a tightness that wasn't usually present. "Our opportunity to expand into Western Europe and China will easily replace any loss in the Americas."

The others nodded, except for Cortez who continued to sit, barely moving, like a hawk on a tree branch waiting for the perfect moment to strike.

"If President Heringten's plan takes off," Guzman said, "it would cripple us... and at the worst possible time. We are broke. If moving the bulk of our drug operations, our families, and our entire lives to Venezuela doesn't work, I, for one, will be destitute. You will find me begging on the street."

Arturo kept his face neutral and refrained from rolling his eyes. He didn't believe Guzman's words for a second. While they had all contributed ninety-nine percent of their profits to the endeavor, one percent of billions was still a substantial amount. And none of them were stupid enough to risk their own secret, personal wealth. At least, he wasn't.

He subtly checked his watch.

Six minutes.

Arturo continued, as anxious as the rest of them to conclude this risky in-person meeting and get back to safer ground. "Thanks to our ongoing plans, we are well-positioned. Yes, losing the United States market could impact the bottom line, but we should keep this in perspective. It is six cities. A year-long experiment. At which time it will be evaluated. With our lobbying arm and various... enticements..."

The men around the table knew exactly what he meant.

American politicians are exactly like Mexican ones—susceptible to bribes and blackmail. Carrot and stick.

"We can still prevail," Arturo concluded. "I have it handled. Lobbying, donations to political action committees, and threats—the usual. But as long as we agree, we should let the experiments go forward and do everything in our power to influence the results. This program will fail. No legislation for expanding it will ever pass. Our lobbyists will portray anyone supporting it as weak on crime. We can also increase the violence, making sure people in these target cities are implicated in horrific crimes. It will be shut down fast."

Arturo looked at each man, getting a small nod as they agreed to his plan—and his handling of it.

"The feint is set up?" Salazar rumbled, moving on.

"Yes," Arturo said. "The American and Mexican forces, working together, will capture our drug mules near Nogales late tonight. Informants have tipped off the authorities."

"I still don't agree with letting them seize the shipment," Duarte whined.

"To keep a dog happy, you must occasionally feed him a bone," Guzman said, making sense for once.

"And because of your objection," Arturo said, explaining the concession he had made to appease Duarte, "the drugs will be our least profitable. The seizure will have a minimal impact on our operations, though it will make for great press for the American and Mexican authorities. The real shipment of pills and heroin will take advantage of their focus on our decoy near Nogales to slip in undetected near El Paso—through a tunnel we have never used before."

Duarte seemed mollified by this and nodded.

There was a pause as Arturo prepared himself to discuss the true reason for the meeting.

Nine minutes. We must hurry.

In the silence, Cortez spoke in his cultured, quiet voice. "None of this is important enough to discuss in person."

Among them, Cortez was the most respected. His operation ran without fanfare, consistently generating more money than the rest of them. He had the politicians, police, and citizens of his area well in hand. He shared his wealth more with the locals than the rest of the cartel leaders combined, constantly building schools, hospitals, and bettering lives in the areas he controlled. His initial reluctance to join their plan and contribute his full share to their long-term joint operation had been a stumbling block that had taken a year to address. When he finally agreed to scale back his charitable operations to provide the funds needed to implement their ambitious plan, the operation became a reality.

Here we go. Of course it would be Cortez who saw the truth behind the meeting.

"Our…" Arturo paused.

Which word to use?

He had worked through the list on the short flight to the airport, but still hadn't decided.

"Our… partner," he continued, choosing the term least likely to cause the others to be annoyed, though the word wasn't quite accurate, "has a last-minute demand."

"I knew it!" Duarte said, pounding the table in frustration. "He—"

"Continue, Arturo, please," Salazar interrupted before the young hothead could go on another of his tirades. Duarte glared at the older man, who ignored him.

"He… requests… we allow a team of his to slip into America with our men," Arturo said, doing his best to keep his tone neutral. He was only the messenger, after all, and didn't want to influence his colleague's attitude toward the information. "He has an assignment for them he claims is unrelated to our business with him."

The four men contemplated the change in plans.

"He has his men staged near Chihuahua, centrally located to easily move where we direct him. He has also requested we provide transport for them—a panel van or similar—once in America. Not a problem, considering we already have plans in place for our men."

"And if we say no?" Guzman asked, a knowing tone in his high voice. They were all experts at making "requests" that could not be refused.

"His courier didn't say, exactly," Arturo said, "but I got the impression the entire deal would be in jeopardy."

Duarte stood abruptly from the conference table, his face flush. "We've paid him one hundred billion dollars and now he pulls this?" He scanned the room, livid, looking for others to share his outrage.

His father had so much more self-control… but my reaction was the same when I heard the news.

With a deep breath, the young man got control of his emotions—somewhat. Enough to speak in a quieter voice. "I say we kill him and insert a different person as president." He sat, continuing to calm down as he presented his plan. "If we pick the right person, our lives would be so much easier than dealing with this maniac."

We aren't so different—aside from the lack of emotional control.

"I agree," Arturo said, knowing he was likely surprising the others.

"But not yet. He offered a carrot, along with the implied stick. He has used our money wisely, he claims. The country's second submarine has been upgraded and is back in service. Both will be at our disposal from day one."

Guzman beamed with lust. The submarines would be his to control and manage, making worldwide delivery of enormous quantities of high-priced drugs easier and undetectable, especially to the lucrative Chinese market so difficult to otherwise access. He nodded slowly. "The man is without honor, but this is a skillful move."

Cortez spoke again in his refined, thoughtful way. "We predicted he would take our money and make a last-minute demand. This is to be expected. It's exactly what we would do if we were in his shoes."

The others nodded.

"And our situation remains the same," Cortez continued. "Despite our best efforts, the United States Drug Enforcement Administration and our own police—at least the few we cannot buy—are closing in. The US-Mexico border is getting impossible to use to smuggle our product. The politicians are listening to the masses who are fed up with the problems they believe our products cause. Change is here. We must continue the plan, abandon our production facilities in Mexico, and finish relocating to Venezuela, where we will be protected—even supported—by the government and its people." He looked at Duarte with a small nod. "No matter who is ultimately the president. As much as we all regret leaving our homeland, and are temporarily beholden to President Villanueva, it must be done for our survival."

With the clock ticking and every second they debated increasing their risk of getting caught, they didn't take long to decide, especially given their lack of alternatives and Cortez's reasoned examination of their situation.

Twelve minutes.

Salazar nodded. "With many of our people and equipment already in his country producing great quantities of product, we have no choice," he agreed. "We are committed."

"I concur. Plus, our dealers are getting antsy," Guzman said. "Because of our scaled back production here in Mexico, their inventory is low. We need this transition to happen smoothly. And we must keep them supplied until it is complete. There is no time to refuse the request. Tonight's resupply must happen. If it means escorting the man's men, so be it."

"Still, it increases the risk," Salazar grumbled. "His men, plus ours... a larger group could be noticed."

Now. This is my chance.

"Perhaps not," Arturo said. "I have a plan. The so-called migrant train has already drawn the focus of the Border Patrol. With a push, it could be a larger distraction."

A mass of people escaping the poverty and other problems of Guatemala and El Salvador had been picking up poor people on their trek through Mexico to the USA border. It was now several thousand people strong and nearing the Texas border near Laredo.

He outlined his plan—but didn't mention it was already in motion—then added the kicker. "We are technology averse out of necessity, but we are not living under rocks. We can use tech as a tool—a weapon against America."

The others were always reluctant to give praise, but as they nodded their agreement, he knew he'd impressed them.

Perhaps I will be their leader at some point, instead of just the first among equals.

And eventually, they would need to do as Duarte said and replace the idiot zealot President of Venezuela.

Why not me? I could be the president of the country. Or at least the power behind the scenes.

They would all be Venezuelan citizens shortly anyway—after, of course, the last-minute favor of slipping the men into the United States, along with the final payment required by the tyrant.

I could be not only the leader of our coalition, but of the entire country of Venezuela.

"Are we in agreement?" Arturo asked, wanting to confirm they were unanimous. "We use the immigrants as a distraction to bring the large shipment through the tunnel—along with President Villanueva's men?"

One by one, the others nodded, then stood and exited the room without a word.

Moments later, with the leaders and their warriors back onboard, the planes taxied out of the hangar and took off.

They had been on the ground less than eighteen minutes.

18

THE WAVE

15 Kilometers Outside Nuevo Laredo
Mexico

The exhausted face of the family's father spoke volumes, easily captured on Roger's small but powerful phone in glorious 4K video.

"Why do we go to America?" he said, repeating the question asked of him. "For my family." His eyes lost their haunted, desperate look for a moment, changing to fierce, protective love as his gaze fell on his wife, standing close to him, holding their baby.

Roger took a step back to capture their other child in the frame, a toddler—about three years old—clinging to her mother's leg and solemnly watching her father answer the *gringo's* questions.

"In our town, no work," he said in simple yet clear English. "No work, no money. No money, no food. No food…" Another glance at the children as a look came over his face, one that would be instantly recognized by any parent: the humiliation of not being able to provide for his loved ones, and the anger that accompanied it.

Roger held the shot, resisting the temptation to zoom in on the man's face. The image of the four hopeful immigrants, one family out of many in the migrant wave, would be viral within an hour if he didn't try to artificially increase the drama with a closeup.

The father bit his lip and blinked hard, fighting back tears.

Roger recorded.

After several seconds, Tim—Roger's boss, friend, and producer—finally spoke. "*Gracias, Señor. Senorita,*" he said with a nod to the man's wife. "Thank you, and good luck on your journey." He shook the man's hand, offered a small bow to the wife, and flashed a smile and a wave at the toddler.

Roger recorded it all, just in case the family had any last-minute words, but he held the phone low, casually, as if he had stopped recording.

"Get the kid," Tim mumbled, barely audible.

Roger dutifully lowered the phone further and switched it to his left hand. Then he stepped forward to shake the father's hand, getting a tight shot of the young daughter's serious face as she naturally turned to look at the phone held in front of her.

This family's never owned a cell phone, Roger thought. *I wonder if she's even seen one.*

Roger glanced at the screen only long enough to make sure the girl's face was centered and had to work at holding back a shiver of delight.

Absolutely perfect.

The girl's cute face, no smile, tired yet curious about the technology in front of her, her wide brown eyes…

Definitely going viral.

The father led the family off, joining the ongoing stream of other hopeful immigrants trudging toward the border.

Roger kept recording from his position on the gravel shoulder of the asphalt highway, bringing the phone higher to better frame them walking away.

Tim, with the wisdom that comes from thirty years in the television industry, stood patiently, letting Roger work.

Finally, Roger hit the red button to stop the recording and turned to Tim.

"Tell me you got that," Tim said.

"Oh, I got it all."

"The kid's face?"

Roger was already scrolling back through the recording as more tired, poor people streamed by, an endless procession of the desperate and hopeful that stretched before and behind them as far as they could see. He stopped on the segment of the child and played it. Tim crowded his shoulder as they watched together.

"Hot damn!" They bumped fists.

"Do you want to end with the whole family walking away or the face of the kid?" Roger asked, already editing the video, cutting out the beginning where Tim asked the father for permission to talk to him and the family and the initial rapport-building questions. He kept only the meat of the interview: the last question where the man's face—and his daughter's—told more of the story than the rest of his words ever could.

"Two versions. Short and long. I bet they both go viral," Tim said. "If we get the go-ahead..." He pulled out his own phone and checked it.

"Yes! We're on." Tim held up the phone. "I got the approval from the client. Prepare to be famous!"

Roger glanced up from editing to grin at his friend. The terms of the last-minute gig were simple. If asked, he and Tim weren't actually hired and paid twice their daily rate to hurry to Mexico in a beat-up rented minivan to record the stories of the would-be immigrants. No, they were concerned Americans, professional video makers interested in sharing the plight of the men, women, and children hoping to find a better life in the United States of America.

In addition to their secret pay, the fame, social media glory, and monetization from the videos were solely theirs—as long as they kept quiet about their employer.

Quickly finishing with the long version of the video, Roger made a few simple edits to cut it shorter, so it ended with the lingering shot of the daughter's adorable face.

He saved that version and held out the phone, showing each to Tim for his approval.

"Perfect," Tim said. "Upload the short one first. All our accounts. The longer version in fifteen minutes, after I send out some texts to my news contacts. Can you cue the ones we've already shot to release every fifteen minutes after that?"

"Already on it," Roger said. The ones from the past days were striking in their own right. Informative, interesting, heartfelt. But not at the level of the lightning they had just bottled with the last interview.

As he worked, Roger felt the presence of their fixer, one of several hard-looking Mexican men who hovered near them. There were dozens more up and down the highway, unshaven and dusty, dressed in the same dirty, ragged clothes as the migrants. They fit in—barely. But the real migrants would have to be blind to not see them for what they were: dangerous men keeping the wave of people moving relentlessly forward. And more importantly to Roger and Tim, preventing everyone from talking to other reporters and activists in the area covering the story, looking to interview people and shape the news according to their viewers' worldviews.

The fixer nodded at a young woman who approached Tim hesitantly, holding twin babies in her arms, her dark beauty obvious despite the grime of countless days of walking, too little food, and a life of hardship.

"I would like to tell my story," she said shyly in decent English.

The fixer stepped away as Tim smiled warmly at the woman. "Of course, and thank you. One moment while my cameraman prepares."

Roger finished uploading the videos and prepping them for release, trying to ignore the unease he felt. The people the fixer brought to them were telling the truth. He had no doubt. No one could fake the emotions they had captured over the past few days.

But not everything is as it seems. Someone's being exploited, and we're a part of it.

But as long as he and Tim presented the truth—and made money—he'd go along with it. He had his own family to feed.

Maybe we're doing some good here. People need to hear these stories.

"Ready?" Tim asked him.

Roger hit the button to start recording, held the phone up, and framed the young woman's face, along with her two sleeping babies she held on her hips. "Recording."

Life is hard, and we do what we have to.

19

A LEAD

National Guard of Mexico Regional Command Center
Monterey, Nuevo Leon
Mexico

Captain Hernandez shifted his weight, trying unsuccessfully to find a position to ease the pain from his healing wounds. In the weeks since the assault he had led on the Hotel Riviera Especial de China, he'd had two surgeries and countless stitches. He had barely survived the several gunshot wounds and the hotel blowing up near him as he sheltered behind a van in the parking lot.

Without the help of the young boy—Juan—I would be dead, he thought.

Gone like the rest of his men. In the past weeks, he had lost eighteen when the Arturo Ruiz cartel's drug lab in the barn exploded. An additional fifty died assaulting the Hotel Riviera Especial de China. Only he lived.

Am I blessed... or cursed?

Around him in the newly constructed, high-tech building, men and women of the National Guard—the national police of Mexico—worked tirelessly, answering phones, writing reports, and analyzing data. From his desk near the window, set aside from the others in deference to his position, he watched—and wondered.

How many in this room are on the payroll of one of the cartels?

The national police conducted random drug tests, frequent polygraphs, and annual background checks, searching for dirty cops, but some undoubtedly slipped through their screens.

Not many of the other men and women were like him, willing to forgo close friendships, intimate relationships, and love, all to avoid providing the enemy with potential leverage.

He lived simply, changed apartments frequently, and had no wife, children, or living relatives to put at risk.

He was as close to incorruptible as humanly possible—especially after watching his men get killed.

No amount of money in the world could prevent me from avenging their deaths.

But his job would be much easier if he could completely trust his fellow police.

A cell phone beeped—the one whose number he provided to a small army of potential informants he had cultivated over the years. Men and women who had struck him as patriots, people who believed more in the country than in the cartels and their endless supply of money... and threats.

The text was from an officer in the air force, stationed at a base near Morelia in central Mexico. Hernandez wasn't sure how he came by his information, but it had proven reliable in the past.

At least 2 heads—Ruiz and Guzman—met at executive airport in Morelia earlier today. Maybe all 5. On location less than 20 minutes.

Another meeting. This was the third in the past six months and the fifth in the past eighteen. There were rumors of more taking place around the country over the past few years.

What are they planning?

And how could he exploit it?

Thank you, he responded.

It was no use asking for more details. If the man had them, he would have shared. Without the man's help, Hernandez would never have known about the meetings to begin with, let alone that their frequency was increasing.

How can I exploit the cartel leader's need to meet in person?

He had his nation's resources at his disposal. Losing so many fine men late last year had brought another level of focus to the war against the cartels. Not that it made much difference. Anything he did, any resources he requested, would be leaked to the enemy. Hernandez walked a tightrope. He had to make progress against the criminals, for himself, his country, and his job. But to do so, he was virtually on his own... except for the Americans.

Whether because of their integrity, distance, or baseline of wealth, the cartels haven't made the inroads in corrupting them as they have with us.

Reasonably sure his computer was safe—the cartels were lacking in cyber capabilities thus far due to their aversion to technology—he searched for the airport the cartel had reportedly met at.

He cross-referenced it with the others from the past year, looking for a pattern.

Useless. There isn't enough information to predict the next meeting location or date.

And while he was decent at technology, he didn't have the skill to analyze the data well or the access to collect more. Only the Americans could.

He took a burner cell phone from his pocket, powered it on, and dialed a number from memory. He'd met a DEA agent who had provided assistance in the past. Maybe he would help—or put him in touch with someone trustworthy who could.

"It's Hernandez," he said in accented English, quietly enough so no one else in the bustling room could overhear. "I have a lead. I need help."

20

A PIECE OF THE PUZZLE

Central Analysis Group Headquarters
Alexandria, Virginia

"Hernandez?" Haley asked, the name ringing a bell. She sat at her desk, noise-canceling headphones temporarily off while she spoke with Gregory on the phone.

"He's a captain in the National Guard of Mexico—their national police," Gregory said while Haley scrambled to look through the intelligence services' many databases for information about the man. "A friend in the DEA vouches for him. He's on line two. Talk to him. We may be able to help him... and it may be the break we need with the cartel situation."

A DEA file popped up on her screen. "I've got it. Captain Hernandez. Oh," she said under her breath.

"What?"

"He was at the Hotel Riviera Especial de China when Axe and Kelton were there. He led the national police assault. Only he survived, and he was badly wounded."

They both sat with the information for a second, then Gregory spoke again. "According to my source, he's one of the good guys. Someone we can trust... probably. Help him out and pick his brain. Play it close to the vest, but don't shut him out. Just... be careful."

In other words, don't risk compromising our operations just to play nice.

"Got it," Haley said, hanging up with him and switching to line two. "Captain Hernandez," she said in English. "How can I help?"

Twenty minutes later, Haley hung up on Captain Hernandez after exchanging contact information.

Through a combination of speaking slowly and using simple sentences in both Spanish and English, Hernandez had given her a piece to the puzzle.

This is big—I can feel it.

The five drug cartel leaders had been meeting in person at great risk. Always, as far as Hernandez knew, at airfields in Mexico. They would fly in on their private jets, meet for less than thirty minutes, and take off again, returning to one of many airstrips in the safety of their home areas where they were protected by bribed police and military leaders.

Hernandez wanted to find a pattern to their meetings, either in time or place, then have the United States monitor other potential sites—for weeks or months if necessary. When the cartel leaders next met, he would attempt to coordinate the arrest of them all.

How he's going to accomplish that isn't our problem.

But she could definitely help with the intelligence. She smiled, the familiar feeling of the hunt taking over. The call came at the perfect time. No progress had been made tying the dead Russian attackers from the restaurant to the dead American assailants from Nalen's farm. She could temporarily put the attacks on her and Nalen on the back burner.

First this, then a nap. I have a feeling it's going to be a busy night.

She hadn't slept since Saturday morning—more than twenty-four hours. But she could slip out to her SUV, roll out the sleeping bag, and rest for an hour or two and be fine.

A change of clothes would be nice, too.

Haley slipped the noise-canceling headphones on, selected an acoustic chill playlist on her phone, and dug in, bringing up a map of all airports capable of landing executive jets, which is what the cartel leaders undoubtedly flew.

Would they want to avoid the quieter airports? The busier ones?

Or would their selection be based on who they had already bribed and the areas they controlled?

The data flowed around her. Her fingers flew on the keyboard and the mouse buttons clicked. Windows opened and closed on her screens, databases and public searches combining to reveal the innermost workings of Mexico's airports, flight paths, and the suspected home bases for each of the cartel leaders.

She learned all there was to know about which planes each man might own—their speeds, range, and capabilities.

Analyzing the airports they had used in the past revealed an important detail—at least one large hangar available for them to hide the planes from view while they conducted their business.

Time passed as she vacuumed up data and compiled a spreadsheet of potential targets. Finally, she had her list.

Eleven likely locations.

Four were in relatively close proximity in the center of the country, convenient for all five men without being obviously advantageous to any of them.

These three they've already used recently. And those two early last year, further away.

She highlighted them in light gray on her spreadsheet.

They wouldn't be likely to return anytime soon, she didn't think. Too much risk.

There was one more in the general area of the others.

No. Too obvious. They'll be more security conscious than that. It would be too predictable to use the one in the same area.

The obvious one got highlighted in red.

Seven more.

It would be possible to monitor them all, but not practical.

She took what she knew and leaned back in her chair, eyes focused on her screen with the map showing the airports in Mexico on the right and her list on the left. A hunch, a gut instinct, was coming to her.

There. Those two close together slightly south of the most recent group of three.

It would be one of those next, then a mid-sized airport to the northeast, near the Pacific coast.

Then number four of the original group, and the other one of these next two after that.

No one, including herself, understood how she got these hunches.

But I'm right more often than I'm wrong. I could be off on the exact order of the airports, but the next will certainly be one of those three.

She relaxed, letting her eyes unfocus for a moment before snapping her attention back to the screen.

That one.

21

A PLAN

"A hunch," Gregory said. As much as he tried, he couldn't hide his distaste. In his fancy executive chair behind his clear desktop, empty except for his computer, he remembered the old days, sitting in a tired cubicle when he first got started.

I used to have hunches too, back in the day, Gregory thought, *but not like she does.*

Haley stood before his desk, more at ease than in the past, but looking too wound up to sit. He scanned the one-page summary of her conclusions and recommendations again.

"Surveillance on all eleven airports would tax our capabilities," he said, "especially given how infrequently they've met. Why not focus on their compounds or areas of influence directly? Even put all our attention on the leader of the group. 'Put all your eggs in one basket... and watch that basket.'"

"They routinely fly the planes all over the place, empty or with decoys, to thwart surveillance," Haley explained. "But we don't have to monitor all eleven—just those three."

"I get it, but I can't sell your hunch to the men in charge of satellites and drones."

"So? Lie."

She makes it sound so simple.

But what if it was?

With the power the president has given me, I could pull it off.

The added responsibility of managing a semi-official direct-action team still felt foreign. It just wasn't how he worked. He collected and analyzed data. He didn't task others with getting it. Nor did he make up intel to justify what he knew was the right thing to do.

Gregory made up his mind and stood, handing Haley's paper back to her. "Fix this. List the eleven as potentials and narrow it down to the three you think are probables. Assign them high percentages of likelihood based on…" He thought for a second.

Go big or go home.

"Call it analysis gathered from a variety of sources, including human intelligence. Then resubmit it to me. I'll do what I can, but full-time drone or satellite coverage isn't practical."

"We only need daylight coverage. They fly when it's busy and they can blend in."

"Still. It's a stretch, Haley. I don't want to begin my direct action career requisitioning assets for a pointless mission stretching over weeks or months. Because even if we see the planes landing in real time, what is Captain Hernandez going to do about it? He doesn't have the manpower to act quickly. He'd have to have teams set up on or near the airports to be effective. But rewrite the report and I'll see what I can do. Maybe the DEA is willing to do it."

Haley nodded and took the paper back. His senses tingled as his own intuition spoke to him.

She played me.

The thought popped into his head with the certainty of fact, not the hunch he knew it to be. Haley was smart enough to create the summary report the way he had just directed her to… but she'd prepared it her way on purpose.

They locked eyes for an instant before Haley glanced away, busted.

This kid's going to have my job one day. Or be my boss.

Haley stood in front of him, clutching the paper, looking like she had something on her mind. "Go ahead, what else?" He sighed and sat back down in his chair. "How much am I going to dislike what you have to say?"

Haley shrugged with a smile. "It depends on how much you want to stick your—our—necks out," she said.

"Tell me what you have in mind."

"One week of daytime coverage on three airports," she said.

He waited for the shoe to drop, but she held out longer than he did. "That's a lot of satellite and drone time," he said.

Haley smiled, and he realized he was still in her trap. "Don't torture me, Haley," he sighed. "Just hit me with it."

"You don't involve other agencies. You do it in-house. Use trusted freelance assets in conjunction with Captain Hernandez. Three men per airport keeping eyes on and ready to go at a moment's notice. Hernandez adds an assault team for each location, ready to go."

Haley was with trying to stay dispassionate, but Gregory could sense her excitement.

It's not the craziest idea...

She must have been able to see him wavering, but not fully convinced, because she sat on the edge of one of the visitors' chairs and leaned forward to close the sale. "One week. Doesn't your intuition tell you a hit is coming?"

Yes, damn it, it does.

"Gregory, we have the possibility of capturing the heads of Mexico's drug cartels all at once." She nodded, using a subtle form of persuasion to get him to say yes, as if he didn't know her tricks.

Still, it's working.

"It's low risk. If nothing happens, no one else knows about it. You pay the contractors and have the gratitude of Captain Hernandez and the national police. But if I'm right, and they meet again soon, think of the success. You'll be starting off the World Intelligence Agency with a bang."

"A bang? That's exactly what I'm worried about!"

She's right. Low risk, but a big win if it works out.

His heart pounded—from excitement and not fear, he hoped. He felt like he was young again, making a difference with his actions instead of writing reports... or lately, supervising others who did the analysis and prepared the papers.

"This is big enough for me to run it by the president—but I just saw him this morning." He stared into space, imagining springing it on the president during their next weightlifting session.

It's a legit mission, well within my mandate.

"Set it in motion," he told Haley, making his decision. "I'll mention it in a day or two when I meet with the president."

Haley smiled and nodded, then got up and left his office.

I hope this works.

Haley paced the short length of Conference Room C, working herself up for the call and trying to ignore her guilt over not giving Gregory all the facts—or the entirety of her hunch.

There's no need for three teams. Just one. If I'm right.

Finally, she took a deep breath and dialed the number from memory.

"I told you never to call me here," Doug "Mad Dog" McBellin whispered before cracking up with laughter. She rolled her eyes.

Out of all the warriors Axe knows, this is the one I'm turning to?

The retired SEAL was a nut job, or at least pretended to be. Haley still wasn't sure if the act was a put-on or a convenient cover to make palatable who he really was. He acted like the class clown, made the occasional crass joke, and took little seriously—except his assigned mission. Even then, however, every interaction seemed to be met with comedy... or at least an attempt at it. But he had helped her out on the last two missions and was solid, deep down inside.

She hoped.

"Hello, Mad Dog," she sighed.

"Blondie, long time no hear. It's been what—a whole month? Let me guess—the world is teetering on the brink and only I can save it," he said.

I sure hope this is an act. If not, the man needs a whole team of therapists.

Despite herself though, she had to smile. Dealing with him certainly brought a change of pace to her day.

"You nailed it. Do you have availability for the next few weeks?"

"For you, Blondie, I would walk through fire!"

She rolled her eyes as he laughed at his own schtick.

"Are you sober?"

He sounded put out. "It's early morning here in California!"

She didn't speak.

Mad Dog sighed. "Yes, I'm sober."

"Perfect. Gear up and stand by. I'll send you the details."

Suddenly, the jokes disappeared, and his voice was that of a serious, professional operator. "You got it, Haley. Whatever you need, I've got your back."

"And you'll need four other guys who are available today. Reliable. Patient—the gig will be mostly surveillance."

"Aww, come on Blondie. No action?"

"Only if I'm right in my analysis. Then there will be plenty."

She had to hold the phone away from her ear as Mad Dog yelled with delight. "Hot damn! Party time!"

22

A DECISION

Joseph Orlov's office was tiny—ten feet by ten feet—and contained only a battered metal desk, an equally old wheeled chair with a compressed, worn green leather seat, a wooden second chair, and a high-tech telephone, which looked out of place in the tired, poorly lit office.

The floor was fifty-year-old linoleum, which used to be off-white but now was a medium gray from wear and dirt. The desk faced the left wall with the simple chair next to it, closest to the door, facing the right wall. There were no pictures. A large map, barely held to the right-hand wall with old, peeling masking tape was the only decoration. It showed the world as Orlov still thought of it, with the Union of Soviet Socialist Republics front and center, including all the countries and areas that had split away when his USSR collapsed.

There was no litter basket because he didn't allow paper to be used in his presence. His desk had no pens, pencils, paperclips, or staples. It was an empty office waiting for a new occupant, but he had been in it eight years.

It suited him perfectly.

He sat at the desk facing the blank wall, his back to the map, a slack look on his fleshy face. Today, as every day, he wore an ill-fitting brown suit and an ugly, unfashionably wide tie that could have been from the 1970s. His horn-rim glasses with scratched, dirty lenses, combined with the rest of the ensemble, made him look like a dim-witted accountant who wasn't good at his job. He cared nothing for style or looks. Only his country mattered to him.

Numerous enemies and competitors had underestimated him or discounted him entirely, all to their ruin. His IQ was off the charts. Were it not for his looks and demeanor, he might have been president. He would have ruled decisively and well, expertly hiding his ruthlessness. Russia would be the world's dominant superpower, instead of the United States of America.

Instead, it was a struggling, economically troubled country lurching from one crisis to another, narrowly averting disaster, filled with a few ultra-rich men who leached off the state. Things would have been different under his guiding hands, his iron fists in velvet gloves.

But while he had the ear of the president—the true one who resigned three months ago, then the egomaniac who had recently died, and now the centrist who made his blood boil, there was only so much he could do. None of them saw domestic, economic, or social decisions as Orlov's department.

Zimalev had been on the brink of welcoming more of his advice. Then, just when Orlov was getting Zimalev nicely trained, the man got himself killed. He'd wanted to show off to the world—and show up the President of the United States.

All my carefully laid plans, gone, he thought.

He stared at the wall and pondered the problem in silence. From outside his office came muffled sounds of the old building—people walking and talking, phones ringing.

I can learn from this.

His enormous decision was a long time coming but now, after all that had happened recently, was easily made at last.

He would no longer train presidents, controlling the men like puppets, making them unwittingly do his bidding. If he wanted more, if he wanted success for his country, he had to do it all himself.

He considered the United States of America, which was to blame for much of Russia's downfall. In the eighties and nineties, America's leaders nearly bankrupted their country, outspending and outmaneuvering Russia to win the cold war, crushing his beloved USSR.

They think they are so superior. That democracy makes them special.

He snorted.

What a joke.

Democracy was an experiment of a few hundred years. Yes, it appeared successful now. But it would never stand the true test of time.

Time is not measured in decades, but in many centuries.

His country had been around far longer and was on nearly equal footing with the United States.

Russia didn't pander to idiots, and did not seek input from various groups of them.

We rule. We control. We do what is needed.

He would finally see Russia rise and the United States of America fall, without fools getting in the way and ruining everything.

From this point on, he would do it all on his own. The president—whoever it was this week—would receive his advice, of course. Would be nudged in the correct direction. But behind the scenes, Orlov would reign. With Dmitry, his trusted right-hand man and eventual successor, he would control the operation against the United States of America.

The previous efforts had failed. The sleeper spy program had come close to succeeding and would still be of great value. Its assets were well placed, and many would survive the coming event.

The invasion of Ukraine had been on the brink of success. The blizzard would have allowed a lightning-fast strike. Seeing the initial success, Russia's allies would have done their parts. Russia would now be in charge of Ukraine, Latvia, and Lithuania, having claimed land and resources. NATO would be in disarray.

In the chaos and confusion, Russia would have excelled.

One man's ego ruined my entire plan.

No more. He alone would position Russia for greatness. Would bring her forward on the world's stage while relegating America's experiment with democracy to the footnotes of history where it belonged. Would finally bring the rich men of the country to heel and return them to their proper roles of support—especially financially.

His expression didn't change. He remained sitting in his worn, old, uncomfortable chair. But inside, his heart soared with joy at his decision.

At last, I will do what I should have done years before.

He had one final trick, six years in the making. The time, effort, and patience involved to bring the various actors to this stage had taken all of his considerable powers.

He would not brief the latest president on the plan he'd put into place years before with the support and consent of the president back then.

He wouldn't explain the many advantages. How America could be destroyed without much bloodshed. The great fortune to come to Russia once it happened. The fail-safes he'd put into place to keep the world from blaming Russia if something went wrong.

There would be no risk of the new president having cold feet, saying no, or wanting to wait until next February.

At last, America would fall.

PART 2

SUNDAY NIGHT

23

THE BORDER

Hudspeth County, Texas
100 Miles Southeast of El Paso, Texas
The Border of the USA and the United Mexican States

Axe scanned the border through the night-vision binoculars. In front of him lay the desolate region of northeastern Mexico. The Rio Grande River meandered between the two countries, creating a formidable barrier—but not an insurmountable one. Ten miles behind him, Interstate 10 ran east to west across this part of Texas. Hard-packed dirt roads wound through the rocky desert terrain on the US side, though the closest one to his hide on top of the hill was a half-mile away, between him and the river.

A small house, long abandoned and looking like it would fall over in a strong wind, stood on a rise several hundred yards into Mexico. The narrow dirt road leading to it disappeared behind small rolling hills every few hundred feet before appearing again for a stretch.

Aside from the river, there was no barrier to entering the United States in the region... though drones monitoring the area, truck patrols by the hardworking men and women of the Border Patrol, and the lack of decent roads on the Mexico side kept this area historically free of people attempting to cross into the United States. There were many other easier, safer, and more convenient places that didn't require a difficult hike on both sides of the border and a dangerous swim across the river.

Not tonight, though—if Haley's right.

Hundreds of miles to the southeast, near Laredo, the Border Patrol had its hands full. Extra bodies were needed to deter the thousands in the migrant wave from crashing the border. Desperate people kept arriving, massing throughout the day and into the night. The news, from radio to TV, internet to newspapers, had non-stop coverage of it thanks in large part to documentary reporting from a team embedded with the group and pushing out four in-depth interviews per hour, every hour.

The president and Texas governor had directed the National Guard and every spare body from the Border Patrol to the area for backup. Some of those agents had been pulled from this area, leaving it virtually unguarded.

Except for me.

As far as Axe could tell, he was the only person in the entire region.

And while he missed having a Team with him, he had gradually gotten used to being a semi-lone wolf.

Admiral William Nalen—call sign 'Hammer'—was driving back and forth on I-10, miles behind him and out of range for any immediate help. He would, however, be Axe's quick reaction force—QRF. They were connected via their new satellite phones and hands-free headsets since cell phone reception was spotty and even military-grade radios wouldn't carry the distance without an AWACS plane circling above them—which they didn't have.

Axe heard the engine noise of vehicles before he saw them creeping around the far hills and up the long dirt road to the abandoned house on the Mexico side of the border.

Who drives across rough terrain on a shitty road without light? Tangos.

No one else would drive on a bad road in the dark after midnight. "Vehicles approaching south," he whispered, though no one could overhear him. Old habits died hard. "Two—correction, three SUVs. Moving slowly, no lights."

"Copy three. I'm at the far end of my zone—turning to head your way."

Axe double-checked his sniper rifle. It waited on biped legs, ready to reach out and touch someone, though his rules of engagement were clear: no international incidents. He could only fire if fired upon. To give him a bit of wiggle room, however, Hammer and he had agreed that any immediate threat to the United States—not including mere drug smuggling —allowed him to engage, as long as his targets were within the USA.

On his left, he had his M4 for closer targets.

From across the river, a scraping noise reached him. The first SUV had bottomed out on a rock. All three vehicles stopped for a moment. Three men exited the SUV, which seemed to lighten the load enough for it to clear the obstruction as it continued on, the passengers following, easily keeping up with its slow progress.

Three other men stepped out of the second SUV and repeated the procedure. But the third vehicle continued without anyone getting out, easily clearing the obstacle in the road.

Interesting. Two heavily laden, one not. What's in the third one?

Haley thought the operation would be merely about drugs. Axe considered the possibilities, wondering about the contents of the third vehicle as he watched the SUVs continue their slow creep to the old house.

Gang members? Guns? No, the United States has plenty already. Weapons of mass destruction?

He held back a shudder.

Enough of a toxic substance dumped into a reservoir or aquifer, and thousands—millions—could die.

The vehicles started up the rise toward the house, shielded from view by a hill. While waiting for them to emerge and park in front of the home, he considered the other options.

It's likely just drugs—a resupply shipment. Maybe the ones in the third SUV are lighter—pills perhaps. I'm not sure why Haley's intuition would be triggered over merely drugs, though.

He waited longer, surprised he didn't see the SUVs.

They should be parking at the house by now.

Could they have gotten hung up on another rock? He waited, another two minutes passing slowly. Something was wrong.

The hill blocks the view from America...

He thought of months prior when he and his former Teammates had snuck into Mexico. A drug cartel formerly occupied a compound that was their target. It had an extensive tunnel network branching from the main house outward for hundreds of yards. Axe and his friend Red had killed the bad guys popping out of the tunnels, then used the well-made passages to infiltrate the basement where the enemy's leader was.

I bet there's a tunnel. They're not going to risk a river crossing— they're going under it.

It would take a while to unload the SUVs and transport the drugs—or whatever—under the river and border. But Axe had to find the tunnel exit before the first of the men emerged. He lowered the binoculars and looked nearby with the NVGs strapped to his head, a bad feeling creeping in. Could his well-chosen hide, with its perfect view of the border area Haley suspected as the crossing, be situated over a network of tunnels?

Or worse, could the enemy suddenly appear behind him, putting him at a major tactical disadvantage?

He surveyed the slope below him, meticulously looking over the desert for signs of the tunnel exit. Then he looked behind him along the top of the small hill and down the back.

Nothing.

In front of him, the rough dirt road on the US side of the border dead-ended a half-mile away, turning into an even bumpier track.

Where would they emerge?

"Vehicles stopped out of view," he whispered over the sat phone line to Hammer. "Possibly a tunnel connects an old house and... someplace on this side."

"Could the tunnel accommodate vehicles?" Hammer asked.

"I hope not."

Hammer grunted softly as they both contemplated the possibility—and difficulty—of a vehicle tunnel between the two countries.

The quiet desert allowed sounds to carry as they would over water at night. Axe heard vehicles behind him far in the distance, the sound of their engines echoing around the hills on this side of the border.

"Vehicles approaching my position from the northeast. Is that you?"

"Negative," Hammer replied. "I'm still at least forty minutes out. They caught me at the end of the run," he said, meaning the far end of the route on I-10 he drove to hide the fact he was patrolling the area, waiting for Axe to need exfil or backup.

"Copy," Axe said and returned to his scan. He watched for the vehicles to come from the north, looking at every dip and rock for signs of a tunnel exit, and wondered what surprises the enemy had in store for him tonight.

24

THE TUNNEL

State of Chihuahua, Mexico
100 Miles Southeast of El Paso, Texas
The Border of the United Mexican States and the USA

Hakimi had been a top Iranian special forces officer for years but had never dreamed he'd conduct a mission in the United States of America. Standing at the entrance to the tunnel, dressed like his seven men in black denim jeans, black shirts, sweatshirts, and thin but warm down jackets covering their plate carrier armor and spare ammunition, he was happy to be out of the SUV. The eight of them had been crammed in with their gear for the long, uncomfortable drive across the northern Mexico desert.

Before him was "El Gato," the leader of the group of six cartel men who would take the drugs across the border to their waiting counterparts. For some reason, the short Mexican had taken an instant disliking to him, which Hakimi had to diffuse. Hakimi and his men needed the cartel members, their tunnel, and the transportation on the other side of the border.

At least for a while longer. He could kill the Mexicans if he had to, but he had been instructed to preserve the relationship if at all possible.

Without jeopardizing his mission, of course.

El Gato was no mere drug mule. That much was obvious. His bearing, professionalism, and attitude made it clear.

This shipment is important to the cartels.

They wouldn't trust the resupply to low-end lackeys. No, this man was a soldier, a warrior. He moved like a cat, hence the nickname, and he had the air of a killer.

"My men have an essential mission tonight," Hakimi argued in his well-practiced Spanish. "They cannot waste their energy helping move your drugs."

The two stood face to face, closer than needed, squaring off in a power struggle Hakimi wished to avoid. Behind them, the Mexicans unloaded the heavy black nylon bags filled with drugs from the first two SUVs and stacked them neatly into carts lined up inside the tunnel. A rough slope led downward north toward the border. While the garden carts with their heavy-duty wheels would be easy to roll downhill, it would take the six cartel men at least two trips to move the entire shipment. With the help of his men, the night would be quicker and easier for the Mexicans.

"I must insist," El Gato said. Or something formal like that. Hakimi's Spanish was good, but not perfect. It didn't come naturally to a Farsi speaker. The shorter Mexican man moved just enough so the red light from his headlamp shone directly into Hakimi's eyes.

Is this him not wanting to work hard, his bosses showing us they are not rolling over completely, or simply his dislike for me?

It didn't matter. His men were highly trained, strong, and had been sitting around a small apartment in the middle of the city of Chihuahua for two weeks, waiting for the mission to start. They had only left the apartment in ones and twos for essential supplies and to keep from going stir crazy. They could handle a little extra work.

"I understand," he said after hesitating long enough to not seem like a pushover. "We will help."

Not waiting for a reply—or the look of satisfaction that surely crossed the other man's face—he turned to his men standing ready just inside the tunnel. Out of training and habit, each had a hand near a weapon—the pistols at their waists or the AKs dangling from slings over their jackets. Near enough to use in an instant, yet far enough to not be overtly threatening.

The Mexicans ignored them, seemingly secure in the belief Hakimi's men were not a danger to them. Their own weapons—also AKs—were securely slung on their backs.

Hakimi spoke to his brother and second-in-command, sticking with Spanish to preserve however much of the illusion remained.

They have to have realized we are not Mexican or Venezuelan, but no need to let them hear us speak Farsi.

While Iran and Mexico were close trading partners, the less known about exactly where he and his men came from, the better. With their skin tones, they passed as South American.

He chose simple words his men would easily understand. They hadn't progressed as far in their language training as he had. "Help them."

With unquestioning loyalty, his brother nodded and turned to help with the bags.

When all the drugs were loaded into the carts, his men helped each other don their heavy backpacks—and the two long, thickly padded sniper rifle cases—then the entire group set off down the tunnel, pushing the carts filled to overflowing with bags of drugs.

25

THE WAITING

Hudspeth County, Texas
100 Miles Southeast of El Paso, Texas
The Border of the USA and the United Mexican States

Three black crew-cab pickups, complete with black bed covers, slowed at the end of the packed gravel road a half-mile in front and left of Axe's hide.

They're shifting into four-wheel drive.

The trucks were the latest model, and he couldn't resist the thought of how nice it would be to have one.

Lights on, they continued carefully onto a rougher dirt trail, bouncing along on their heavy-duty suspensions.

The lead truck stopped for several seconds, pulled forward ten feet, stopped again, and flashed its lights. It then pulled forward, drove in a circle, and stopped facing back the way it had come, poised for a quick getaway. The other two maneuvered into the desert, turned around, and joined it.

Outside of range for the M4, but well within striking distance of the sniper rifle.

"It's on," Axe said to Hammer.

"I'm still a ways out."

"No sign of the tangos from across the water yet, so there may be time."

"I'll hurry."

"Not too fast. I'm fine here. I'm out of their range, but with the long gun, I can take them out if needed. Besides, there may be sentries stationed at the interstate exit or in the desert watching for you hurrying this way."

"Copy. Agreed."

The three drivers had lowered their tailgates and removed shovels from the backs of the trucks. One toyed with what appeared to be a GPS device, then used his shovel to outline an area in the dirt. All three started digging.

Smart. The tunnel isn't complete. No way to discover something that's not there yet.

Axe removed paracord from his pack and prepared for what he sensed was the coming confrontation.

I saw six guys on the Mexico side—three per SUV. If the other vehicle wasn't carrying drugs, there could have been three or more people in it. Say four to eight. That's ten to fourteen tangos, including these guys.

He'd be outnumbered and exposed as long as he was on the top of the hill.

"What about backup?" he asked Hammer as he crawled fifteen feet to his left. "My gut tells me Haley's right. This isn't just a drug run."

"No one to call. The Border Patrol is overwhelmed elsewhere. I got a text from Haley—the migrants are marching. They're at the border fence, protesting and raising a ruckus. TV and the internet are eating it up. 'Crisis at the Border,' they're calling it. We have our guys lined up in riot gear, and the National Guard is also on its way. And in California, the DEA and company have their hands full with the other thing. They sprung the ambush about ten minutes ago. Sorry, we're on our own."

"Copy that."

What else is new?

Axe finished his preparations and crawled back to his original position, carefully stringing out the cord behind him. His decoy plan might not be needed, but he had the time—and it might buy him a few extra seconds in what he bet was the coming firefight. Then he scrambled back, keeping the small boulders that dotted his hill between him and the tangos still digging a half-mile away, and repeated the preparations before returning to his original location in the middle of the other two firing positions.

The sound of a shovel hitting wood carried easily across the desert air.

They found the tunnel.

If he dug a tunnel he didn't want discovered, he would leave it mostly complete except for a roof or trapdoor several feet underground. When it was time to use it, the rest could be easily excavated either from below or above. In the meantime, there would be no danger of collapse.

The men cleared a square about four feet by four feet, mounding the dirt to the far side, away from the pickups. At last, they put their shovels back in the trucks and waited.

Now we find out what this is all about.

26

THE LADDER

Hakimi stopped pushing the gardening cart piled high with black duffel bags, grateful they were at the end of the tunnel. The trip had been harder than expected because the floor wasn't as smooth as he thought it would be. Many times along the way, bags would fall off the carts, forcing a stop to pick them up and for everyone to rebalance their loads.

Bungie cords or rope would have helped. Making two trips, carrying fewer bags per cart, would have as well.

But they were done with the bullshit assistance job and about to start their real mission. He checked his watch.

Still on track.

As long as they were finished by dawn, they would be fine.

Hakimi clicked off his headlamp, killing the red glow. Immediately, his men did the same, switching to their night-vision goggles. Then their jackets were unzipped, and weapons double-checked, all without him saying a word.

El Gato and his men worked at the base of the sturdy, homemade wooden ladder leading twenty feet to the surface. One hoisted a duffel bag and climbed up to what looked like a trapdoor, which he knocked on. A few seconds later, something clunked on the other side of the door—an answering rap with what sounded like a shovel.

The man at the top of the ladder stepped lower, fiddled with a latch, and pushed. Fresh air flowed into the tunnel and Hakimi breathed it in gratefully. He hadn't known he was slightly claustrophobic until several feet into the tunnel when his skin prickled and he started sweating. While he acknowledged it could be a feeling of impending danger—like he'd felt before—he guessed it was actually the realization he hated being underground... or in this case, underwater, as part of the journey had been beneath the river flowing above.

The Mexicans lined up on the ladder, holding on with an arm looped through the rungs, and handed each bag up to the man above, one by one, until it was hoisted out of the hole by men standing outside at the top.

"Ready?" he asked his brother, Rahmin, in Spanish. He nodded in the green glow of the NVGs, the long sniper rifle jutting above his head from its position on his back. The rest of the men did, too. While none of them were expecting trouble from the American Border Patrol or the Mexican drug runners, now was the time to be even more careful.

Their mission could not fail.

27

THE SOLDIERS

Axe watched as bag after bag was carefully loaded into the full-size beds of two of the pickup trucks, filling every inch in two layers before the bed covers were secured over them. The remaining bags filled the backseats of the crew cabs, then the passenger side of one of them.

That's a lot of drugs. The SUVs must have been packed to the brim.

As the three men who had driven the trucks finished, other men appeared from the tunnel, levering themselves out.

The ladder ends well below ground.

After the second man emerged, he could tell they weren't other drug mules or migrant workers being snuck into the country. They moved fifteen feet from the hole, spread out, took a knee, and aimed AKs outward in a classic perimeter security move.

Those guys are experienced operators. Likely special forces. This is the threat Haley sensed.

"Trouble," he said, more quietly than before, hoping Nalen could still pick up his voice over the call.

"Send traffic," Hammer said, reverting to familiar radio jargon during a mission.

"Two… three tangos, so far. Military, professionals, armed with AKs emerging from the tunnel."

They took their places, fanning out around the trucks, and even looking back at Mexico, covering their rear. They wore dark clothing—not tactical, but functional, with down coats against the bite of the cold desert air. No matter what they wore, however, it was clear they were military— and at least one grade above the common soldier.

The fourth man to emerge caused Axe more concern. In addition to the large backpack the others carried, he had a long, black padded bag.

That's a carry bag for a sniper rifle.

Axe had a similar one a few feet behind him, out of the way.

The fifth man out of the hole had one as well.

Axe tucked himself in tight to his own sniper rifle and prepared to fire on the fourth and fifth men.

I'm out of range of the AKs, but if the sniper rifles come out, I'm vulnerable.

He spoke into the hands-free mic, giving Hammer an update. "Five men so far, arranged in a defensive perimeter, two with sniper rifle cases. Permission to engage?"

His finger was on the trigger, fully expecting Hammer's go ahead.

"Hold," Hammer said instead.

Damn it.

Still, he followed orders. "Holding. But we have to take these guys out. Drug runners don't carry sniper rifles and fan out in a perimeter. These guys are a danger to the country, well within our ROE." The reason for the comprehensive pre-mission briefing they'd conducted was exactly for this purpose—so everyone understood the rules of engagement and could act in the heat of the moment. Why were they hesitating now?

Another man came out of the hole. "That's six. Permission to engage?" he repeated.

"Not unless you're under fire or they are an immediate threat. It's a close call, but what you have so far isn't enough. Sorry. Direct from the big guy."

"Copy. Not unless under fire."

I think I liked it better when we were lone wolves and the president had no idea what we were up to. But this isn't unexpected… and I'm well prepared.

There was a wooden thump from the area of the men.

The trap door being closed.

He took in the scene. The three original men who had driven the trucks were arguing with the sixth man, who seemed to be in charge. They were holding out a shovel to him while he shook his head firmly.

They want the soldiers to fill in the hole. Perfect.

Axe didn't have to take his eye off the scope to find the cord with his left hand. But he double-checked the location of the two small, cheap plastic remote controls on the dirt next to it.

If the Commander in Chief needs me to take fire before killing these assholes, I'll take fire.

He yanked on the cord. Fifteen feet to his left, the bottom rock of the small cairn he had built earlier moved, sending the rest of the stones piled on top of it toppling over, making a racket. The men facing him in the security perimeter swung toward the noise.

An instant later, he pushed the top left button on the first cheap remote control. Immediately, behind the fallen rocks, a small LED party light pulsed, the red strobe throbbing. He hit the second remote and the other light joined the first one, blue alternating with the red, creating the perfect illusion of police or Border Patrol lights.

One man fired a short burst from his AK, though he was well out of range.

A natural reaction, but it shows either a lack of discipline, which is unlikely... or orders to take no chances.

"Taking fire," Axe reported calmly to Nalen. "Engaging." He fired at the fourth man, on Axe's right of the group's security perimeter, who had already unzipped the rifle case. The tango had the long gun halfway out of the bag as Axe's round penetrated the top of his head, exploding it like a watermelon hit by a hammer.

28

THE SNIPERS

Hudspeth County, Texas
100 Miles Southeast of El Paso, Texas
The Border of the USA and the United Mexican States

One second Hakimi was arguing with the stupid, stubborn man about filling in the hole to the tunnel. The next he was flat in the dirt, rifle pointed at the flashing blue and red police lights on the small hill almost a kilometer away, outside the effective range of his weapon. One of his men had fired before realizing they didn't have much hope of accurately hitting anything from that distance.

On the far side of the perimeter, a man collapsed, followed an instant later by a gunshot. He shouted to his brother in their native tongue. "Sniper! Rahmin—engage him!"

"Rahmin is down," came the word as they all opened fire on the man shooting at them. Despite the range, bullets impacting the sniper's area might prevent him from taking such careful aim.

He called to his two fastest men. "Assault the hill." To the rest, he yelled, "Covering fire!"

The men picked up their rate of fire as the two he had called out sprang to their feet and ran for their lives, not bothering to fire as they went. They only had to close a few hundred meters before they could take cover and put rounds on target effectively.

Hakimi saw his second sniper slump to the ground, the rifle out of its case, pointed in the right direction, but unfired.

"Get on the long gun," he called to the man nearest the dead sniper.

One of the men sprinting toward the hill stumbled, then fell. He rolled to the side until he came to rest behind a small boulder.

Injured, not dead. Whoever is shooting at us is gifted... but fallible.

Damn.

Axe had winged the runner, but not killed him, possibly hitting his shoulder.

Bullets struck the hill several yards in front of him, but most of the fire was aimed at the decoy position to his left, exactly as planned. Still, after three shots, it was nearly time to move.

Have to get the last man running at me.

Axe had instinctively worked the bolt of the sniper rifle, so all he had to do was find the second man, moving surprisingly fast up the slope to his right... lead him... and fire. The man dropped.

Axe rolled to his right, just in time. A high-velocity round impacted the boulder inches from where he had been.

Someone has gotten to the long gun.

"Taking sniper fire," he called to Hammer, no longer whispering. Distantly, he heard a "Copy" from the other end of the line.

He kept rolling, working the bolt of the weapon as he landed in his new position behind several head-sized rocks he had arranged further back on the hill. He got ready to fire, visualizing where the two men with the sniper rifles had been, aware one or both might have moved.

One hadn't. Axe aimed and fired quickly, more a deterrent than a kill shot, instantly rolling to his left, against the slope of the hill, hidden from view by the small rocks. He felt another round pass overhead.

Three feet to the left were two microwave-oven-sized rocks. He crawled, positioning himself well behind them. The gap between the boulders would allow only a narrow field shot, but it should be enough. More sniper rounds impacted where he'd been.

Right... there.

He breathed out, held, and fired, watching the man drop dead. Then he ducked, grabbed the cord laying in front of him, and yanked. Fifteen feet to his right, an even taller pile of rocks toppled as the bottom stone was pulled by the cord tied to it.

The AK fire shifted to that area, along with more sniper rounds. But as Axe looked through the small opening between the two rocks that shielded him, he couldn't see where they were being fired from.

He heard the sound of trucks starting. The covering fire from the AKs kept coming, but the sniper gun went silent.

They're disengaging.

He had to get rounds into the trucks to disable them. But as soon as he moved to his left, accurate sniper rounds would be on him. He was forced backward, slightly downhill on the back of the rise, where he was safe… but couldn't return fire.

"They're making a break for it and I have no shot," he reported. "Three black crew-cab pickups with black bed covers. How copy?"

"Solid copy. I'm coming to you."

"Negative. Stay on the trucks. These guys are professionals. I don't know what they have planned, but they're a threat to the country. If I don't stop them, you have to."

There was a pause from Hammer, long enough for Axe to worry he'd lost the connection. Finally, as he crawled further left around the hill, hoping for an angle where he could fire on the trucks without exposing himself to excessive risk, he heard Hammer's terse reply.

"Copy."

29

THE BACKUP

Haley's head slumped to her chest. She leaned back in her office chair with her feet on her desk, resting in a way that allowed her to be conscious and ready while conserving energy—a trick discovered by necessity over the past year. Despite a short nap in her SUV in the CAG parking lot hours before, the lack of sleep, along with the adrenaline spikes and crashes of the past twenty-four hours had definitely caught up to her.

The only easy day was yesterday.

Her mind flashed back to the restaurant the previous night, adding more men to the total number she had killed. Then she let it go. She'd have time to deal with those memories after the crisis.

We're all feeling exhausted.

Nancy and Dave had been woken up in the middle of the night to come into the office and hadn't gone home yet, though they had squeezed in quick naps at their desks late in the afternoon.

Gregory had a couch in his office, which he'd taken advantage of. The last Haley had seen of him, he looked okay, though she got the sense he was still feeling out of his depth running assets in Texas along with Mad Dog and his team on their way to Mexico.

The phone ringing with a call from Hammer gave her a jolt of adrenaline—which would fade at some point, leaving her to deal with yet another crash. After a quick update from him, she rushed to conference room C, where Nancy and Dave worked at their stations and Gregory sat at the conference table, his own laptop up and running.

"Axe is in contact with an enemy at the border," she said after shutting the door carefully. The night shift knew something was going on in the conference room but asked no questions. "They have sniper rifles, AKs, and heavy backpacks."

"Drug runners?" Gregory asked, alert and all business.

"Hammer says no. Axe believes they are professional military. Possibly special forces—and are a separate group than the cartel people."

"What do they need?"

She had asked the admiral the same question.

"Nothing at the moment, but Hammer thinks they may need surveillance help. There are multiple vehicles they may not be able to disable or intercept."

Gregory hesitated only a second, but Haley saw it. The thought had been brewing for a while, and it hit with a certainty she couldn't shake.

He's not yet ready to be a direct action manager.

He called to Nancy, who sat ready for orders at her computer. "Get me Holloman Air Force Base. Tell them to spin up the Reaper. The previously approved 'training mission' is a go. Patch them into Haley," he said, giving her a questioning look. She nodded back, happy to play liaison with the drone pilot and Hammer.

The reconnaissance drone—unarmed, for their mostly legal in-country "training mission," wasn't the armed attack helicopter she had wanted on standby for Axe and Hammer, but it would have to do. At least it would be another set of eyes for them.

"Get your computer," Gregory told her as Nancy worked the phone. "Time to work from here."

Haley hurried back to her desk, hoping Axe was okay.

Hang on, brother, we've got eyes coming to help.

30

THE ESCAPE

Hudspeth County, Texas
100 Miles Southeast of El Paso, Texas
The Border of the USA and the United Mexican States

Hakimi sped away, going faster than prudent over the rough Texas desert terrain, one of his men bouncing around exposed in the truck bed with the sniper rifle pointed back the way they had come, just in case.

Perhaps I didn't give the Mexicans enough credit.

In the middle of the firefight, the trapdoor to the tunnel had sprung back open. El Gato and his men poured out, adding their firepower to Hakimi's men and that of their three Mexican comrades firing from behind their trucks laden with drugs. Then El Gato ordered half his men forward, assaulting the hill from the front and flanking both sides under covering fire from the others.

For a moment, Hakimi had thought they were coming to his rescue. As he had collected the essential heavy backpacks from his dead men, along with the long rifles—and crushingly left the body of his dead brother behind—he had realized the truth.

The enemy has seen the tunnel and the drugs. El Gato has to eliminate him. It's not for my mission or to avenge our losses at all.

Still, the Mexicans acted swiftly and bravely, even yelling at Hakimi to hurry and take off, letting him out of the fight before the two trucks full of drugs could leave.

He angled toward the rough-packed desert road which would lead him to I-10, according to the map he and his men had spent countless hours memorizing. From there, it would be easy to fulfill his mission, slightly behind schedule because of the unplanned firefight.

How can I complete my assignment now?

Unfortunately, there wasn't a centralized point where all the oil and natural gas pipelines came together. It wasn't that easy. But pipelines in certain areas of west Texas were so prevalent that a small team of dedicated men—armed with maps, GPS locators, minimal digging equipment, and plenty of C-4 explosives—could wreak havoc. Oil and natural gas deliveries would be hampered for years. The environmental damage would set back the construction of new pipelines across the country—and the world. Their work tonight would demonstrate the vulnerability of putting essential, unguarded—and unguardable—miles of pipeline through both remote and populated areas... then telling everyone, friend and foe alike, exactly where those pipelines were.

One night of effort with a trained, motivated team could accomplish more than a battalion of soldiers in an open conflict. It would be simple, cheap, and untraceable. And that was before the next mission—their true reason for being in the country.

Unfortunately, Hakimi no longer had his small team of dedicated men. He had a wounded man, himself, and two others. Half the men planned for the first mission, which already was fewer than Hakimi needed, a fact he had told those above him.

And for their second objective, every living man meant a better chance of success for the more important targets on the other side of the country.

Plus, there was a deadly, unknown enemy, possibly still out there, who may or may not be alone.

There could be reinforcements on the way right now. Helicopters. Police. Troops.

The first order of business was ditching this vehicle. Whoever killed his men would have reported the truck. And while they were very common in Texas—even he knew that—tonight was not the night for driving one if he wanted to complete his mission and avoid being apprehended.

And get my revenge for the death of Rahmin.

31

THE DESERT

Hudspeth County, Texas
100 Miles Southeast of El Paso, Texas
The Border of the USA and the United Mexican States

Axe ran down the hill, sniper rifle slung tightly to his back, its protective bag abandoned. He held the M4, happily trading the reach of the first weapon for the firepower of the shorter weapon for the rest of the evening.

He hated the idea of abandoning the high ground as well as letting the trucks out of his sight, but one look at the advancing men and he realized he'd had no choice.

I'm not running from the fight—it's a tactical retreat.

No matter what he called it, though, it annoyed him.

I'd rather stay and fight. But with these odds, I'd lose.

If he had his Team, it would be a different story.

His NVGs gave him an advantage, even against the men coming for him and whoever was left near the tunnel. But his priority had to be incapacitating the three trucks.

We can't let the trained soldiers escape.

"I'm on the move," he said as his long legs carried him down the slope, practically flying from step to step to put distance between him and the attackers. "Northeast to evade men attacking and attempting to flank me. How long until backup?"

"I'm still not at the highway exit, so I'm effectively out of the fight. ETA twenty minutes. We have a drone on the way, but it's unarmed—this is American soil, after all. But we'll be able to keep the trucks in sight. It's coming from the north—Holloman Air Force Base. I'm on the other phone with Haley, who is on the line with the drone pilot. But I keep losing her to bad cell coverage."

"Time to target?"

"Hold on," Hammer answered. Axe heard him query Haley, then they waited.

At the bottom of the hill, he angled right, hoping to outflank his flankers... and maybe switch back to the sniper rifle for a few shots at the trucks.

"It hasn't taken off yet," Hammer said with a sigh. "It's about to go. We're still on our own for a bit. But we also have a sheriff from the closest town. He's a ways out too, though, and won't be able to provide immediate help."

"Copy that. Going silent, be right back." Axe dove behind a medium-sized boulder, suddenly convinced he was in more danger than he realized. He extended his senses, feeling, listening, and looking, his head barely poking around the corner of the rock as he lay prone, gun out and ready.

He couldn't see his pursuers, but he heard them. They were on the side of the hill to his right, just out of sight due to the lay of the land.

How did they get there so quickly?

For a second, he wondered if they had an ATV or another vehicle he hadn't seen, or if they'd jumped into one of the trucks, but then the truth hit him.

They're much younger—and faster—than me.

No matter how hard he trained, he wouldn't be as fast as a man half his age who also worked hard at staying in fighting shape.

I'm not going to outrun them.

Could he set up an ambush? Lay in wait for a sniper shot?

I don't have time. At least one truck has already left—probably the soldiers, but maybe not.

Using the large boulder and other smaller ones scattered throughout the area, he moved slowly away at an angle, getting more distance from his former position and the enemy searching for him. In sniper school, he learned being invisible was more than merely picking a good hide and staying still. It was using the terrain to your advantage, keeping out of sight with a sense of where the enemy was and what they could see from their vantage point. Thinking spatially from another's perspective was difficult to teach and harder to learn. It took months of practice to get the hang of, but Axe had excelled at it from the start. He could put himself in the enemy's shoes, envision what they saw, and use the knowledge to conceal himself both in stationary positions and on the move.

He used those skills to his advantage now.

I may not be as fast as them, but I'm more experienced. Better, basically. I hate to brag, but it's true.

Then again, there were a lot more of them.

Outnumbered and outgunned. What else is new since leaving the Teams?

"Drone is airborne," Hammer said in his ear. "ETA your position..." he hesitated. "One hour."

He took a second to tap his finger twice on the microphone, acknowledging the report without having to speak.

An hour? I could be dead and in a shallow grave by then.

Nalen pushed the truck faster.

We should have risked being caught by surveillance and kept my route closer to Axe. What was I thinking, agreeing to drop him off in the middle of the desert alone? SEALS are called Teams for a reason. We don't go into combat alone.

In a rare sign of his frustration, he slammed the heel of his hand against the borrowed beat-up truck's steering wheel and tried to get a few more miles per hour out of it. He had less than ten minutes to the turnoff from the quiet rural highway to the dirt road leading to Axe's area. Ten minutes to decide whether to let Axe deal with the pursuers by himself and hunt the black truck or go to the aid of one of the bravest and most capable men he'd had the pleasure of knowing.

Ten minutes is an eternity on the battlefield. I have time to make my decision.

The truck would never be the same after tonight, but Hakimi didn't care. All he needed was to get to the highway, then to the interstate, then to a gas station, rest area, or somewhere else to switch vehicles.

He pushed the truck harder over the little-used trail—it couldn't be called a road—driving faster as he approached the highway. In the bed, his man—Kabiri, a wiry veteran—hung on for dear life, cursing from time to time as they hit a large pothole or tilted on a rut in the road. But he protected the sniper rifle more than his body, preventing it from banging against the truck.

The other team will need the weapon after we're done with it.

Next to Hakimi in the front was Dehdari, also holding on despite the seat belt he'd clipped when ordered. He looked both pissed off and devastated by the loss of life. None of them had expected to meet such strong resistance so early in their mission. And leaving the bodies of their comrades behind on the battlefield was against their creed.

In the backseat, the man he had ordered to run up the hill—Tir—lay stretched out, silent. Hakimi had all his attention on the road and avoiding the worst of the ruts and holes. There would be time to worry about him soon.

He didn't slow as he neared the highway. Though he'd seen no helicopters, no patrol cars, no backup for the warrior near the border, it didn't make sense.

The Americans don't operate alone. Where are the rest of them?

32

THE FIGHT

Hudspeth County, Texas
100 Miles Southeast of El Paso, Texas
The Border of the USA and the United Mexican States

Halfway across the bare section of desert, with only a few scrubby bushes and a small dip in the desert to shield him, Axe froze.

Something's wrong.

Another hundred yards would bring him to a pile of rocks, half the size of a compact car. From there, he guessed, he'd have a limited line of sight on the trucks and, if it wasn't too much of a risk, he could get back to sniping, taking out the vehicles and more men.

But right now, he melted into the ground, shut down his energy, aura, or whatever people wanted to call it, and went dark. He thought he'd been getting away, but as he lay on the cold ground, his gut told him he may have underestimated his opponent.

What if the men running up the hill and flanking me were only a distraction meant to flush me out of my position?

A clever enemy might have sent other men farther out to the sides, anticipating his escape into the desert.

With the tiniest movement of his right hand, he felt for the phone in his pocket. His thumb moved, finding the volume button on the left side and pushing it repeatedly until the sound of Nalen breathing and the noise of the truck on the other end of the line disappeared. Then he shut down completely—no thoughts, no feelings, nothing—as he first sensed, then heard a man walking across the desert near him.

———————

The turnoff to the gravel road appeared in Hammer's headlights, right where he knew it would be, having passed it several times over the course of the night as he went up and down the deserted highway waiting for Axe's ambush to pay off.

Finally.

He took the turn fast, flying onto the road, then slammed on the brakes. A truck barreled toward him.

In an instant, he was out of the truck, M4 in hand as he took aim and fought his conscience.

It has to be one of the trucks Axe reported... right?

The vehicle wasn't slowing. They had to have seen him.

If I'm wrong, there goes my reputation, my career... and my soul, if I kill innocent people.

But how many innocent people drove brand-new black trucks from the direction of the Mexico border in the middle of the night?

The truck changed angle, moving onto his side of the road. It would slam into his door and kill him if he didn't act. It grew closer and the driver flipped on the high beams, trying to blind him.

Clear and present danger. Self-defense.

Hammer fired at the front tire, destroying it, then pumped several rounds into the engine block. The truck kept coming.

The M4 isn't powerful enough to stop the vehicle before it hits me.

He squinted into the glare of the headlights, sighted the driver, and fired.

Heaven help me if I'm wrong.

The truck swerved, turning hard and going straight into the shallow ditch on the far side of the gravel road. It gradually slowed to a stop as it hit rocks and bushes in the desert.

Hammer moved around the front of his truck, putting the engine block between the tango vehicle and himself, ready for return fire.

———————

Axe kept his energy to a minimum, staying relaxed in stealth mode as the tango crept past him, less than two feet away.

A little closer, that's all I need.

Before moving, he let his senses reach out. If they were smart enough to send people on a wide perimeter, they might have a person on overwatch, keeping an eye on the entire area.

He felt nothing and couldn't wait any longer. He rose silently, taking his time. A quick turn and three quiet steps brought him up behind the wiry man straining to see in the dark. He had a headlamp on his head, but it was off. No night-vision goggles.

Axe clamped one hand over the man's mouth as his other arm snaked around the man's neck. In twenty seconds, the man was dead, lifeless in Axe's arms, having never made a sound.

Now for the rest of them.

After several seconds of no movement or return fire, Hammer cautiously approached the truck resting twenty yards into the desert, engine still idling, though steam had started to come from under the hood.

At least a few of my bullets hit home.

The bed had a black cover over it, and aside from the dead driver with a bullet hole in his forehead, the inside was deserted. Instead, black duffel bags filled every spare foot. He had a bad feeling.

Damn it.

He moved to the back and opened the tailgate. The entire bed was stuffed with neatly arranged black duffel bags. Opening one, he saw a thick plastic bag containing thousands—tens of thousands—of small white pills.

Another bag contained wrapped blocks of what might be heroin but could be any other drug—he didn't have the experience to even guess.

This is one of the trucks, but not the one with the enemy soldiers.

He grabbed one bag as evidence and dropped a second one half under the side of the truck. Stepping back, he fired several shots until gasoline flowed out of the fuel tank, quickly saturating the nylon bag of drugs. He lit it on fire with his classic, decades-old lighter before quickly kicking it under the truck—and the stream of fuel.

Then he ran, looking back toward the highway.

Either they haven't come this way yet, or I'm too late and they went north. If they had turned south, I would have seen them.

He called out to Haley via the cell phone in the holder attached to the heating vent as he drove away. "Blondie—the truck with the enemy soldiers may be headed north on the highway, heading toward the interstate. Have the sheriff on the lookout but tell him to be cautious. These guys are pros, Axe says."

There was silence from the phone. He touched it, which revealed the home screen… and no cell reception.

I need to use the sat phone to call her—but I can't do it while on the line with Axe.

Behind him, the truck exploded.

"Axe, sitrep," he ordered, putting the truck in reverse.

I bet they got ahead of me.

He would check on Axe, call Haley, and pursue the bad guys.

There was silence from the satellite phone as well.

Things go wrong. It always seems like if it's not the intel, it's the comms.

Or Axe was in a bad situation and couldn't reply.

He sat with his foot on the brake, debating for a split second. Then he threw the truck into drive and hit the gas. The tires spun on the gravel road and the old truck lunged forward.

There's the sheriff on the way. And whatever the tangos have planned, it's probably at least a few hours off.

He had to go help Axe.

But first, he had to call in the warning. If Axe couldn't talk, he didn't need the phone line open. Hammer hung up with Axe and dialed Haley's cell.

She answered on the first ring. "Go."

"Axe is off comms," he reported. "And I'm going to help. I took out one of the trucks—one EKIA. The bed and cab are filled with bags of drugs. But I think the truck with the soldiers might have slipped past me. If it did, it's going north on the highway, headed to the interstate. You have to get ahold of the local sheriff who is heading in this direction. Warn him to follow the truck, but to not try to apprehend them. They're heavily armed pros. What we really need is intel, not an arrest. And vector in the drone to fly along the interstate from west to east."

"Copy, I'm on it."

"We're also going to need more support. If Axe's report is accurate, we have some sort of kill team or saboteurs on the loose in the country. Get your boss on board with more resources... or do it yourself on my authority. How copy, Blondie?"

"Solid copy, Hammer. Good hunting."

"Hammer out." He hung up in the hopes Axe would call back.

Hang on, Axe, I'm coming.

33

THE HIGHWAY

Highway 90
Culberson County, Texas

Hakimi resisted the temptation to go faster. He was already driving ten miles per hour over the speed limit north on the highway toward the interstate. Every few seconds, he had to ease off the accelerator as his speed crept up. Stealth was more important for the moment. The last thing they needed was to draw the attention of any bored police on the highway in the middle of the night.

His gamble had paid off. Taking the slower, horrible trail through the desert might have helped them avoid backup coming down the main gravel road to the border.

He took a breath and spoke into the silence of the luxury pickup to his man lying in the back seat "Where are you injured?" he asked in their native tongue.

"My shoulder," Tir replied, his voice weaker than Hakimi had expected.

"I've dressed the wound, but it's still bleeding," Dehdari, his other man, added from the passenger seat. With a quick exchange of glances, Hakimi knew Tir wouldn't make it.

"Just rest," he said. "We'll stop soon and do more," he lied.

"I have an idea," Tir replied, "if we can stop at one of the roadside fueling depots." He sketched out his plan, which Hakimi had to admit wasn't half bad.

"I approve—if we find the right location and you believe it necessary," he said.

"It's necessary. Hurry." Tir went silent.

Conserving his strength for his idea—one last mission.

Hakimi glanced at Dehdari stewing in silence, anger radiating off him.

Better to get it out in the open now.

"What is it?" he asked, though he guessed what was on the man's mind. It was on his, too.

"We should not have left them behind," Dehdari said, his voice tight with frustration and rage.

"I agree. But our missions take priority. The Mexicans will capture or kill the sniper and take the bodies of our comrades into the tunnel."

This seemed to calm his man. "I am sorry about Rahmin," he said. "He was a courageous fighter."

Hakimi forced his face still, letting neither his anguish nor rage show in the dim glow of the dash lights.

My brother. I will complete the missions, avenge his death, then return for his body.

"Thank you."

Ahead, the red and blue strobes of a police vehicle crested a small rise, then dipped from view again. A few moments later, it was obvious—the car was coming quickly toward them.

"Get ready."

The patrol car sped by them, and Hakimi thought for a moment they were in the clear.

Then it slowed, pulled onto the shoulder, and made a U-turn to follow them. Hakimi didn't speed up, allowing the car to gain on them.

"Take him out," Hakimi ordered. Dehdari knocked on the rear window. Seconds later, Kabiri, likely freezing in the bed of the truck, fired a burst with his AK.

The police car instantly slowed, dropping behind them and coasting to a stop in the ditch, its red and blue lights still flashing frantically as Hakimi and his surviving men drove away.

34

THE AFTERMATH

Hudspeth County, Texas
100 Miles Southeast of El Paso, Texas
The Border of the USA and the United Mexican States

Axe lowered the body of the strangled man gently to the ground. Figuring he'd already exposed himself to anyone watching, he ran as quietly as possible to a small rise. As he got closer, he crouched, then crawled until he could peek over the top. His chin scraped the sand and gravel of the Texas desert.

A man guarded one remaining truck. He was short and wiry, but from a few hundred yards away Axe got the sense he was a capable warrior.

Shoot him from here and risk bringing the others running? Or sneak up and risk getting caught in the open by him?

The ground between the truck and his tiny rise in the land—a bump more than a hill—was mostly flat, though there were plenty of scraggly bushes.

He scanned the hill he'd been on earlier but didn't see any of the men sent to kill him.

If the keys were in the truck, or on the man guarding it, could he get away before coming under fire from the men out looking for him?

It's my best bet.

He lined up the shot, using the M4, and fired, sending a bullet into the man's head as he stood on the far side of the truck.

Then the race was on. Axe sprinted forward, putting all his training to the test. It wouldn't take long to get to the truck, but the enemy had heard the shot. Gunfire came from the distant desert.

They're too far away to be effective. As long as they don't get lucky—or have one of the sniper rifles—I'm okay.

He made it to the truck without getting shot, though a few bullets whipped by uncomfortably close. Jumping into the luxury vehicle, he noted the key fob in the cup holder, started the engine, and stomped on the gas.

As he drove out of range, bouncing over the desert, he pushed the button to roll down the window, stuck his elbow out, and grinned.

Score one point for the old guy.

El Gato's remaining men stood together over their leader's lifeless body with a hole in the middle of his forehead. Near them, the tunnel to Mexico beckoned.

But as they watched the truck disappear around a distant hill in the Texas desert, driven by the enemy they had allowed to escape, they knew it contained not only the drugs they'd been tasked to deliver, but each of their lives, as well. While it could be argued that none of this was their fault—they'd been ordered to deliver the drugs to Texas via the secret tunnel, which they'd done. They'd even come to the aid of the men on this side of the border. But tonight's mission would be perceived as a huge failure. And since they were the men left alive, they would be the ones punished.

A man spoke in the darkness. "We can't return home."

The others nodded. They all knew it was true.

"Our families…" another said.

They contemplated the dilemma.

"We dump the bodies in the river," the first said, proposing a course of action that would allow them to live—as long as they disappeared into America and never contacted their loved ones again. "Some will be found, but not all. The boss will think we died as well, and our bodies are missing."

"We will start over," a third said, warming to the idea. "Work and save money."

They nodded. It could work if they got lucky.

"Help me get everyone to the river," the first said. "And fill in the hole over the trapdoor. Maybe the bosses will believe it was the soldiers who killed us." Left unsaid was the thought on his mind and surely a consideration by the others.

Maybe we can use the tunnel to bring our families safely to us someday.

35

THE HEADLIGHTS

Hudspeth County, Texas
100 Miles Southeast of El Paso, Texas

Hammer slowed to turn off the packed gravel road onto the trail through the desert leading to Axe's position. He stopped when he saw the high beam headlights bouncing toward him a mile away, too far to distinguish whether it was another of the cartel's trucks filled with drugs, the team of soldiers Axe warned him about, or kids from town raising hell in the desert.

He got out of the truck, slammed the door, and moved into the darkness alongside the road, hoping the driver of the truck couldn't see his movements.

The truck closed the distance quickly. The driver was clearly in a hurry. Hammer checked his weapon and got ready. He couldn't engage until he knew without a doubt the truck contained the enemy.

As it neared, the headlights flashed.

That's Morse code. A—X—E.

He stood, revealing himself, though he didn't lower his rifle yet.

More light flashes.

O—K.

The truck slowed to a stop and Axe stepped out, his raised hands leading the way. "Nice night for a drive! Beautiful country down here, don't you think?" Axe called to him.

Hammer couldn't help but smile.

"I thought you needed me to rescue your ass," he said.

"Sorry to disappoint. We could go back… I left you a few tangos."

"No, no, I'm sure there will be enough to go around," Hammer said. Turning serious, he added, "I stopped a truck with one tango in it and a lot of drugs, but the soldiers are in the wind. Either they got ahead of me or took another route—maybe overland instead of the road. Let's get a move on—we can talk on comms while we go. I had to hang up on you to call Blondie."

"Copy that. I had to turn off the volume, anyway. An acquaintance got all choked up."

Hammer guessed the meaning behind the statement as he got back into his truck.

He's crazy—but in a good way. And I'm glad he's on our side.

36

THE SITUATION

Off Highway 90
Culberson County, Texas

"I'll be right behind you," Hammer told Axe as the younger man's newer truck pulled away from him. With the go-ahead, the black truck surged ahead on the gravel road.

"And never mind the burning truck up ahead—that's my handiwork," Hammer added. "No sense letting those drugs fall into the wrong hands."

"Perfect," Axe said over the sat phone line. "So where are we?" he asked.

"The sheriff is on the way, looking out for the truck. The drone will be flying along the interstate shortly and will see them if they're going west. What do you think they're up to?"

The frustration in Axe's voice was clear. "I don't know. But they're highly skilled—likely some type of special forces. They also had two sniper rifles, and everyone was a solid marksman, not just the two snipers I took out. Also worrying was they all had large, heavy backpacks. They were too big for merely spare ammunition unless they were looking at a protracted siege or something."

Hammer's mind went through an alarming list of possibilities. "Explosives. RPGs. Bigger weapons like machine guns and plenty of ammo."

"Radioactive dirty bombs," Axe said, voicing a fear Hammer hadn't wanted to admit out loud.

"Why, though? Were they part of the cartel?"

"Unsure. They didn't act like it. The US-side cartel guys wanted the special forces leader to help put sand back into the hole to hide the tunnel —likely a pissing contest. They got into an argument. Doesn't sound like they're fully on the same team. But other cartel guys popped out of the tunnel real quick once I started shooting. They were the ones who went after me while letting the special forces get away, so you do the math."

"Get the brains of the organization on it," Hammer said. "Call Haley once you're back in cellular range."

"Good idea. She'll figure it out. Tonight, once again, she was right. Nailed it—the location and the date."

"At least we intercepted the drugs."

"And we confirmed the location of a formerly secret tunnel," Axe said. "But I didn't get them all. Not the drug runners or—worse—the hit squad."

"How many are left?"

"Of the really bad guys? I took out four, I think. That leaves three, including the one I thought of as the leader. Plus one I winged. I don't know how badly I hit him—things got pretty hectic there."

"So they're at half strength. That's excellent work for one man in one night, Axe."

"Thanks. Again, I got kind of busy, but I know they collected both sniper rifles. And there were no backpacks lying around when I stole the truck."

Hammer tried not to let his imagination get the better of him as he pictured what a few highly trained American special force operators could do in a foreign country with backpacks filled with various deadly items.

What can the remaining enemy accomplish with whatever they have?

37

THE EXTRA PIECES

Central Analysis Group Headquarters
Conference Room C
Alexandria, Virginia

Nancy reveled in the additional space of the converted conference room, along with the privacy. She and Dave had been using the room when necessary for the past few weeks, whenever they needed to discuss sensitive issues for the newly formed World Intelligence Agency that they couldn't risk the other analysts overhearing.

She had her work area at the end of the room furthest from the door. Her two new, huge monitors matched the ones Haley used.

Dave's workstation—and his new, larger monitors—was set up near the door. In the middle of the room, a third person could work at the conference table.

I'm happy Haley came back.

Five weeks before, Haley had returned to the office with no discussion of why she had quit—or the video footage of her abducting Victor Baranov. With the Russian president dead in a freak helicopter crash, the Ukraine crisis appeared to be over—for now.

But Nancy wasn't stupid.

Haley quits, and later that day abducts Victor Baranov. The drug we suspected was in his company's beer is used in Las Vegas, but death and destruction are mostly averted because of a group of retired veterans who "happened" to be in the city. Then, a few days later, the Russian president dies under strange circumstances, averting a war.

There was a far-fetched possibility she couldn't get out of her mind.

Haley and her asset, Axe, killed President Zimalev of Russia— somehow.

But they didn't talk about that. Dave had started to bring it up once, but Nancy had silenced him with a look.

And now Russian gangsters try to kill her in a restaurant. Does she really believe we don't know what's going on?

Some things, however, were better not discussed, even in their top-secret realm. To speak of it made it real—and no one wanted that if it could be avoided.

Gregory stood behind her, watching as she updated the master spreadsheet listing Russian sleeper spies on a separate, special laptop, chained to the wall and incapable of connecting to the internet or any network. In the midst of this other drama with the attacks on Haley and Admiral Nalen, the cartel's drug smuggling actions, and the terrorists that had snuck into the country, a report had come in. The Russian sleeper spies continued to be monitored by a group of field agents hand-selected by Gregory and a friend of his at Homeland Security considered above reproach.

She highlighted the final name on the list and changed the cell color from blue to red, indicating the man was indeed a Russian spy.

The rest of the spreadsheet listed the remaining suspects. All were highlighted with a color.

Many were pink. These were probable sleepers suspected of being clueless, uninformed of the situation by their families so they could escape detection.

Others were red. Nancy, Dave, and Gregory considered them to be actively in touch with Russian handlers, ready for operations of some sort —or already involved.

Orange names were sleepers they had already begun to turn into unwitting double agents. Gregory had chosen a counterintelligence colleague to run the operation with him and the president.

"Well done, Nancy," Gregory said. "Could any of this," he continued, gesturing to include the terrorists and drug cartel situation, "be a part of the sleeper program?"

"I don't see how, but it's worth a look." She logged off and shut down the machine as Gregory walked away to sit at the conference table and work. Only she, Gregory, Dave, and the president could log into the laptop, and it took two of the four of them to access the data stored on it. But with this work done, she moved to her other computer to poke at the problem.

None of this made sense. Why would a Mexican drug cartel get involved with the Russians by helping Victor Baranov?

Victor Baranov had confirmed the cartel's involvement in the procurement and disappearance of test subjects for Dr. Edgars, along with the kidnapping and guarding of Carol, the nurse who knew too much.

But why take on a project like that?

For the money? No. They were a drug cartel—money wasn't a problem... except for the recent reports they were struggling financially.

That could be it.

Or could they want a connection to Russia? Possibly, but how would they have known who had hired them, and the source of the funds? Baranov had said his handler, an American of Russian origin just like himself, had done the initial contact and negotiations. The Mexicans would have believed an American organization was behind it, not a Russian one.

She frowned, annoyed.

There has to be an explanation. A logical motive. And why would the cartel import a group of soldiers along with their drug shipment?

Dave appeared at her side, surprising her. She'd been lost in thought. Falling into the zone was getting easier and easier. "Making any progress?" he asked.

She frowned and shook her head. "You know those puzzles that contain extra pieces to throw you off?" she asked. He'd gotten her one for Christmas a few years before. She had both loved and hated it. "We have a situation exactly like it with the Mexican drug cartel angle. The picture is complete on the first puzzle—the abducted nurse who knew too much and Dr. Edgars' lab in the hotel in Mexico—but there are these other pieces that don't fit. They can't because the puzzle is finished. But obviously, it's not. There's another, bigger puzzle. I went from thinking I had a few extra pieces to realizing I don't have enough."

38

ROADBLOCKS

Central Analysis Group Headquarters
Conference Room C
Alexandria, Virginia

"Get the word out to everyone," Gregory ordered Haley, Nancy, and Dave. "FBI, Homeland. Highway Patrol, local sheriffs, whoever they have. Someone get me the governor—maybe he can make things move as fast as we need them to."

He looked at the map of West Texas displayed on the room's big monitor. "I want roadblocks on I-10, well before El Paso. We can't let those guys get into a populated area."

Seconds before, Axe had reported a sheriff badly injured but clinging to life on Highway 90, south of Van Horn, Texas, and Interstate 10. The terrorists—which is what they officially were now—had shot him. Admiral Nalen rushed him to the local hospital while Axe was heading for I-10 at top speed.

"Nalen brought the sheriff to the hospital from the south. He didn't see them, so the terrorists are likely heading north to the interstate. We need another roadblock to the east. Preferably here," he said, pointing at a spot before the first exit from the freeway. "If not, we need one here, before I-10 splits, or one on each. Make it happen!"

He no longer felt the hesitation he had earlier. The fear of doing the wrong thing was gone. In its place was a certainty. The CAG—or WIA, whatever they were calling themselves—was essential to saving the country. While part of him would rather keep the operation small, confined to his three trusted analysts and the bare minimum of people needed to capture or kill the men who had infiltrated the country, shot at Axe, and tried to murder the sheriff, help was needed.

This is a time for action.

He sat at his laptop and ran the calculations himself, figuring average and maximum rates of speed for the truck. Next, he mapped the information and noted the times the roadblocks had to be in place by.

Come on, come on!

The hunt would get exponentially more difficult if they couldn't get roadblocks set up and catch the men before they got off the interstate.

39

TRUCKS

Hakimi stopped near the entrance to the large truck stop.

This will do.

A combination of a convenience store, two different fast-food restaurants, a small coffee shop, and seemingly endless fueling areas for both cars and semis.

Best of all, a long row of semi-tractors idled to one side.

"Are you positive, my friend?" Hakimi asked Tir, the injured man. They weren't really friends, but that wasn't important now. The man would be dead soon.

"Yes," Tir said, holding back a sob from the pain as Dehdari helped him sit up in the backseat of the pickup. His face was covered in a sheen of sweat. "If I must die, let me go with dignity and help the mission."

Hakimi nodded, impressed and pleased. "Ready yourselves," he said to his remaining men.

He looked at the row of eighteen-wheelers and selected two that looked promising. They were set apart from the others by several empty rows and had one empty space between them.

Perfect. It will shield our actions from view.

Circling the parking lot, he pulled between the idling trucks.

Hakimi left his rifle behind as he exited. A noisy gunshot would ruin the plan. He moved to the passenger side of the semi closest to him. Kabiri prepared to assault the other one.

He made eye contact with Kabiri as they both stepped onto the running boards of the big trucks. It was time.

Hakimi checked the door.

Locked, but not a problem.

He broke the window with the butt of his knife, sure the noise wouldn't be heard by the occupants of the other nearby trucks over the idling diesel engines. Reaching in, he opened the door, climbed inside, and slit the throat of the trucker who stuck his head conveniently through the curtain shielding the sleeper bunk to see who had broken his window.

Moments later, Dehdari passed him the heavy backpacks from the rear of the pickup, which he piled in the sleeper compartment, avoiding the dead man he'd pushed into the back corner.

In the second semi, Kabiri hit the sleepy trucker repeatedly until the man was unconscious. Then he exited and helped Tir up into the truck's seat, trying but failing to be gentle. "You will be remembered, brother," he said as the dying man arranged himself behind the steering wheel.

"Any of us would do it," Tir gasped, but Kabiri didn't think so.

Would I have the courage and strength, or would I beg for morphine and slip away in a haze of bliss?

"Do you need him?" Kabiri asked, gesturing at the truck driver. The man slumped in the sleeper compartment, coming around with a groan. "I can make him show you how to operate the vehicle."

"No. I trained in the army," Tir said, sounding weaker by the moment. "Go. Hurry, while I can still do this."

Kabiri nodded, drew his knife, and stabbed the trucker until the man stopped making noise.

"Good luck, brother," he said as he slipped out the passenger door.

Tir pulled the tractor-trailer forward, shifting with a great deal of effort. His eyes watered from the pain, and he fought to stay conscious.

Not much longer now.

He never thought he'd live this long or achieve so much. And he'd realized his biggest—though secret—goal: to see America.

At least for an hour.

He drove across the large parking lot, gaining speed.

The faster I'm going when I hit, the better.

In the distance, at the front of the facility, Dehdari had already started filling the black pickup provided by the cartel with gasoline. They locked eyes as he turned toward the fuel pumps. Dehdari directed the flow of gas into the cab of the pickup for a moment, then placed the hose back into the tank. It overflowed immediately, spilling fuel onto the ground. Then the man casually walked toward the street... where the other semi with Hakimi and Kabiri was idling.

Tir felt himself weakening as he pushed the gas pedal to the floor. The heavy truck responded sluggishly but started picking up more speed. The pumps grew closer.

As soon as Dehdari jumped into the cab of the semi, Hakimi pulled forward, signaled, and turned onto the frontage road for the interstate.

I would love to watch—and honor Tir's sacrifice in person—but we can't risk it.

He smoothly cycled through the gears, picking up speed and watching in the side mirror for the explosion that would come any second.

The pain woke Rick Murrey, Marine combat veteran turned truck driver. His stomach and chest felt like when his Humvee had taken an RPG round, leaving him filled with holes and gushing blood.

I've gotta get out of the Humvee and return fire, or we're all dead.

He pushed himself forward as he opened his eyes, confusion hitting him.

How the hell are we still moving?

Reality came crashing in.

I'm in my rig, not the Humvee.

He'd been stabbed, not shot with an RPG. And this was Texas, not the Sandbox.

In a moment of clarity, he took in the man driving his semi directly at the center passenger vehicle fuel pumps of the truck stop. They would hit in a moment. There was no time to be a hero, grab the wheel, and turn. No matter what he did, the truck was going in. But he could possibly save himself.

Acting on instinct, he flung himself out the passenger door, the pain ignored until he landed on the ground and rolled. The agony came crashing back, but it only hurt for an instant before he blacked out again.

Tir's consciousness faded as he fought to hold the truck straight... then the dead trucker tumbled from the sleeping compartment and out the side door.

What just happened?

A moment later, the semi plowed into a compact car at the fuel island, pushing it forward. The car hit the concrete median where the pumps sat and scraped along until it slammed into the cartel's black pickup—and the fuel covering the ground around it.

All it took was one spark for the gas to catch fire. The explosion sent a huge fireball into the air. The truck, car, and semi were engulfed in flames... but Tir was already dead.

Hakimi said a prayer for his comrade, softly echoed by the other two men as they watched in the side mirrors as the flames leapt high into the night. Then he turned, avoiding the freeway entrances, and drove south on Highway 90, back the way he'd come, safe in their new transportation, going in a direction none of the Americans would think to look for them.

40

CAMERAS

With the fire still blazing, the lights of the emergency vehicles flashing, and what seemed like half the state standing in the parking lot watching the spectacle, it didn't take much for Axe to get what he wanted.

He held up his fake Homeland Security credentials to the grandmotherly woman at the cash register inside the convenience store section of the truck stop. "I need to see all your security footage," he said in his most official tone.

She tore her eyes away from the firefighters and the circus outside and barely glanced at the badge, though she checked out his plate carrier with extra magazines, knife hanging upside down from its sheath at his shoulder, and the M4 he carried on a sling.

"You think this is terrorists?" she asked, sounding more excited than scared.

"Not sure yet, Ma'am. But there might be more of them on the loose, and it's my job to find them. The security footage?"

"Oh, of course. Marvin!" she yelled at the top of her lungs. "The manager," she explained.

A twenty-something kid with acne opened a door in the back corner of the store, near the hallway to the bathrooms.

The manager?

Axe looked at the older woman, who caught his meaning and shrugged.

"What, Phyllis?" Marvin asked with an exasperated look. "I'm on hold with corporate."

He's having a rough night and is way over his head.

"Homeland Security thinks this is a terrorism plot," she said as Axe walked to the back.

"Terrorism?" Marvin said with a skeptical look. "Come on, seriously? It was some drunk or sleepy trucker. But whatever, dude, come on back." He turned, causing the door to swing closed automatically. Axe had to hustle to catch it before it latched.

Several color security monitors were stacked on shelves above a messy desk in a room more like a broom closet than a manager's office.

A grimy telephone handset lay on the desk and soothing jazz came from the speakerphone part of it. "I call this in, and they put me on hold. Can you believe that shit?" Marvin asked, waving his hand at the phone.

"I need to see your security footage from about fifteen minutes before the incident," Axe said, trying to sound more like an official Homeland Security officer and less like a retired Navy SEAL.

Marvin hesitated. "Yeah man, I'm happy to help and everything, but... lemme ask corporate. If they ever pick up again," he muttered.

"I don't have time for all the red tape," Axe said. "We think—"

"Sorry to keep you on hold," a stressed woman's voice came from the phone. "We're—"

Axe reached over and hung up the handset.

"Hey!" Marvin yelled.

"Kid, I just saved your ass," Axe explained as patiently as he could. "You would have asked for permission to let me see the tapes. They would have said no, or at least, to wait." He took a step closer to Marvin, invading his space. "But then I would have made you show me the footage, anyway. Get it?"

He's a night manager of a large, popular truck stop. He's probably smarter than he seems, despite the place being in the middle of nowhere, Texas.

"Between the accident and not waiting for their permission, they would have plenty of reasons to fire me," Marvin thought out loud, trying his best not to cower too much against Axe's crowding.

"I imagine there aren't a lot of great jobs way out here in the boonies, am I right?"

"You're right," Marvin sighed. "Okay, let's look at the footage, but quick-like. Before they get their act together and call me back."

***

Axe allowed himself ninety seconds to grab a pre-made sandwich, the largest cup of coffee the store sold, and an assortment of trail mix, candy bars, and sports drinks before hurrying outside to the truck.

It's going to be a long night... and killing bad guys always makes me hungry.

Haley answered his call, sounding tired but focused. "Where are you?"

"Leaving the truck stop. The explosion was a good diversion, but this place has a better security camera setup than most banks. The manager was kind enough to let me look at them without a warrant."

"I bet all you had to do was ask nicely," she said dryly.

"I think all the bad guys are in a semi-tractor now, not the black truck. They blew that up with another semi, likely driven by the tango I wounded. It's what I would do."

"But you're not sure?"

"No. There's a blind spot in the camera coverage. If the trucks park just right, their cabs can't be seen and recorded. The manager said it's in case they have... visitors."

Some people get lonely, I guess.

"Visitors? Who would— Oh. I get it," Haley said, catching on.

"But an enemy walked away from the pickup truck after overfilling the gas tank right before the semi rammed into the fuel island. Another camera caught the semi I think he got into leaving the parking lot, but he was out of range to know for sure. Best guess—they switched vehicles to stay off our radar but didn't account for the security cameras."

Axe gave her the license plate number and description of the big rig he hoped all the remaining terrorists were in. "How are we doing on the roadblocks?" he asked, starting the truck he'd stolen. "Which direction do you need me to go?"

Haley considered the question for a second. "The drone was looking for the black truck, so might have missed the semi, but it hasn't been long. If they're going northwest toward El Paso, the roadblock there will get them. So will the ones to the east. They're already searching every vehicle. No one shoots a cop and gets away with it."

"Where aren't we covered, then? Or what do you think they're doing?"

"I haven't figured it out yet. The heavy backpacks are concerning— were any of them in the burning truck?"

"Unsure because of the blind spot in the cameras, but it was a pretty well-executed spur-of-the-moment action, so I bet they still have the backpacks."

"Okay, I'll put the description out. Now that we have everyone on alert and the roadblocks up, I have some time to look at the problem. Even if they're caught, it will be good to have an idea what they were after, in case there are others coming in for the same target."

Others? Damn. I hadn't thought of that.

"Otherwise, the only place we don't have a roadblock—yet—is Highway 90, but you and Hammer were just on that, so we didn't prioritize it. And between the truck stop blowing up and the other roadblocks, we're out of manpower for now. Day shift police are being called in, but it'll be a while."

Axe thought of his race to the burning truck stop and the route he took. He'd driven the eastbound frontage road, separated from the westbound road by the elevation of the freeway.

They could have gone right past me, and I wouldn't have seen them.

He shook his head at the time he'd spent arguing with Marvin, watching the security footage, and—he rolled his eyes—buying food and drinks.

How far ahead could they be?

His foot pressed the gas pedal to the floor, sending the truck lurching out of the parking lot of the truck stop. One of the duffel bags of drugs filling the cab fell off the pile on the passenger seat and landed on his lap. "We need a roadblock on Highway 90 ASAP," he told Haley. "That's where they're going." He sailed down the westbound interstate frontage road, slowed at a red light to check for cross traffic, then sped through the intersection without stopping.

Haley paused for a second as she yelled at someone in her office, repeating Axe's instruction.

It's not going to happen quickly enough... and I'm too far behind to catch them.

"But why?" Haley asked a moment later. "They couldn't know we don't have a roadblock there, too."

Axe turned onto Highway 90, passing under I-10, and ran more red lights as he pushed the truck to its limit.

"Because they guessed we wouldn't prioritize that direction since it's where they—and we—came from. It also could be where their target is, but they didn't want to go that way until they'd switched vehicles. You need to figure out what their target could be and vector me in. Quickly."

41

DOUBTS

Central Analysis Group Headquarters
Alexandria, Virginia

Haley settled into her desk chair, foregoing conference room C for the quiet of her desk and the large monitors.

This shouldn't be as hard as it's been in the past.

For their previous missions, she had suspected attacks on the country. From there, she had to put together the whole puzzle, relying on hunches, leaps of logic no other analyst would be comfortable making, and sheer willpower to understand the threat.

At least this time I have hard facts—a foreign kill team is at large in the United States of America.

She also had a clear question: what could a small group of trained men do in southwest Texas, a place with few people? And nothing against Texas, but it had no high-value-target cities, little water, and few resources.

Basically, all they have in West Texas is desert, oil, and natural gas.

Her stomach flipped.

Oh no. Oil.

Another part of her mind had been quietly chewing away at the problem of who attacked Nalen and herself the night before. Now, it started to fit together.

If Russia still wants the country weakened and or injured, taking out our oil and natural gas infrastructure and pipelines would do it.

Her fingers flew on the keyboard, pulling up maps. If anything happened, the United States, already barely keeping up with demand for its natural gas export, would be unable to supply its current obligations, let alone set aside extra for a future crisis in Europe.

And less production in-country means we stop being a net exporter and return to importing oil. Which means the world would turn to whoever could produce extra supply... like Russia.

But she and Axe had handled the Russian threat. Permanently.

She paused her research as the thought hit her. She remembered lying in the shallow "grave" next to Axe on the mountain outside Sochi, Russia, five weeks before. The crack of the sniper rifle as Axe took the shot that forced the Russian President off his skeleton sled and onto the ice of the bobsled track. The sight of President Zimalev's body crashing headfirst into the padded column. A man covering the president's face and body with a coat.

What if we assassinated the wrong person?

42

MARVILLE

Route 90
Marville, Texas

It was Officer Mariana Rodriguez's first roadblock, and she felt ridiculous. Her car angled across both lanes of Highway 90, just past the fancy "Welcome to Marville" billboard the Chamber of Commerce had installed the year before. It was a lovely sign but completely out of place along the desolate road a few miles from town. It looked strange, like a joke.

Might as well say, 'Welcome to the middle of nowhere.'

She'd been born and raised in the town, sent to the nearest big city's police academy, and returned as one of the eight officers—plus the chief—on the town's force.

Now I'm out here ready to stop a group of terrorists.

Sighing, she shook out her long black hair and redid it into a tight bun at the back of her head.

Terrorists, here? What a joke.

Still, the job beat working at the grocery store. And the roadblock was different from the usual. At least she wasn't rolling slowly through the RV park, making an appearance to prove to any night owls their precious rigs were protected from the outlaws of the area. Which consisted mostly of the Porter siblings—boys and girls—who were known to pour a few beers down their underage throats and graffiti the local buildings or, on more than one occasion, the side of a fancy RV. Once, they'd stolen the same RV they'd graffitied the night before and took it for a joy ride. They made it to the edge of town before the traumatized snowbird tourists in the back bedroom mustered the courage to yell at them.

They're just going to have to keep themselves under control tonight.

She checked her watch.

They're likely in bed by now, anyway.

She sat in the patrol cruiser, engine off, windows down like she'd been taught—can't hear cries for help or gunfire with them up—even if it was freezing out. The red and blue flashing lights lit the flat, barren desert and long stretch of old asphalt highway. Keeping her eyes focused up the road, she daydreamed of stopping the terrorists, becoming a hero, and getting the hell out of this town for good.

When she heard the faint whine of what sounded like a plane taking off from the airport north of town, she thought nothing of it. Not even the Porter kids would steal an airplane.

The semi-trailer blocking the highway—without the tractor that had been attached to it—proved Axe's hunch. The terrorists had come this way.

They ditched the trailer to make better time… and slow down pursuers.

But Axe had advantages the police didn't—he had not only a four-wheel drive, American-made pickup truck, but it wasn't his and he didn't care what happened to it. He cranked the wheel, bouncing down the shallow ditch, through the desert, and back onto the road without losing much speed. He figured he was less than an hour behind the kill squad and had to make up the time if he had any hope of catching them.

Surprisingly, Mariana was enjoying the evening. After tonight, she'd have to pick a spot—maybe this one—and hang out.

There are only so many times a night I can patrol the entire town.

Usually, she'd park by the grocery store, or the RV park, to deter the Porter kids, but out here was much more peaceful.

Miles away, headlights appeared. It didn't take long to see they were coming much faster than a car usually drove on the road.

Holy shit, I'm actually catching someone!

She never considered the shotgun resting in its mounting bracket. Not when she'd been issued the sleek, deadly-looking weapon on the seat next to her for the night. Living so close to the Mexico border, with the threat of illegal immigrants and drug traffickers ever-present, Homeland Security had seen fit to fund the purchase of a semi-automatic rifle for every member of the force. After a few hours at the range shooting shit up, the chief promptly confiscated them and locked them in a gun safe in his office—the "armory." But once the dispatcher woke the chief up with the news they were needed for a statewide roadblock, and he called the higher-ups to confirm it wasn't a sophisticated prank by the Porter clan to waste his time and make the whole force a laughingstock, the chief had called her in from patrol, handed her the powerful gun and several spare magazines, and said, "Don't shoot anyone who doesn't need shooting."

If this guy doesn't slow down and stop, I'm lighting him up.

The thought was mostly just bravado, but she'd be able to tell the tale more convincingly later if she practiced now.

This is a great night.

She wondered if she'd get to do stuff like this more often as a police officer in a bigger town.

Or the Border Patrol. They'd take me in a heartbeat.

All she had to do was find the guts to pick up and leave the only home she'd ever known.

She grabbed the rifle and slid out of the car, crouching behind the relative safety the engine block would provide if she got into an honest-to-God firefight with terrorists.

What am I forgetting?

She had to call it in! "Base, this is Unit 1 by the Welcome sign. There's a vehicle approaching my position at a high rate of speed." She tried to keep her voice casual and professional but guessed she had failed miserably. She was excited, a little afraid, and ready to rock and roll.

Mariana aimed the weapon up the highway. Her finger rested lightly on the trigger, then tighter. She forced herself to ease off.

Relax. Remember what the chief said. No killing anyone who doesn't deserve it.

Axe had seen the patrol car's red and blue flashing lights from miles away but didn't slow.

Please don't let it be another dying cop, shot by those assholes.

Hammer had reported to Haley, who passed along to him that the sheriff was in rough shape and undergoing surgery. His ballistic vest had caught three rounds from what was probably the AK the men carried. If they'd shot him with the sniper rifle, he'd be dead. As it was, the soft LEVEL II armor normally worn by police wasn't rated to stop rounds from automatic rifles. His distance from the terrorists when shot had saved him.

But as Axe neared what was obviously a roadblock and not an injured officer in a shot-up car, his senses tingled. There was danger ahead.

They could have killed the cop and left a guy behind to ambush me.

He slowed quickly, still outside effective AK range... but already close enough for the sniper rifle.

Axe clicked off his high beams and took a chance. The tingle didn't feel the same as it did when facing the kill squad in the desert. He opened the door slowly and stepped out, his hands raised—but his M4 dangling within reach. He had a better chance at putting rounds on target—or near enough from this range—than the terrorists would with the less powerful AK.

And if it's one of them on the sniper rifle, I'm already dead.

"Alex Alexander," he yelled, using the fake name on his fake credentials. "Homeland Security. I'm the one who requested the roadblock."

He held still, hands up, feeling certain he was in someone's crosshairs. He hated it, but what else was there to do?

"Yeah? Prove it!" came the response from behind the patrol car. The female voice sounded nervous and excited.

"I have a badge—can I come toward you?"

"No!" She hesitated. "What's the capital of New York?"

Seriously? A challenge question?

He had to think for a second.

It's not New York City, right? No. What was it? Buffalo? No...

"Albany?"

There was another pause. When the woman spoke again, she sounded disappointed. "All right, come forward slowly."

Mariana felt robbed. Her one shot at action and she catches a Homeland Security officer.

I'm definitely not telling it the way it's going down.

When she told the story, she'd have to change it around to make it sound less like she was an idiot holding a gun on a fellow officer and more like the guy had needed her help.

The well-built, moderately tall man—six foot, maybe six-one, she figured—walked toward her. He moved with a weird sort of grace she'd never seen before. He had dark hair and rugged features.

That is the sexiest man I've ever seen in my life.

True, she hadn't traveled much, but still. She was thirty years old and single in a town with few viable prospects.

A girl can dream—and what a dream.

"Alex," he said as he neared the car. He slowly pulled a credentials case from his rear pocket and held it up. It looked legit, as far as she could tell from fifteen feet. He certainly acted the part and didn't seem like a terrorist.

She couldn't help the sigh of disappointment that slipped out.

"Fine, put your damn hands down," she told him, standing and lowering the gun she hadn't gotten to fire.

"Thanks, Officer…"

"Rodriguez."

"Thanks, Rodriguez. No semi-tractors through here?" His question had an urgency to it now that she wasn't going to shoot him.

She shook her head.

Nothing, unfortunately.

"How long have you been set up?" He shook his head when she told him.

"Anything unusual happen?" It sounded like a last-ditch, throwaway question, and she felt the story of her short lifetime slipping away.

This isn't how it was supposed to turn out.

"No. Nothing much happens here, except for a family of pain-in-the-ass kids who run around at night and raise hell."

The memory of the sound of the airplane taking off popped into her mind.

"What?" the guy from Homeland said. "What did you just remember?"

"It's probably nothing. But shortly after I got set up, I heard a plane take off from the airport," she said, nodding her head north of town. "But it's probably just a local guy named Randy leaving early to fly to Austin for the day or something. Maybe there's a concert this afternoon—he likes music."

Shut up! I must sound like an idiot. No, worse—a hick.

Homeland turned and sprinted back to his truck. "Move your car, Rodriguez! Lead the way to the airport—and get your dispatcher to call Randy. Wake his ass up and get him to the airport."

"I told you," she yelled, "he flew to Austin or wherever."

"No, he didn't. Those were the bad guys!"

It took a second to fully hit her, but then she was moving. The gun went on the seat and the car was in gear before she had the door fully closed, spinning a donut in the middle of the highway.

Now this is more like it!

43

EXPLOSIVES

Hakimi kept the overloaded airplane low to stay under radar. He had been selected to lead the operation for his experience and versatility—including his ability to drive or fly nearly anything—and it was paying off now.

The desert passed below them with only the occasional light to break up the darkness. The eighty-mile flight wouldn't take long—much shorter than a two-hour drive and the roadblocks that would be set up by now.

Maybe I should have considered this option from the start, instead of wasting time with the trucks.

His original mission plan hadn't called for stealing an airplane except as a last resort. Then again, he hadn't anticipated a sniper shooting five of his men the moment they stepped onto American soil, either. But with the authorities of the United States surely searching for them, desperate times called for desperate measures.

The American Navy SEALs consider themselves so special, but they aren't the only ones who would rather die than fail.

The plane had been easy to steal, though they'd lost some time when Hakimi insisted on a contingency for their second mission. While he broke into the plane, the men found a suitable place far enough from the tarmac, then used their collapsible shovels to dig a shallow hole for the spare sniper rifle and one of the backpacks filled with explosives, pistols, and knives.

Now, behind him in the cramped aircraft, his men were preparing the rest of the explosives. While he didn't expect to encounter any guards or roving police patrols at their targets, there was no way to know how much time they'd have once they landed the plane. He had to make the best of having fewer men. They would still accomplish the mission, though they would likely not be able to take out as many targets as originally planned before continuing to their next operation.

And somewhere along the way, I will avenge my brother's death. If I can't kill the man who actually pulled the trigger, then I will end the lives of others. Many others.

44

PIPELINES

Haley had been terribly wrong in her assessment of how easy it would be to find the terrorists' target given what she already knew.

On one of her monitors, a map of Texas showed all the oil, natural gas, and other pipelines crossing the state. Overlaid were oil wells, refineries, and liquid natural gas sites. The volume overwhelmed her.

Talk about a target-rich environment.

Could her analytical superpowers pick out the best target based on her limited knowledge of the attackers and the overall situation? She didn't have a good feeling.

Work the problem.

With a rare sense of hopelessness, she opened a spreadsheet on the other monitor and started.

High-value targets grouped closely together for maximum impact.

With the big backpacks Axe had described, the terrorists wouldn't be content with one facility. And with three or four men left, they couldn't hit multiple locations at once.

The packs have to contain explosives.

Missiles wouldn't fit into the backpacks. RPGs would, but the launcher would be more easily carried outside of a pack.

And where would they get enough material for so many dirty bombs?

No. Her guess would be plastic explosives.

But backpacks full of the stuff? How much would really be needed?

She eliminated the facilities from her map. The terrorists no longer had the manpower to attack a refinery or gas processing site.

They could have an inside man...

She clicked a button to display them on the map again and chose the biggest refineries close to the western part of the state.

If they wanted the port facilities or bigger sites in south-central Texas, they would have snuck across the border somewhere closer, like between Laredo and Brownsville.

Haley recalled her success weeks before using public search engines to find the data and connections she needed. After setting her search parameters in the classified databases looking for intel on vulnerable oil and gas sites, terrorist chatter about potential strikes, and any other tidbits picked up by the country's massive intelligence network, she switched to a web browser and entered a search. A few clicks revealed the cold, hard facts she didn't want to see.

It all comes down to Pecos County, Texas.

Another search brought up the maps and driving time.

About ninety minutes from where they stole the eighteen-wheeler... if they had taken I-10.

The trip was longer using the route the terrorists might have taken to evade the obvious roadblocks, but the back roads would still get them there.

She sprinted to conference room C with her laptop.

"We need more roadblocks," she said to the startled—and exhausted-looking—Gregory, Nancy, and Dave. She plugged in her computer so the maps would show on the big screen on the wall. "Here," she said, pointing out several locations. "No matter how fast the hit squad is moving or what route they take, we can catch them with enough manpower at these places."

"Why there?" Dave asked, already picking up his phone to enact her plan, not bothering to wait for Gregory's approval.

"They're going to hit the oil and natural gas pipelines," she said with conviction. She knew it in her gut like she had felt so many times before when she was right.

"Where?" Nancy asked, bringing up her own map of the region and the pipelines snaking through the whole state.

"The Waha oil field area," Haley said, trying not to let her concern show.

Nancy zoomed in. The hundreds of pipelines in the region glowed green on the map. "Yes, but where exactly?"

Haley bit her lip in frustration. "That's what we have to figure out."

45

DEPUTIES

Axe watched the local rich guy with annoyance.

"Officer Rodriguez, where the hell is my plane?" Randy, fifty-something years old, gone doughy in the middle, his bed head hair flying everywhere except the thin spot at the top, had his hands on his hips and a furious look on his face. The shorter policewoman, with her powerful, stocky build, wasn't backing down from him, though she kept her mouth shut and let the man vent. He'd gone from annoyed at being called out of his bed to full-on rage when he saw that his plane had been stolen.

The three of them stood on the tarmac of the tiny airfield next to Axe's truck, Rodriguez's patrol car, and the spot where Randy's plane normally rested.

Time to nip this in the bud.

"Randy," Axe said, "like you were told, we suspect terrorists have taken your plane. What we—"

"Terrorists? They were serious about that?" he asked Rodriguez, in her face and ignoring Axe completely.

Axe sighed.

There's no time for this.

He stepped closer to Randy, getting between him and the police officer, who looked like she was having a lot less fun than she'd hoped tonight.

"Randy, I can get your plane back for you."

Probably, Axe thought.

Randy clearly wasn't used to people invading his personal space. He took a step back, which Axe matched. Randy's eyes narrowed and he didn't step back again. "Explain yourself, mister…"

"Alexander, Homeland Security. It's simple—we go get it."

"We… what?"

Axe nodded to the nearby hangar. "The officer says there's another private plane in there. A fast one."

Randy laughed uncomfortably and shook his head. "Yes, but that's Norman's." He hesitated a second, then said, "Mr. Darrian."

"I'm aware—and he's in Europe?"

Randy looked at Rodriguez like she'd been sharing secrets.

He knows where this is going.

"Yes. On a cruise, I believe," he admitted uncomfortably. "We could call him and ask—"

"Can you fly it?"

"Well, yes, I could, but—"

"You want your plane back, right?"

Randy's eyes narrowed, and he nodded sharply.

"Then come on," Axe said, grabbing the man by the arm in a firm but not painful grip—yet. "Let's go get it back. Your country needs you. As of this moment, you're officially a deputy agent in the Department of Homeland Security."

Utter horseshit, but by the time he finds out, I'll either be long gone or dead.

Randy allowed himself to be dragged toward the hangar. He looked like he wasn't sure whether he should protest or feel proud of his newfound position.

"Rodriguez," Axe looked over his shoulder at the woman still standing by her patrol car. "Can you shoot that rifle?"

"Hell yes!"

"Then grab it. You're coming along."

The thrilled look on her face in the glow of the flashing red and blue lights was priceless.

I just made her day. Now all I have to do is not get her and my new 'deputy' killed.

46

TARGETS

Central Analysis Group Headquarters
Alexandria, Virginia

"Axe says the terrorists are now airborne," Haley said as she disconnected the satellite phone. "He's stealing a plane to follow them—and his plane might be faster than theirs. But he needs a direction. Quickly, before they take off and we lose comms."

"He can fly a plane?" Dave asked, impressed.

"No, he's deputized a local pilot."

"He can do that?" Dave muttered.

Haley shrugged. "He does a lot of things that he might not formally be allowed to do. It's necessary in the field."

She moved to the large monitor and pointed at a spot on the map where dozens of pipelines crossed.

"There," Haley said. "What do you think?" She turned to look at her team. One by one, they nodded.

"But isn't it a little obvious?" Dave asked, ever the skeptic.

"They weren't planning on being intercepted the moment they set foot in our country," Nancy argued.

"Would they have a set of backup targets?" Gregory wondered. "If they were compromised—like they are now—or if they arrived on target to find the situation changed? Like police in the area or new fencing not accounted for?"

Haley zoomed out, showing the area where the terrorists were last reported—southwestern Texas—and the nearest facilities for oil and gas, along with the pipelines connecting everything. "With a plane, they could get a lot further. This spot is the best I can figure. If they want to do the most damage at one time, and not spend all night moving around, risking capture, this makes the most sense. But here and here," she said, clicking on the other points near the first where smaller groups of pipelines came together, "these could be potential alternate targets."

"What happens when a natural gas pipeline explodes?" Nancy asked.

"It's like an atomic weapon going off," Gregory answered.

"And if they blow up a dozen?" Nancy asked in a quiet voice, looking at the massive nexus of pipelines at the first target Haley identified.

No one answered.

"There are also highly volatile liquid and crude oil lines crossing at that location and the others," Dave pointed out.

Haley had already dialed Axe. "Are you mobile?"

"We will be in a minute. I found us a fast plane."

I'm not going to ask.

"We've identified three priority targets, in order of likelihood. But they could be going anywhere, including Corpus Christi, where they could attack a port facility from the air and do a lot of damage."

She read him the coordinates, throwing in street names and landmarks they might be able to see from the air. Then she hung up. He was in a hurry.

"Let's get whatever police and security we can to the locations, in order of priority," Gregory ordered. "Maybe they'll be able to help."

Haley, Dave, and Nancy reached for their phones and started calling in whatever cavalry wasn't manning the now useless roadblocks.

Axe will take all the help he can get.

47

REVENGE

Over Texas

"Fly it like you stole it," Axe told Randy over the microphone in the headsets they wore, which canceled out much of the engine noise. Axe had his backpack and sniper rifle on the seat next to him in the back of the sleek, single-prop plane.

"We did steal it!" Randy said. He seemed to be quickly gaining comfort with the plane, but not with the idea of "borrowing" it.

"So it should be easy. We need to catch up to terrorists who want to blow up oil and natural gas pipelines."

Randy and Rodriguez—sitting in the copilot seat—both turned at the same time to look at him in the dim glow of the fancy instrument panels.

"Pipelines?" Rodriguez asked.

Randy didn't adjust any of the controls. "Randy, seriously, max it out. Get us there in one piece, but I don't care if the engines have to be replaced after we land. The bad guys have a head start. This plane is supposed to be fast. Let's do it."

Randy pushed the throttle and the tiny plane seemed to leap forward.

That's more like it.

Hakimi frowned at the police cars speeding by ahead and below him, heading toward his primary target.

How did they know?

He banked the plane slightly, changing course.

"We will try the secondary target," he told his men in the back. "I want you both digging down to the pipeline the moment we are on the ground, understand?"

They responded, but he was already thinking through his approach and landing.

The small plane rattled and shook. The engine strained.

"I understand about the terrorists, but we should really slow down," Randy said, his voice shaking.

"Are we in danger of crashing?" Axe asked, entirely serious. "Blowing the engine?"

"Honestly, I'm not sure," Randy said. "But... yeah, maybe."

Axe could see the glow of a large town ahead and to their left.

"Do you need an engine to land?"

Randy's head snapped around to look at him, his eyes wide, but he didn't answer.

"Well, do you?" Axe asked.

"Not... technically, but it makes it easier!"

"Then we keep it maxed out. I have complete faith in you."

I've been in helicopters that have lost their engines after being shot up. It can't be any worse in a plane.

More police patrol cars surrounded the secondary target site, but the towns in the area were small. How many officers could they have available this early in the morning?

"Someone has betrayed us—or the Americans have an extremely gifted intelligence analyst. We're going to skip numbers three and four and go to target five. If they're guarding that one, too, we'll go down the list until we find at least one we can eliminate."

The silence from the back was telling.

They're worried now.

The plan all along had been for the men to cram into the crew cab pickup while one huddled in the bed with the backpacks. They would endure the uncomfortable ninety-minute drive to the first target, where two men would be dropped. The next two would be left at the second target, and so on. As each team set their charges—spacing them out so there would be multiple points of damage, making the eventual repairs more difficult, costly, and time-consuming—Hakimi would pick them up and shuttle them to the next site. All the targets were conveniently in a small geographical area.

A team of men, working on a coordinated plan over several hours, would destroy the region's ability to transport oil, natural gas, and highly flammable liquids like propane. By morning, the country's pipeline infrastructure, representing the majority of its ability to transport the essential energy products, would be eliminated.

Once all the charges were set, they would have linked up with the second team for a long drive across the country and the next part of their mission.

But as he lined up the plane on approach to the long, straight road next to target number five, Hakimi refused to let his anger show. The men needed cool, calculated leadership, though it was the farthest thing from his true emotional state.

First, they kill Rahmin. Now this?

He wouldn't stop until he destroyed the pipelines here and the targets on the east coast.

This part of the mission can still be a success.

"Take us a little higher, then circle the area," Axe told Randy. Even through the headsets, the engine strained and sounded horrible, but they kept flying—and hadn't slowed down. "Rodriguez, look for the enemy plane. It will be at a lower altitude and won't have running lights on."

Axe had a paper map out and his headlamp on, using its red light to preserve their night vision in the airplane's tiny cabin. He matched the major roads and prominent ground features—a strip mall and two round, irrigated fields next to each other.

Okay, we're... here.

The top three targets from Haley would be spread out over a large area in front of them. From this altitude, he could just make out the flashing lights of patrol cars at one of them to the far left.

Haley has them covered. So where else will they go?

He should have gotten more targets, but then again, the whole area was a target. Above- and below-ground pipelines crisscrossed the region.

"Papa, Papa, this is Reaper One-One. Papa, Papa, this is Reaper One-One. Are you on this frequency, over?"

Axe recognized his alternate call sign, jokingly assigned to him by his former Team when he'd rejoined them for a mission nearly a year before.

Now we're talking! The drone pilot.

"Reaper One-One, this is Papa. I'm here, over."

"Blondie sends her regards," the man said. "And says that the bogey we're looking for is in your airspace." He told Axe the altitude of the enemy plane and the direction to look.

From the right-side co-pilot's seat, Rodriguez shouted. "There!"

Her outburst caused Randy to flinch, which made the plane tilt crazily for a moment until he brought it back to level.

"I see it—there's a small plane down there," Rodriguez said. "It's... it looks like it's going to land on that road."

Axe followed where she was pointing and saw it. "Reaper One-One. Copy, we have it. Can you do me a solid and take it out?"

The drone pilot laughed. "It's the same thing Blondie asked. No, sir, I'm on an unarmed training mission. Just helping out."

Training mission? Good one, Blondie.

"Copy that. Interrogative... how about ramming it?"

"What, are you two related or something? Same answer I gave Blondie. This is not a thirty-two-million-dollar bullet."

"Copy. I had to try. We'll take care of it. Can you help Blondie vector in backup to our position?"

"Already on it, Papa, but it'll be a while, Blondie said. You're on your own for a bit, but I'll stay on station as your eye in the sky."

"Thanks, Reaper One-One. Papa out."

At least we found them in time.

"Randy, get ready to land," Axe said.

"Land where?" Randy asked, doubtful. "On the street?"

The poor guy has lost his sense of adventure—assuming he had one to begin with.

"Yes, on the street. If they did it, so can we. But don't slow down until you have to."

"But we've caught up to them," Randy argued as he banked the plane and lined up on the road stretching out in front of them. "We did it."

Axe thought of all the combat insertions he'd been a part of, the huge aircraft spiraling down—fast—to avoid groundfire in Iraq, Afghanistan, and other war-torn areas.

"Yes, we did. So it would be a shame if they shot us as we landed."

His remark caused Randy to shut up and focus on bringing the plane in fast.

Hakimi slowed the plane and turned it off the highway, bumping onto the dirt and weeds next to the road. He'd seen no police cars from the air, and the location seemed deserted from the ground, too.

The plane easily drove through the three strands of barbed wire connected to old, weathered posts. The fence was likely used years ago to keep cows contained. It was never meant to stop anyone from gaining entry to the area.

They couldn't have made it any easier.

After the fence, the ground was level and free from obstructions. They bumped over a mound several inches high—leftover dirt from a buried pipeline running mostly north-south. "Highly volatile liquid line," he told his men. They had studied and likely knew what lines were where as well as he did, but communication never hurt. "Propane. Not on our list." It would blow up on its own if they did their job right on the other, more important pipelines. His superiors had made the objectives clear: oil first, natural gas second.

Luckily, this target has both.

A hundred yards ahead was the first of the many pipelines. Half buried —not fully underground.

"This is target number five. The pipelines on either side will need to be uncovered, but you probably will not need the shovels. We will place charges spaced well apart, set the timers, then use the plane to drive to target six, and so on until we accomplish the mission. Then we meet the others for the drive east."

The two men voiced their understanding, packs in hand, ready to get to work the moment he stopped.

He turned slightly north, then felt the next bump.

"Go," he told his men as he braked, but they were already out the door.

Randy throttled back, bringing them in for a perfect landing on the highway.

"Drive along the road to where they turned," Axe told Randy, pointing. "And can you go faster without taking off?"

"I guess."

"Well, do it. Before they turn their engines off and hear us."

"Wait—what happens then?"

"They shoot at us!" Rodriguez said. She was practically bouncing out of the plane, gripping the rifle and raring to go.

Axe lowered his NVGs and instantly felt better.

I wish I had a pair for Rodriguez, but even in the dark, she'll be able to see her target easily enough.

"Faster!"

The plane shot ahead, closing the distance quickly.

A half-mile ahead, the enemy plane slowed. Two men carrying backpacks hopped out before it stopped.

"Rodriguez, you shoot the shit out of that plane and the guys near it, if you can see them. Aim, but you're mostly covering fire. You're outside effective range with your weapon unless we get closer. Don't shoot near the pipelines, though. I'm not sure what would happen if you hit one."

Axe had his sniper rifle out and ready to go. "I'll target the terrorists. You keep them from effectively firing back. Be careful. At least one of them has a sniper rifle, too."

"Copy that, Mr. Alexander."

"Just Axe, please."

"What do I do?" Randy whined.

"Hide," Axe said as they closed the distance. He debated getting closer, which would help Rodriguez put rounds more on target, but would also be more dangerous for them.

"That's it?"

"Praying would be smart, too," Axe said.

This close, if they blow even one pipeline, we're all dead.

But better not to spell that out.

The other plane came to a halt. "Stop the plane and turn it off!"

Randy slammed on the brakes, jolting them forward, and killed the engine.

"Everybody out now!"

———

As Hakimi scrambled out of the plane to assist his men, he had a feeling. The quiet of the flat, empty, bare-dirt area, despite being relatively close to a large town, told him nothing, but he couldn't shake the sensation of danger.

Then the rifle fire started from the road.

"Down!" he yelled at his men. "Behind the pipeline—and keep working!"

He didn't want to believe his first instinct, but his gut had never failed him before. What it told him didn't seem fathomable, but…

It's him. The sniper who killed Rahmin. Who else could it be?

It didn't seem possible, but somehow the man had tracked him all the way from the border.

He dies here.

Bullets hit the plane as Hakimi reached in to retrieve the sniper rifle, but he ignored them. Instead, he grabbed the long gun, prepared to complete the mission—and get his revenge.

48

AUTHORITY

Central Analysis Group Headquarters
Alexandria, Virginia

"What do you mean, I have no authority?" Haley yelled into the phone. "We need those pipelines shut off right now!"

Axe was engaging the terrorists at a location not on her target list.

Now she was on the phone, as were Dave, Nancy, and Gregory, all yelling at once, trying to figure out a last-ditch way to turn off the flow of whatever was in the various pipelines at that location. Just in case.

Axe has never failed before.

There was a first time for everything, and this morning would be a terrible time to be defeated.

"I'm sorry, ma'am, we can't help you," the voice on the other end of her phone told her. "I don't have the authority to do what you want."

"No," Gregory's command voice cut through the chaos. "All the pipelines through that area. It's a matter of national security. Make it happen. Sir," he added hastily.

He stood in the center of the room, straight and tall, all the exhaustion from the late night long gone. At some point, he had smoothed his longish salt and pepper hair, taming the strands that had gone astray.

"Yes, I'll hold." He caught Haley's eye and covered the mouthpiece. "The sleep-deprived and overwhelmed governor of Texas," he whispered.

"No luck on my end," she said. While Nancy and Dave tried various government agencies, she had gone directly to what her map indicated were the owners of the pipelines. Using one of the many databases at her disposal, she had called emergency contact numbers. All took her seriously but understandably refused to comply with her request to shut down pipelines through the area first and get questions answered—and authorization—later.

"Thank you, sir," Gregory said into his phone. "Let's hope it's enough. I'll be in touch."

"He's on it," Gregory said, hanging up. "The only question is how long it will take." He looked at Haley. "We've done what we can." Then he sat heavily in a chair at the conference table, his tiredness back.

With nothing left to do, Haley sat at her computer and tried to figure out what was behind this, but her mind had a hard time focusing. Instead, her thoughts were on Axe.

If I was out there with him, would it make a difference?

She'd come so far as an asset in the months since the fateful night in May when she'd been abducted from her apartment—and rescued by Axe. Was she more use here or in the field?

I vectored in the drone. I got the pilot on board with the hunt for the plane and convinced him to use his resources to contact Axe.

Could Nancy and Dave have done it? Would they have thought of the ideas she'd had and been willing to act on them?

There was no way to know. All she could do now was hope.

Come on, Axe. It's up to you.

49

DUEL

Axe lay flat on the ground, trying for a shot, but the terrorists were smart and skilled. They kept working despite the gunfire directed at and near them. And they did it while lying on the ground behind the pipeline.

What happens if I shoot the pipeline?

Would it cause a major explosion, killing him, Randy, and Rodriguez, along with the men next to it?

I can't blow up the pipeline trying to kill them. It would be doing their job for them.

The pipeline hiding them ran mostly east to west. If Axe could get further north, he'd be level with them for an easy shot.

A bullet zipped past his ear. He immediately rolled to his right and kept going until he reached the tiniest of dips in the ground. He was perhaps an inch lower than before, but it might be enough.

I have to take out the sniper first.

Rodriguez was putting rounds on target—the airplane—but without night-vision goggles, she hadn't seen where the two other men dropped to the ground, nor where the man with the sniper rifle lay behind the smallest rises right next to the plane.

Another bullet zipped past him, close enough to feel.

The second I raise my head to aim and return fire, I'm dead.

"Rodriguez," he called.

Another bullet, closer than the last.

There was a berm ahead, maybe a foot high, running northeast.

If I can get to that, I'll have a tiny bit of cover to move up.

"Aim at the ground three feet right of their plane and pour it on!"

An instant later she started firing and Axe moved, hoping it was enough to keep the enemy sniper's head down for a few seconds.

He crawled for his life, staying low but giving up safety to move faster. As Rodriguez's mag ran out of bullets, he made it. While he still didn't have a shot on the sniper or the men undoubtedly planting explosives on the pipeline, at least he had cover.

Axe stuck his head up an inch, exposing it over the hard-packed earthen berm, then ducked immediately.

The bullet hit the ground inches above his head, spilling dirt into his eyes. Instantly, he started crawling, face scraping the ground to stay as low as possible. Two seconds later, he stopped.

Now.

The bullet skimmed the top of the berm an inch in front of him and would have grazed him if he hadn't stopped in time.

That's five.

From the firefight at the border, he knew the sniper used the same high-quality, precision weapon he did with a ten-round magazine. All he had to do was get the man to miss five more times. Then Axe would have a moment when the sniper had to reload.

That's my window.

Time seemed to slow down as the cat-and-mouse game continued. Axe varied his speed and stayed low, moving ever north behind the scant dirt cover. He relied on his sniper instincts, timing, and finely honed sense of danger to stop, start, and stay undercover as the man continued to fire at him. After Rodriguez's initial burst, the tango must have realized he was safe from her because he kept shooting at Axe despite her cover fire.

A bullet penetrated the top of the miniature dirt wall, so close Axe felt it.

Nine.

The berm ended a few feet ahead.

And if the last round was any indication, the cover is thinner here.

He scooted backward two feet as he gripped the rifle and prepared.

The tenth round zipped past him, flying through the dirt berm an inch in front of his face.

I hope I counted right.

He brought the rifle to bear as the man in the distance rose, reaching for the open door of the airplane. The figure filled the scope. Just as he had on countless ranges and battlefields over fifteen years, Axe exhaled, held, and shot.

Hakimi lay on the ground, uncertain for a second how he'd gotten there. Then the pain hit… but only for a few seconds before his body went into shock.

The sniper.

He felt the sopping wetness at his stomach and knew the end was near. There was simply too much blood to survive. The bullet had hit just below his protective armor—not that it would have been very effective against the powerful weapon at this range, anyway.

He could still prevail. He would never give up on the mission. All he had to do was get to his feet, reach inside the plane for a spare magazine, and shoot the man who had killed his brother.

Then he would allow himself to die.

He got a hand under him and pushed.

Axe took no satisfaction in watching the enemy struggle. He aimed again and fired, putting him out of his misery.

50

ALTERNATIVES

Pecos County
West Texas

Kabiri had set his first charge, then hid behind the pipeline. It was only half-buried, covered in dirt but sticking out of the ground at knee height—had he been standing and not hugging the ground. There was no sense running across the open ground to the next pipeline, about thirty steps away.

When this one goes, everything around it will, too, he thought.

He resolved to be very far away when it happened.

I'm a coward.

The thought hit him hard, but it was the truth. It hadn't always been this way. He'd been on more missions than he could count and been recognized for valor repeatedly, which is why, he guessed, he'd been selected for this essential yet dangerous mission.

But he had "forgotten" to notify his superiors, and his fellow soldiers, of the son he'd had with his girlfriend. They had a so-called "white marriage," which was cohabitation before marriage and technically illegal under Iran's strict religious laws. The birth of their son was a major problem since their legal rights as parents were different than if they'd been married. The authorities kept records of such births. The boy might have trouble getting certain jobs in the future. While the issue had become more common lately, there were many legal hurdles to deal with. So, right or wrong, they had told few people.

Nothing had prepared Kabiri for the feelings he had when he held his son. The idea of the boy growing up without him—and of his beautiful girlfriend struggling on her own—flipped a switch in him.

A switch he didn't realize would cause a problem until he came under fire along the river earlier... and he had wanted to jump back into the tunnel instead of fighting.

So when a second shot from the distant sniper rifle rang out, he knew what he had to do.

He'd watched Dehdari use his hands to dig down to the pipeline and attach his charges. The synched timers meant they couldn't linger—they had to get away soon or return to the charges and stop the clocks.

Kabiri crawled quickly to his comrade as the man finished attaching his last charge—redundancy, or overkill, considering what would happen when even one went off. The pipeline would explode like an atomic blast. Having more charges planted would only make the rebuilding process a little harder, causing slightly more damage to the actual pipeline but having no other impact.

"Hakimi is dead," Kabiri began.

"Yes. There are at least two men out there," Dehdari said as he unslung his AK. He was two years older and next in command. "We'll lay down covering fire, leapfrogging forward. We will eliminate them, then drive to the next target."

"Can you operate the plane?" Kabiri asked, reluctantly unslinging his own rifle.

Maybe there is still a way to succeed.

"Not to fly, but we should be able to start the engine and drive it like a car. We must destroy more targets to ensure the mission's success, then meet the others."

Does he not realize we are going to die?

"Or..." Kabiri said, hoping the man wouldn't make him say it.

They stared at each other for a moment, NVG to NVG. Then Dehdari said, "You're suggesting we blow the pipeline now?" It was clear he was surprised at Kabiri's proposal. "I see that only as a last resort. If we are both injured."

He misunderstood completely.

"What? No! We should surrender!"

For a moment, neither moved. Then they turned their rifles on each other and fired at the same time.

———

Axe had run north, outside of accurate range for the remaining men's AKs, but pushing himself just in case. There was still a second sniper rifle out there. He made it several hundred yards before he heard the sound of AK fire.

He dropped to the ground, already calming himself for the shots he needed to take. He brought the rifle to bear and saw two men, prone, facing each other next to the pipeline.

They weren't moving.

They shot each other?

He couldn't worry about their internal dispute. One or both could still be alive and preparing to blow the pipeline.

———

Kabiri clung to life long enough to see Dehdari struggling for the detonator he had in his pocket to manually blow one of the charges. Then his eyes closed, and he slipped away, his last thoughts on the son he would never hold again.

51

FOUR MINUTES

Pecos County
West Texas

Dehdari acted on instinct, fighting the pain and fog overwhelming him. The only thing that mattered was completing the mission. The idea had been hammered into him from day one of basic training—failure was not an option.

With his last bit of strength, he fumbled for the detonator in his pocket.

I thought I had the drop on the coward, but he got me.

But he smiled at the thought of overcoming the odds—including being shot by his brother-in-arms—to blow at least one pipeline despite the mission going badly from the start. Surely there would be a special place in the afterlife for him.

One tango struggled to move, his arm reaching toward the pocket of his black pants.

Axe pulled the trigger, sending a bullet into the back of his head easily at this range. He put another round into his body, at the base of the skull, just to be sure. Then he shot the other man twice as well.

Can't be too careful when detonators and explosives are involved.

He scanned the area through the high-powered scope and extended his senses, searching for other terrorists, but came up empty.

Those three should have been the last of them.

The only questions remaining were how many charges they had set and whether the charges had timers or manual detonation.

And if there are booby traps.

"Rodriguez," he called as he stood and started running. "Don't shoot—I'm moving forward."

From behind him, by the airplane, she called back to him. "Can I come?"

"Affirmative."

The more the merrier.

It didn't take long to reach the dead men by the pipeline. He carefully searched the pocket the first man had been reaching for and came up with a remote detonator. If the guy had pushed the button...

Cheated death again.

"Um, Mr. Axe?" Rodriguez said from further down the pipeline, her voice shaking.

That doesn't sound good.

"I found a timer thingy. And a lot of explosives."

"How much time do we have?" he asked as he ran to her.

"Four minutes," Rodriguez said, sounding solid and focused, not scared. "Shouldn't be a problem, right?"

Axe turned to look at the pipeline stretching into the distance. "No. Well... depending on how many charges there are."

52

GO

"Go," Axe told Rodriguez. "Take Randy and the plane and get out of here."

"Randy!" Rodriguez yelled at the top of her lungs toward the road. "Get in the plane and go! Get as far away as you can. Right now!"

For once, Randy didn't argue.

"Not exactly what I meant," Axe said to the young officer as he knelt to examine the explosive device and timer.

"I'm staying. You need help. Besides, this is the coolest thing I've ever done in my entire life."

"What are you, twenty-five?"

"Thirty," she said, sounding put out. She paused and knelt next to him. "How old are you?" she asked in a low voice.

"I'm taken." The device attached to the pipeline looked simple enough, and he couldn't see any booby traps.

The airplane's engine started. Axe glanced at the silent officer. "Still want to stay?"

"Definitely," she said, but without her original conviction.

"Great."

Would a cell or sat phone signal detonate the bombs?

He didn't think so and was ready to take that risk.

Axe pulled the satellite phone from his pocket, pressed a button, and handed it to Rodriguez.

"Talk to Haley. Tell her we need an EOD—quickly."

"EOD?" she asked, taking the phone.

"Explosive Ordnance Disposal tech. She'll understand."

He retrieved his cell phone from a pocket, recalled the face of the young man he'd worked with the previous summer and used a mnemonic technique he'd been taught by a memory expert brought in by the brass one time. After a second, he recalled the number and dialed. Would the man be stationed overseas or home on rotation? And would he answer a random call this early in the morning or have his phone on do not disturb?

"Hello?" the young tech said, sounding awake.

"This is Axe—'Papa'—we met last summer when we went on vacation down south together." He didn't want to say too much on an open line with no idea who was around the man or what country he was in.

"Papa? I never went on vacation... oh! The working vacation to that cute little village on the coast?"

"That's the one. Sorry to drop this on you, but I need immediate help. How copy?"

The man switched instantly to all business at the familiar phrase. "Solid copy. Send it."

"I'm looking at a block of plastic explosives. A small, white electronic timer is attached to it."

"How much time?"

"Three minutes, ten seconds."

"Just one?"

"No, I'm not sure how many. Wait."

Rodriguez was holding the sat phone, but he got her attention. "Tell Haley I have a tech, then hang up. Go back and look for more bombs. Mound dirt next to each one you find so we can locate them again. Hurry."

"Sorry," he said back to the EOD tech. "I have someone looking now. I suspect there are at least a few. To me, it looks pretty straightforward, but I don't want to do something wrong and blow it."

"Copy. Can you send a picture?"

Leave it to the kid to think of the obvious.

He didn't bother to reply, but hung up, hit the buttons on his phone until the camera was up, and took a picture, closing his eyes so the flash didn't blind him. Then he sent it.

The timer kept counting down.

After a few seconds, the kid called back. "What does the explosive smell like?"

"Like C-4. Motor oil," he added.

"Okay. I agree with you. From what you sent, it looks straightforward. All you should have to do is remove the blasting caps, which should be attached to the timer. Lift the timer off carefully—and tell me what you see."

Axe put the phone on speaker and set it on the ground, then did as ordered.

"It looks like a setup I've used before, only with the timer switched in."

"Did you find a manual detonator onsite?"

"Yes. I've got it. The bad guys were reaching for it."

"Then at least one of the devices has a manual detonator instead of a timer. As long as they all look like this, I think you're good. Just cut the wires to the blasting caps—but get them as far from the C-4 and the target before the timers go off, just in case. You know the drill."

"Got it. And thanks."

"Go easy, brother. I'll stay on the line, just in case."

Axe shoved the phone into his pocket and turned his attention to the C-4 and timer. The roar of the airplane faded into the distance. Randy wasn't worried about saving the engine at all anymore.

Rodriguez had three mounds of dirt and was bent over, inspecting the pipeline for more as Axe reached for the timer.

Would she want a warning?

No.

If it doesn't work, better to not see it coming.

The timer showed two minutes left.

He pulled his knife and sliced the wires between the timer and the blasting cap in the brick of C-4.

53

TEN SECONDS

Pecos County
West Texas

"I count three, plus that one," Rodriguez said, out of breath from the running she'd done.

"Great," Axe said, kneeling next to the second charge attached to the pipeline, several feet from the first one he'd disarmed. "Good news is they're not booby-trapped. Bad news is if we miss even one of them, we die. So check the other direction for more. And, obviously, be thorough, but hurry."

"Got it," she said, and took off past the first one Axe had already disarmed.

One minute, forty-five seconds.

Axe noted the time on his watch, then cut the wires and removed the blasting cap from the second one, shoved the timer in one pocket and the cap into another. He stood, his knees creaking noisily.

When did that start?

It had been a long, hectic night of hiking, laying prone in the desert, running, killing, sitting in the truck, and being crammed into the rear of the airplane, but he still didn't like hearing his body make noise.

It won't matter if I don't take care of the explosives in time.

Axe sprinted to the next charge, dropped to his knees in the dirt, and repeated the process. Then he ran to the final one Rodriguez had marked, pushing as hard as he could, the exertion of the night finally getting to him.

Forty-five seconds.

Plenty of time.

He cut the wires, pulled the blasting cap, and stood, ignoring his knees this time.

Denial is not just a river in Egypt.

"Axe!"

Uh-oh.

He ran toward Rodriguez, who was frantically mounding dirt into a pile to mark the spot. She set off further down the pipeline, bent low, looking for more explosives.

He slid to a stop at the mound of dirt like a man stealing second base.

This setup looked different. There was no timer.

According to his watch, though, he had eighteen seconds left on any other timers out there.

It's just the standard remote detonator.

He and his Team had used them often over the years.

Nothing to worry about.

He hesitated, checking his intuition.

Nothing.

Ten seconds.

He cut the wires with a sinking feeling.

If there's another one, we're dead.

Axe looked at Rodriguez, still bent forward as she jogged away, and counted down in his head.

Four. Three. Two. One.

54

TROUBLE

Pecos County
West Texas

The sirens wailed as the column of patrol cars approached, blue and red strobes lighting up the night. Axe looked at Rodriguez, who seemed to be having the time of her life—now that the pipeline hadn't blown up. They jogged to Randy's plane—the one the terrorists had stolen.

Does she understand how close we came to dying?

"Is it always this intense?" she asked as the police cars squealed to a stop on the road.

Axe picked up the dead tango's sniper rifle next to the stolen airplane.

Axe seriously considered the question. "Yeah, I guess it is," he shrugged. "But you get used to it."

"Cool!"

She and Haley are cut from the same cloth.

"The locals aren't going to shoot us, are they?" Rodriguez asked, eying the police spilling out of cars, drawing their weapons and spreading out.

"They won't get very close at all," Axe answered. "Not with C-4 in the area."

Haley had dispatched an EOD tech to make sure there were no hidden booby traps and to handle the explosives. The local police would set up a perimeter and preserve the scene.

But looking at the dead enemy on the ground who had nearly killed him, Axe had a feeling. He needed to satisfy his curiosity, though he hoped his gut was wrong. A question bothered him.

Why didn't they use both sniper rifles?

Every tango along the border who picked up the long gun had been adept with it. Was it an oversight—the men getting out of the airplane didn't realize they were being pursued, so hadn't bothered to bring it? Sure, the weapon was long and heavy, but they'd been so professional all night. It just struck him as odd.

With two long guns, we wouldn't have had a chance.

He searched the plane for the second rifle but came up empty. He gave Rodriguez his night-vision goggles and ordered her to scout the area.

While she looked next to the pipeline and the other dead men, he followed his other hunch and counted backpacks.

Damn it!

He removed them from the rear of the plane, lined them up on the ground, and opened every compartment of the aircraft, front to back, including the engine. He counted the packs again and came up with the same number. All were filled with C-4, timers, blasting caps, and some extra ammo.

"I only found these," Rodriguez said, holding up the two AKs. "But it's almost dawn. We can get the officers to help look once it's light."

His look must have given him away. "This is bad?" she asked.

"Yes. We're missing one sniper rifle and a backpack of plastic explosives."

55

THE MARINE

Van Horn Hospital
Van Horn, Texas

Hammer stood at the foot of the hospital bed, waiting. He felt naked without the M4 but had left it locked in the truck to not cause a stir in the hospital.

Marine-turned-truck driver Rick Murrey's pain medicine was due to wear off, and the doctor had reluctantly agreed to allow Hammer to ask a few questions when the man woke.

Hammer had visited the truck stop and watched the security camera footage of the scene at the gas station, marveling at the man's ability to survive. Murrey had sailed out of the semi-truck cab and rolled upon landing. The semi-trailer had protected him somewhat from the explosion a second later, but he'd suffered burns to his upper body.

And the Marine did all that while only half alive from multiple stab wounds. Glad he's on our side.

Hammer didn't go in for that service rivalry bullshit. Well, aside from the occasional good-natured ribbing. To him, warriors were warriors—it didn't matter which branch they served.

The injured man's eyes flickered open and slowly focused on him, taking in the black pants and top, along with the camouflage plate carrier and pistol in a drop holster on his leg.

"How are you doing, son?" Hammer spoke gently and quietly, but the man reacted, struggling to straighten himself in an effort to come to attention.

No hiding the command voice.

"No, at ease. You're in the hospital, but you'll be fine."

The Marine-turned-truck driver relaxed. He winced in pain.

Hammer nodded gently at the man's bandaged stomach. "Couple of new scars to go with the others, and those burns are going to hurt like hell for a while," he added, looking at the man's arms. "But you'll live. I expect nothing less from a Marine. You all are damn near indestructible."

The truck driver licked his lips and whispered, "Oorah."

"Now, you're awake because the pain is hitting, I'm sure. And I hate to make you wait on the next dose of meds, but I need whatever intel you have for me. Can you help me out, Marine?"

Rick's lips moved, but no sound came out. Hammer moved around the bed to lean close to the man. "You can do it. A little louder."

"Iranian," Murrey whispered, audible this time. "One or more got away."

Haley had looked up the man's history and read the highlights of his service record, but Hammer didn't see how the Marine could know the terrorists' origin from his brief encounter with them. While the man had served in both Afghanistan and Iraq, he likely hadn't come into contact with Iranians.

"Yes, we're tracking them down. But how do you figure they're Iranian?"

"Spoke Farsi."

Murrey grimaced in pain again.

"And you know the difference between Farsi, Dari, or any of the other languages spoken over there?" Hammer tried to keep the skepticism from his voice but didn't think he succeeded.

"Bored. Made friends with a terp who spoke them all. Taught me words. Accents are different. Pronunciation, too."

He befriended an interpreter on deployment and worked on languages? Impressive.

Hammer could have Haley verify it with the man's commander or other members of his squad.

She might have to wake them up in the middle of the night, but we'll need to confirm his story.

A nurse entered the room and hurried over to the bedside, frowning at Hammer. "It's time for the pain medication."

"Not yet," Murrey whispered, though it clearly cost him.

The nurse hesitated.

"Just another minute," Hammer said as he turned back to the Marine. "How sure are you, son? I mean, no bullshit. This is as real as it gets."

Murrey's eyes focused on Hammer, clear and steady despite the pain. "One hundred percent, sir. Heard him speak to the other one. Caught a few words and the accent."

"Well done, Marine. You rest now. We'll take it from here."

Hammer nodded at the nurse, who fiddled with the IV.

Murrey's eyes closed as he waited for the pain medicine to flow into his system.

"Sir?" he whispered.

"Yes, son?"

"Kick their asses for me." Though faint, the Marine's voice had an edge of steel to it.

"You're damn right we will."

56

THE NEWLYWEDS

As an Iranian sniper, Jafar never thought he'd ever visit Texas. America was his country's great enemy, the target all his fellow soldiers dreamed of attacking.

And now, here I am, he thought.

Jafar navigated as his fellow sniper Cyra drove through the night. They stuck to back roads and spoke little. Jafar glanced at her, marveling at how the glow of the dashboard lights made her look feminine and sweet.

Not so much. She's neither.

With her short black hair, sharp features, and fit body, no one would ever call her soft or delicate, but he appreciated her skill, dedication, and expertise.

He wasn't sure what she saw in him. Maybe his dark, full beard and hair he'd been allowed to grow out, along with his black, brooding eyes, appealed to her.

Or maybe it's just the mission fueling the attraction.

They left the airport behind, then the city. The miles and hours slipped by.

There was nothing much to say, though they jokingly discussed a short detour through the small Texas town of Iraan. It was pronounced "Ira-

Ann," not like their home country, but it would have made a nice anecdote when sharing the success of their mission with comrades once they returned.

The airport coffee had long grown cold, but they sipped it anyway, making it last. They would only stop for gas when absolutely necessary and avoid needlessly exposing their faces by going inside. If they needed to stay awake, the two large coffees each from the worldwide chain in the airport concourse would have to do for a while.

They had a quiet familiarity in keeping with their cover as newlyweds. *I'm more interested in her than she is in me.*

They'd had sex twice—Jafar wouldn't call it making love. It was for sport and stress relief, but mostly to make their cover story look and feel realistic. They both had partners back home, though they didn't talk about it other than to acknowledge that what happened on the mission would stay on the mission. They'd done it once at the conclusion of training, and again before the travel that took them from Iran on a convoluted route, culminating in their final flight landing hours earlier in Dallas with perfectly forged Kuwaiti passports.

The grumpy customs official had looked at their passports while they held hands and lied about spending their honeymoon touring the desert southwest. The man stamped their documents, handed them back, and said, "Enjoy your visit to the United States."

Their first order of business was picking up the backpack full of C-4 explosives Jafar needed and the sniper rifle Cyra would use in the assassination.

"What kind of name is Marville?" Jafar wondered out loud, not expecting an answer from Cyra. She rarely spoke.

They had expected to meet the other special forces team at a truck stop along I-10 but had received a message on their encrypted communication app of a change. They were to pick up the items needed for their mission further away than planned—and the two men expected to ride with them wouldn't be coming.

It wouldn't jeopardize their timeline, but it made for a much longer drive... and had Jafar wondering.

Why the change of plans? What were they concerned enough about to leave the explosives and rifle unattended—buried—nearly two hours away from the rendezvous?

After the cryptic message, there had been no other communication, which was also odd. By now, they should have received confirmation of the mission's success.

Unless they failed.

If the men of the other team were injured or dead, his job would be much more difficult. Cyra would be fine, but he'd expected to have help for his mission.

He had the radio on low, hoping for news of explosions in the region, but so far there had been nothing.

"Through the town, then turn right," he told his partner. "The airport is only a few miles away."

There was only a single nod from Cyra, but it didn't bother him.

What else should I expect from a woman who has killed so many?

PART 3

MONDAY

57

THE HOLE

Gas and Go Travel Center
Van Horn, Texas

After getting the Marine's intel about the possible Iranian soldiers to Haley, the rest of William "Hammer" Nalen's night had been safe—but miserable. He had no part in the ongoing mission, and it annoyed the hell out of him.

Still, the evening hadn't been a complete waste. Speaking with Murrey had helped figure out the terrorists' origin and their mission.

Hammer had also helped save the sheriff's life. His high-speed driving had gotten the lawman to the hospital just in time. It looked like the officer would pull through.

But after that, Hammer had felt useless. He was out of the loop while Axe pursued the terrorists and Haley worked the intel.

If I'm going to be in the field, I want to be part of the fight.

In the end, with nothing better to do, he'd settled back in the pickup and got some sleep. Having a well-rested team member was often an overlooked asset.

But he was thrilled when his sat phone woke him with a call from Axe.

"Good times?" Hammer asked, sitting up in the truck and cracking his neck on both sides to get it back in line.

"The best. You available? I'm out of range and we have an issue."

"Tell me," he said, starting the truck.

"Where are you?"

"Off I-10, down the street from the truck stop that got blown up."

"Perfect. Update: we eliminated the threat. Three more enemy killed in action. No damage to the pipelines."

"Well done. But?"

"At the river, each tango had a black backpack and there were two sniper rifles. We only count a total of seven packs and one long gun here."

"Those types of things don't get left behind by accident."

"No, nor do they disappear or fall off the truck."

"Where are you thinking they went to?"

"My guess is they were staged for another team. Maybe sleepers or people coming into the country as tourists. I figure the gear is somewhere between the river and the Marville airport."

"That's a lot of ground to cover," Hammer said, putting the truck in gear and pulling onto Highway 90 south.

"No doubt. But they wouldn't have left it in the desert by the border. They would have thought I had backup nearby and the area would be crawling with the authorities. I doubt they'd risk it."

"So the airport?"

"Or somewhere along the way. It'd be easy to pull over along that dark highway, near a mile marker or sign, dig a shallow pit and drop it all in. The other team would pick it up and drive on. The airport seems riskier. It's a small airport, but people are there every day, coming and going. A team might stick out, especially if they have to dig."

"Unless it's already done."

They pondered the possibility.

Hammer broke the silence. "The airport seems the most likely to me. It's an identifiable location. No chance for a mix-up. One guy could have dug while the others secured the airplane."

"Makes sense. Can you check it out?"

"Already driving. You okay?"

"Good to go. And," Axe's voice lowered, "I may have a line on a new team member. A little green, but fierce. You and Haley are going to love her."

Interstate 20
Outside Abilene, Texas

The rising sun blinded Jafar. He tilted the car's visor down to block the brightness. In the passenger seat, Cyra stirred in her sleep.

Beautiful.

In the trunk, the sniper rifle in its padded case lay waiting for her. In front of it, partly hidden by their matching roller suitcases, the dusty backpack filled with C-4 explosives, two pistols, knives, and spare ammo would be ready for them at the end of their long journey.

His stomach rumbled, and he took the last sip of his coffee. They would drive through one of the many anonymous fast-food restaurants along the interstate as they neared Fort Worth. He shook his head in wonder at what he'd seen so far. The prosperity of the country shocked him. Tehran, his home, was his country's largest city. But it didn't compare with America.

I will relish this time. These sights. But when the mission is done, I look forward to returning to my homeland—and girlfriend.

He glanced at the peaceful, sleeping face of Cyra.

But maybe we can 'perfect our cover story' another few times before then.

In the meantime, they had twenty-eight hours of driving—across two-thirds of the country—before they would arrive in the nation's capital of Washington, D.C.

Marville Municipal Airport
Marville, Texas

The sun warmed Nalen as he stepped out of the truck near the abandoned airplane tie-downs at the edge of the tiny airport's tarmac. He rubbed his eyes. Despite the brief nap earlier, he felt every one of his sixty-five years. But he consciously shook off the fatigue, stood up straight, adjusting the plate carrier he still wore, and slung the M4 that had felt a part of him for decades.

He walked off the asphalt and into the desert between where Axe said the stolen airplane had come from and the hangar, considering a search pattern. Ten feet straight in, however, he abandoned the plan.

The hole wouldn't be obvious if he hadn't been on the alert for it. And anyone other than him who saw the disturbed dirt carefully smoothed over wouldn't have thought twice. The entire southwest portion of Texas was dirt, rocks, and small shrubs. Desert. Who cared about freshly disturbed ground the length of a sniper rifle and the width of a large backpack?

No one besides me—and the people that dug it up before I got here.

He walked back to the tarmac and scanned the area, praying for a miracle.

Maybe they're still around, ready to make a break for it. Or in town getting gas?

Doubtful. He knew wishful thinking when he did it.

How long ago were they here?

It had been hours since Axe had left, chasing after the terrorists. The second team could have arrived any time afterward.

They could be hundreds of miles away by now.

Would the Texas authorities accept more roadblocks? He pictured the many back roads, highways, and interstates crisscrossing the state. He expanded the map in his mind to include New Mexico and Arizona to the west. Oklahoma to the north. Or Dallas, San Antonio, and Houston. Large cities where the new terrorist team could easily fade into the background and disappear.

No. There were too many roads and he didn't know the number of people or the type of vehicle to look for.

I'll get Haley and her team on it. Maybe they get lucky with a traffic camera or something. But at this point, we're back to square one.

He frowned and pulled out the satellite phone to call it in.

"Gregory? It's not over yet. We have a big problem."

58

THE ZONE

Haley sat at the desk in her cubicle and contemplated her screens, preparing to slip into the zone.

Gregory had informed them all of Axe and Nalen's assessment. Despite the heroic actions of the evening to stop the team of terrorists, the country was likely still under threat of another attack.

And it's my job to figure out what might happen, where, and who's doing it.

Axe had also reported no intelligence gleaned from the backpacks, weapons, or C-4—though Nancy was working on tracing the explosives and other equipment, in addition to fingerprints and pictures of the men— at least the ones whose heads Axe hadn't destroyed.

Haley slipped her headphones on and started up some quiet background music to help her focus and further block the world around her.

What do the attacks on the pipelines tonight and the kill teams hitting Nalen and I Saturday have in common?

On one screen, she started a spreadsheet and listed potential enemies.

Russia. The Mexico drug cartels. Iran. A dead-man switch from Todd "The Assistant" Burkley.

She paused, then added an unlikely—but more alarming—threat:

A dead-man switch or an associate of "The Boomer" bomb maker.

Her mind slipped into analysis mode, leaving behind her desire to be out in the field, running and gunning with Axe and Nalen.

The zone welcomed her.

All I have to do is sift through an overwhelming mountain of data, find the hidden pieces, and put the puzzle together.

All before the next attack.

She started a new column and added notes.

There's a threat to the country.

It likely had something to do with energy.

Oil and natural gas so far, but I can't rule out other forms.

The most obvious targets—but also the most well-protected—were nuclear power plants. The country had more than eighty active ones.

Including a few in Texas, Arizona, and southern California. All within reach of another team.

She closed her eyes and pictured the eight-man team Axe had reported.

Could they successfully attack a nuclear power plant?

The maniacs Todd Burkley had trained launched a hit at the nuclear plant north of New York City. Their drone strike might have succeeded if not for the additional security team she got in place before the attack. Could the missing black backpack contain a drone and explosives to repeat that type of assault?

My hunch is this is a small-team action. One drone, or an assault by a few people, wouldn't get past the everyday security.

Still… She dashed off a quick email to Gregory recommending the area nuclear plants raise their alert levels as a precaution.

What else?

The power grid was extremely vulnerable.

A few dedicated teams could take down high-power transmission lines out in the middle of nowhere.

While it wouldn't destroy the country, it would wreak havoc and be a big story.

Would terrorists target windmills? There were a few facilities near southern Texas as well as scattered around the United States. While electricity from the wind grew every year, it didn't seem like a high-value target.

Not unless they're going for optics. Toppled windmills would be the lead on every TV news program.

What about solar farms? They were unprotected.

Not likely. Poor optics and not essential—backup, additional power for the most part.

Hydroelectric?

Blowing a dam would be spectacular if they pulled it off, but they were well protected and difficult to impact.

Haley sighed, frustrated. She was missing something, getting lost in the potentials instead of flowing with the data and allowing it to lead her to the answer.

I guess that means speed reading and seeing what my intuition picks up.

She minimized the spreadsheet and opened databases. FBI. CIA. CAG. DEA. The newer databases that much of the raw information from the various agencies fed into. They filled her screens. She started running searches, skimming the latest intel summaries, letting her instincts guide her.

Time slipped by, but she was unaware of it. Her ears ached from the headphones, but she couldn't remove them and let in the sounds of the world. Haley rubbed her eyes and fought off sleep. After a while, she could ignore her bladder no longer and rushed to the bathroom, stopping at the kitchen on the way back for a two-liter bottle of soda.

She read human intelligence reports—HUMINT. Electronic intercepts. Her focus wasn't on the obvious—the big clues. Other agencies and analysts were already all over them, pulling at the threads to see what unraveled. Since nothing big had come onto the radar, she would find her answers in the minutia. The offhand comment overheard by an embassy employee in a foreign country's local dive bar. An odd spike in internet traffic from suspected terrorists to a new contact. Or the group who dropped off the radar and suddenly went silent.

Haley blinked and sat up straighter, slowing down to take in the information she had almost skipped before her gut told her to stop.

An agricultural report?

Venezuela had improved its agricultural production for three quarters in a row, reducing the constant hunger struggles much of the country had experienced over the past several years.

She dug further, intrigued and guided by her intuition.

Poverty there has been reduced gradually but steadily over the past four years.

Not by a lot, true, but enough so it had been reported and logged into the State Department's database.

Morale in the military had improved after soldiers had received one year's worth of back pay they were owed.

The country had signed a deal with Russia—one of its few allies, aside from Iran and Mexico—to work together to improve and modernize Venezuela's aging, failing oil production infrastructure. They would finally be able to export more oil than ever before.

Haley's whole body shivered.

That's it.

The puzzle pieces appeared before her and seemed to assemble themselves in her mind.

Mexico—the cartels and their vast amounts of money.

Russia—oil and natural gas along with an ongoing desire to torment the United States.

Iran—the injured Marine reported the terrorists in Texas had spoken Farsi and his story checked out. The interpreter working with his unit had been fluent in Farsi, Dari, Arabic, and conversational in other languages. The Marine and the interpreter had been friends—Murrey's commander had confirmed everything. The Marine-turned-truck driver's intel could be trusted.

Finally, Venezuela. It all made sense—President Heringten's hard line against Venezuelan President Villanueva, the sanctions against the country, and now the inexplicable influx of wealth over the past few years.

The pieces fell into place. She finished the bottle of soda, replacing the hunger pangs in her stomach with the burning of acid, and continued reading. She now had a roadmap—a theory to either support or tear apart. But her intuition told her she was on the right track.

I don't have it all yet, but I'm very close.

59

THE PARTNERSHIP

Presidential Office
Caracas, Venezuela

President Esteban Villanueva loomed over his desk. His six-foot three-inch body-builder bulk required a custom leather chair. It creaked whenever he shifted his considerable weight. He'd gone soft in his fifties when he stopped working out but kept eating as if he were still training for world-caliber weightlifting tournaments. When he turned sixty, the softness had turned to flab.

But he'd recently started working out again, lifting weights every morning to return to his glory days—or at least a semblance of fitness.

With his tailored suits, dark hair, and perfect white teeth, he could be charming when needed, despite his fleshy jowls and small, beady eyes. But his casual cruelty was known to all. His mood also wasn't helped by the incessant chanting of protesters on the streets outside his office.

They will be silenced.

The throngs of people had shown up twenty minutes ago, surprising everyone. They had somehow kept the details from his country's secret police and countless informants.

"Change, now! Change, now!" Over and over. The repetition threatened to drive him crazy. But he couldn't do a thing about it at the moment except trust his security forces to keep him safe and the national guard to disperse the crowd using tear gas and rubber bullets—as usual.

An aide standing at a small desk along the wall nodded to him, then rushed from the room, closing the thick door firmly behind him. Villanueva picked up the telephone and spoke pleasantly to his contact. They certainly weren't friends and barely trusted one another. But mutual respect and a feeling of shared purpose cemented their relationship.

"Good day," Villanueva said in accented but passable English, purposefully not using Orlov's name. His people assured him the Americans couldn't listen in to the conversation because of some technology mumbo jumbo he didn't pay attention to, but he'd followed Orlov's lead from the start. If the Russian spymaster didn't use names, he wouldn't either.

"Is that... chanting?" Orlov asked in his methodical style.

Damn those people!

"Yes. My apologies. They took us by surprise this morning but are being dealt with as we speak." He hated explaining himself and rarely had to. But even the most powerful had to play the game at times.

Orlov chuckled, an evil sound even to Villanueva's ears. "We no longer have protests," he said in acceptable but imperfect English. "Here is free but very valuable advice, the same I shared with my president," Orlov said in acceptable English. His slow manner hid a devious mind. "You need gulags. Distant labor camps to send prisoners. Killing leaders of movement creates martyrs. Arrest them in the middle of the night, stage a short trial before finding them guilty. Sentence them to ten years of hard labor. That is the way to stop dissent." Another low chuckle. "Make sure the work is brutally hard but give them a pencil and one piece of paper per month. Make them write letters home. Censor those, of course. If they write the wrong things, they get less water and food. But encourage them to say how difficult work is. The conditions horrible. Works like magic."

Not a bad idea.

Villanueva made a note on a legal pad in front of him with an expensive Swiss pen.

He couldn't resist twisting the knife, though he knew it wasn't wise. "Valuable advice indeed, but which president do you mean? The new one, the one who bumped his head and died, or the one who resigned in disgrace?"

For a moment, he thought he had gone too far. Then the slow, low chuckle came across the line. "The one who reigned longest—so, yes, three presidents ago. But that's the wonderful thing about men in power—they are so easily replaced."

The threat hung between them for several seconds before they both moved on with the reason for the call. "I was expecting news today," Orlov said, his tone mild.

"I, as well," Villanueva said but did not elaborate.

Let the man ask. He may think he has total power over me, but he is wrong.

"The Americans have a saying: no news is good news. In this case, however, I think they are incorrect," Orlov said.

"I agree. In the meantime, the other plan proceeds," he said.

There was a long pause. As the silence grew uncomfortable, Villanueva resolved not to be the one to break it. He knew the power of silence. He had used the tactic his whole life.

The weaker man speaks first.

He doodled on his notepad, sketching bars, then a cube, and adding a stick figure inside the bars of the prison he had drawn.

"If certain results are not produced," Orlov finally said, his voice betraying no note of impatience or concern over having to be the one to break the silence, "certain other items may have to be returned."

Villanueva slowly placed the pen on the desk next to the yellow pad and sat up straight.

My one weakness.

Everything else he could lose. The help to modernize his oil drilling and refining capabilities, the steady supply of military hardware at near-wholesale prices, the increased trade between the countries, even the huge uptick in Russian and Iranian tourists.

But not that.

For a moment he didn't know how to respond. As an independent head of state? An equal in a mutually beneficial business transaction? Or would the powerful man respond better to him begging like a dog?

His instincts kicked in, ignoring the desperate need to hang onto the items secretly supplied by Orlov.

"I understand and will make sure you are happy in the end," he promised.

After another pause—this one a more common length for the slow-to-speak Orlov, the Russian responded. "Good. We will speak again soon. I have no doubt."

There was a click, then silence as the man hung up on him.

After Friday, he won't be able to get the material back no matter what he threatens.

"Change, now! Change, now!" From outside the thick windows, Villanueva could still hear the peasants, as he called them. Each day they demand both more—and less. More food. More jobs. More security. Less inflation. Less crime. Less persecution.

They don't appreciate me and all I have done for them.

Hadn't he already sacrificed billions of the initial drug cartel payments, pouring the money into the country's economy?

Might as well try to fill a well with pebbles.

Hadn't he directed back pay to the police, doctors, and soldiers?

Probably just stolen by those under me before it reached the needy… or squandered on whatever idiotic things stupid poor people buy.

No. The mistake had been trying to help at all. He should have left well enough alone. Let them all suffer.

But I had to be ambitious, didn't I?

He wanted—needed—international recognition. To the country's west, Columbia prospered… and took in his poor and desperate.

The other country mocked him with their wealth and success.

The Americans had insulted him with their hurtful words, sanctions, and lack of support. Meanwhile, his country spiraled ever downward.

Venezuela should be celebrated for all we are. Instead, they deprive us. Stifle us. Pity us.

And that he couldn't tolerate. To fix it, he wasted billions on anti-poverty programs. On feeding the poor, tackling inflation, and improving the economy. But with all the money spent, he still had little to show for it. The country had fallen so far over the years. Billions more dollars were needed.

The money will continue to roll in.

As long as his ambitious plan worked, that is.

He would have his revenge.

Orlov and the rest of the world would have a prize beyond their wildest dreams: a vulnerable, defenseless United States of America.

He smiled at the thought, his small eyes lost in his fleshy face, his brilliant white teeth flashing.

The feeling faded as he turned his mind to the problem at hand. There had been no pipeline explosions. No reports of vast infrastructure damage in Texas. No word at all from the team provided by his allies in Iran.

The next phase of the plan will succeed.

But even if it didn't, the final part of the operation would. Nothing could stop it.

The protester's chants turned to cries as they were dispersed. He caught a faint hint of tear gas despite the closed windows.

That should shut them up for a while.

He smiled again and picked up his phone. It was time to turn one of the country's prisons into a gulag.

60

THE MENTOR

Orlov hung up the phone and contemplated the call with Villanueva.

There was a single knock on the closed door. A second passed, then Dmitry, Orlov's deputy, entered. A tall, forty-year-old man who looked like he missed more meals than he ate, he had listened in to the call with President Villanueva, as ordered.

Dmitry—the son Orlov never had—quietly took a seat on the plain wooden chair to the side of the desk. He then stared at the map on the opposite wall and said nothing.

They sat like this for minutes without speaking.

"Begin," Orlov said eventually.

Dmitry didn't speak for another minute. Then he said, "The man cannot be trusted."

Orlov nodded his head slowly. "Few can."

"He is so focused on revenge he could be dangerous."

"Yes," Orlov agreed after a moment. Though he kept his face impassive, inside he was impressed. He didn't confide in Dmitry—only allowed him to watch the master at work. The man was proving to be a quick learner and adept at deceit.

"Continue."

"You provided the warheads in a way it could not be traced back or blamed on Russia. But he does not know this and is not clever enough to wonder. Those beneath him would work it out and suspect a trap, but he is too egotistical to share the information and plans with anyone smart enough to question him. Only a few fanatically loyal men will know, and they are not encouraged to think, let alone voice their suspicions. You threatened to take back the missiles to keep him moving forward and prevent cold feet."

"And the results?"

"He will go through with the plan, never realizing how much he is being used. The plan has a probability of success. America will be in tatters."

"If it fails?"

"The beauty of it. Villanueva is blamed, of course. But the Iranians will take the fall for providing the missiles and the 'special' warheads."

"Well done, Dmitry."

Dmitry nodded once, acknowledging his mentor's praise. "If the plan succeeds, what is our move? What do we do?"

A cruel smile spread across Orlov's face, changing his image from a dumpy-looking accountant to a menacing predator in an instant. He answered much quicker than he usually spoke. "Absolutely anything I want."

61

THE THREAT

Haley couldn't pull it together. She had most of the pieces to the puzzle, but the overall picture eluded her.

She had been so close but was now stuck. It didn't happen often, but she felt like she had slammed into a brick wall.

A brick wall...

An image flashed through her mind. Former Russian President Zimalev's body, seen through her binoculars, crashed into the blue padding covering the concrete pillar.

I need sleep.

She crossed her arms on the table, put her forehead on them, and was asleep.

What felt like a second later, she felt a hand on her shoulder.

"Haley?"

Her mom was trying to wake her up.

It must be time for school. I overslept again.

"Five more minutes, Mom," she grumbled.

Mercifully, her mother left. She was almost back to sleep when a thought occurred to her.

Mom?

Her mother and father were in hiding, protected by the Secret Service. And she wasn't in her childhood bedroom.

This is conference room C at the CAG.

She came fully awake with a start and stood up quickly.

Nancy was a few feet away, hands out before her in a calming gesture. "It's okay, Haley, you're at work. You fell asleep." The older woman's eyes had dark bags under them, and her gray hair stuck out in all directions, filled with static.

She looks as bad as I feel.

"Put your hands down. I'm not going to shoot you," she muttered. As soon as the words were out of her mouth, she regretted them. "Sorry. I'm exhausted. I know we all are."

"No problem," Nancy said. "You've got..." she gestured at her face.

Haley swiped the back of her hand near her mouth, rubbing a trail of drool.

Oh, great.

Her face burned with embarrassment, but Nancy smiled. "You got it. Are you awake? Gregory's coming back in—time for a meeting."

Gregory walked into the room. He, too, looked like hell.

"First things first," he said. "Sleep. We have a lot of work to do but we can't function on empty. Grab it as you need it." He glanced at his watch. "I'm converting conference room E into an 'employee wellness room.' Yoga mats, pillows, blankets, the whole deal. The stuff will be delivered shortly. Use it."

Gregory paused, took off his glasses long enough to rub his bloodshot eyes, then replaced them. "The country has been attacked and there's at least one other team of terrorists in the wind. We won't be getting out of here any time soon."

He looked at Haley first, then Nancy, then Dave. "I've just been working out with the president," he said. "He's been briefed. The entire nation's intelligence services are on this now. We're no longer in charge —" He held up his hand at Haley before she could protest. "Which is fine. We don't need to be. Our role can be to find out what's going on. We excel at it."

They sat around the small conference table Haley had been asleep at moments before.

"Let's do a check-in," Gregory continued. "What do you all have?"

Haley started explaining her hunch. "My working theory is a

connection between Russia, Venezuela, Iran, and Mexico—or at least the cartels there." She laid out her reasoning and the pieces she had so far. "But I'm stuck. I can't quite see what the motives are or where they're going with it. Assuming I'm correct," she added in a tired voice.

"Sabotaging our oil and natural gas production or delivery would directly benefit all of them," Dave agreed. He looked at her like he had a few times before—like he didn't know if she was a brilliant analyst with incredible intuition or a spooky witch who received messages from the beyond which allowed her to know the future.

He's an analyst. He should know better than to believe in voodoo, witchcraft, or whatever it is he thinks I do.

Was there an argument to be made for her hunches being more than the work of her mind?

It's only my subconscious pulling together stray bits of intel my conscious mind could never connect.

Nancy cleared her throat and looked worried. "That could fit well with an intel tidbit I read last week. Dave and I went out for dinner, and I felt a little off a few hours later, which made it jump out at me the next day. The entire kitchen staff of a natural gas tanker ship got food poisoning while on leave. They were so sick they ended up in the hospital. They literally missed the boat. One of them kept complaining they were poisoned on purpose, and he demanded the United States look into it. Completely crazy, but it got logged in the system because the energy company is based in the USA."

"A liquid natural gas tanker would make an effective bomb and fit in with what the first terrorist team attempted to do by hitting the pipelines," Dave said. He went to his laptop, typed and clicked, and projected a map onto the big monitor screen on the wall. "Here are the biggest LNG shipping ports." Several were in southern Texas.

Nancy worked her computer for several seconds, then stood in front of the monitor and pointed to a location in the Gulf of Mexico near the coast of Texas. "That ship is here now—with a replacement kitchen crew."

Nancy, Dave, and Haley turned to Gregory, who rubbed his chin with his hands.

"Do we have anything else?" he asked. "Info on who the new crew members were? Any proof this could be what we're looking for?"

Nancy shook her head. "Not yet."

Haley felt for Gregory.

This is all supposition. Guesswork. But it fits.

What would he do with the information?

"Can we send Axe and Nalen to inspect the ship?" Haley asked, thinking out loud.

Gregory shook his head. "No. They have the training, of course, but it's a job for more than just the two of them. If we think this is a genuine threat, we need more." He stared into space, lost in thought.

I'm not sure he's cut out for this type of work.

Gregory had been an analyst his entire career. He'd done well so far, but the strain of taking action, instead of just passing off the intel to others who had to make the tough decisions, clearly weighed on him.

"How long until the ship gets into port?" he asked Nancy.

She checked her computer. "They're behind schedule. They were expected to arrive early yesterday, take all day to fill up, then depart before dark. Now it looks like they'll be in port this morning."

Gregory nodded. "Work the problem," he said to them. "I want an assessment in thirty minutes. Is this a threat—another one in the same campaign? A different potential hit? Or nothing—a coincidence, the guys all ate some bad fish or whatever? Make calls, wake people up, rattle cages. But balance it with subtlety—if it's the real deal, it would be nice for our boys to have the element of surprise if they have to hit the ship."

Nancy and Dave hurried to their small desks in the room, but Haley stayed sitting with Gregory.

"We're missing something big," she said to him in a low voice.

"The sniper rifle and the backpack."

"No. Well, yes, but it's more than that."

"The liquid natural gas tanker." Gregory nodded at the map of Texas and the Gulf of Mexico still displayed on the screen. "It fits."

She nodded. "Yes, I think Nancy's on the money. But there's more." She shook her head in frustration. "It's just out of reach. I can't see it."

"Your hunches have been solid," he said. "Help Nancy and Dave on this, then follow your gut. It's up to us to stop this... whatever it is."

62

THE SETBACK

Bar Ocho
Tampico, Mexico
Five Hours South of Brownsville, Texas

"*Jefe*," Hugo said, his face grave. "The drug shipment never arrived."

Arturo sat in the bar's small office at a messy desk strewn with bills, receipts, and notes. On the other side of the reinforced interior door, the bar was dark. The stools made with horseback riding saddles had looked sad and uncomfortable as he'd walked in. Tourists wouldn't be laughing and enjoying the kitschy decor for several more hours. But this morning, as one of his many legitimate businesses, it served as his temporary office. Aside from his home, which he was convinced was unknown to the authorities—or at least so well defended they would never risk attacking it —he never used the same location twice in one month.

"None of it?" Arturo asked, not angry. It was just one more puzzle to solve, one more problem to overcome.

"None. And all the men are gone. A source reported two were found shot, floating in the river downstream from the tunnel," Hugo explained.

"And the others? The rest of our men and the guests?"

If the men Villanueva made us escort into America took the drugs or killed our men, there will be hell to pay.

"Gone, *Jefe*. I have not made further inquiries in case they are hiding, or you wished the matter to remain unmentioned."

A smart man.

"No word from America's Drug Enforcement Administration? Nothing on their news?" They always bragged about their successes.

"Only about the decoy shipment, which was intercepted as planned. It is all over their media."

"So what happened? Where are the drugs, our men, and those foreigners?"

I suspected allowing the soldiers to accompany our shipment would be a mistake.

"I have no information. Our sources say no reports have been filed by the Border Patrol or police. Except..."

"What?"

"Along the highway near the tunnel, a police officer was shot last night by an automatic weapon. He lived and reported being fired upon from a black truck—which is what we had supplied to our men and the foreigners. Also, a black truck was destroyed when a semi drove into a fuel pump at a truck stop in the small town nearest the tunnel."

Arturo's skin burned, which always happened when he felt rage and didn't allow himself to express it.

Our men would only shoot Americans as a last resort.

It had to be the soldiers sent by Villanueva.

His next thought chilled him, cooling the fire on his skin but leaving it just as uncomfortable, if not more.

What would the members of "The Five," as he was calling the other four drug lords and himself, do when they heard?

They will blame me, though we all agreed to allow Villanueva's coercion.

Arturo would have to find a solution on his own, put it into place, then inform the group. Failing to handle it would doom his position as leader.

"Take our current stockpiles and ship them immediately."

"But the scanners at the borders and the dogs—"

"No, we will do it differently. Call in favors and find out when the dogs won't be working. Distribute the drugs among many people. Fill cars and minivans. Offer bonuses to mules who are willing to risk the drive across the border. Plant the drugs in the cars of unsuspecting people for transport. We will work when they are least likely to catch us... and overwhelm them.

Several will get caught. The rest will slip through while the others are inspected." He nodded, warming to his plan of attack. "Shift the immigrants at the border near Laredo further out of the city. Get our people to spread rumors of a mass crossing tomorrow. This will focus the Border Patrol on containing them and away from other points of entry. Then, flood the border crossings with drugs tomorrow at multiple points. We will get them through with sheer volume. Much could be lost, but enough should get through to hold us over until next week when the larger, safer shipments begin from our new country."

"Yes, *Jefe*. But…" Hugo waited for permission to speak his mind.

"Yes, say what you need to."

"We have so much ready to deliver," Hugo said slowly. "It is just waiting, at our labs in Venezuela. Couldn't we also begin the process of those shipments today so they will arrive next week?"

Arturo considered the logical question.

Technically, it would violate the agreement with Villanueva—but hasn't he already broken the deal by insisting on sending the mercenaries through the tunnel?

They had their own fast boats ready to use. Why wait a week until the formal beginning of the agreement?

Who needed the assistance of the Venezuelan Navy? The tacit approval of Cuba, who Villanueva had promised would look the other way as their small boats transited their waters on the way to America? The submarines, which could sneak into shallow waters from the Gulf of Mexico to the northern state of Maine, packed with drugs, delivered quickly to their ultimate destinations with minimal risk?

He frowned in frustration. No. They had spent so much, put their futures at stake with this deal. They had much to gain by completing the last few steps as agreed. They couldn't break the agreement. President Villanueva had them by the *cojones*. If they were going to speed up the timeline, he had to get the approval of the other cartel leaders… and think of an enticement or argument the Venezuelan president would agree to.

"No, my friend," Arturo said. "Continue as I have instructed. But also send runners to the other leaders. I must meet with them to discuss our options. And get the secure meeting container on the road." He told Hugo which airport—the next one on his list—and the day and time for the emergency meeting.

Coming together again so soon is also a risk, but a manageable one.

He would know if the national police were on to them. No local police —the few who weren't bought and paid for—would dare try to arrest them. Besides—in the worst-case scenario—as long as they stayed on the ground only a short time, no one could get a tip and rush men to the area in time.

I will turn this setback around. We will get what we need from Villanueva... or Señor Duarte will get his way—we kill him and take our chances with the next president.

No one was irreplaceable.

63

THE SLAM DUNK

Central Analysis Group Headquarters
Conference Room C
Alexandria, Virginia

Gregory returned to the conference room exactly thirty minutes after he'd told his team to work the problem of the liquid natural gas tanker. Nancy stood next to the big monitor, looking ready for a presentation.

If it's conclusive, I'm fine. But if they're not sure, what the hell do I tell the president?

Could Gregory send a SEAL team to board the ship?

He had the authority now, but to take that step felt foreign to him.

I'm supposed to be the one providing the intel reports and letting others decide, not ordering strikes on ships.

He was further outside his comfort zone than he'd ever been before.

"What do you have for me?" he asked Nancy as he sat at the conference table. Dave joined Nancy at the monitor while Haley stayed at her seat on the far side of the table.

"This is it," she said with conviction. "Eight of the crew members got food poisoning bad enough to be admitted to the hospital in their previous port of call. They claim they ate different food, though all were at the same restaurant."

"A server with the flu? Bad sanitation at the place?" Gregory asked.

"Unknown. But the one who made a fuss has disappeared. Checked himself out of the hospital earlier than the others and vanished."

"Suspicious."

"Definitely. We think he was either disappeared or paid off. Also, Dave got info on the replacement workers. Nothing jumps out except one minor item." She pressed a presentation clicker and the screen changed, showing security footage of eight men walking along a dock. "Do you see it?"

Gregory examined the jerky footage of a camera capturing fifteen frames per second instead of a high-quality video's normal thirty frames per second.

At least it's in color and isn't too grainy.

"They look like a unit. They're trying to disguise it, but they're soldiers."

"Yes. If we weren't already suspicious, no one would have caught it. They did an excellent job. Very professional, but the clues are obvious now," Nancy said.

"Could this be confirmation bias?" Gregory asked. "We're seeing it because we suspect it, not because it's there?"

"Look closer."

Dave clicked on his laptop, and the short clip ran again.

Damn. The backpacks.

"Identical black backpacks," he mumbled.

Nancy nodded with a grim look on her face. "Still think it's confirmation bias?"

"No. Can you get a—"

"Already done," Haley said. "Axe confirms it looks like the same style, size, and shape as the ones he recovered. And no, it's not standard issue with any military. They aren't special backpacks, but most LNG crew members carry duffel bags or regular suitcases, so this is unusual."

Gregory pondered the information, then asked, "Anything else?"

"When the kitchen staff got food poisoning, the call went out for replacements. These men were supposedly on leave from another ship with a different company and got scooped up. They had experience and proper documentation. Further checking, though, turns up no personal connections. No one I spoke to had ever met them. I didn't have much time, but it's a relatively small community. Someone should have recognized at least one of their faces."

"Sir," Nancy said, "this is as close to a slam dunk as we get. The eight guys are up to something. It could be nothing, but I believe they're out to hijack it. They'll sink the LNG tanker before it gets to port, to completely block the shipping lane. Or, if they're smart, they wait until it's full and blow it in port."

"What happens then?"

"We're still working on that. But if they do it right, nothing good, obviously. Block part of the shipping channel, destroy the LNG facilities, cause massive damage, kill a bunch of people."

"What about other ships? Are there others we need to worry about, like the other planes on 9/11?"

Dave shrugged. "We're about to work that next."

Gregory nodded as he stood. "Excellent work. Get to it. I have to call the president."

This is bigger than intelligence gathering. Whether I have the authorization to order this mission or not, the president has to be informed.

64

THE TORNADO

Central Analysis Group Headquarters
Alexandria, Virginia

Haley's eyes snapped open, the dream fading. Her cheek rested on a hard surface and a long object dug into her face from her jaw to her ear. Lifting her head, the pen she'd been laying on stuck to her for a second before clattering to the desk in her cubicle.

I fell asleep again.

She used the sleeve of her jacket to wipe drool off her face and the puddle from the desk.

This has to stop.

She'd researched tanker ships for an hour after the team meeting before falling asleep for a few minutes. So far, it appeared no other ships had new crew members. With any luck, the terrorists were only on the one —empty—liquid natural gas tanker.

But she'd been awake for over forty-eight hours.

She stood to take a proper nap in conference room E, as Gregory had ordered.

He's right. We can't win this if we're too tired to think.

As she walked down the hall toward the conference room though, she remembered her dream. She had been standing on an oil drilling platform, a calm sea far below her, the warm sun on her face.

An oil platform?

Over the last two days, she'd read so much, consumed pages and pages of information, vacuumed up thousands of tiny details. Was her dream based on intel... or a meaningless movie her subconscious played for whatever reason people dreamed?

She opened the door to conference room E. Yoga mats and blankets beckoned. The exhaustion demanded that she rest.

The dream has meaning.

If she slept now, would she lose the thread? Or wake refreshed and better able to think? She made a deal with herself.

Thirty minutes. I'll give myself half an hour to figure it out, then I can sleep.

Turning, she hurried back to her cubicle, somewhat reinvigorated.

I can do this.

The zone welcomed her instantly as she typed, entering the search terms her dream dictated.

'Venezuela' + 'oil drilling platform'

Her tired eyes scanned both public and confidential information.

The information appeared.

Her gut told her she had nailed it... but her mind had to admit she didn't know what 'it' was.

From start to finish, the process had taken only five minutes.

Time to take this to Gregory.

She hurried to the bathroom, brushed her hair, washed her face, and touched up the tiny amount of makeup she wore. It wasn't enough to be smart or right frequently. The presentation—how she sold herself and the analysis—mattered.

I still look like hell, but it's better than before. Maybe he won't notice the fading outline of the pen on my cheek.

Gregory awoke with a gasp in his darkened office. The couch along the back wall had proven more comfortable than it looked, and he'd been asleep for...

He sat up and checked his watch.

Seventy-five minutes since informing the president about the tanker ship.

Not quite a full normal ninety-minute sleep segment.

What woke me?

His phone hadn't rung, his watch alarm hadn't beeped, and he hadn't heard a knock at his door. He didn't think he'd been dreaming, or at least he didn't remember any dreams. But some feeling had caused him to suddenly awaken.

It felt like when he was ten years old, at home with a babysitter on his parents' weekly night out. He stood at his house's front door with the sitter, a fourteen-year-old neighborhood girl who looked after him. Together, they watched in awe as the huge, black mass of a tornado turned toward the subdivision. It came closer so fast, with a noise like a freight train.

The tornado sirens went off, wailing and scaring him more.

"Run to my house!" his babysitter had yelled, taking him by the hand as they ran down the block—toward the tornado. Behind them, his screen door had started banging, then the wind ripped it off and it flew away as he glanced back.

They made it to the sitter's house, joined her parents in the basement, and were safe as the tornado veered away from the suburban subdivision and demolished acres of nearby cornfields instead.

Absent the sirens, the howling of the wind, and the freight train sound of the tornado, he could be living the moment again. Or at least, that's how it felt.

Too much stress, too little sleep. I'm not sure I'm cut out to be a direct-action manager.

He was reaching for his glasses on the small side table when a quiet knock came from the door a few feet away. He knew in an instant, without a doubt, what his feeling and the knock meant.

Haley.

65

THE DREAM

Central Analysis Group Headquarters
Alexandria, Virginia

Gregory gestured for Haley to sit, as usual, though she didn't—also as usual. So he just leaned back in his chair, rubbed the sleep from his eyes again, and waited for her to begin.

I can no more control her than I could the tornado when I was ten.

His youngest, most talented analyst looked horrible. Bags under her bloodshot eyes, and what could only be the fading indentation of a pen on her cheek, though her face looked washed, and makeup touched up.

She's made an effort to clean up. This is bad.

"What do you have for me?" he asked her.

I can tell already that I'm not going to like it, he thought.

"No, you're not," she said.

Now she's reading my mind?

"Well, yes, kind of," Haley admitted with a tired smile. "You're too exhausted to hide your thoughts and feelings like you normally do. And they are easy to guess. We've been here before, right?"

Gregory closed himself down. Not all the way—she was right. He was much too tired, and his relationship with the analyst had progressed to a point it wasn't absolutely necessary. But out of long habit, he did it anyway.

You never know when you're going to need to hide a thought or emotional response.

In his business, especially at the director level, keeping his cards close to the vest was mandatory.

"Impressive," Haley remarked at his change. "You've got to teach me that."

"You've improved over the past year. Now—what is it?"

Haley opened her mouth, paused, then tried to speak again. Finally, she sighed and sat heavily on the chair in front of his desk.

That's never a good sign.

"I had a speech all planned," she said in a soft voice. "Point one, point two, justification, a logical argument. But I'm going to cut through the bullshit. I have a very important question for you."

Oh, shit. Here it comes.

"Go on. Ask it."

"How much do you trust me?"

He surprised himself with a sudden chuckle. "Don't mince words, Haley. Just dump it all out there."

He got another small smile for his efforts.

Turning serious, he paused before speaking, then hit the ball right back into her court. "As your boss, I should ignore the question and just have you spit out whatever crazy idea you've come up with. But as you said, we're way beyond that bullshit. The truth is, I trust you completely. But," he said, interrupting her before she could jump in, "that doesn't mean you have a blank check or a green light to do whatever the hell you want. It's my ass if things go south around here. I'm in charge. You're still a young analyst, even if you are a prodigy and have been right on more big calls than basically anyone else, ever. Now, why don't you tell me what your wild plan is? I'll try hard to go along with it."

Here's where she tells me she has a gut feeling.

She brushed her blond hair out of her face, tucking it behind her ear. "I had a dream," she began. "Of an oil platform in the ocean. And... well, I don't remember any more than that." The words came rushing out, an admission filled with frustration and regret. "But I must have gotten the idea from intel I read. I went back and started a search," Haley continued, warming to the story. "Venezuela has one remaining functional oil drilling platform at sea in the east... and a brand new one off the coast of Caracas. There's a report about it in the databases—a fisherman's offhand complaint of soldiers firing warning shots at him as he neared the rig." She held up her hand. "And yes, before you ask, he was in a bar, drinking. The new oil rig means they've at least restarted their oil exploration and extraction, which takes a lot of money. Plus, I can understand a guard or two, but armed soldiers firing at a fishing boat? Something is up."

Gregory took it in, his mind finally coming fully back online after the nap. "There's no good reason to prevent fishing in the area, is there?"

"No, not at the small scale it sounds like this guy does."

"I see where you're coming from, but it's not enough," he said as gently as he could. "Do you have more?"

She shook her head.

"A hunch, at least?" As much as he hated her gut feelings, crediting the lead to a hunch was much better than admitting she'd seen a vision in a dream.

"Yes. My intuition tells me it's important, but no, I don't have more than that."

"We could re-task a satellite, or…" He stopped thinking out loud when the realization hit him. "Oh."

"Yeah."

He knew in his heart this was his moment. The decision he made next would make him or break him, regardless of the results of the action.

"You want to send Axe."

Haley nodded.

"We can't send a team in," she said. "I don't have my usual confidence in this hunch. All I know is that we need eyes on." She hesitated, then continued. "It's your call, of course, but I'm not sure we should tell the president, either. This has to be black, off the books, so he—and you—can deny it, if necessary."

Gregory shook his head. "We don't have to operate that way anymore. We're official."

"Officially unofficial," Haley pointed out.

"If you have enough conviction to send Axe, we need to take it seriously and send in a team of SEALs—or at least former SEALs. Get Nalen and Axe to put together a team or pull Mad Dog out of Mexico."

"No," she said. "A team will get caught. A flyby or drone might provoke a mess of an international incident—not what the president needs right before the State of the Union address."

"Axe—as good as he is, against whatever is waiting on the platform? If you're correct that something is going on there, and I bet you are, it's heavily defended."

"True, but the defenses can't be too obvious, or people would know something's up. There will be a balance of protection and concealment. Axe is perfect. He can get in and assess the situation. We'll rely on him to make the call—send in the cavalry if needed or back off." She barely hesitated, but he'd had just enough sleep to pick up on her tell.

Here comes the rest.

*"*And I'll be there to help."

"No, absolutely not."

"But—"

"No," he repeated, his voice firm. "I promised the president. You stay in the country and preferably in the office. You'd be too valuable as a hostage or a victim. And you're much too important as an analyst to be out gallivanting in the field if you ask me. You're incredibly talented. Embrace it."

There was a long pause as they both digested the discussion. Finally, Haley sighed. "Fine. I get it. But he needs backup nearby… and I have the perfect man for the job—with your approval."

She outlined her plan to him. It was high-risk, but if anyone could pull it off, it would be Axe.

This is it. Yes or no. Go big or go home.

It didn't take more than a second. He trusted Haley's instincts, or hunches, or now, apparently, her dreams. It was risky but the plan and cover were both solid.

"Approved on one condition. You lay it out to Axe. He's going to be way off-grid. And I will deny knowledge of his actions if he gets caught or killed," he added, his voice cold and firm.

I'd have to. There would be no other way than to call him a rogue former Navy SEAL acting on his own.

"If he agrees to the mission, we'll get him most of the way, then he's on his own. And don't con him," he told her as sternly as he could. "Tell him the truth and let him decide."

Haley nodded once, stood, and left his office without another word.

A phrase Admiral Nalen had used a few weeks ago during one of their early morning workouts at the White House came to mind.

All in, all the time.

He didn't know if it was in his blood to be in charge of a direct-action team… but he had to try.

66

THE SHIP

LNG Vessel *Orion's Belt*
Corpus Christi, Texas

Saman hadn't noticed the sunrise when the tugboats maneuvered the ship to the terminal. He and his staff had been busy in the kitchen, preparing breakfast for the crew. He'd missed the morning as well when they prepped for lunch. But now he had a moment to step outside onto the deck next to the galley for a breath of sea air. The sun felt nice on his forehead's receding hairline. He rubbed his close-cropped beard and smiled sadly.

Not a bad life.

Cooking nutritious meals for a crew with such diverse tastes was a challenge, but he'd spent years in the military doing the same for his countrymen. For this mission on the natural gas tanker ship, his day-to-day existence had changed little... aside from hiding his true identity and purpose.

With a few different choices, this could have been my life. Safe. Predictable. Lasting.

He stood straighter, unconsciously returning to his military roots. In the past days, he'd slipped easily into the role of civilian cook, but now those days were over.

The bright afternoon sun reflected off the water. Onshore, the liquid natural gas terminal sprawled with its miles of pipes and gigantic storage tanks. The January air was cooler than usual for this area, according to what he'd overheard the crew saying at the lunch tables.

A good day to die.

He contemplated his fate. While there was a plan to get his team off the ship before the explosion, the others had been kept in the dark about how unlikely it was to work.

No, they had been deemed expendable.

At least we will die martyrs.

He opened the metal hatch to return to the kitchen. It was nearly time to prep for dinner service. While his men cooked, he would use the afternoon to casually walk the ship and place the charges where he had been trained.

He walked through the galley, nodding to his men. They knew what time it was and gave him solemn nods in return.

They must suspect this is the end, though none of them have questioned the escape plan.

Later, after hours of loading time, he and his men would blow up the ship and its full tanks right before it left port, taking America's newest, largest LNG terminal with it.

Inside the walk-in freezer, he moved to the back, shivering in the cold. Moving cardboard boxes of frozen hamburgers and stuffed pasta, he worked his way back to a box marked **Vegetables**. No one on the ship would ever seek out a box of frozen veggies.

He left the freezer and the kitchen without another glance at his men, though it was likely the last time he'd see them. At least, until the afterlife.

Red, an active-duty SEAL Team leader, had gotten the last-minute call to drop everything and assault the ship with his men. And this time, for once, his former Teammate Axe didn't demand to join the mission.

"One tango on the deck just returned to the galley," Red heard over his radio as he climbed the narrow metal ladder at the stern of the ship on the bay side, away from the prying eyes of the terminal.

Not that we're invisible here.

Surely people could see them. An assault during the daytime was not ideal. But the word had quietly been circulated to the ship's captain, the tugboat operators, and the people in charge of the terminal. The Navy

SEALs were conducting a training mission. Keep it quiet and stay out of the way.

Yep, never mind the eight heavily armed men boarding your ship. Nothing to see here.

He swung his legs over the ship's railing and stepped lightly onto the deck, moving to his position on the security perimeter, covering his sector until the rest of his men boarded. The big question on his mind was whether the terrorists had moles in place to warn them.

Or are they careful enough—and have the freedom of movement while undercover—to put lookouts in place?

He didn't dwell on the larger, more alarming question: had they already placed explosives or were they waiting until closer to when the ship was filled with the liquid natural gas?

Best guess: they wait until the last minute to place the charges. It's what we would do.

"Last man," came the call from Rocky, the K9 handler with the dog strapped to his body. The man and Enyo, the Belgian Malinois with brown and black fur, looking like a thinner, more compact version of a German Shepard, would assist in searching for explosives once the terrorists were killed or in custody.

"Move," Red said quietly into the radio. As planned, they split into two four-man teams. One team would secure the bridge, leaving a man there to ensure the ship stayed put and no damage was done from the control room, then start searching for the eight terrorists.

With his bushy red beard, Red led the other team—wiry Thor, strong and steady Ronnie, and hulking Link—directly to the door the terrorist, disguised as the chief cook, had recently passed through.

In their briefing for the operation, intel indicated all the terrorists should be in the kitchen at this time. But they couldn't rely on that. Haley and her team, who had conducted the briefing, had only guesses.

They stacked up outside the red door with the round, silver wheel, which needed to be spun to open.

At least we don't have to worry about locks or breaching charges.

They waited, their pulses only slightly elevated. Ready to capture or kill the enemy. They had the faces of the terrorists memorized from the video provided by Haley. Their short-barrel M4s were locked, loaded, and the safeties off. Years of working together had instilled trust in their abilities and each other.

They were a finely tuned team of warriors at the top of their craft.

"Breaching the bridge in three," came the call from the higher deck.

Two... one...

Red tapped Ronbo, who tapped Thor, who spun the metal wheel and yanked the door open.

Ronbo slid effortlessly and soundlessly through the opening with Red shadowing him and Link right behind. Thor swung around, checking their rear, then followed.

The door opened directly on the end side of the kitchen. Ahead on the left, one man spread dirty white dishes on a conveyor belt moving slowly into an industrial size dishwasher, like a miniature car washer.

Terrorist "Three."

The man, mid-thirties with dark features, looked up from his work without much surprise—until he realized who, and what, the men rushing toward him were. His eyes widened in surprise, and he turned to run.

Ronbo slammed the butt of his M4 into the man's head, knocking him down—and out.

"Don't move—don't move—don't move!" Link yelled in his booming voice as the SEALs rushed into the room. The sound filled the surprisingly spacious kitchen.

The other men, in various stages of cleaning, prepping, and cooking, turned to look at the four SEALs. The face of the man nearest Red changed from shock to dismay, to anger, then defiance.

"Down on your knees!" Red yelled, rifle up and aimed at the man's chest. Ron, Thor, and Link were repeating the phrase at the men closest to them. But as Red locked eyes with the cook who had been cutting carrots, he realized this wasn't going to go as easily as he hoped.

My guy isn't going down without a fight.

Time seemed to slow as the knife in the man's hand swung toward Red. There was only an instant to make a decision. Close and engage, taking the man alive but risking injury, or shoot him and move on?

Instinctively, Red planted his left foot and kicked with his right, putting all his strength and forward motion into it.

The man's eyes widened before shutting tightly in pain as he dropped the knife and fell to the floor in a heap. He curled into a ball. Quiet, pitiful cries of agony came from him as Red expertly dragged his hands away from his groin and zip-tied them behind his back. Then he kicked the knife away and assessed the situation.

Red counted seven men on the ground being zip-tied, including his.

Damn. Where's the last one?

67

THE EXPLOSIVES

LNG Vessel *Orion's Belt*
Corpus Christi, Texas

As Saman left the kitchen, he heard a commotion from the other side of the door. He half-turned, ready to go back and see what the trouble was. But his instincts saved him. He hesitated a moment, trying to place the feeling. He hadn't seen combat—he was a cook and always well back from the front lines. But he'd had plenty of training and been around enough hardened warriors to guess what was going on.

I'm in danger.

A few seconds later, he faintly heard yelling through the thick metal door.

That sounded like someone yelling, "Don't move" over and over.

Without thinking, he turned and ran through the corridors of the ship, carrying the cold cardboard box from the freezer.

We have been discovered somehow.

He desperately tried to figure out where to plant the explosive charges. He wouldn't have time to place them as planned. But was there one location where, if they were detonated at once, the damage would be enough to ensure a chain reaction?

It was all up to him.

I will not fail.

Were his men brave enough to fight back, giving him enough time to reach whatever spot would do the most damage?

He wasn't sure. The men had been selected from the armed forces for their dedication, yes, but to go undercover convincingly, the planners of the mission had been restricted to cooks and those with previous kitchen experience. Because of this requirement, he didn't have special forces or front-line warriors. He had rear-echelon support personnel—just like him. And while they'd spent two weeks training together, none of them were killers.

One, maybe two, will fight.

They all would have done their duty later in the day, helping him place the charges. But most would surrender.

I don't have much time.

His only advantages were his familiarity with the ship's corridors and the knowledge that his life was over one way or the other.

I will do my duty and go out with a bang.

"We're missing one," Red said into the radio, running down the corridor as he balanced speed with a desire to not get shot or stabbed at every corner and doorway. "Where are Rocky and Enyo?"

"We're clearing the crew quarters," Rocky replied. "Nothing so far."

"Meet me on the kitchen level, stairwell two. Ronbo, sitrep."

"Seven in custody, IDs confirmed," came the terse reply from Ronbo. "Area secured. We're searching it now."

"See if any of them will talk. Ask them where the last guy is, where the charges are, all that."

"Copy."

Saman headed forward to the nearest location where he had decided to plant all the explosives. No matter what happened, at least the ship would be destroyed and the terminal damaged. If he got lucky, the LNG would explode as well, taking out the entire facility.

He heard pounding footsteps behind him. There were only so many places on the ship where the charges would do enough damage, so it was no surprise they were on him so quickly.

All they had to do was work their way forward.

But there was another sound that confused him. A clicking noise. Then it dawned on him.

No. Not a dog.

He hated the unhygienic animals. A stray had attacked him and a friend as they played outside as children, causing an irrational fear of them since those early years.

For a moment, Saman almost put down his box and ran to save himself. But as he hurried down a long, straight corridor to the vulnerable area of the ship where he would live his last moments, he got himself under control with the perfect plan. If he succeeded, he would not only destroy the ship, but the facility, and his enemy.

I'll kill the dog, too.

The idea gave him strength and made him smile.

Red could hear the terrorist just ahead of them.

It has to be him. No one else is running around in the ship.

Enyo the Navy SEAL dog looked back, trying to see around Red to make eye contact with Rocky, her handler. She clearly wanted to be allowed to run farther ahead.

They approached a half-closed heavy door, meant to seal the section of the ship from fire or water. Red slowed as he neared it, taking one side as Rocky took the other without either of them having to speak or gesture. Enyo stood in front of Rocky on the hinge side of the door.

Red took a knee, M4 up and ready, then nodded. Rocky pushed the door open enough for the dog to slip through.

"Enyo, go!" Rocky called softly. She leaped through the door and sped down the hallway as he pushed the door the rest of the way open.

At the far end of the hall, a matching door started to close. Red caught a brief glimpse of a man, gone before he had a clear shot.

We're not going to make it.

The dog tore down the corridor in a blur.

"No shot!" he called to Rocky.

"Enyo, kill!" Rocky bellowed.

Speeding like a bullet, Enyo darted through the narrow opening just before the door slammed shut.

"Enyo!" The quiet, desperate cry slipped from Rocky.

The dog could take care of herself as well as—or better—than any other member of the Team. But both Rocky and Red reacted the same as if Ronbo or Link were locked on the other side of the door with an enemy. With single-minded purpose, they rushed forward. They had to back up their teammate.

68

THE BOX

LNG Vessel *Orion's Belt*
Corpus Christi, Texas

The screams of terror started seconds after the door slammed shut. They were quickly replaced by cries of pain. By the time Red and Rocky ran down the hallway and worked the door open, the anguished sounds had stopped. It was all over.

As they stepped into the compartment, Enyo looked up at them, panting happily, tongue out, eyes bright. Her muzzle and neck were dripping blood, but it wasn't hers. Nearby, the terrorist lay on his side, blood still flowing from the gaping wound that used to be his throat. His dull, dark eyes stared at nothing.

Enyo sat next to the large cardboard box labeled as frozen vegetables and stared expectantly at Rocky.

"What do you do when she finds the explosives and kills the bad guy?" Red asked as they took in the scene in front of them.

"Give her two treats," Rocky said. The relief in his voice was clear. He was reunited with his partner—who had saved the day.

"Good girl," Rocky said, feeding the dog first one, then a second treat. Enyo accepted them with relish, then waited expectantly, ready for more action.

Red checked a large cardboard box on the floor near the terrorist's body, peeling the tape off and opening it carefully. Inside were wrapped packages of C-4 and everything else needed to blow the ship sky-high, packed tightly together. The tango hadn't had time to open it or set any charges.

"Take her and search the ship. Top to bottom, front to back. Just to be sure."

"We're on it, boss man," Rocky said. "Come on, girl. Let's go. Search!" They returned the way they had come, Enyo leading the way, leaving a faint trail of blood drops on the clean white linoleum floor in her wake.

"Get the EOD down here," Red called on the radio. The explosives ordnance disposal tech waiting onshore would secure the box and any other materials Rocky and Enyo found. "Team two, continue the search. Team one, question the prisoners. We don't leave until this ship is safe and secure."

69

THE SHIRTS

Hotel Nuevo Uruapan
Uruapan, Mexico

"The timing will be tight," Mad Dog told his men—four former SEALs—sprawled around the modern hotel room. They had worked together recently in Las Vegas and jumped at the chance to get back into action again.

The hotel offered the perfect vantage point of the airport runway to watch for the cartel jets, potentially for days on end, without having to loiter in a van near an international airport. It was Mexico, so perimeter security wasn't as tight as it was in the US, but they still took protecting their airports seriously and *gringos* hanging around would be noticed.

One man—"Johnboy"—sat in a chair in the window, his back to the rest of the group, clocking every plane coming in for a landing. A sticky note on the window had the tail numbers of the suspected cartel planes. Another below it had outlines of what each model looked like. If two of the correct types of planes landed and taxied to the expansive, private hangar building north of the commercial terminal, they were on standby, regardless of the tail numbers. Three jets and they were a go.

"It's one minute down the stairs to the vehicle at full tilt," Mad Dog continued. "Six minutes of crazy driving to the airport fence closest to the target hangar. Eight to nine if there's traffic or we're slow." He kept his face straight for a second before he couldn't hold it anymore. The men laughed with him. They wouldn't run anyone over, but the last thing they would be is slow.

"Then it's breaching the fence—'Rook' and 'Bishop,' that's you." The two men, one short and squat, one tall and thin, were swim buddies from BUD/S many years ago who had stuck together over the years. They were hard, reliable men who would make short work of the chain-link fence with the new bolt cutters they'd picked up at the big-box hardware store a block from the hotel, or simply cut the strands of barbed wire at the top if time was tight. All the men were capable of getting over a fence quickly.

"A one-minute run through the woods to the hangar," Mad Dog said, pointing at a satellite view of the route and airport taped to the room's mirror above the desk. "We should be in place by the time the final plane finishes taxiing to the hangar. Then the party starts."

"Enemy forces?"

"Heavy," Mad Dog admitted. "Figure five to ten heavily armed, highly motivated tangos per plane. Five planes."

"Twenty-five to fifty against..." Rook made a show of slowly counting the men in the room, "four guys?" He held up his hand before Mad Dog could correct him. "You don't count, you're brass."

There's one in every group, Mad Dog thought.

The irony wasn't lost on him that, usually, he was the smartass in the room.

"Rook, that's cold. I'll be there, rockin' and rollin' right by your side. Yes, it's bad odds. But we'll have surprise on our side, and we're getting more help later this morning."

"Blondie?" Bishop said hopefully, his eyes lighting up.

"No, sorry, not Blondie. But she told me to tell you hello—she actually remembered you from Vegas," Mad Dog explained.

Bishop looked thrilled. "Really?"

"No, you meathead, not really. She has other things on her mind than retired Navy SEALs, okay? And besides, she's one of us. Hands, eyes—and minds—off her." He glared at the men, not an ounce of humor in his tone or look.

Instantly, the men replied. "Copy that," they said, one by one.

Mad Dog let the mild rebuke hang for a moment, then continued. "We're getting Mexican national police. They're in charge." The men didn't groan out loud, but Mad Dog could sense the change in the room.

He wasn't thrilled to have a non-SEAL in charge, let alone police officers instead of military. "Cut it. It'll be fine," he said.

I hope.

"They're due here any minute. The main guy is—"

Two firm knocks came from the hotel room door. The men were up instantly, hands on pistols hidden beneath the Hawaiian print shirts they wore.

"Relax," Mad Dog told them, and opened the door.

Captain Hernandez took stock of the American who opened the door. The short, barrel-chested SEAL looked like a cross between a bear and a man. Thick, dark beard, strong muscles, dressed in a horrible red shirt with green palm trees, but he had a surprising sparkle in his eye.

Hernandez didn't speak. Neither did the American. They sized each other up for several seconds, then the shorter man stepped back and held open the door.

Hernandez stepped through the entry area to the main room, stopping near the corner of the bed. In front of him, lined up by the window, were four men. One sat with military-grade binoculars watching planes approach and land at the airport. All were strong, clearly warriors to his trained eye, and wore similar gaudy, button-down tourist shirts.

They looked like clowns. Dangerous clowns, to be sure, but still.

This is what I get? Five men that have no hope of blending in?

The short man from the door moved past him and turned to stand before his men. "Mad Dog," he said.

"Hernandez," he replied, shaking hands with the American.

The man nodded and smiled. "Call sign?"

It took Hernandez a second to process the words and accent. His English wasn't as good as it could be, but he figured out the meaning.

I'm a police officer. We don't have call signs.

The man clearly expected an answer.

"Captain," he said, staring into the man's hard eyes.

They assessed each other for a moment. He'd always believed he could read a man from looking him in the eye. In Mad Dog, he liked what he saw.

Apparently, the other man did as well. He chuckled. "Well, Captain, welcome to Operation Just Cause. We're at your service."

With a look and handshake, Mad Dog saw the warrior spirit that lived in the Mexican police officer.

The man has been there and done that.

And he still carried the pain. Mad Dog could sense it in him, like a heavy burden.

It's weighing him down.

But he still had a sense of humor.

'Captain.' What a fantastic comeback.

With his dark hair and unshaven face with several days of dark stubble, Captain Hernandez didn't look much like a strait-laced, clean-cut American police officer. But his muscles showed how strong he was and the way he moved proved he could handle himself.

Mad Dog introduced him around, then asked, "Where are your men?"

"Only me," the Mexican said.

Mad Dog paused. "I thought you would have a team. We need more men."

Hernandez hesitated. Yes, more men would be ideal.

How do I explain to him the reality of the situation?

They didn't need to know that all his trusted men were dead.

How he'd led them into cartel ambushes.

That he'd overheard the quiet use of his new nickname—Captain Death.

Keep it simple.

"I am on vacation," Hernandez explained. "Officially. My boss knows I am setting an ambush. With the cartel and the bribes..." he shrugged, wishing his English was better. "Better to be careful. But we are legal, approved. You as well," he reassured them, though they were the type of men who looked like they didn't care as much about the legality as he did.

If the operation resulted in a firefight or any intelligence gain, the Chief Inspector would submit backdated paperwork that had been "mislaid," approving Hernandez's mission. No one would be hung out to dry. And as long as the Chief Inspector wasn't corrupt, they should be safe —and have a chance at catching the cartel leaders.

Between his English and the American's Spanish, they eventually worked out the explanation to everyone's satisfaction. The Americans weren't happy to be potentially outnumbered against the drug cartels' men, but it was what it was—and they accepted it.

Welcome to my world, my new friends.

"Why those shirts?" Captain Hernandez asked once the briefing was over, and he'd told them his plan.

"No hiding men like us."

Hernandez nodded. "Hide in the open."

"Exactly. We say, 'in plain sight.' We are American entrepreneurs. Start a global sports website. Stay at cheap Mexico hotel for company conference." He'd resorted to speaking in short, easy sentences, which beat butchering the language with his elementary Spanish.

"Smart."

"And now," Mad Dog announced, pausing for effect, then spinning to look at the window, "we attack!"

The men, including Hernandez, looked surprised and turned to the SEAL staring through binoculars at a plane landing.

Several seconds passed before the man at the window shook his head. Mad Dog chuckled and shrugged. "Someday, that's going to work. People are going to be amazed!"

70

THE CALL

The Nighty-Night Motel
Pecos County
West Texas

Axe finished the last of the pushups as his phone vibrated on the nightstand. It didn't matter that he'd only slept a few hours. Every day was either a workout or a mission... and sometimes both. The Texas sun was setting and it was time to get up, work out, and start the new day. He picked up the phone.

Haley. It's taken her longer than usual to come up with the solution to this puzzle.

"What do you have for me?" he asked as a greeting.

"One good, one bad, and one you're going to be pissed at me," she said, her voice rough.

He paused for a second, much more concerned about how she sounded than her words. "When was the last time you slept?"

"You sound like my mother. And my boss," came the terse reply.

Ouch. Well, then.

"Okay," he said slowly. "Then let's start with what I'm going to be pissed about."

Haley sighed. "I'm sorry. You're right, I haven't slept much. Only a few minutes in the last two and a half days. And I know, I have to sleep.

It's next on the list, I promise. But I have to get you in motion first. Or rather, talk to you about whether you'll do it."

"Of course I'll do it," Axe said, moving to the bathroom to dry the sweat off his face with a hand towel.

"Wait until you hear it first, then decide. But let's get this out of the way. While you slept, your former Team hit a liquid natural gas tanker ship near Corpus Christi. The decision was made to send them in without you or Hammer. First, you both had a busy night. Second, it's been years since you've trained on that type of mission."

Red—that bastard. He kept me off the mission.

"And before you go blaming Red," Haley continued in her tired voice, "it was Gregory and the president. And me. You want to be pissed at someone, it's me."

Axe took a breath, held it, then released it slowly, letting the annoyance dissipate.

I would have slowed them down.

"You're right, I'm wrong. It makes sense and I'm not mad. What did they do?"

"Caught eight more terrorists undercover as the cook staff on the tanker. Kept them from blowing it up, along with the LNG terminal, miles of pipelines, and killing several dozen people."

"Not bad for a day's work. Your intel, I assume."

"Team effort. Seriously. We're all going non-stop here."

"Are they as tired as you?"

"Yes. But Nancy is sleeping now, then me, then Dave. Gregory got a nap before I woke him up. We're good to go."

"What's the good news?"

"The ship not blowing up is the good news. The bad news is we don't have a line on the missing backpack, sniper rifle, or who might have them. We're completely blank, but Dave's on it now and Nancy will take over when she's awake. We'll figure it out." She didn't sound very convincing.

In fact, she sounds like she's at the end of her rope.

He knew her well now.

There's something else.

"But that's not what's bothering you, is it?" he asked.

"No," she sighed. "I had a damn dream."

She's pissed again.

"What's wrong with a dream? It means you slept a little, at least."

"The mission I want to send you on? It's not a hunch or an educated guess. It came to me when I was sleeping."

Suddenly, she sounded less like the prodigy intelligence analyst turned killer field asset and more like the young woman she was.

"Do the four-count breathing with me twice through. Then tell me all about it."

He heard her sigh, then start the breathing exercise with him. It was designed for centering and gaining focus.

Several seconds later, Haley continued, sounding more sure of herself.

"I did a ton of speed reading, then couldn't continue so I put my head down and slept. I don't know how long. But I dreamed, and when I woke up, I remembered it. Don't worry," she added hastily. "Once I woke up, I worked it. The facts check out. There's something going on in Venezuela. I just…" She paused. "It feels stupid that the idea came from a dream."

"We take them where we can get 'em. You know what I say."

"Always trust your gut."

"Exactly. So, where is your dream sending me? Venezuela?"

"Yes, and I'm making a call to a friend next. How do you feel about Kelton and the yacht backing you up?"

"Can he get there in time?"

"Yes, you go in tomorrow night. I can't get you there with the intel and gear you'll need until tomorrow, anyway."

"The last time I almost got him killed," Axe said, recalling their trip to Mexico, the run-in with the cartel soldiers, and Kelton getting dosed with Dr. Edgar's drug.

And I lost the young scientist when the cartel shot him instead of me.

"And Kelton almost killed you while under the influence of that drug, so I say you're even. If it's a problem—or if he says no—we can work something out with a local. But I'd feel better with a trusted team member there, not a hired hand."

Can I allow Kelton to risk his life again?

He recalled what the man had said during that operation as they approached the hotel where all hell would break loose.

He wanted to atone for the things he'd done.

"I guess it's up to him. If he's in, I'm fine with it."

"I'll ask him. And I'm bringing Nalen back to D.C." She lowered her voice to a whisper. "Gregory is struggling with being in command. Having Hammer around would really help."

"Good plan. I'm all in," he said, wondering how to broach the delicate subject he wanted to bring up.

———

Central Analysis Group Headquarters
Alexandria, Virginia

Haley sighed in relief. She'd had a gut feeling the call with Axe wouldn't be easy for some reason.

I'm not sure what I was so scared of. Axe has always believed in me and had my back.

"Okay," she told him. "I'll get you details and call Kelton. Look over what I send. Let me know if you need anything not included in my gear list."

She'd gotten a boost of energy from talking with him.

I'll handle these details, then sleep. Finally.

It felt good knowing she could rest soon. And she'd be able to do it with nothing on her plate for the time being.

"There's one other thing," Axe said in a tone of voice she'd never heard from him before. She froze.

"You there?" he asked.

"Yes," she managed to get out. Warning bells flashed in her mind.

"I drafted a cop from Marville to help at the pipeline," Axe began, then stopped.

"Okay. You think he should go with you? You need the backup?"

Whew. No biggie.

"It's exactly what I was thinking. We worked pretty well together. I wouldn't have gotten it done without her."

The last word, spoken with a slight emphasis, hung in the silence between them.

"But I wanted to run it by you. I know you're stuck in the office. You're exceptional there."

He's replacing me.

"And don't worry, I'm not replacing you," Axe said, reading her mind.

Emotions flooded her tired psyche.

I'm in this office, staring at computer screens, while he's out running and gunning. And apparently, finding a better partner.

"In fact," he continued, but she barely heard him, "I think you'll like her."

"It's fine," she choked out, suspecting she wasn't fooling Axe one bit with her reassurances. "Let me know what gear you think she needs. I'll make it happen."

I have to get off the damn phone before I lose it in front of him.

"I have to call Kelton and get him moving, then send you the mission brief. And sleep. God, I need sleep. Talk later." She hung up on him.

Not my finest hour.

She breathed in for a count of four, held it, then breathed out four. She held her breath again, and repeated it, trying to stay in control.

I'd be okay if I weren't so tired.

She wasn't being replaced. If anything, having another member of the team was a smart decision. Axe shouldn't have to go on a dangerous mission with only the civilian Kelton Kellison as backup.

But it should be me. I'm his partner, not some small-town cop who barely knows her ass from her elbow.

Nancy and Dave could handle the analysis. She could leave right now, collect her gear, and meet Axe in Aruba.

No. My place is here.

Haley took another breath.

One second, it all made sense.

The next moment, all her fears came crashing back. She'd be stuck in an office for the rest of her career, always supporting the mission, never a part of it.

She closed her eyes and repeated the breathing exercise, trying to calm down.

There goes my peaceful sleep.

71

THE BACKUP

Axe knocked on Rodriguez's motel room door as the afternoon sun set behind him.

Am I doing the right thing?

Rodriguez had training—but as a police officer, not an asset.

And she's never taken a life.

He didn't need to ask—he could tell. She wasn't a killer.

But I need backup.

If Haley was right—and she had been every time he'd worked with her—he needed another person along for the mission.

Kelton can't handle this alone.

He needed a shooter. Someone who could lay down covering fire or take out a target in an emergency.

With Admiral Nalen returning to Washington to assist Haley and Mad Dog in Mexico with several of the people Axe would consider calling on for help, he was out of good options.

Any of the warriors who assisted in Las Vegas with the drugged tourists could help.

But he wasn't on close enough terms to call and ask them to drop everything to go on an overseas op with him.

But this mission is so far off the books, is it fair to ask Rodriguez to go?

The door opened, revealing Rodriguez in her patrol uniform pants, shirt, and bullet-proof vest—the only clothes she had with her. She looked put together, awake, and ready to conquer the world.

Ah, to be young again.

He felt like shit. The running and gunning of the previous night was messing with his knees. His back ached. And while the body-weight workout followed by stretching had helped, he would give a lot to take ten years off his body.

"Come in," the young officer said, standing back and pulling the door the rest of the way open.

Uh oh.

He wasn't much of a ladies' man, but he could hear and sense the invitation behind the two little words.

"Let's walk," he countered.

She covered it well, but Axe caught the quick flash of disappointment on Rodriguez's face.

She grabbed the keycard, slipped on her patrol coat with POLICE in yellow capital letters across the back, and they started walking. Axe led the way through the parking lot. They'd circle the small, cheap motel where they'd been dropped earlier that morning after dealing with the local police, then the FBI, and finally a whole host of other departments at the scene of the shooting with the terrorists.

Away from the room, Axe felt more comfortable. And he was fine with the conversation he had to have.

It's going to be more difficult for her than me.

"Am I in trouble?" Rodriguez asked bluntly. She didn't sound worried or scared—curious, more than anything.

"Not with me, but we do have to talk."

"Yeah," she said sheepishly. Out of the corner of his eye, Axe noted her blush. "I'm sorry about inviting you inside like that. I know you said you're taken, and you're so much older, but I don't get a lot of good prospects in Marville."

'So much' older?

Between his sore body and the matter-of-fact way Rodriguez spoke, the hits just kept on coming.

But yeah, almost twenty years older than her. I get it.

"Thanks. Yes, I'm quite happy in my relationship. But let's drop that from now on."

"There's a 'now on'?" she asked. She sounded thrilled. "I checked in with my department. My chief got a call saying I had been temporarily reassigned to Homeland Security. If he was smart, he'd keep his mouth shut, not ask questions, and welcome me back with open arms when and if I wanted to return." She chuckled. "It sounded like they tag-teamed him. First, a woman bluntly told him how it was going to be. Then her boss got on the line and asked if he had questions. But not asking, you know? The chief said they both sounded exhausted, stressed, and like they would go to Marville and mess him up if he objected."

Haley and Gregory working well together.

"And that's a good thing?" Axe asked, knowing the answer.

"Are you kidding? What we did... stealing an airplane, chasing another plane, a shootout with terrorists, finding and disarming explosives, saving Texas? Best night of my life!"

"Want to keep doing it?"

Rodriguez abruptly stopped, forcing Axe to stop too.

"That's an option?" she asked.

She doesn't quite believe it—but she's desperately hopeful.

"It is... but there's a catch. Or two," he warned. He nodded his head in the direction they'd been going and started walking. She hurried to catch up.

"Dealbreakers?"

"Possibly. Depends on you. Here's the first one—absolute secrecy. No one gets told the story. No bragging, no explanations, no hints, raised eyebrows, or winks. Stone cold silence." He paused, then added quietly. "That's a big problem for some people."

Rodriguez chewed it over as Axe had guessed she would.

She might be one of those people who needs the glory more than the satisfaction of a job well done.

They occasionally had to deal with it in the SEAL community as well. But they handled it, taking the "Silent professionals" part of their code very seriously.

When she didn't say anything, he continued. "I'd prefer you say nothing about last night, but that's up to you. If we go forward, though, last night—and anything else—are off the table. Eventually, you'll go back to Marville. People will ask questions, and you'll smile politely and say you can't discuss it. Then you'll change the subject."

This time, he stopped. They were in back of the rural motel with the tan desert stretching out behind them.

"If it's any consolation," he said, "people will see you've changed. That will speak volumes... at least, to the ones who matter. They won't have to ask. They'll know."

She nodded, but he could see her mind churning over the decision.

"And before you answer, here's the other part. This you can't tell anyone, no matter what. If you do, you'll end up in a world of hurt. I'm not Homeland Security."

Rodriguez's eyes widened and she whispered, "I knew it! CIA?"

"Something like that. Three initials, yes, but it doesn't matter which ones. We're a very small, exclusive, clandestine direct-action force. We're official... mostly. What we do skirts the border of legality at times. When we briefly cross the line, if something happens..."

"Nobody knows your name or what you were up to."

"You got it."

"Hence the secrecy."

Axe nodded. "Best to keep it all quiet so we don't worry about what was sanctioned and what wasn't."

"And now?" Her excitement was still there—but tempered with what looked to Axe like an understanding of the real-world consequences if things went bad.

"Now I could use some backup. Out of the country, where a fluent Spanish speaker might come in handy. Unofficial. You wouldn't be a cop. In fact, you'd be playing the role of either the young girlfriend of a rich guy or his hired help."

Axe caught the smallest tell, a micro-expression of unhappiness.

I've hit a nerve there on one of them.

But he waited patiently for her to process the information.

"And if we're caught or get into trouble," he continued after a moment, "your story would be that you're a former police officer from Texas who gave up her career for love—or a cop who couldn't handle the heat and left it all for an easier life as a maid. You might even be portrayed as going rogue, using your police training to turn to a life of crime and violence. It wouldn't be good, Mariana."

Once again, Axe had to wait while she considered the ramifications.

If she's right for this position, I know what she'll be wondering.

"What about the potential action?" she finally asked, as he had hoped she would.

"Strictly backup. I'm going into a rough, delicate situation. You'll be on standby—at a distance. At most, you'll offer covering fire as you did by the pipelines."

"That's it?"

"Don't get me wrong, Rodriguez. You're good, you've got the right attitude, but you're green at this type of operation. And we haven't worked together much. Play your cards right and it might turn into something more. We're looking to expand our roster and you're a solid prospect."

He turned and started walking toward the front of the hotel and the street. There was a fast-food place up the road. He was hungry and needed to fuel up before the night got underway. "Come on, let's get some food. I'll give you until after we eat to make up your mind."

The shorter woman jogged a few steps to catch up to Axe, a serious, determined look having replaced the earlier excitement. "I won't keep you waiting. I'll give you my answer now. I'm in."

PART 4

TUESDAY

72

SEARCH

U.S. Customs and Border Protection Port of Entry
Laredo, Texas

The line of cars, as usual, stretched as far as he could see, though the shift had barely started. They had eleven border entry lanes open this morning, and all were beyond busy.

Kyle loved his job as a canine handler for the U.S. Customs and Border Protection. Yes, it was often hot, boring work that still required attention, a careful eye, and trusting his intuition. But he had health insurance, including dental, and a government pension.

And he had Benji the Drug Sniffing Wonderdog, a Border Collie who, Kyle suspected, was smarter than he was.

He wasn't the only person who worked with the blue-eyed, white-and-black bundle of energy. But in his heart, he knew he and Benji had a special bond—one that the part-time handler couldn't possibly share.

With all the passenger cars, vans, and SUVs backed up already, at least he and Benji didn't have to worry about the semi-tractors—they crossed further up the river where they were scanned with the new imaging tech installed over the past two years.

The morning was cool but walking up and down the line of cars kept him warm, and he delighted in the joyful focus Benji brought to the job.

"What do you say, boy? Another day, another dollar. Am I right, or am I right?"

Benji gave him a quick, almost dismissive glance over his shoulder, then faced front, ready to move down the line of cars as they crept forward and stopped, over and over.

The dog works harder than I do, and he does it for praise and treats. God help us if they figure out a way to train the dogs to do the job on their own, without handlers.

Thanks to a program initiated by the president four years before, backed by a Congress miraculously in agreement for a change, Kyle and Benji were part of a program that was finally widely operational. The number of dogs used at the border had shot up with the authorization of additional funding. Most ports of entry now had at least one dog team. They had already proven their worth, at first catching multiple cars per shift, then fewer, until finally, the cartels must have realized it wasn't profitable to smuggle drugs hidden in vehicles. They still occasionally tried, though. There weren't enough dogs to cover every hour the border crossing was open.

Gotta keep us on our toes, probably. See if we let our guard down.

Well, not on his shift.

"You and me, we're on it, right, boy?"

This time, Benji just ignored him.

He's gotten used to my chatter.

Kyle was starting two hours earlier than scheduled because he'd forgotten to ask for time off to go to his niece's birthday dinner. Thankfully, his boss had let him flex his hours at the last minute.

Lately, since the cartels cut back their shipments, the job had been more of a grind—a long day of walking without much excitement or reward. Still, it paid the bills and got him some exercise.

"Sure beats working for a living, buddy," Kyle told the dog. They reached the head of lane three and turned down lane two. They'd already been to the far side—lane eleven—and were almost done with a full circuit. At each lane, he'd lead Benji past ten or fifteen cars, come up the next lane, turn, and repeat all day. Sometimes he'd do fewer cars in one lane, sometimes more, depending on his instincts and whether there was an interesting—or suspicious—car to check out.

As Kyle meandered down the long line of vehicles, he counted his blessings. He didn't see Mexicans commuting to work or American tourists returning home from a vacation, trip to the inexpensive dentist, or getting their prescription drugs filled at a fraction of the price they could in the US. No, he saw job security.

The tension on the leash jolted Kyle back to reality. Benji sat near the trunk of an upscale sedan, panting happily, staring hard at him.

"Come on, seriously? That's like an eighty-thousand-dollar car. Let's go."

Benji refused to move—exactly as he'd been trained.

Kyle pressed the transmit button on his shoulder-mounted mic. "Alert in lane two. Black sedan."

"Copy," came the immediate response from his dispatch officer.

"Good boy, Benji, good boy," he said, giving the dog the required treat for doing his job.

Kyle stopped the car in lane one from moving forward and tapped on the windshield of the black sedan to get the attention of the driver, a well-dressed man who was idly scrolling on his cell phone as he waited in line to cross the border.

"Sir," he called in English, "Please drive carefully to the pullout. There," he said, pointing. They had a multi-vehicle staging area on the side where they could do quick inspections. They could take cars to other areas for more in-depth searches, but that wasn't usually necessary.

The man nodded but didn't look scared. Bored, if anything. Not concerned at all.

"You better be right, buddy," Kyle muttered to the dog.

He didn't relish the idea of having Benji taken away for retraining.

They'll stick me in one of the damn booths, sitting on my ass all day, looking at passports.

Kyle walked backward into the gap left by the car in lane one as it moved ahead. He kept his eye on the driver of the black car as he gestured him forward. There was nowhere to run to, really, but that didn't always stop the guilty from trying.

Once again, the tight leash brought him up short.

The dog stood in front of the next vehicle in lane one, sitting and staring at Kyle in the obvious alert signal.

"Again? Come on."

What the hell is wrong with this dog?

Right or wrong, he had a strict protocol to follow. He had to call it in.

"Alert in lane one. Blue minivan." Inside, the female driver looked surprised and nervous, which wasn't unusual. No one relished the delays and questions of an inspection, even if they were innocent.

"Another one?" the dispatcher, a woman he'd been interested in for a year but had never asked out, fearing both a rejection and concerned about being inappropriate at the workplace. "Did you forget to feed the poor thing this morning?" she teased him.

"No." He wanted to say something witty but had never been quick with comebacks. So he just shut up and did his job. He gave Benji another treat, got the second driver pointed toward the pullout inspection area, and prepared to follow both vehicles. Benji would be needed to narrow down where they should inspect so the whole vehicle didn't have to be ripped apart to find the hidden drugs.

He got down on a knee so he could have a heart-to-heart with Benji. "What's gotten into you today, boy? You feeling okay?" He touched the dog's nose, got his hand licked, and Benji's tail wagged happily.

Poor thing's probably just as bored as I am.

"We all need a little fun in our lives, don't we?"

The black car and blue minivan were pulling to a stop on the side as four other Border Patrol officers—two inspection teams who were also likely bored already this morning—descended on them.

On a lark, he keyed his mic. "We'll be over in a second. Just want to check something out."

He didn't wait for an argument. "Come on, Benji, let's go! Search!"

They took off, jogging between lanes one and two. He let Benji have the full length of the leash. The dog ran happily past two cars, then stopped abruptly and sat next to a beat-up car in lane two.

"Good boy!" Kyle gave him a treat. "Search!" He ran further but only made it three cars before the dog again stopped next to the front tire of a small SUV in lane one.

More praise, treats, and running later, Kyle and Benji were twenty cars back, both panting.

"Um," he said into his mic, then composed himself. "Multiple alerts in lanes one and two," he began, then paused. Around him were more than one hundred cars waiting patiently to cross into the United States. In two lanes alone, Benji had alerted at nine vehicles.

"Either the dog has gone crazy, or like every third car is filled with drugs."

73

REDEMPTION

Aboard *Mine, All Mine*
Williamstad Marina
Williamstad, Curaçao

Kelton tossed the stern line to the marina's young dock worker, then went back to the bridge to finish docking the boat. He shut the engine down while the kid hopped aboard, grabbed the bow line, and jumped back to finish securing the boat to the dock.

Hustling for a good tip, no doubt. As if the cost of filling the enormous fuel tanks wasn't enough.

Not that it mattered. The United States government was paying. But since losing most of his vast wealth, Kelton had become much more aware of how much things cost, from boat fuel to the tips expected from people in his position: the supposed super wealthy owner of a multi-million-dollar yacht.

Around him, the small "mountains" of Willemstad didn't exactly loom, but they looked lovely. He'd never been to the island just east of Aruba and northwest of Venezuela, and he wouldn't have time to enjoy it today. He was exhausted from the nearly twenty-four-hour solo cruise from St. John, and Axe would be here any minute. They'd have little downtime, according to the briefing Haley had given him. Axe had somewhere to be—and it would be Kelton's job to get him there, and back, safely.

Kelton stayed on the bridge. The dock worker and another one who had joined him would fuel up both fuel tanks, top off the water, and other workers would be on the way with provisions. Haley had managed the entire operation.

He moved to the stern to supervise—and be seen. With the tan skin, beard, and longer hair, he didn't look much like his old corporate self, but people would notice him. Some would know who he was. And it might help the mission for him to be remembered.

He still moved slower than before his adventures with Axe in Mexico. The drug in the beer five weeks before had left him changed. He felt different and still woke up sweating every few nights, his body craving more of the spiked beer.

The memory of coming back to life on the mucky shore of the Mexican lake would occasionally overwhelm him and he'd lose five or ten minutes staring into space, reliving the experience.

He had a recurring vision, like a scene from a movie filmed in black and white. From ten feet above his limp body, he watched as Axe yelled at him while pounding on his chest, trying to bring him back to life.

He'd felt light. Detached. Like sitting in the backyard on a sunny afternoon, seeing the wind blow through the trees, and thinking, "Ahh, that's nice." No more concern than that, though he knew he was dead. Nothing mattered. He was leaving his old life behind without regret.

As he rose, insubstantial, like fog or a cloud, he felt a tug. Not like falling back to his body—it had been much more violent. He was yanked, pulled from the air and forced back into his skin, which is when he coughed out water. Coming to, it had felt like he'd swallowed half the lake.

At least once a day he relived the moment. Sometimes right after waking up, or before falling asleep when his mind relaxed and drifted. Other times it was more problematic, like when he was in the middle of a conversation, and he briefly checked out.

He wasn't sure whether or not he regretted coming back to his body and living. It went both ways, depending on the day.

But as long as he was alive, he figured he should make the best of it. He had skills, shares of his former company, and a will to redeem himself for the harm he'd caused, actively and inadvertently, to New York City nearly a year before.

A month earlier, as he recovered from his experience, Haley had told him her friends Bec and Cody could use help running the maniac Stefan Conroy's Movement. They needed a big-picture guy to offer advice.

That he could do.

And this time around, unlike running his company, he took no credit. Stayed behind the scenes. Offered help where needed. The rest of the time, he'd lived on the yacht and enjoyed the beautiful island of St. John.

It had gotten a little boring but was a chance to give back while continuing his recovery.

He stared off into space, not seeing the green of the island in front of him or the blue of the water to the sides.

I should have died on my superyacht when Todd Burkley shot me.

Axe had been there and saved his life.

He should have died again in Mexico.

Technically, I did.

Once again, Axe had saved him.

Maybe today I can return the favor.

He smiled, coming back to the present moment. When Haley had called and asked for his help, he hadn't hesitated. It had been less than thirty minutes from the time she called to when he unhooked from the mooring ball in Francis Bay of St. John and turned southwest toward Curaçao.

I'll help out no matter the cost. For Haley and Axe, of course—and for me.

74

CRUISE

As Mariana walked on the dock of the upscale marina, surrounded by expensive boats of all kinds, she couldn't believe her luck. The warm sun, cool breeze, and the feel of the air, so different from the desert southwest she was familiar with, thrilled her.

I'm in Curaçao!

She was the farthest from home she'd ever been.

When Alex had told her where they were going, she had freely admitted she didn't know where the hell the island was, but she was ready to go.

Especially when she looked over the gear list assembled by his partner. M4s, tons of ammo, military-grade night-vision goggles and armor, pistols, and knives.

She was in heaven—and that was before she'd provided her sizes so a full wardrobe of swimsuits and casual yacht cruising wear, along with tactical clothing, could be bought for her.

I feel like I'm dreaming.

Behind her, a pair of dock workers pushed carts with their duffel bags inside. Except for the special ones that she and Alex carried—the bags filled with weapons.

The yacht ahead of them wasn't a superyacht, but it was big. Huge, really. It fit in well at the fueling area of the luxury marina and yacht club. It had to cost several million dollars—and she was not only going to cruise on it but play an important role in a secret mission.

Geez—I have to pull myself together. I sound like an excited little girl.

Which, in a way, she was.

But I don't have to act like a backwoods hick who has never been away from home.

She glanced at Alex walking next to her and adopted the same expression he had—relaxed and happy yet alert.

And... he and his team want me. Need me.

That alone made up for the one major drawback.

It's a bummer I won't be able to tell anyone about this.

The risks didn't bother her.

If I'm dead, I'm dead. But as long as I don't fail and let Alex down, I don't care.

"Your friend looks a little like Kelton Kellison," Mariana whispered to Alex as she did her best to keep up with his long strides. "See the resemblance?"

Alex chuckled. "Yeah, he gets that a lot."

Axe knew the moment he greeted Kelton with a hug that all was not well. The man gripped him in a tight bear hug... and didn't let go.

"You alright, brother?" Axe whispered, easing up on his own hug in hopes Kelton would take the hint and do the same.

"Fine, yeah. Just good to see you."

Is he... crying?

He chose to overlook it for the moment. They had to get moving, but he'd have to assess the man's ability to continue the mission before they got too far from shore.

What do I do if he's in no shape for this?

Axe could operate the vessel, but Kelton was a master. He'd grown up around boats and had proven his abilities weeks before on a river in Mexico. Rodriguez had never operated any boat before, let alone a seventy-five-foot yacht.

No problem. All I need is for him to get me close, then pick me up when needed. How hard can it be?

Kelton steered the boat surely out of the marina, cleared the no-wake zone, and opened her up to a decent cruising speed—not fast, not slow. They weren't in a hurry. The course plotted to Tortuga's gorgeous white sand beaches and calm water showed them passing the point where Axe would leave the boat right on time. Axe couldn't arrive at the oil platform until after dark, anyway.

Kelton felt better already. Axe's calm, capable presence had helped immensely. So had Mariana. Knowing he wasn't alone, solely responsible for being Axe's unarmed, untrained backup made him feel better—a little, at least.

"I'm really worried I'll let you down again," Kelton said from the helm to Axe as they stood on the bridge while Mariana unpacked her clothes in the primary suite. After some initial awkwardness upon meeting him and realizing he was, in fact, the world-famous Kelton Kellison, she'd come around. She decided she was comfortable with the role of his fake girlfriend for the mission.

"You didn't let me down! You nailed the mission on the river, backed me up at the hotel, and—"

"Nearly got us both shot, drank spiked beer, and tried to kill you." He paused. "And died."

"Yeah, how about we avoid all that this time?" Axe asked with a small smile.

Kelton chuckled. "You've got yourself a deal. And thanks for bringing Mariana. It's reassuring to have a police officer along. She seems capable —and nice."

"Keep in mind that she has firearm and police training, but technically, you've been on more real-world operations than she has. And you were a successful CEO of a multi-billion-dollar company."

"But this is a pretty easy operation, right? Drop you off, pick you up?"

Axe spoke almost immediately. "Absolutely."

I'm just going to ignore that moment of hesitation before he answered.

75

TROUBLE

Aboard *Mine, All Mine*
Southeast of Williamstad, Curaçao

"Axe," he heard Kelton say. "Axe, wake up. We may have a problem."

Axe had been dozing, feet up, in the luxurious second chair on the bridge as Kelton navigated their passage. He never passed up a chance to nap, especially before what was likely to be a long night.

"What's up?" he asked, coming to quickly.

"I haven't checked the binoculars, but my guess is some kind of Navy ship. They might have changed course slightly. I... My gut tells me they're going to check us out."

They're inspecting boats in the wide area of the oil tanker platform, Axe thought. *Maybe Haley is on to something after all.*

"On it," he said, standing up. "Remember, you're Kelton fricking Kellison, billionaire—"

"Former," Kelton interrupted.

"Whatever. Former billionaire playboy, disgraced former billionaire, however you want to play it. But you're still rich, you're still you. I'm your bodyguard. Mariana is your new girlfriend and you're out impressing her. Be yourself."

And don't think about the small arsenal of weapons and assorted other gear hidden in the forward berth.

But best not to say that and plant the idea in his head, Axe decided.

"Mariana," he called as he headed aft, through the small dining area, past the living room, and out onto the stern where he had left her to take her own nap under the cover of the upper deck.

"Wake up. Time to go to work—a little earlier than planned." She came to quickly and sat up.

I hope she can act. It would suck to get all this way and blow the mission before it even got started.

76

QUESTIONS

Central Analysis Group Headquarters
Alexandria, Virginia

William was surprised by the reception he got outside the doors of the nondescript modern office building that houses the CAG.

"Glad you're here, Hammer," Haley said in his ear, giving him a crushing bear hug.

Odd. She's not usually a hugger.

"Everything okay, Blondie?"

This has to be about Rodriguez.

"I'm fine," she said, turning to lead him into the building. "Act important," she said over her shoulder before opening the door. "You're a VIP intel guy on an inspection tour."

They entered and worked their way through security—which thankfully allowed him to keep both his primary pistol on his hip and smaller backup weapon on his ankle, along with his pocketknife. He'd left the rest of his gear in the car provided for him after catching a ride on an FBI jet from Texas to D.C.

When they made it to the conference room, William saw why Haley was happy to have him there. Gregory looked like hell. His graying hair, longer than expected for a man in his position, was normally perfectly in place with some magic products William couldn't fathom. Even when working out with the president at the White House, Gregory somehow managed to maintain his look. This afternoon though, strands were out of place, absently being brushed out of the man's eyes every few seconds. There were dark bags under Gregory's bloodshot eyes.

Both he and Haley look like they've had a harder time of it here in the office than Axe and I had in the field.

"Gregory," he said, shaking the man's hand. "Thanks for the invitation."

I have to remember that despite my experience, he's in charge.

The last thing William wanted to do was take over. It wasn't his mandate—or his desire.

But I can advise—if he wants or needs help.

"Let's sit down and bring William up to speed," Gregory said to the group of analysts.

I don't know what Haley is so worried about. He seems tired and stressed, but in command. Unless he's putting on a brave front for me...

Gregory locked himself and his feelings down.

No more indecision or worry. I can do this.

And if not, he had Admiral William "Hammer" Nalen by his side to back him up.

"Haley—you start with the backpack and the weapon," Gregory said as they took seats around the conference room table.

"Still in the wind," Haley admitted. "No other targets have been hit and we have no leads. The top political and business figures in Texas, New Mexico, California, Louisiana, and Oklahoma have been alerted. Extra security is in place for them, along with all facilities even remotely connected to the oil or natural gas industries. We have increased police and private security presence patrolling likely pipeline targets. Airports, shipping ports, trucking—especially gas, oil, and other flammable or dangerous liquids—are on alert. We've tried everything to find and trace their vehicle but haven't had any luck." She took a breath and sighed, rubbing her eyes. "We're stuck, and so are our sister agencies."

There was silence around the table for a moment, then Gregory spoke again. "In Mexico, we have a contracted SEAL team led by—" His eyes closed for an instant as he hesitated, then shook his head. "Mad Dog."

William watched it all, taking it in. The fatigue, worry, and frustration.

Gregory really doesn't like this direct-action stuff with the call signs, gear, and weapons.

"Axe, Kelton Kellison, and Mariana Rodriguez are on their way to Tortuga?" William asked with a subtle glance at Nancy and Dave.

"They know all about it," Gregory said with a nod. "Yes. Axe should arrive at the oil rig just after dark, local time."

No one spoke for a moment.

There's something not being said.

"So aside from the missing backpack and sniper rifle, we're okay?" he asked.

Nancy spoke for the first time, looking around the table at the rest of the WIA team, her eyes finally coming to rest on William. "We're all feeling strange," she said softly.

Dave, sitting next to her, nodded. "Like we're missing something."

"It started with me," Haley admitted next. "I just can't shake the feeling there's... more."

Gregory took in a long breath, then sighed, shaking his head. "I hate to admit it, but I feel it, too. A big part is we can't figure out how it all fits together. Haley briefed you on the Iran, Russia, Mexico, Venezuela theory of hers?"

William nodded. "It makes sense they would work together, and I agree they're likely behind it. At least, thanks to the Marine in the hospital, we know the Iranians sent the team Axe took out. The drugs I destroyed—and Axe's truck filled with more drugs, which the local police have—are proof the Mexicans and Iranians are working together. Russia and Venezuela being involved are more tenuous, but it feels right," he admitted. "Iran and the drug cartels wouldn't hook up on their own."

"But what about the attacks on Haley's parents?" Nancy brought up. The mood in the room changed, but William wasn't sure if anyone but he and Haley noticed it.

Let's not go there.

But Nancy seemed like she had more to say, so after a nod from Gregory, William turned to her.

Best to get it all out now. Like ripping off a bandage or popping a shoulder back into the socket.

"Go ahead. Ask."

Confronted, Nancy glanced at Dave, then looked across the table at Haley, sitting next to William. She blurted out, "What happened after you abducted Baranov? There are missing pieces here, and they're driving me crazy."

Hell. Here we go.

77

PLANES

Hotel Nuevo Uruapan
Uruapan, Mexico

"Heads up," came the call from Ty "Johnboy" Johnson at the window. The tall African American was smart, steady, and had the patience of a saint, so he'd spent the most time at the window, earning the rest of the team's gratitude. "I've got one plane on the ground that matches the description, though the tail number is different. And I have another on approach. Can't make out the number, though."

Mad Dog put his thick paperback novel down on the bed and moved to the window next to Johnboy.

Hot damn. Party time.

"Ten-minute alert," he said, then knocked three times on both the left and the right walls. He received three knocks back from the guys in the rooms on either side as he stripped off the ridiculous Hawaiian-print shirt and stuffed it into the waiting duffel bag.

"I've got a feeling this is it." It was the second time he'd given the ten-minute alert since yesterday. The previous one turned out to be a false alarm, but this one felt right.

"Bingo," Johnboy said, satisfaction in his voice. "Tail number on the approaching one almost matches Señor Salazar's plane. A '1' has been turned into a '4.' Looks like someone got lazy and didn't change the whole tail number. And I have another private jet on approach—too far away to be sure yet, but it looks like this is it."

Mad Dog knocked twice more on the walls and slipped on his plate carrier containing the extra magazines, zip ties, long knife, and everything else a well-stocked SEAL needed for a mission. His M4 got slung over his shoulder, dangling exactly where he liked it, and a dark windbreaker covered it all. They would all look a little out of place running down the stairs to the minivan with their zipped jackets, but less so than with their guns, ammo, and armor on display.

He took the big binoculars from Johnboy and relieved him at the window, focusing on the plane descending to the airport. Johnboy shrugged off his own shirt and grabbed his duffel bag, repeating the same process Mad Dog had completed. When he finished, he opened the door. Mad Dog heard the rest of the group enter.

"This is it?" Captain Hernandez—or "Captain" as they'd called him from the start—asked, coming up behind him.

"Hold on," Mad Dog said. The plane came close enough for him to see the tail number. "Wrong number, but…" He compared it to the outline of the known cartel planes. Salazar's was confirmed on the ground. Inside the hangar was the plane they suspected was Arturo Ruiz's based on its profile.

"This could be Duarte's. It's the right type of plane." He turned to Captain and handed him the binos. "Look. The first one is in the hangar now. Taxiing—moving—is second one. Landing is number three. Number four—same type as Duarte's—lands soon. Confirm?"

He probably understands English well enough. I don't have to speak to him like he's stupid.

Captain took his time, but finally lowered the binoculars and handed them back. "Confirmed. We go. As planned, yes?"

"Right you are, my friend. Let's roll, people," Mad Dog said and moved to the door after grabbing his bag. The men headed to the hallway while he held the door and waited.

Johnboy finished wiping the room with the microfiber towel and stepped into the hallway. They'd wiped the rooms every four hours, even overnight, to keep up with it. But each room got one last wipe down for fingerprints before they could leave. "The rest of you—your rooms are clean?" Mad Dog asked to confirm. "Fingerprints, trash, all gear? We're never coming back."

He got nods in return from the men in the hall.

Captain peeled the plane identification info from the window, folded it carefully, and stuck it in his cargo pants pocket, then joined Mad Dog at the door.

"Clock is running. Let's go," Captain said.

Johnboy wiped the doorknobs one last time. Then they were off, rushing along the hall, down the stairs, and out into the late afternoon sunshine.

78

BOATS

Aboard *Mine, All Mine*
Southeast of Williamstad, Curaçao

A rigid-hulled boat left the Venezuelan Navy coastal patrol ship and sped toward them. Six men, wearing armored plate carriers and helmets, their rifles pointed down, approached the yacht.

"Act friendly, but it's okay to be a little nervous," Axe said to Mariana and Kelton as they stood on the bridge. "Our guns and gear are well hidden. If they want to search the boat, we let them."

They both nodded. Kelton looked scared, but Mariana seemed like she was on the adventure of a lifetime.

"Be yourselves. And if things go bad, leave the violence to me."

A few minutes later, the boat was at their stern, swinging expertly alongside the small swim platform at the rear.

"*Hola!*" Axe said, walking to the back deck. "Hello. I'm sorry, I don't speak much Spanish," he continued as two men jumped aboard holding lines. Two others—a tall one and a short one—stepped onto the yacht, holding their rifles expertly in the low ready position. The other two stayed in the boat.

At least their fingers are off the triggers.

"Passport, papers," the taller one said.

"Of course. Mariana, Kelton?" Axe called back.

Mariana appeared from the bridge, looking radiant in a white beach coverup dress over a modest bikini. Kelton followed behind, smiling. "Welcome," he said.

Mariana spoke Spanish, greeting the hard-looking men. Axe couldn't follow the rapid-fire words, but within a minute she had all six men smiling back at her.

"They want to see our passports," she said. "Alex, would you run to the safe and get them, please?" Despite their age difference and the fact this was her first undercover operation, she nailed the commanding tone of a rich guy's girlfriend ordering around a servant.

Axe nodded and immediately turned, heading into the galley where one of the ship's two wall safes was located. As he left the stern, he caught Mariana's offer for the entire group to join them for beers... and the tall sailor's polite—reluctant—refusal.

All six men were on board when he returned with their paperwork. He had a fake passport for Mariana and himself but opted to provide Kelton's real one.

It paid off. When the tall sailor saw the name, he looked up sharply at Kelton and asked if he was the businessman Kelton Kellison, to which Kelton nodded with a smile.

From there, the cell phones came out. The tall sailor got a solo shot with Kelton, then Axe took a picture of Kelton with the whole crew standing on the swim platform.

Two of the sailors performed a cursory inspection, confirming there were adequate life jackets and safety equipment on the boat. Then they were off, returning to their ship, smiling and waving as they left.

"That has to be the first time young men ignored me in favor of a guy," Mariana grumbled, waving at the sailors as she, Axe, and Kelton made their way back to the bridge to resume their journey.

"Let's hope they clear the area," Axe said. "We can't risk getting closer and drawing more attention. I'll have to go in the water sooner and swim farther."

79

STREETS

"I knew this was a terrible idea," Mad Dog muttered from the passenger seat of the minivan. When they briefed Captain on their mission plan, Hernandez had made a few suggestions, along with two demands. First, he had to drive.

"My country," Captain had said. "My people. I drive."

Mad Dog's arguments—the hours of evasive driving training, years of experience handling everything from dune buggies to Humvees around the world, plus his time as billionaire Kelton Kellison's chief of security, which often entailed navigating through difficult and dangerous traffic conditions around the world—fell on deaf ears. Hernandez wouldn't take no for an answer.

"Holy shit dude, that was close!" Johnboy called from the seat behind him as they skidded around a corner, narrowly missing a car coming their way.

"Captain, this is a one-way street," Mad Dog said, his knuckles turning white on the handle above the door. "And we're going in the wrong direction." Cars honked and swerved out of their way, but Captain didn't seem bothered at all.

"Other street blocked. Traffic," he said.

Mad Dog had noticed the slowdown on the street they'd mapped out as their best route but had figured it would clear.

"MD?" Johnboy said, using the shortened version of his call sign.

"Yes, Johnboy?"

"I don't want to die in a damn minivan."

Captain chuckled as he swung the van onto the sidewalk, scattering a group of children dressed in school uniforms on their way home. He muttered several choice words while glancing over his shoulder at Johnboy and the other SEALS in back.

"MD," Rook said with a soft laugh, "my Spanish isn't as good as yours, but did he just call us a bunch of—"

"Two minutes," Captain interrupted. Then they tore around another corner. At the end of the road—the surprisingly empty road, Mad Dog had to admit—there was a tall fence topped with razor wire.

Mad Dog removed a signal-blocking cell phone case from the pocket of his black cargo pants. He shook the phone from it and quickly typed a text to Haley based on the code they'd worked out before he arrived in Mexico.

Guests are arriving. Party is about to start. Wish you were here.

The last sentence he added just to mess with her.

Poor thing, trapped in an office. That's no place for a warrior like Haley.

The fence around the airport grew closer by the second.

"We're almost here," Mad Dog said. "Get ready with the bolt cutters. Just as we planned. Slow is smooth and smooth is fast."

"Slow is smooth and smooth is fast," they repeated quietly. Even Captain joined in.

80

SECRETS

Haley froze, unsure what to say to the direct question from Nancy about the events five weeks earlier. What could be said about the previous mission without admitting she had helped assassinate the Russian president? A second ticked by, feeling like an eternity.

Last time, Gregory stepped in and shut this down. 'Need to know' and all that.

But it looked like this time neither Gregory nor Nalen would stop her from answering.

Does Hammer really want me to go there?

She took a breath, but Nalen beat her to it. "We parachuted into Senator Woodran's ranch in Utah and rescued her. She had already been shot. Haley and I drove her to the hospital, saving her life."

Haley looked at Nalen, nodded, and looked back at Nancy.

Excellent answer. But will it be enough?

"Do they know..." Nalen started, looking at Gregory.

"Yes, everyone in this room is read into the Russian sleeper spy program. In fact, Nancy is the keeper of the database we're using to track them. There are no secrets here."

Haley kept her face neutral.

Well... there are still some secrets. No one in this room knows where Axe and I went or what we did after Utah. Nalen suspects though, I'm sure.

She thought of Nalen's reaction to Senator Woodran and their recent courtship. Had he been interested in her before that night? They'd met in previous years at least once. The senator had recognized Nalen when he stepped into her office doorway.

"Wait! What did you say?" she asked Nancy, interrupting Nalen before he could continue discussing the Russian sleeper spies. Frantically reviewing the conversation seconds before, she tried to bring into focus... something. It felt like when a word is on the tip of your tongue and you can't quite get it, but much, much bigger. An idea. A revelation.

"What?" Nancy asked, confused. After a second, she corrected herself. "Sorry. I asked about the attack on your parents, but I meant the attack on Admiral Nalen and you."

Could it be as easy—and as petty—as that?

Haley turned to Nalen. "Would you say you're the president's best friend?"

He was caught off guard and clearly uncomfortable, glancing around the room quickly.

"Well, I, ah..."

"Hammer, answer the damn question!"

His eyes narrowed.

She backpedaled and softened her tone. "Sorry. Please, just answer the question?"

"I suppose I am, yes." He glanced down, then back at her. "I'm out of the political loop, and from the old days when he was a SEAL."

That's it!

"Nancy, you're brilliant!"

Everyone around the table looked at Haley like she'd finally lost it.

Maybe I have, but this feels right.

"I wasn't the target. And neither were my parents. It was only my mom." Haley turned back to Nalen. "They hit the president's best friend— you—and the First Lady's. My mom. That's the connection. It's not about me or—"

She stopped herself from saying "Russia" just in time.

"It's personal. This whole thing is. The target is the president himself.

Not the whole country or 'the President of the United States.' Well, maybe in part. But my guess is that James Heringten is the one in the crosshairs."

"Literally? Like, the missing sniper rifle?" Dave asked.

"Maybe, but no, my gut says he's not the target of the sniper. His protective detail is way too good to let him be exposed to a long-range gunshot. But the rest makes sense. So we have to ask, who—personally—has it out for James Heringten?"

"I don't think we have enough time to get into that list," Dave said with a small smile. "He's the leader of the free world. He's popular with some, vastly unpopular with a lot of others." He used his fingers to tick off the list. "North Korea. Iran. Maybe China. Various people in the Middle East he's annoyed or pissed off. Different fanatics in the United States, from—"

"President Villanueva of Venezuela," Nancy interrupted. Everyone turned to look at her. "Remember? Four years ago, right after Heringten was sworn into office? He pushed further sanctions into place against Venezuela. There was a lot of rhetoric and some harsh words. Some of it was personal—before President Heringten learned to be more diplomatic. What if Villanueva took them to heart?"

Haley nodded. "It all fits."

"I agree," Gregory said. He looked decisive again, like the leader Haley knew he could be. "Let's work through this with the theory President Villanueva is personally behind this and see how it shakes out. What could the targets be for the sniper rifle and the explosives if he's out to specifically get the president?"

"While also pleasing his masters," Dave added, "because there's no way he's doing this on his own, right?"

"True," Haley agreed. "Not even with Iran. They wouldn't dare."

"It has to be Russia," Nalen said, breaking his silence. He locked eyes with Haley.

He's guessed what Axe and I did... and that we might have taken out the wrong Russian.

The team stood up from the table to work the problem.

Nalen and I need to talk, but not before I take care of this other situation.

She gave him a nod and a look to wait, which he picked up on easily.

"Nancy, I have something for you at my desk that might help," she said, and held the door for the other woman. But as soon as they were in the hallway and the door closed behind them, Haley stopped her with a light hand on the shoulder.

"What I'm about to tell you goes no further, understand? Not to Dave, Gregory, or anyone else." Haley's voice was ice cold, and the look she gave Nancy would have made anyone think twice about messing with her.

Nancy gulped and nodded her agreement.

"I need your word," Haley said, her voice low and firm.

"I give you my word," Nancy said. She sounded shaky, like she wasn't sure she wanted to know what Haley was about to tell her.

Haley leaned forward and whispered into Nancy's ear. "I will never tell you—or anyone else—about what happened after I abducted Victor Baranov, and we rescued Senator Woodran, so don't bother asking again," she said, speaking quietly and calmly. "It's a secret I'll take to my grave." She started to pull away, then leaned back in and spoke even more slowly. "And if you can't guess what it is from that, you're not the analyst I think you are."

Haley pulled away—and waited.

Nancy stared at her for a few seconds, then nodded as if confirming what she had already guessed.

She's got it.

Haley didn't bother to give the older woman anything else. She just turned and walked to her desk. There was a lot of work to do. Mad Dog was assaulting the airport in Mexico, and she needed to find out where the missing backpack, sniper rifle, and terrorist team were.

81

PLANS

Near the Uruapan International Airport
Uruapan, Mexico

Captain Hernandez turned off the main road into the neighborhood near the airport. Small houses and working-class apartment buildings filled the area.

Another turn had them once again facing the airport's fence and the trees behind it. From here, there was little to show a major airport terminal was a mile southeast, or that a huge, private-plane hangar was only one hundred yards from the end of the street, on the other side of a wooded area.

A quick glance at the Americans confirmed they were ready. All it took was a nod to their leader, Mad Dog, and they were off.

This was the way. A small team of dedicated warriors. Men who couldn't be bought. Who, for whatever reason, were beyond reproach, beyond corruption.

With a few hundred men like them, I could turn my entire country around.

But for today, these five would do.

While they didn't exactly blend in—the fit, intense *gringos* would stand out anywhere, even in the tourist areas of Cancun or Mexico City —they didn't have to. The street was mostly deserted at the moment, as it ended at the road running parallel to the airport. Further south, a busier road led directly to the airport's entrance, but here, a mile north, it was a poorer residential community of people who could handle the noise coming from the planes landing and taking off half-mile to the east.

Hernandez led the way on the sidewalk, past an empty lot with overgrown weeds, a wall painted in several shades of gray to cover graffiti —and the new graffiti already sprayed on it.

There were other cars and small trucks parked along the street, which reassured him. They didn't have the manpower to leave a man behind to guard the vehicle. He fished out the keys to the minivan from his pocket and handed them to Mad Dog, beside him on the narrow sidewalk as his men followed behind, trying not to walk like they were on their way to a combat mission.

No words were needed as Mad Dog accepted the keys and pocketed them.

I'll either be dead or will stay behind while they escape.

"The fifth plane," the dark-skinned SEAL said quietly from behind him. Looking up, he saw an expensive private plane about to land. Seconds later, it disappeared from view.

This is it.

Uruapan International Airport
Uruapan, Mexico

Arturo looked up as Hugo cleared his throat from the hallway behind the jet's cockpit. "*Jefe,* Señor Guzman has just landed," his right-hand man said.

Surrounding the plane were ten of his best warriors, the most trusted men in Arturo's security detail, fully armed and ready to die defending him if needed—from either the police or the other cartel members, which he could never disregard.

Hugo had drilled various scenarios with them over and over, and they were given a level of autonomy rare in the drug cartel world. Using their instincts, experience, and training, they would do what needed to be done without orders from either him or Hugo. He trusted them implicitly.

Unfortunately, the other four cartel leaders had the same type of men.

With any luck, the mutually assured destruction of any one of them trying to take control would prevent it from happening.

As for the police, there was little risk. No one knew they were here. The hangar and area around it should be deserted per his request, but if anyone looked, the scene wouldn't raise too many eyebrows. Armed guards weren't unusual in Mexico, especially for wealthy, security-conscious people.

But the Americans' electronic capabilities were legendary. Hence the electronic eavesdropping-proof building waiting for them in the hangar.

I will not be caught or killed because I underestimated American technology, no matter how much the others think I am too careful.

Arturo nodded. Hugo would escort Arturo to the portable secure building—which looked like an expensive shipping container—that had been delivered in the middle of the night on the back of a flatbed semi-tractor trailer.

"A few more minutes, *Jefe,*" Hugo said, checking his pistol's magazine before securing it in the holster at his side.

The cartel guard, who looked alert and put together, didn't see Mad Dog laying on the ground in the thick bushes. The tango walked from the huge, gaping doorway of the airplane hangar, along the south wall of the metal building, his rifle at the half-ready position. Between the edge of the hangar and the street one hundred yards away was an area filled with trees, bushes, and patches of grass.

I hope no one notices the hole where we cut the fence.

In the United States, he was sure security would be on the way to investigate the intrusion. Here, no one had come yet.

Pressed against the southwestern wall of the hangar, out of sight from the guard, Captain Hernandez waited, holding a long, wicked-looking knife.

This should be interesting.

He and Captain had discussed, in their broken English and Spanish, the rules of engagement. Mad Dog had gone into the meeting assuming he'd be disappointed—he'd have to play by cop rules, not war rules. He'd left the conversation pleasantly surprised. The gloves were off, even by the standards of war. Captain said they didn't need to announce their presence, identify themselves as law enforcement, or wait to be fired upon.

"This is assault," Captain Hernandez had said last night. "We ambush. Kill... or capture. They are enemy of the state. Legal."

Mad Dog wasn't sure about the legality and didn't much care. Haley said it was legit from the USA side and that was good enough for him. But he'd seen the pain in Captain's expression and realized what the attack really was: payback.

Captain had come with multiple contingencies for getting inside, but it looked like they wouldn't be needed. The guess had been the cartel leaders would keep a relatively low profile and send only a few guards outside the hangar to watch for police or other unwelcome visitors. Hernandez thought most of the guards would stay inside, near the airplanes—more concerned about the potential threat of betrayal from one of the rivals than an assault from outside.

Right again. Only one man at the north side opening and one at the south.

The cartel guard stepped past the corner of the building to check out the west side.

Captain's knife flashed.

Blood spurted, the man sagged, and the Mexican police officer lowered the lifeless body to the ground.

Impressive.

Captain slipped off his windbreaker and put on the dead man's plate carrier, then slung the man's rifle, instantly assuming the identity of a trusted guard. They had similar builds and hair. From behind, at a distance, there was a reasonable chance Captain would pass for the guard.

Nearby, at the northwest corner of the building, Johnboy had killed his guard but didn't bother changing clothes or gear. If all went according to plan, they wouldn't need disguises.

Mad Dog scrambled from the bushes and moved to his pre-planned position next to Johnboy.

So far, so good.

The whine of the last jet's engine filled the afternoon air. The noise decreased slightly as the plane swung into the hangar. Captain gave the signal, leading Bishop and Rook around his corner of the building.

Mad Dog followed Johnboy and Cooper, one of his other SEALs, around their corner toward the large opening on the north end of the building, hating being out of sight of the other group.

The radios will work fine but won't be as good over the airplane noise... and because we don't all speak the same language.

As they got closer to the open door, the engine noise increased. There were five expensive executive jets in the hangar, all with their engines idling.

Johnboy stopped four feet from the opening—close enough to rush in, but out of sight from anyone inside.

Captain's best guess was that the cartel leaders would send out their soldiers, wait until the all-clear sign, then get escorted to a table, vehicle, or possibly a room in the hangar for their meeting.

They agreed there was little chance the criminals would board one of the aircraft. No one would want to be a guest—at best—or a prisoner, at worst, in one of the other cartel leaders' planes.

By now, Captain Hernandez would be near the doorway with his back to the airplane hangar, looking like the guard he'd killed. The airplane doors would be folding open to reveal stairs. The other cartel leaders' guards would be taking up defensive positions around the planes.

After that, it was anyone's guess. They didn't have the intel to be certain, but it wasn't hard to predict. The principals—the drug kingpins—would exit and go... somewhere.

That's the part that bothers me the most. We're going in blind, not knowing where the targets are.

But even that didn't matter much. First, the guards had to be eliminated.

I hope Captain's plan works.

82

TRAPS

Uruapan International Airport
Executive Jet Hangar
Uruapan, Mexico

Arturo met the guard who drove and guarded the semi at the door to the Sensitive Compartmented Information Facility—the long, modular shipping container on the back of the flatbed trailer in the middle of the hangar.

"Secure?" he asked, and the man nodded.

"Yes, *Jefe*. I did not stop the entire way and have swept it twice for listening devices."

"Good man. You may wait in the airplane," Arturo said. The man nodded his gratitude and hurried to the plane until the meeting was over when he would drive to a secure Ruiz cartel location and await the next time the secure meeting room was needed.

Arturo stood at the portable stairs leading to the door of the SCIF, a small, welcoming smile on his face to greet the powerful men coming toward him. A step behind him, Hugo stood at parade rest.

No words were spoken as the four cartel leaders mounted the stairs one after another.

They aren't happy to be here—as usual—but especially so soon after last time.

He would have to win them over to his idea of moving up the drug shipment timeline from Venezuela.

It shouldn't be difficult, given how annoyed they already are with President Villanueva—and news of the emergency shipments I sent out being discovered by the damn drug-sniffing dogs will help.

He could also nurture Duarte's idea of eliminating Villanueva.

But only after I position myself to take over the presidency... or at least be a trusted advisor to whoever we install as the next leader.

It would be a difficult conversation, but he was ready.

It is my time.

As Salazar, the oldest and slowest, reached the top of the stairs, Arturo heard a shout.

What the hell?

Then the gunfire started.

***

Captain Hernandez had stood in the sunlight, his back to the hangar, feeling exposed. At any moment, he expected to feel bullets slam into him when the guards in the hangar discovered he was an imposter. But no one had said a word. With any luck, the brightness of the late afternoon sun had made him more of a silhouetted shape than a distinct person.

A quick glance over his shoulder had confirmed the cartel leaders were nearly at the long, beige shipping container on the back of a flatbed semi-trailer in the middle of the vast hangar.

Perfect.

He had been afraid the men would meet in one of the jets despite the drawbacks or go to a secure room in the hangar he and the Americans would have to fight their way to. But upon seeing the semi the first time he'd glanced in, his plan had come together.

Almost there. The Americans have gotten me this far. Now it's up to me.

He had counted the seconds, hoping the operation would work and that this wasn't his last day on earth.

Finally, his gut told him the time was right.

"Now," he said into his radio so the two men pressed against the building to his right and the other SEALs on the north would know.

He spun around to face the interior of the hangar. "It's a trap!" he yelled at the top of his lungs to be heard over the noise of the jet engines. "Kill them!"

He opened fire on the nearest guards, hoping he was shooting men belonging to a different cartel than the man he was impersonating.

At such close range, he killed two easily and directed his fire at others, further away, guarding a different executive jet, hitting at least one.

Other gunfire sounded from the north side of the hangar as the Americans yelled out the Spanish for "traitors," and "It's a trap," doing an excellent job with the accent and tone of outraged anger.

Nicely done, Mad Dog.

He spun to the side, away from the opening, hidden from view by the side of the hangar—though not protected from the bullets which came a second later. By then, though, he was already flat on the ground, watching the two SEALs on the other side of the large opening shoot the men inside who were busy shooting at him.

Next, what he had hoped for happened. The natural distrust of the five sets of guards, combined with the sudden attacks from two different directions, along with the subterfuge of the yelling, took on a life of its own.

Screams of, "Kill them!" and "Open fire!" mixed with gunfire from dozens of weapons as the cartel guards turned on each other, doing his job for him.

We'll give them a few minutes, then go in and mop up.

83

BREAKTHROUGH

Central Analysis Group Headquarters
Alexandria, Virginia

Haley once again stared at her screen and tried to enter the zone, but she was exhausted. She opened a new spreadsheet and started her analysis.

Assuming I'm right and it's a personal attack from Venezuelan President Villanueva against President Heringten, what could he target next?

The president's other friends and family, of course, but Gregory was already on the phone with the Secret Service, telling them about their assumption and requesting a stronger security presence around key people in the president and First Lady's orbit.

Would they hit the bookstore that Uncle Jimmy buys presents from each Christmas? His high school or college?

She doubted it, but added her concerns to the list, anyway. You never knew what would trigger another idea.

They attacked Nalen and Mom—and failed, which probably surprised them.

The enemy wouldn't bother with another small assault. Whatever came next had to be bigger.

The next target has to be the president himself.

She shook her head, hesitating to enter the information into her spreadsheet.

He's too well protected.

And besides, tonight was the State of the Union address. The speech would begin in a few hours, broadcast live from the Capitol building. Washington, D.C., and the President of the United States were heavily protected on an average day. At the Capitol, with the entire government of the United States gathered, no one was getting in.

Only a sniper rifle and a bag of C-4? Good luck.

Unless… If the Russians were helping, or the Iranians…

What if there's an insider, a Russian sleeper spy we haven't identified yet?

She couldn't see how even the most trusted person could smuggle explosives into the White House, Capitol building, or somewhere near the president, but it had to be considered. She added the idea to the list. Then she sat, frustrated, staring at her screen.

I'm stuck. Again.

It wasn't like her to not find the answer. Sure, she made leaps of logic that terrified Nancy, Dave, and especially Gregory, but she went with the flow of the data. It always led her to an answer. But not the last few days.

Have I lost my touch?

If so, it had been a pretty short—but spectacular—career.

If I'm done here, would that give me the push I need to get out of the office for good? Go undercover as a field asset?

She shook off her daydreaming and set an alarm on her watch. Maybe an artificial deadline would help her. If not, at least she wouldn't get lost in the endless flow of data and lose hours while the others made progress.

She opened databases and filled her huge monitors. Starting randomly, she typed in *President Villanueva* as a wide search parameter in one and *Russian attacks* in another. Then she dove in and let her intuition guide her.

Thirty minutes later, she emerged from the ocean of data, disturbed from her hunt by an annoying beeping noise from nearby.

My watch alarm.

She blinked several times, typed a few notes into the spreadsheet, then unplugged her computer and took it to conference room C.

There's a kernel of intel here we can use.

Maybe, working with the others, they could get to the bottom of it.

But I hope to God I'm way off base.

84

AMERICANS

As the shooting started, Arturo was yanked away from the SCIF by Hugo. While still unsure of what was happening, Hugo pushed him to one of the hangar's offices along the east side of the massive building.

As Arturo stumbled away from the shipping container, trying not to fall as Hugo rushed him along, the SCIF door slammed shut behind him.

They locked me out.

Seconds later, he crouched next to Hugo, hiding behind the office's solid oak desk. He could smell Hugo's sweat.

If Hugo had pushed me up the steps, would I have made it in time?

Or would he have been too late? He wasn't sure he would have made it inside before his fellow leaders closed the door.

Would they have actually left me outside?

"Did anyone see us?" Arturo whispered, then felt stupid, a rare experience for him. Between the noise of the engines from the idling jets, the firing could barely be heard in the room. They could speak freely—no one would hear their conversation.

"I don't think so, *Jefe*. But we shall leave in a moment, just in case."

The exterior door was only a few feet away. It led to a walkway to the public terminal. They could be gone before anyone realized they were missing.

I can't go until I know for sure our men have lost.

"Leave?" His anger flared. "No. We will not flee like cowards!"

"*Jefe*, whatever is happening out there has destroyed your coalition. Whether it is a power play from one of the others, rogue guards, or a police raid—" Hugo gave him a look that stopped the protest on his lips before he could get it out. "As unlikely as that all is, it will take time to figure out what happened," Hugo said, much of the usual deference in his voice gone, replaced with a patient, respectful, but take-charge tone Arturo had never heard before. "Our best move is to leave this instant."

What he says makes sense, but I can't leave until I know more.

The other leaders had locked themselves safely in the SCIF container —possibly before he could have gotten inside.

Were they in on it?

Had the men banded together against him? Did they mistake his long-term goal of leading them with an intention to take over?

I can fix this.

The office's window, which looked onto the hangar floor, shattered as gunfire hit it. With the sound barrier removed, the noise level increased. The engine noise dominated and mostly drowned out the guns, but he still heard many rifles firing.

They're shooting at each other.

The jet engines whined, changing from idling, standby speed. They were ready to rush their owners away from the killing taking place on the hangar floor... but the principals were safe in the bullet-proof container. The planes wouldn't leave without the cartel leaders.

The gunfire continued, gradually slowing as, Arturo imagined, more and more men were killed. Then steadier firing started. Something about the rhythm of the shooting made him exchange a look with Hugo. There was a controlled precision that suggested mopping up or...

Extremely well-trained professionals.

His men, and those of the other cartels, were pros. All were ex-soldiers from the Mexican army and special forces. But what he now heard was another level entirely.

"Could be the national police," Hugo said. "But it sounds..."

"Better," Arturo said, and Hugo nodded.

The airplane engines shut down one by one and the sound of a man yelling came to them. A man used to calling out orders but butchering the Spanish language.

Americans.

For the first time in many years—decades—Arturo felt fear. He couldn't be caught by the Americans. Handcuffed, imprisoned, put on trial. He would not suffer the loss of freedom. The indignity.

Hugo was right. It is time to leave.

85

TACOS

Uruapan International Airport
Executive Jet Hangar
Uruapan, Mexico

The Mexican warriors had done the work for them, just as Captain Hernandez had predicted. Dead bodies of the guards from competing cartels lay in pools of blood, spreading across the spotless white floor of the hangar.

Mad Dog crept forward, ready, willing, and able to apprehend any injured men who had survived the initial fight if they were willing to lay down their weapons.

None of them were, despite him, his men, and Captain Hernandez identifying themselves as police and ordering them—in Spanish—to surrender.

As the SEALs took inaccurate fire, they returned it with focused precision, eliminating the remaining threats.

The pilots watching from the airplane cockpits wisely shut down their engines in response to the rifles aimed at their heads.

"Clear north," one of his SEALs yelled.

"Clear west," came an answering call.

"Clear south."

"Check the planes for other guards," Mad Dog ordered. "Johnboy, with me. We have to clear the offices and rooms on the east side."

"Copy," Johnboy said, forming up one step behind him to his left as they headed to the first room, with a desk near the door, facing the hangar, along with two comfortable-looking leather couches, and a coffee table. Its large window was destroyed, likely hit by bullets during the firefight.

They moved past a SCIF on a trailer, a bullet-proof shipping container turned into a secure conference room designed to thwart even the highest-tech eavesdropping and other spying. Captain Hernandez stood on the metal steps positioned outside the door to the room.

"The cartel men. Went inside when shots fired," he said. He looked focused—like the mission was far from over.

For him, it's just beginning.

But his face changed to a predatory smile as he reached to the side and grabbed the large metal door which made up the end of the shipping container. Mad Dog realized the smaller, normal-size door built into the SCIF was there to make it both easier to enter and secure, but the entire container had to be sealed for shipping as well, hence the exterior door to close the whole thing up.

With a resounding clang, Captain shut the door. The metal locking arm swung down. From his cargo pants pocket, Captain pulled a large padlock, easily four times bigger than an average one designed to go on a gym locker. It looked like it would take an acetylene torch to cut it off. With an air of finality, he ceremonially put the lock through the hole in the metal arm and locked it.

Mad Dog and Johnboy advanced to the first room, clearing it and the others along the side of the hangar. All were empty.

His men were in defensive positions at the large north and south doors to the hangar. A shake of the head from them showed that once again, Captain Hernandez's plan had worked. No one was coming to investigate.

The jets' engine noise covered the sound of the shootout.

The action had gone unnoticed by the outside world.

Someone's in for a shock when they come back.

All five planes sat on slashed tires, courtesy of his men—another part of Captain's plan. The pilots were bound inside their aircraft, zip-tied in the passenger compartments.

The detachable staircase had been pulled away from the rear door of the SCIF. The powerful diesel engine of the semi started up with a rumble.

Mad Dog stepped onto the running board of the driver's side. Captain Hernandez stuck his hand out the window and they shook.

"My thanks to you," Captain said "And the woman. Haley."

Mad Dog nodded. "Our pleasure. Good plan. Until we meet again."

At this, Captain smiled. "Until we meet again," he said.

Mad Dog hopped down from the semi-tractor and Captain put it into gear, carefully pulling the trailer with the shipping container past the silent, multi-million-dollar executive jets, out the south door, and away to wherever he planned on taking his prisoners. He hadn't shared that part of the mission plan with his American teammates.

"All right, gentlemen. Let's put some distance between this place and us, then stop for tacos before we get on a plane out of here. I'm buying."

86

REGRET

Axe had miles to go before reaching the oil drilling platform. And since they weren't sure how close they could bring the yacht without coming under more scrutiny, he had gone into the water far out of sight of the rig.

Hence the dive propulsion vehicle and the top-of-the-line re-breather gear.

Being officially unofficial has its perks.

So does cruising on a yacht with a former billionaire. The Venezuelan Navy men hadn't batted an eye at the pricey gear.

The DPV was on its lowest setting, pulling him along at a slow speed. He had to conserve the battery, along with his limited supply of air. So he was using his snorkel for the moment, barely below the surface, kicking with his fins to supplement the DPV. The muscle memory had brought the skill back quickly despite not conducting any swim or scuba training in quite some time.

After an hour, he knew he was in trouble. The current was stronger than anticipated.

The intel is always wrong.

There was no one to blame but himself. He'd looked at the data and determined the best spot to leave the yacht. But with the patrol boat and risk of discovery, he'd gone into the water earlier than planned. The swim was longer and tougher than he'd expected. Maybe the forecast had changed, or the currents were trickier than he'd thought, but he was having to work harder than planned. He kept the DPV on low and used his fins to make up some of the speed.

'The only easy day was yesterday.'

Another big problem, as always with most of the insertions he and the Team had done, especially via the ocean, was boredom. There was nothing to see in the water except for the frequent compass, depth gauge, and dive chronometer checks. If he got into a real bind, he could use a handheld marine GPS to figure out where the hell he was. Otherwise, he swam on, making the best of it.

He had too much time to think, so he sang songs in his head, remembered every line and freckle on his girlfriend's face, and recalled past missions.

After the second hour, Axe was seriously regretting the mission. He'd fully submerged, figuring his air would last, but it made the swim even more boring.

I should have parachuted. Sure, it's riskier, but at least it's not this endless darkness and exertion.

When he was in training, the one thing he didn't want was to be deployed on a SEAL Delivery Vehicle Team. Operating the open water mini-submarine vehicle for hours on end would have driven him crazy.

He checked his time and figured the distance. He should be getting close—or at least within visual distance.

Now I can see how rusty I am at this.

He surfaced for an instant. Thankfully, his navigation was on target. The well-lit oil drilling platform was ahead, still quite far, but impossible to miss and mostly where it was supposed to be—he was about ten degrees off.

The structure was immense. It loomed out of the water like a skyscraper floating above the ocean. Four huge, round yellow pylons supported the multi-layer platform—Axe guessed the entire facility was at least ten stories tall. There were cranes, helicopter landing pads, miles of pipes, tens of thousands of square feet of operational space, storage, and living areas. In the darkness, with hundreds of lights glowing on the facility, the craziness of the mission hit him hard.

How am I supposed to find out what's going on here?

He should have fifteen other guys, at least, supported by a follow-on force to do a proper search. Instead, he had his aging, tired self. One man against this beast of a facility and whatever the potential enemy was up to.

A moment later, he was underwater again, his exhausted legs protesting as he turned off the DPV. He didn't know what type of defenses the rig had and doubted they could detect the near-silent propulsion device, but better safe than sorry.

Another half-hour. An hour, max. No problem.

He continued, fighting the current, daydreaming done, focused on getting to the facility without being detected.

87

THREATS

Central Analysis Group Headquarters
Conference Room C
Alexandria, Virginia

Haley stood in front of her team of four—Gregory, Nancy, Dave, and Nalen—and tried not to look as nervous as she felt.

Just be honest. Come out with it.

She took a breath and started. "Sorry, people, I'm not in the zone. I... The data..." She sighed. "I have a lead, but I'm stuck," she said, putting it as bluntly as possible. "I need you. We have to figure it out together."

No one said a word for a moment. Then she caught a kind smile on Nancy's face. "Let's do it," the older woman said. The others nodded. "What do you have?"

Reassured, Haley started her presentation. "Several possibilities to work through. One," she said and clicked a button on the pointer. Behind her on the large TV, the screen changed to show a diagram of a portable nuclear device. "A suitcase nuke. It would fit in the missing backpack."

No one spoke, so she continued. "Based on the drive time from southwest Texas, the terrorist team could be in D.C. by now."

"Would the yield be enough to take out the Capitol building?" Gregory asked.

"Doubtful," she and Nalen said at the same time.

She nodded to him, and he continued. "They couldn't get it close enough. Not in the time they had between when they must have picked it up in Texas and now. The building and entire area have been locked down. It would do damage and kill people outside, but we should be safe."

Gregory abruptly reached for the phone and dialed a number from memory. "It's me. I need a full accounting of all our guests. Both right now and any movement near the Capitol building or the White House, including the routes the president would take, in the last twelve hours." He paused. "Fine. Call me back, but hurry."

"That was the man in charge of keeping tabs on the confirmed and suspected sleeper spies. Just in case one has more access than we were aware of. Continue," he said to Haley.

"Between eighty and one hundred former Soviet-era suitcase nukes could be missing, so this isn't an idle threat. We have active detection measures, but we need to consider the possibility."

"I thought that claim was discounted," Dave said. "About the missing nukes. It's like an analyst's Holy Grail—discover the missing nukes and save the world."

"Opinions vary," Haley conceded. "I haven't had time to fully dive into it."

"I'll take it," Dave said.

"Great, thanks. Next, drones. Iran, especially, has been working hard on them. A concerted effort, using multiple drones at once might work. We need to run an assessment. I know the military says they have it covered, but it's a possibility, no matter how remote." She shrugged. "Nine months ago, the terrorists in New York tried it on the nuclear power plant and could have pulled it off if they had more drones. With Iran possibly joining forces with Russia and Venezuela, they might have enough to make an impact. It's how I would do it," she added.

"I'll take that one," Nancy volunteered, and Haley nodded.

"Last, but not least," she said, and hesitated.

"Here we go," Gregory said under his breath.

"Yes. Chemical and biological. Smart, well-funded people could make it happen from scratch. And we know Russia had programs they claim to have shut down. The know-how or the materials could be easily shared with Iran or Venezuela."

"Anthrax, smallpox, botulism," Nalen said, thinking out loud. "They could all be put into missiles, or a bomb the size of the backpack. Even grenades. But they're slow to work, and if we truly believe this is personal, that Villanueva might be behind a direct attack on the president, it wouldn't be effective. Or at least, not immediately dramatic."

"What about a cruise missile?" Dave asked. "Russia has tons of them. So does Iran. They can also be bought on the arms market."

"Our people would likely shoot them down," Nalen said, shaking his head.

Haley doubted anyone else had caught the tiny pause before he spoke, but she knew him well enough now to notice.

"Likely? Not one-hundred percent?" she asked him.

"Some of the technology is cutting edge," he admitted. "And there is conflicting evidence about the success rates against cruise missiles. But given the protection level around D.C., and the number of missiles we can shoot at any incoming target, it shouldn't be a problem."

"What if there are a lot of cruise missiles?" Gregory asked.

"Then it gets tougher," Nalen said. "But it doesn't fit with what we've seen: a small team at the border—only eight men. One missing sniper rifle and a backpack. That doesn't sound like the D.C. sky filled with incoming cruise missiles."

As Gregory, Nancy, Dave, and Nalen continued to brainstorm and debate, Haley's mind slipped away.

During the Iraq and Iran war, both countries used chemical weapons.

Libya and Iran traded chemical weapons technology starting in the '80s and early '90s.

Iran's nuclear program was well known by the public, but its development of missile technology and chemical weapons research was more feared by those in the know.

Mustard gas. Nerve agents.

Her senses tingled. It wasn't the same as when she sat at her desk, fingers flying, ingesting incredible amounts of data, letting her intuition guide her in unexpected directions and to surprising—though accurate— conclusions. But the feeling was the same.

In her gut, she knew.

Or do I? This is as bad as the dream that sent Axe to Venezuela.

There was no proof—not the tiniest hint. Her very premise—that Russia, Iran, and Venezuela were working together—was guesswork. This just added to the potential house of cards.

It makes complete sense, though.

"I think we have to call off the State of the Union address," she announced, interrupting the ongoing discussion. She blinked, coming back to the room.

"What did you say?" Gregory asked her. "You mumbled something."

She checked her watch. Two hours until the start of the speech. The president would still be at the White House.

"I think we have to call off the State of the Union speech," she said again.

"What's going on?" Gregory asked.

"Mustard gas causes blistering of the skin and lungs and results in death," she said, not sure if she was trying to convince herself to follow her intuition or talk herself out of it. "Tabun is a fast-acting toxic nerve agent. Both were used in the Iraq-Iran war." She looked around the room at the faces of some of the smartest, most diligent people she knew. "If Russia, Iran, and Venezuela are working together, this is what they'd do. They have the know-how, resources, and motive. If it's them out to get us, they'd fire cruise missiles armed with weapons of mass destruction."

Gregory stared at her, thinking it through. He opened his mouth to speak.

"No, damn it, I don't have any proof!" she said before he could get the question out. "None at all," she muttered.

"Does it feel like one of your hunches?" Nalen asked.

"Yes," she said. "But… it's built on a house of cards. I could be wrong at any stage. The terrorists with the sniper rifle and backpack could be in Texas, California, or New York City. They were focused on oil and natural gas pipelines and the LNG ship and terminal. Maybe they're targeting more of that. Refineries. The CEO of energy companies. We just don't know."

"Missiles armed with weapons of mass destruction are a logical possibility," Dave admitted. Then he asked the question on Haley's mind. "But is it enough to recommend calling off tonight's speech? Rescheduling would be a big deal."

Nods came from everyone around the table. Canceling the annual address would be international news. The media would want to know why. Congress would demand to know what intelligence caused it to be called off—and whether they were in danger whenever they went to work. The president would look weak or like the boy who cried wolf instead of a careful, concerned leader.

"The D.C. area is well-protected on a regular night," Gregory said. His eyes drilled into hers. "Tonight, it's locked down. Without proof—or at least more than a hunch, even from you, President Heringten isn't going to cancel the speech. He would take too great of a political hit. You know that—and you know him."

"Still," she said. "Can we risk it? The entire government? No." She shook her head, ponytail flying.

"We have slightly less than two hours until the speech," Gregory said slowly, his gaze not on her, but off into the distance like he had an idea of his own. "It's entirely possible, logical even, that tonight is a target of our enemies. It could be an intercontinental ballistic missile from Russia, a team of terrorists with car bombs or mortars, or the options we've already discussed—the drones, suitcase nuclear device, or the cruise missiles," he added with a nod to her.

"Admiral," he said, turning to Nalen. "You and I will call the president now to let him know our concerns." Nalen nodded at him.

"Haley," Gregory continued, "you know how much I hate your gut feelings," he added with a rueful smile. "Especially when they come from thin air with nothing to back them up. But something about this feels right to me, too. I don't know how they think it could be successful, but the threats need to be evaluated." He turned to Dave and Nancy. "Take the suitcase nuclear device angle. Consider a dirty bomb scenario as well. And the drones. Keep in the back of your mind the chemical or nerve agent possibility, as well. Get on it."

The indecisive Gregory, reluctant to lead, was finally gone.

Thank God he's taking charge.

"You take this idea and run with it," he said to Haley as the other two analysts hurried to their workstations. "Work it as you've never worked anything else. You have thirty minutes."

"Thirty?"

"Yes. I have a feeling of my own. If I'm right, we're going to need time to deal with it."

Gregory has a hunch?

"But before you start, get word to Axe. If he sees cruise missiles, he is to immediately take them out by any means necessary, along with any nearby enemy. That oil platform would make the perfect launch facility. We wouldn't dare bomb it—there would be ecological devastation if they are actually using it for drilling."

She nodded absently while berating herself. Why hadn't she caught it earlier? The Venezuelan's new oil drilling platform off the coast of Caracas was in a subprime location for oil production. There would be oil there, but the country's proven reserves were hundreds of miles to the east and south.

Farther away—out of cruise missile range of D.C.

She composed a text to Axe, worrying about how long it would be before he got the message. He'd be arriving at the platform about now if all was going according to plan. But he would surely have the satellite messaging device on silent mode.

Please let him check it right away.

"You have twenty-nine minutes," Gregory told her. "Admiral?" he said, turning to Nalen. "Let's go to my office. We have a phone call to make."

88

DECISIONS

The Oval Office
The White House
Washington, DC

James had finished a light meal and was about to change into a fresh suit for tonight's speech when Chad David, his tireless chief of staff, called the residence. He was needed in the Oval Office immediately.

Minutes later, he and Chad shared a concerned look. "How likely is this, Gregory?" James asked, processing the potential threat his newly installed World Intelligence Agency director had shared with him.

"Sir, we have no concrete intel of any kind. At this point, we're frantically working off what I would hesitate to call a hunch. It makes complete sense, but the logic is built on several layers of supposition and guesswork. It's a house of cards." Gregory said.

There's more he's not saying.

"But?"

"It comes from Haley," Admiral Nalen said.

Haley. I knew it.

"She has a perfect record so far," James said, thinking out loud.

"Yes, Mr. President, she does," Gregory agreed. "But this time, she's not convinced, either. I'm sorry, sir, I wish we had more for you. We're working hard to uncover more intelligence—Venezuela buying cruise missiles from arms dealers, Iranian scientists arriving in the country, arms shipments to Venezuela, anything really—but so far we have nothing. It could be this, it could be another form of attack, or it could be nothing, I'm afraid."

His words say one thing, but he wouldn't be on the phone if it were nothing.

"Admiral," James said, going formal with his best friend. "If this happens, if someone fires a cruise missile at the Capitol building during my speech, how likely are we to get hit?"

There was an uncomfortable moment of silence when no one wanted to speak. "Come on, spit it out. I'll get the experts on the phone, given time—but I want it straight from someone I trust with my life."

"Mr. President," Chad said before Nalen could answer, "if this is a credible threat, we should reschedule the speech."

"Don't give me that! How good are our defenses? Seriously."

"We can't say, sir," Nalen admitted. "The problem isn't one missile or which country is behind it. What if they send twenty, fifty, or one hundred? At some point, our Patriot and National Advanced Surface-to-Air Missile System—NASAMS—systems could get overwhelmed."

"And the risk…" Chad added, "It's the entire government."

"Not the Secretary of Agriculture," James joked grimly, having second thoughts about the man he'd selected as the designated survivor. Sure, Secretary Clifford Lelberger could handle the job—James wouldn't have picked him for the role if he had serious doubts—but he wouldn't be the first choice to run the country.

Gregory cleared his throat on the other end of the line. "You have something to add, Gregory?" James asked into the speakerphone.

"I'm working on getting confirmation, but there is a possibility the chosen designated survivor name leaked ahead of time, sir," Gregory told him. "I'd rather not say more on the phone."

Could this all be connected to the Russian sleeper spy program?

That they were on a secure line and Gregory was still reluctant to speak about it directly meant it had to be.

James ran the threat assessment in his head the same way he'd made decisions as a Navy SEAL, first as a new guy and later as the man in charge of the missions. Risk versus reward. Preparation and planning versus the uncertainty of the enemy's actions.

Can I risk the entire country's political leadership just so they can hear me speak for an hour?

What if it wasn't real? If he called it off and nothing happened, he'd look horrible. He couldn't easily admit there had been a potential security threat. The other side—hell, even some of his own people—would destroy him for being weak on national security, overly cautious, or "letting the terrorists win."

Probably all the above, at the same time, from every different direction.

And someone would surely accuse him of staging the whole threat for... whatever reason they cooked up to suit their current argument against him.

Basically, I'd be a weak, scared coward who is a horrible president and a worse human being.

All for doing what was probably the right thing.

But our enemies would be emboldened. They'd have a grand time threatening us, laughing as we ran into hiding whenever they rattled their sabers.

James forced himself to consider what would happen if he didn't cancel the speech, the attack occurred, and their defense systems didn't work as promised.

Mass destruction. Our government decapitated. Thousands dead.

He thought of the senators, representatives, and judges who served the American people. Most were good men and women. Even if they disagreed vehemently about which direction the country should be heading, they were passionate about their love of democracy and the union.

A few in Congress were money-grubbing, power-mad jerks who cared for nothing but themselves. He wouldn't wish any of them dead though, including the few nuts he hoped got voted out of office at the earliest possible moment.

But with all of them gone, the entire government destroyed, what happens to the country?

The Secretary of Agriculture would rise to the occasion—if he wasn't also killed by a different attack, which is what Gregory was hinting at.

In the end though, the American people would rally. If necessary, the military would take charge temporarily and protect the country until fair elections could be held.

Losing all three branches of the government would be a national tragedy, but America's ideals were strong enough to withstand it.

"This is perhaps the hardest decision I've had to make as president, and you all know how difficult many of the others were," James said gravely. "Chad and William," he said to his closest advisor and his best friend, both retired SEALs, "what did we do when we suspected our mission was actually a setup? That we were walking into an ambush?"

"We planned for it. Contingencies, adding or changing personnel, whatever it took," Chad answered promptly.

"And then we did the mission anyway," William added.

"Exactly. We continue as planned, gentlemen. You have," he checked his watch, an old analog monster he'd worn back in his active SEAL days. "Not quite two hours. Find out if we have a legitimate threat. If we do, I'll gladly call the whole thing off. One of your contingencies is to think of an exceptional excuse in case we need it—Chad, you take that. Maybe I have a sudden stomach bug. Otherwise, we trust our multi-billion-dollar military hardware and dedicated personnel to do their jobs. We don't run and hide from every threat, gentlemen."

There was a chorus of acknowledgment from the men. "I have to get ready," he said, finishing up. "So get going. If you need me, I promise to take your call," he said, chuckling at his own dark joke.

He disconnected the line, thought for a second, and spoke to Chad. "Make sure key military leaders are in bunkers by the time my speech starts. Call it a readiness drill. And get me Senator Woodran on the phone."

"Of course, Mr. President," Chad said, and left to speak with Mary Beth, the hardworking presidential secretary, still at her desk outside his office.

He thought of contingencies, appearances, and loyalty—to the country, not to him.

Barbara would make an excellent president in the first elections after the attack. And Admiral Nalen would be an exceptional chief of staff... or 'First Gentleman' if they get married.

89

SECURITY

Off the Coast of Caracas, Venezuela

As Axe questioned the life choices that led him to the long, boring swim, he sensed one of the oil drilling platform's support pylons ahead. He corrected his approach angle a final time. Moments later, he surfaced behind one of the huge yellow columns. The DPV, run at the lowest speed, still had juice left in the battery. He'd be able to use it to escape to the rendezvous with Kelton and the yacht in the morning. The current would carry him, and he'd need to swim, but with the mission hopefully accomplished, they could risk a closer pickup than dropoff.

Axe attached the DPV along with his dive belt and other gear to a line and moved silently through the water until he found a place he could secure the equipment on the rung of an access ladder. All supplies, including food and other equipment, would be brought onto the facility via boat and one of the crane arms. But there were still metal rungs bolted to the structure's supports, rarely used but available for emergencies and small-boat access.

Since Axe didn't have his Team, a boat, and a portable ladder to directly access one of the higher levels of the structure at a location well-chosen for its stealth or surprise, he had to assault the huge platform the old-fashioned way, via the emergency ladder.

He climbed out of the water, his tired legs protesting, and continued until he reached the first level of the oil platform, dimly lit and filled with thick pipes leading in every direction.

If this rig is what Haley thinks it is, there should be at least one guard down here.

With his head just below the level of the metal open honeycomb deck, he saw the guard and rolled his eyes. The man, dressed in camouflage fatigues, sat in a chair with his head tilted back underneath a staircase leading to the next levels of the massive structure. A paperback novel lay open face down on his lap and he wore earphones connected to a small music player. His eyes were closed, and his head and body moved to the music only he could hear. An AK leaned against the wall next to him.

You've got to be kidding me. Jamming to music?

He understood the kid's situation. Guard duty was boring and took its toll. Days or weeks of nothing happening, sitting down here with no action, no threats—no purpose—and no one to talk to. Why not rock out? Why would anyone want to sneak onto the platform—and who could do it without their boat being seen?

Still, Axe rolled his eyes at the lack of discipline. If their various enemies ever wised up and treated the mind-numbingly boring job of guard duty with the seriousness it required, the SEALs would have a much tougher job.

But I'm not complaining tonight.

With this mission being about shaking the tree and finding out what was going on—if anything—on the oil rig, he didn't have a mandate to start shooting. Stealth was required. He'd have to get past the man.

Before climbing higher, he surveyed the area for security cameras, but the area was clear.

He calmed his mind and let all his emotions go; the excitement and joy of being in the field, doing what he did best, the hope for a successful mission, the concern he was risking his life and an international incident for nothing, that the oil platform was merely the result of a country with huge oil reserves getting its act back together and drilling once again. With a few breaths and mental effort, it all melted away, leaving him empty— and hard to sense.

Axe put his hand on the deck and mantled his way up and off the ladder, grateful as always for the daily workouts which let him effortlessly make the move.

His feet, still covered with the swim booties, squished softly as he stayed in the shadows along the edge of the platform.

Slow is smooth and smooth is fast.

It had taken him years of practice, and the combined instruction of his expert SEAL mentors, to learn how to move quietly across any terrain, from a forest to a desert, a city block to a boat deck. The hard work paid off now as he stepped past the guard keeping time to the music. Then he lightly ascended the stairs, passing within a foot of the kid's head. If the guard opened his eyes and glanced to his right, he'd be staring directly at Axe's ankles.

A moment later, Axe reached a landing and turned, moving up the next series of steps, out of danger—for the moment.

A guard implies this is more than a mere oil drilling platform.

But a kid listening to music suggested the security wasn't taken very seriously.

An interesting situation. It's definitely worth investigating.

One slow, quiet step at a time, he continued up the stairs, looking for a place to unpack his dry bag. He had a hunch he'd need more than the dive knife strapped to his ankle tonight.

90

PATIENCE

Iranian sniper Jafar pressed the explosive charge to the underside of the vehicle—a cross between a small truck and a Humvee—exactly as he'd been instructed. The pressure-sensitive tape allowed it to stick firmly, even with the small countdown timer, already ticking down the minutes until detonation. This smaller, mobile missile launcher was the closest to the Capitol. Blowing it up was essential.

He'd set the charges at other large, permanently fixed NASAMS sites before dawn, immediately upon arriving in the area from the long cross-country drive. Then, as soon as the sky had darkened in the early afternoon, he'd been at it again, infiltrating two others—including a mobile site near where Cyra was preparing for her mission.

He'd cut fences, crept through woods, and crawled across fields to affix the blocks of C-4 to multiple missile launchers at each location.

The guards on patrol at those positions had been good, but he was better. And none of them suspected a lone man would painstakingly approach missile launchers.

But each intrusion had taken longer than he had hoped. The American guards were much more alert than he'd been told they would be. It had taken all his skills, learned over a lifetime as a special forces sniper, to plant the explosives and get out without being detected.

It was better the eight men from the Texas team had disappeared instead of helping on this part of the mission.

Would they have gotten caught? he wondered.

He had trained for the mission with them. They had skills, but he wasn't convinced they would have succeeded. One might have been discovered and the whole operation ruined.

As Jafar prepared to slide out from under the mobile missile launcher, positioned so close to the Capitol building, he froze. Someone was nearby.

Tan military boots stepped toward him. For a moment, he thought he'd been caught.

Without moving, he prepared for a confrontation. The knife would be preferable. He could kill this one and drag him under the truck, then sneak away.

The pistol would be noisier, but with his marksmanship abilities, he could eliminate all the soldiers and run.

How long after they missed a check-in would the alarm be sounded? Would their radios be blamed? Would another unit be sent to investigate right away?

The boots stopped nearby and turned.

He's admiring the Capitol building in the distance.

Jafar relaxed and avoided looking directly at the man's feet. Tension created vibrations. An alert, experienced warrior might pick up on them and be compelled to investigate further.

Placing the charge at this launcher near a bridge over the Potomac River had been important enough to take the risk. The Capitol was only a mile away, rising beautifully above the surrounding area. Jafar had parked nearby, jogged along the sidewalk like a few other people out exercising in the cold but manageable February evening, then dropped to the ground when the vehicle's guards weren't looking.

His black clothes and skill had allowed him to follow the barely perceptible contours of the cold ground to remain hidden. The guards must have thought the nearby streetlights provided enough illumination for them to see anyone approaching. Or that here, in the middle of Washington, D.C., extreme vigilance wasn't needed.

They were wrong.

This would have to be the last missile launcher of the night. But if he hurried, he might hit a major radar installation guarding the area.

Or he could return to Cyra's position and be her security backup.

Not like she needs protecting.

Two feet away, next to the vehicle's tire, the guard stomped his boots to stay warm.

Jafar couldn't see the timer in the darkness under the truck. It didn't have large, easily seen red numbers counting down the seconds. But he had a sense of how much time he had until this one and the others ticked to zero.

I have time. No need to worry or risk exposure.

The guard would move eventually. Already, as the night grew colder, the men on duty here took turns sitting in the warm cab. Soon it would be this man's turn. The warm one would take a tour of the perimeter. Another would return to the truck, just as they had before. Jafar would use the changing of the guard to crawl, inch by inch, down the slope of the hill, further into the darkness, until he could stand and continue his jog—just another American living in the shadow of the awesome United States government buildings.

Jafar had already accomplished his primary objective of planting the explosives on other missile launchers around Washington, D.C. The more he destroyed, the better, he'd been told, but not all of them needed to be blown up. They couldn't be, especially without the other men and his strict orders—do not get caught.

Better to sabotage fewer of the high-tech launchers than to be seen or apprehended—dead or alive. He'd done enough, he hoped.

So Jafar lay on the frozen ground, ignoring the cold, and mentally kept track of the countdown.

I have time.

91

CONTINGENCIES

The Oval Office
The White House
Washington, DC

James sat at his desk in the Oval Office to make the crucial phone call.

"Senator Woodran, sorry to bother you," he started. He'd gone to the residence, gotten dressed in record time, and returned to the office.

"Never a problem, Mr. President," the tough-as-nails woman said. He could picture her in her Senate office, ready for the evening—and probably wearing cowboy boots. As a prominent western senator, she'd surely be featured on camera by all the news media, especially given the recent failed assassination attempt at her home. Boots would be perfect to remind people of her independence and western roots.

James hesitated. He hadn't prepared a speech and was suddenly at a loss for words.

"Mr. President? Are you still there?"

"Yes," he said, clearing his throat and having second thoughts about both the call and the bigger decision to not reschedule the speech.

Am I making the right decision?

"Sorry. Yes, I'm still here. Barbara?" In person, with few others around, they were on good terms. First-name terms, at least on his side. She could be a stickler for protocol when it suited her.

"Yes... Mr. President."

"James," he corrected.

"Mr. President," she said firmly, but her smile came through the phone line.

"Barbara, I need a big favor."

"Of course, Mr. President. If I can do it for you, I will."

"Not so much for me I'm afraid, though it's me you'll have to trust."

I'm blabbering.

The senator didn't speak, waiting him out.

"I would like you to skip the speech tonight," he said, coming right out with it. "In fact, I'd like you to leave your office, get on a plane, and fly to your home in Utah. Or at least go to your townhouse in Georgetown."

Will that be far enough away from whatever might be coming for us?

There was a long pause. Finally, he had to ask. "Barbara, did you hear me?"

"I did, Mr. President," she replied. "What's going on? Why would I do what you're asking?" She sounded both suspicious and concerned.

"Perhaps one of your family members is ill," he said, ignoring her question. "Or you aren't one-hundred percent tonight, given your recent injury."

"Try again, James," Barbara said, cutting to the chase and making a point of using his first name. Her voice wasn't exactly sharp, but she was obviously done playing the game.

Okay, now we're talking.

"I can't tell you. I won't tell you. But your president is asking a favor of you. Actually," he said, "your country needs you to do this. I'm just the messenger."

There was another pause, but shorter this time as Barbara digested the request. "There's a threat, but you don't know how seriously to take it. I'm your contingency plan," she said thoughtfully.

He remained silent.

"What is the timeline? Should I leave immediately?" she asked, then continued without letting him answer, planning out loud. "I would love to make an appearance on the floor of the Senate. Then maybe I feel the pain of the surgery. Let it show. I get a little tired but stick it out, showing how strong and brave I am. Eventually, though, I reluctantly let myself be talked into going home to Georgetown and having a doctor check me out."

The timing would be tight, but it should work.

"As long as you and I are not in the Capitol building at the same time, I think that would be fine," he said.

Barbara drew in a sharp breath. "Are you sure this is the right plan, Mr. President?"

Am I?

"Yes, Senator, I am."

"Then may God protect us all."

92

TECHNOLOGY

Off the Coast of Caracas, Venezuela

Eighty feet below Axe, on the other side of the yellow safety railing, the dark ocean rose and fell, making a rhythmic sound he found reassuring. Crouched in a dim corner of what he was calling level two of the enormous oil platform, he prepared for the next phase of the mission, opting to leave on the wetsuit. It was matte black and allowed him to blend into the dark corners of the facility, though he'd be instantly marked as an intruder if anyone caught a glimpse of him. He could steal coveralls or take the camo fatigues from a guard if needed.

He strapped his pistol and belt around his waist, slipped on his usual plate carrier with lighter armor, which had been easier to bring on the swim than his maximum level plate, and slung his short-barrel M4.

Normally, he would sneak in, get the intel, and get out, but tonight there would be an extra step. Thanks to the fancy electronic device in his dry bag, he had two-way text communications with both Haley in the CAG and Kelton on the yacht.

Gotta love technology.

A plane or drone overhead allowing direct radio contact would be ideal, but for this fact-finding mission, they had rejected the idea. After all, he was here because of a dream Haley had. The lower the profile, the better.

Axe removed the handheld satellite communicator and navigational device from his dry bag. It was shaped like a sturdy walkie-talkie, with a yellow rubber grip surrounding the color screen. Powering it on, his back to the facility, he held it close to his stomach in case it made noise. It was set on silent, but electronics had minds of their own half the time.

A few seconds later, he checked it. On and searching for a satellite. He held it back against his stomach. He didn't want a loud, obnoxious *ding* to ring out when it connected. It was a new gizmo to him and consumer-grade, not military. Once it was fully up and running, he'd navigate the menus and make sure they were still set on silent mode.

A noise from behind distracted him. Two men were talking and coming in his direction along the walkway.

He slipped the device back into the dry bag, praying it wouldn't make noise. He had nowhere to go. While he was in a dim corner, if the men walked nearby, they would see him. Sniper mode wouldn't protect him here.

With no other choice, he swung his legs over the chest-high railing and lowered himself down. His feet dangled over the open water far below.

Holding on with one hand, he grabbed the next lower railing with his free hand, then matched them. He repeated the process two more times, lowering himself until his hands gripped the bottom railing.

Is this enough?

If he went into sniper mode and disappeared, would the men coming his way notice his face at foot level?

He couldn't risk it.

Carefully, he let go of the railing and clamped his fingers on the edge of the platform.

His second hand joined the first as he brought his head below the level of the walkway.

This should be good—unless there's someone walking by next to my dangling feet on the next level down.

93

RESENTMENTS

Miraflores Palace
Caracas, Venezuela

President Villanueva sat at his expansive desk, feet up, waiting.

Alone. He'd sent all the lackeys away. The guards were outside the doors. He had a TV, but it remained off for now.

For once, mercifully, there was no chanting of protesters reaching through the windows to annoy him. It was dark, and the peasants were at home, doing whatever the little people did in the evenings.

Football on TV, no doubt, he thought.

His mind turned to the horrible things said about him four years before by the then-new President of the United States.

"President Villanueva is a horrible leader and a worse person. He doesn't care one bit about his citizens. The people of Venezuela can do better," President Heringten had said.

The people of Venezuela can do better.

The phrases had been stuck in his mind ever since.

President Villanueva is a horrible leader and a worse person.

He remembered the looks people gave him after President Heringten had spoken so bluntly about him and the way he ran the country.

He considered the sanctions placed against the country and him personally when he'd helped shape the voting results of the most recent presidential election to make sure he remained in power.

How leader after leader around the world had turned from him because of what one man—President Heringten—thought of him.

A horrible leader and a worse person.

Tonight, the long ordeal would be over.

There were no orders to give. His commanders would conduct what they believed to be a drill. Their men would practice a training exercise starting in less than an hour.

Orlov had warned him to keep the details of the plan to as few people as possible, which made complete sense to him. Most of his men were idiots, anyway. The commanders thought the missiles were aimed at a derelict oil tanker well past its prime, being sunk off the coast to form an artificial reef for tourists to visit.

That they believe this shows either their loyalty or ignorance.

Either was fine with him.

None of them have a clue that the missiles on the oil drilling platform are armed with weapons of mass destruction.

His secret warheads made the anticipation even better.

He glanced at his watch. At long last, his revenge was near.

President Heringten's final speech started in ninety minutes. He pushed down his impatience. He had his resentments—and his dreams of the future—to help him pass the time.

94

CHOICES

"We don't have time for presentations or formality," Gregory said to his people as he joined them around the conference room table. Nalen sat next to him, neither of them revealing how their conversation with the president went.

Better to hear their unvarnished opinions before telling them the president doesn't want to cancel the speech.

"Make it short and sweet. Nancy, you first," Gregory said.

"D.C. is well protected from drone attacks," she said. "There are multiple rings of radar, several types of weapons systems all working together to locate, target, and destroy them. If there were hundreds of drones, we might be in trouble, but even then, most would get shot down. They couldn't carry much destructive power—from conventional, biological, or chemical weapons." She took a deep breath but looked resolutely at him. "In my opinion, the Capitol building is safe."

Gregory nodded once at her, then turned to Dave.

"The missing suitcase nukes," he said, sounding reluctant, "were likely real. But we have no way of knowing for sure. Still, it's been decades. There are valid questions about why they haven't been used before now.

Our enemies have the money and would pay dearly for them. If they existed, they would have been bought and used by now. It's possible they are not functional after all this time."

He paused, then plowed on. "On the other hand, a dirty bomb is possible. Our enemies have the capacity to build and transport one. But they wouldn't get away with it. We would use the unique signature of the material—after the fact, of course—to determine who attacked us. Our country wouldn't rest until we annihilated those responsible. And besides, we have systems in place to detect the material."

He, too, took a deep breath, paused a second, then spoke. "In my opinion, the Capitol building is safe."

Gregory turned to Haley.

My tornado. Uncontrollable and awe-inspiring—if you're not in her path of destruction.

Surprisingly, she offered them a small smile. He relaxed. Then she spoke, her voice calm, clear, and convincing. "The Capitol building is not safe. An attack is imminent—likely already in progress. We just can't see it yet."

What did I ever do to deserve this?

"And your proof?" he asked, knowing the answer. "Intel? A morsel. Give me something."

The damn woman, the best analyst he'd seen, shook her head, looking composed and certain. "Absolutely nothing."

Gregory didn't know whether he should laugh, cry, or throw his hands up and walk out. None of his management training or years of experience had prepared him to work with this genius.

He opened his mouth to speak, but no words came out. He didn't know what to say or do.

A glance at Admiral Nalen didn't help. The man, only a few years his senior, had decades more leadership experience under the toughest conditions in the world. He'd sent men into battle and, likely, some to their deaths. He was studying a laptop, examining what looked like locations of missile batteries and radar installations in the greater D.C. area.

He should be in charge here, not me.

But all he did was stare at the computer and chew on his lip.

Is he thinking, staying out of my way, or as lost as I am?

Gregory met Haley's eyes. Her beautiful, model-perfect exterior hid an incredible mind.

She's been right over and over and over again.

Finally, he knew what he had to do. "The president refuses to cancel or reschedule the speech unless we have something firmer than we do," he told them.

Nancy's face visibly paled.

"He pointed out that the nation spends billions on defense for situations just like this. Contingencies are in place already, with the designated survivor safe, far from the capital."

Gregory's options flashed through his mind.

I could lie to the president and say we have proof of an attack. I'd be a hero if Haley's right or take the hit if nothing happened. Retire early.

Another possibility was to accept the decision of the Commander in Chief and let the cards fall where they may.

Or he could man up and take charge.

Gregory looked once again at Nalen, hoping he'd glance up and offer to take over, but he was lost in the map on the laptop.

Nothing.

He took a deep breath, making up his mind. "Haley, there's always a first time for you to be wrong, and I hope this is it. But given your track record, I bet you're right again. So we have to figure out a way to stack the deck in our favor."

He made eye contact with her, then Dave, Nancy, and finally Nalen looked up, his expression neutral.

"We do everything in our power to make sure the attack fails."

One by one, his team nodded at him, looking determined.

He felt better having made the decision to work behind the scenes to get to the bottom of the attack and keep it from succeeding.

"First. Admiral, I want you to—"

The phone on the table rang, and Gregory snatched it up. "Go."

He listened to his counter-espionage leader in charge of monitoring the Russian sleeper spies. The man was short and to the point.

"Understood. Thank you."

Just when I thought it couldn't get any worse.

He hung up the phone slowly.

"What is it?" Haley asked, her voice barely above a whisper.

He turned to her. "One of the Russian sleeper spies is missing. She would have been in a position to know, days in advance, who the designated survivor is for tonight. The person who takes over if the entire government is destroyed is in danger. My guess is that's who the sniper is after."

95

WEAPONS FREE

Off the Coast of Caracas, Venezuela

Axe grabbed the rungs of the safety railing and pulled himself up once the two men had passed. He took a knee and once again retrieved the satellite communicator from the dry bag. There was a text from Haley.

Possible cruise missile attack on DC planned w unknown WMDs. Orders: find and destroy any cruise missiles on platform immediately by any means necessary. If missiles found, all ppl considered hostiles. WEAPONS FREE.

Whoa. Cruise missiles? Weapons of mass destruction?

His mission had gone from a simple shaking of the tree to a full-on assault mission. He replied with a simple, "Copy," and returned the device to the bag. He glanced up at the enormous facility. Pipes ran in every direction. Square red shipping containers took up the length of two sides of one level. There was a crane, two helicopter landing pads, at least ten levels, workers who weren't likely to be the enemy, and guards who were.

How the hell am I supposed to find cruise missiles here?

Then it all came together.

Tonight is the State of the Union address. The entire government will be in one place for at least an hour.

He checked his watch. The speech would start in forty-five minutes. He had to hurry.

96

ORDERS

"Does the identity of the designated survivor being in the hands of our enemies early enough for them to plan an operation change the threat assessment for the president?" Gregory asked Admiral Nalen.

"Absolutely. It means the risk is real," Haley jumped in. "It's the proof you said he wanted."

Gregory nodded absently at her. He agreed, but he was interested in how Nalen perceived it.

"Haley's partly right," Nalen said. "But we don't have proof the sleeper spy passed along the information, or that it is being acted on, so it won't change his decision. Not yet. Just because there's a plot or possibility of an attack doesn't mean it will succeed."

Exactly my thought, too.

Gregory stared into space, frantically processing the situation.

First, he had to tell the president and let him make the call.

Second, he had to continue assuming the president wanted to proceed with the speech.

This is another life-altering moment. A chance to rise to the occasion or punt and allow others to take responsibility.

His eyes snapped to Nalen and Haley. "I'll call the president first, then alert the Secret Service about the possible threat to the Secretary of Agriculture."

Gregory paused and called to Nancy sitting at her computer. "Get me the location of the designated survivor, including all possible sniper points within…" He glanced at Nalen.

"Two thousand meters," Nalen and Haley said together.

"Though fifteen hundred is more realistic," Nalen added.

"Two thousand meters."

"The Secretary of Agriculture is at his daughter's house," Nancy came back immediately. "About forty minutes south of us in Fort Washington, Maryland."

"Fort Washington?" Nalen asked, sounding surprised. "There's a major mobile NASAMS setup near there."

"Admiral," Gregory said, feeling more sure of himself and fine with ordering around the older, more experienced man, "you call whoever you need to. On my authority, initiate an immediate hardening of our defenses of all National Advanced Surface-to-Air Missile System—the NASAMS assets. Plus the Patriot batteries, Avenger short-range air defense systems… everything on the ground that's up and running. Assume we're under attack not only by air. The missiles and radar installations themselves may be at risk. The best way to get cruise missiles through would be to attack and take out our land-based defenses first."

Nalen nodded and turned to the phone.

Gregory looked at Haley, trying to make up his mind, knowing that the clock was ticking and every second counted.

All security personnel were maxed out tonight. There were no extra bodies to search for a hypothetical sniper. And he couldn't tell them about the Russian sleeper spy program, which is why he believed the threat was real.

It has to be Haley. She's a hunter, whether it's looking for data at her desk—or in the field.

He could sense the desire and readiness radiating from her.

She'll be safe with Nalen. The two of them can get this done.

The situation had gone beyond intelligence analysis. It made sense to have Haley as an operational asset.

"Take Nalen," Gregory told Haley. "The Secret Service will be there, but they won't be staffed to actively search for a shooter. You'll probably be too late, but it's worth a try. If the Secretary is still alive when you get there, your job is to find and eliminate the sniper. And don't die, understand?"

Haley looked like she was about to give him a thank-you hug, but she nodded instead, then checked her phone. "Axe copies the orders," she said. "And tell Hammer to meet me at my SUV," she added as she turned and ran from the room.

God, please don't let anything happen to her.

97

DEADLINE

The Venezuelan soldiers and missile crew had traveled in relative comfort in their insulated, specially outfitted shipping container. They had a chemical toilet behind a privacy curtain, sleeping pads, old-fashioned portable DVD players and dozens of movies to watch, books, water, limited alcohol, a crate of various flavored MREs—Meals Ready to Eat— and tiny ventilation ports they could open on warmer days or when the room got stuffy.

Vasquez, one of the two missile technicians, had experienced some sea sickness the first day, but the provided acupressure wrist bands had worked surprisingly well. He'd joined the army because Venezuela's navy didn't amount to much, but here he was, on the country's new, secret, clandestine navy vessel.

Their officer, Quintero, had kept them occupied with calisthenics twice a day. But otherwise, the week-long trip had been a relaxing—though confining and occasionally boring—vacation for the men.

Beneath their temporary home was a stack of nine other identically sized containers, painted green, orange, blue, and white. Another blue container was right across from theirs. They could open their door, reach out and push open the matching door across from them, allowing them access to the missile launch controllers.

"Disperse," Quintero had ordered the guards fifteen minutes ago. Wearing the same baggy beige coveralls the ship's crew wore on duty, the four men had exited the container and climbed along the outside of the other ones nearby. There was little risk of anyone attacking them and trying to stop the top-secret launch, one hundred feet above the deck of the massive ship, but orders were orders.

Vasquez stood by the door, enjoying his first real fresh air in days. The other tech, Delgado, stood next to them. The sky was pitch black, making the stars shine brighter than he'd ever seen them before.

"Start the launch."

Vasquez was startled out of his reverie of the night sky at Quintero's order but reacted quickly. They were on a deadline. The exercise was being judged on stealth, accuracy, and timing. He stepped to the doorway, leaned out, and used the key that had hung around his neck for the past week to open the lock on the door of the launch container.

He pushed open the door and stepped across the narrow gap between the containers, not daring to look down at the deck far below. Once inside the tiny entryway, he hit the button on the console to turn on the lights and power up the electronics and hydraulics. The system had been outfitted with lithium batteries specifically for the mission, and they worked perfectly. The lights came on and the console lit up with every display in the green.

Delgado joined him in the room a minute later, having undone the latches holding the top of the container in place. At the touch of a button, hydraulic arms slowly raised the metal roof, tilting it up along its length like a giant footlocker being opened.

When the panel showed the green light indicating the cover was out of the way and locked in place, Delgado read the next item on the checklist, though they both had it memorized. Procedures were to be followed to the letter. "Raise the launch tubes," he said.

Vasquez pushed the next button on the panel. The noise which followed sounded exactly like it had on land during their training exercises, and his heart rate picked up.

Finally, after all this training, I get to fire a live missile.

Cruise missiles were expensive, especially for his poor country under crushing sanctions from the United States of America and her allies. There was no budget to test-fire them often, which is why this training mission had them so excited.

That the missiles would fly hundreds of miles, destroying an ancient ship off the coast of his country to form a barrier reef and, eventually, a world-class scuba diving destination to bring tourist dollars to his homeland, filled him with pride.

I am helping to make my country better.

The launch tubes locked into place with a clang and a green light on his board.

"Launch tubes in place and locked," he said.

"Arm the missiles," Delgado read from the laminated checklist.

One by one, Vasquez turned the old-fashioned knobs from SAFE to ARMED.

"Missiles one through four are armed."

"Confirm location," Delgado said, raising his voice.

Behind them, Quintero held a small GPS device. The ship's captain and bridge crew had been very well paid to ensure the ship's accuracy, but mistakes happened. "Location confirmed," Quintero called.

"Initiate firing sequence?" Delgado asked.

"Initiate firing sequence," Quintero ordered.

Vasquez flipped up the clear plastic cover and pressed the recessed red button underneath it. "Firing sequence initiated," he called and knew his voice betrayed his excitement.

"Firing sequence initiated," Delgado said. He sounded excited as well.

"Firing positions," Delgado said, reading the last item on the checklist.

"Firing positions," Quintero said, issuing the order.

Delgado put the checklist into its holder along the wall, then stepped into their container. Vasquez joined him a second later, again ignoring the long drop below him, turned, and closed the door to the control room. Then he joined Delgado and Quintero inside their living quarters. There was little danger from the launch—the missiles were not ICBMs that released a thunderous trail of fire. His country, unfortunately, didn't yet have such weapons. The small blast from the launch should be kept within the shipping container as designed.

"Fifteen minutes," Quintero called, checking his watch.

Right on schedule.

98

30 SECONDS

Off the Coast of Caracas, Venezuela

Axe snuck up the staircase, grateful for the size of the structure.

Four levels up, he heard the slow footsteps of a person before they came into view, which gave him time to press himself into the darkness between two pieces of machinery.

A bored guard, armed with an AK dangling from its strap, passed by two feet in front of him.

I don't get it. Guards—but not many. Patrolling, but not on alert.

It didn't make sense.

Axe was on the sixth level, which was half the width of levels one through five. He moved in the opposite direction of the guard, making his way silently to the railing overlooking one of the helipads and the lower levels. He hated the well-lit outdoor passageways, but there seemed to be few guards on this level, and he hadn't seen any security cameras.

If Haley's correct, the cruise missiles should be easier to find than I first thought.

He didn't have to find missiles. He only had to find the launchers, which were large, hard to hide, and by necessity would have to be out in the open.

Two levels below him, six soldiers walked briskly across the helipad to the large deck next to it. A long, blue shipping container sat out in the open on the platform at the edge of the landing zone.

Found it. That was easy.

The Russians had designed and perfected a portable cruise missile launcher built into a standard shipping container. The rest of the containers on the ship were different—square and red instead of the lone dark blue rectangle the soldiers were walking to.

It's been sitting out in the open the whole time.

Assuming the men were about to open the container and prep the missiles for launch, it meant the gloves were off. All people on the facility could be considered hostiles, though Axe wouldn't go out of his way to shoot those who looked like regular oil rig workers if he could help it, no matter what the rules of engagement allowed.

But if anyone stood in his way of stopping the launch, they were as good as dead.

He ran, trading stealth for speed, moving to the far end of level six, overlooking the ocean. Thirty feet below and a hundred feet to his right, the men were reaching the container. Four stopped on the helipad while two men, both tall, but one burly and the other thinner, proceeded to the front of the container and fiddled with a padlock.

Shoot first, then destroy it? Or the other way around?

Axe wracked his brain, trying to remember how long it took to prepare to fire. Did they have to start equipment? Allow it to warm up? But he either never learned those facts or had forgotten.

Shooting six men before any of them returned fire worked in the movies but was risky in real life. One or two would target him. He would lose the element of surprise. Other guards would come. They could keep him pinned down and proceed with the launch.

He had to take out the launcher first, despite the personal risk. He would happily die saving the United States, especially if the warheads contained WMDs.

Running down a staircase, likely into the bullets of other guards, wasn't an option. Leaning over the railing, he ignored the water over one hundred feet below. If he had his former Team with him, at least one of them would have a rope, which would allow a quick rappel two levels down. But he'd been selective in what he brought on the long swim and climbing equipment didn't make the cut.

This will work.

The facility had thick pipes everywhere, equipment, and safety railings.

Plenty of stuff to grab onto.

He swung his legs over the railing and started lowering himself down. A slip of a hand meant a fall to his death; hitting the water from this height would feel like falling on concrete. He'd break both his legs—at least. Most likely, he'd fall off-kilter, splat against the surface, and be killed instantly.

Best not to dwell on that.

Axe's foot found purchase on a metal clamp holding a thick pipe to the wall. Move by move, he'd made his way down the two levels, unseen by the guards. The two men who had unlocked the shipping container's door had done something to open the roof of the container. Hydraulics whined, slowly raising four long gray tubes from inside.

Once Axe reached the correct level, he realized there was no easy approach that would keep him hidden from the guards. The four men were facing outward, weapons in hand, but not expecting trouble. They glanced behind them often, watching the progress of the missile tubes.

If I shoot them now and run, I have a chance. I'd have a clear shot at destroying the container, but again, the element of surprise would be lost. The mission would succeed, but I'd die.

The tubes rose slowly. He had time.

He lowered himself further until his hands were clinging to the metal deck of level four. His feet dangled over the ocean; there was no level directly below him for toe holds. Carefully, inch by inch, he moved his hands to the left, going as fast as he could without risking the long fall into the water.

His fingers slipped, and his left hand let go. Before he could make a desperate grab for the edge, the fingers of his other hand, having to suddenly support the entire weight of his body and gear, started sliding off as well.

His left hand slapped the platform floor and clung just as the right fingers lost their grip. The process started to repeat itself.

With another desperate grab, he got his right hand back on the platform and stopped moving, holding tight to the edge.

He'd tried to go too fast. The damp sea air made the edge slippery.

A little slower is good.

Refusing to think about the deadly drop below his dangling feet, he steadied himself with a favorite line from the SEAL ethos.

'In the worst of conditions, the legacy of my teammates steadies my resolve and silently guides my every deed. I will not fail.'

He carefully moved his hands slower than he'd done before, continuing his sideways progress.

The hydraulics stopped and the missile tubes locked into place as Axe reached the far end of the shipping container. He lunged up and grabbed the railing, then matched hands. He repeated the move, his legs dangling uselessly with no footholds to use. When his hands grasped the third railing, he could finally use the edge of the platform for a foothold, which made things easier. He climbed over the railing into the narrow walkway between the shipping container and the safety railing lining the edge of the level.

Forty feet away, the operators at the front of the container recited a checklist in Spanish, though one sounded different.

That sounds like a Russian accent.

Axe quickly crouched and unslung his dry bag. He was hidden from view as long as neither man poked his head around the corner.

First, take out the launcher. Then escape and report what I found.

He removed the two blocks of C-4 he'd liberated from the backpack of the terrorists in Texas.

Sure glad the Venezuelan Navy didn't find this when they searched the yacht.

The pistols and rifles hidden on the boat would have gotten them into a lot of trouble, but the explosives in his hand would have escalated the situation quickly. Americans are known for their love of guns and the weapons could almost be explained away—a billionaire on an expensive yacht needed protection, after all. Axe's fake passport came with a legend portraying him as former special forces and a licensed bodyguard.

But there would have been no good excuse for the incredibly powerful explosives and countdown timers.

He had training in explosives like all SEALs, but he was never the go-to guy for demolition.

Place both charges? And where—low or high?

Given the destructive power of the C-4, one should do the trick, but using both would be best.

'Two is one and one is none.'

And if there was another launcher elsewhere on the platform?

They are in the process of launching the weapons. I won't find any others in time.

He pressed one of the blocks against the metal wall of the container, sticking it into place halfway up.

Four launch tubes, arrayed two by two across, meant he needed to risk exposing himself to the guards on the far side if he was to place the other block where it would do the most damage. The explosives would destroy the launcher and missile bodies but leave the warheads intact.

He set the timer on the second block to thirty seconds, then did the same on the first one, already attached.

Will that be long enough to get clear?

At the far end, the men sounded like they had finished their checklist.

"*Listo,*" one said.

They're nearly ready to launch.

Axe was out of time. He pressed the start button on the timers, then hurried around the back of the container. Exposing only his arm, he stuck the other block of explosives as high as his hand could reach.

He had to get as far from the explosion as possible, but as soon as he left the concealment of the container, the guards would see him and open fire.

He raised his M4, stepped out, and started shooting, hurrying across the helipad as he went.

99

LAUNCH

S-34 *Tiburón*
Mid-Atlantic Ocean

"Prepare to fire," Captain Contreras said in his quiet, commanding voice. Around him on the cramped bridge of the submarine, his men sat and stood at their stations. He could feel their excitement. He suspected that, like him, none of them believed the mission was a training exercise.

"Missiles ready, Captain," came the instant reply.

A digital timer counted down.

"Fire missiles," he said.

His ship gave the tiniest shudder over and over until all ten missiles were launched.

"Missiles away, Captain," a crewman said.

"Well done. New course and speed," he said, rattling off his pre-planned escape from the area. They were in the middle of the Atlantic, but the acoustic signature of a missile launch might have been heard by the American's extensive sonar capabilities.

The ship sped up and dove, the crew executing his orders with precision.

They had launched the cruise missiles as ordered at exactly the right time. He and the crew could be proud of that, no matter what the real target was.

Training exercise? he thought. *Not a chance.*

———————

Container Ship *Petrel*
Mid-Atlantic Ocean

Vasquez kept track of the time on his cheap digital watch.

Please let it work as it's supposed to.

"Ten seconds," Quintero called.

Delgado looked at Vasquez, his eyes wide with anticipation and excitement.

"Five, four, three, two, one, launch," the officer called.

The four missiles *whooshed* as they launched.

We did it!

100

PAIN

Axe shot the guards from left to right, killing the first two with headshots.

The third got his rifle up as he turned to face Axe but took two rounds to the chest and a third to his face before he could fire.

Axe wasn't so lucky with the fourth guard. The man managed to get rounds off before falling to Axe's precision shooting.

An instant later, a sharp pain in his chest made Axe stumble. He felt a bullet barely miss his head as he fell gracelessly to the ground, turning toward the end of the shipping container. The thin missile technician had a pistol in both hands, carefully aiming his kill shot.

Axe fired the M4 without aiming, walking the bullets onto the target.

The enemy's shots struck the metal deck around Axe and ricocheted away harmlessly.

The tango fell back as Axe's fire struck him.

Axe sensed a presence coming fast from his blindside. An instant later, his ribs exploded in pain.

The burly technician loomed over him, preparing for a second kick.

There was no time to bring the rifle to bear. Instinctively, Axe rolled away. The kick connected but didn't have the impact of the first one.

Smart—he closed on me under his buddy's covering fire.

With a roar, the man was on him. Axe got his arms up in time to spare his face but was too slow to protect his stomach. The punch hurt—a lot—causing him to falter.

Instantly, his head took a blow, then another. More followed to his stomach. He couldn't keep up with the huge man kneeling over him. He was losing the fight.

He's too fast.

Axe would have doubled over if he could have when another punch got him in the groin. But the giant above him didn't allow a second of mercy, following up with more punches to his stomach, face, and head.

On the verge of blacking out, Axe did the only thing he could. Using all his strength, he grabbed the man's jacket and pulled, got his arms around the enemy's beefy body, and clenched him tight.

With a snarl, the man tipped his head back and slammed forward, delivering an expert head-butt.

Axe saw stars and fought to stay conscious. He tipped his chin to his chest, trying to avoid the next strike as the man fought to escape Axe's weakening grip.

He only had to hang on for a few more seconds.

The timers were about to go off.

Was he far enough away from the explosives? He wasn't sure. It would depend on the force of the blast, the shrapnel, and whether the cruise missiles detonated as well.

At least I'll stop the launch—I hope.

He hugged the bigger, stronger, faster man with the last of his strength and waited for the boom he'd never hear.

So this is how it all ends.

101

PREPARATION

Haley finished strapping on her plate carrier, then loaded the M4.

Hammer had parked right next to her. He was a few seconds behind her in getting ready.

"What if it's more than the sniper?" she asked him. "If they knew the location, could they have planted some C-4?"

"The Secret Service will have checked the area for explosives with a bomb-detection dog," he said, finishing his own preparations. "All we have to worry about is the long-range shot. They'll take care of the rest."

Haley checked her extra ammo magazines on the front of her plate carrier, then the knife hanging upside down in its sheath. Another knife was attached to her belt, hanging horizontally at the small of her back, no longer covered by the black fleece jacket she'd been wearing for days. A smaller folding knife was in her front pocket.

She inserted a small earbud into her ear. Nalen did the same.

"I'll be right behind you," he said, opening the door of his borrowed car.

102

HAMBURGER

Off the Coast of Caracas, Venezuela

Axe came to slowly. His entire body hurt, the pain deep. Crushing. He had a sharper pain on his right side. A cracked rib, maybe.

The lucky shot from the tango with the pistol.

The lightweight armor had stopped it—he hoped—but the impact hurt. His head pounded.

From the explosion? Or maybe the blast flung me, and I hit my head on the helipad?

Both, probably.

The air smelled like a bomb had gone off.

The C-4.

Axe gasped as he felt a poke in his stomach, and he finally mustered the energy to open his eyes.

A man dressed in camouflage fatigues stood over him, face red, eyebrows together, glaring.

Looks like I'm still alive—barely. And that I've pissed some people off.

The guard called out something over his shoulder in Spanish, then yelled accusingly to Axe, but Axe didn't catch the words. Normally, his Spanish wasn't bad, but his mind wasn't focusing well at the moment.

"Um, just an ice cream sundae, please. Extra hot fudge, no cherry," he answered in English.

The man screamed at him again in Spanish, not amused.

Tough crowd.

Though still in a world of hurt, Axe prepared himself for what was coming next. The guard shifted his weight, preparing to deliver a kick to Axe's side.

With a rush of adrenaline deadening the pain he felt, Axe grabbed the man's planted foot and yanked.

The guard, off-balance with one foot back for the kick, gasped as he fell backward. The dull thud of his body hitting the deck was followed an instant later by the sickening sound of his head slamming into the ground. He lay still, groaning.

There were guards everywhere, but Axe thought he might be seeing double and triple, so it might not be as bad as it looked. He drew his pistol and fired at the nearest ones, then got his feet under him, ready to run for cover.

He wasn't prepared for the sight near him. What once had been the muscular missile technician that had attacked and nearly killed him was barely identifiable as a person. It looked instead like a pile of hamburger meat roughly molded into the size and shape of a human.

The man he'd fought had taken the brunt of the blast and shrapnel as the two of them had been flung several yards across the helipad.

Axe gagged at the site even as he turned his body to fire in the general direction of the other guards he'd seen. He kept shooting as he stumbled away from the enemy, trying desperately to orient himself. He moved as quickly as his broken body would carry him toward the side of the helipad overlooking the rest of the facility below it. Maybe there would be a ladder or a way down that didn't involve fighting his way through the men emerging from doors in the middle of the rig.

Bullets zipped by him. Axe had no cover, nothing to hide behind.

Staggering to the edge of the helipad, he dropped to his stomach and peered over. The next deck was thirty feet below. Too far to fall.

But there were pipes running horizontally about fifteen feet down.

A bullet grazed his leg, then another hit his hip.

He tipped himself over the side, aiming for the pipes to avoid dropping the entire way to the deck.

This is going to hurt.

103

STRENGTH

Miraflores Palace
Caracas, Venezuela

Villanueva finished the last of his whisky and sat back in his leather desk chair, finally feeling a sense of peace.

At this moment, normal cruise missiles from the ship and submarine were flying toward America. They would impact in the middle of the State of the Union address when all of America's leaders were gathered in one place.

From the oil drilling platform, four extra missiles with very special warheads followed a few seconds behind, ready for the *coup de grâce* once the others had destroyed the United States Capitol building.

He felt a huge weight lift from his shoulders. In an hour, America would suffer. And, more importantly, President Heringten.

In the end, the cartel's money, the economy, the peasants—none of it mattered. All Villanueva cared for was revenge for the slights directed at him by the American president.

The rest of Orlov's plan was merely perks: Russia, Iran, and Venezuela forming a new bloc where they would all flourish. The return to oil drilling and exporting, which would help Venezuela become a superpower over the next few years as America struggled to put the pieces back together—assuming Russia and China didn't take the opportunity to invade and divide the country in two.

Yes, there were risks. But Orlov was a genius, and their culpability would be difficult to uncover.

And so what if they find out?

The Russian spymaster had promised more chemical and biological warheads for the cruise missiles once this initial attack was successful, and their partnership cemented. Orlov's point was valid; the world only knew strength. Possessing weapons of mass destruction, even if his scientists couldn't produce them on their own—yet—made Venezuela impossible to invade or mess with.

Gaddafi gave up his WMDs and development program and look where it got him.

No, whoever led America after tonight would think twice about retaliating—assuming they even found out who was behind the attack.

He turned on the huge TV on the wall of his office and switched to an American news channel featuring commentary prior to the big speech. It was time to savor every morsel of news, every pundit discussing what the president would say.

They have no idea what is coming.

104

AGONY

Axe came back to consciousness to the sound of yelling and pounding feet on metal stairs. He was facedown on level two of the oil drilling platform. The pain he thought was unbearable before was a sweet memory compared to the agony he felt now. His nose ran and a sob escaped his lips as he rolled from his stomach to his side, then to a sitting position. His pistol was in his hand, the M4 still on its sling, but who knew if it was functional.

As he scooted backward to hide between two huge metal boxes housing some type of equipment, he replaced the empty pistol magazine with a new one and aimed at the nearby stairs.

Probably would have been easier to walk down than leap. Except for the assholes shooting at me, I guess.

His focus faded for a second. When he came back, a soldier with his AK raised stalked forward, searching for him. Another stepped off the lowest stair, while two more were close on his heels.

Axe breathed, focused, and killed the first two before they turned toward him.

He scooted back, his body screaming in agony. Bullets pinged off the metal boxes around him.

He leaned out, shot the third man in the leg, and ducked back before either could shoot him. A moment later, he heard the sound he'd been hoping for. Both men were out of bullets.

The guard on the ground could wait. He was awkwardly fumbling for a fresh magazine as Axe focused on the fourth one, trying to head for cover while reloading, doing neither well—nor fast enough.

Axe shot him in the face.

Just as guard number three got the fresh mag in, Axe put a bullet through his head, too.

There are sure to be more.

He wasn't waiting around to face them, though he didn't look forward to what came next. Holstering his pistol, he crawled as fast as he could to the edge of the platform, confirmed he was only fifteen feet from the water, and pushed himself off the edge.

105

CURTAINS

Potomac High School
Fort Washington, Maryland

Iranian assassin Cyra lay prone behind the powerful rifle, motionless, as she had for an hour. The two-story brick school wouldn't normally have worked as a place to shoot from. But the gym was an extra ten feet high—and the air handler on top of it gave her just enough angle for the twenty-five-hundred meter shot—one-and-a-half miles the way they measured distance in this strange country.

The road from the school to the target's house—at the end of the street's T intersection—was straight enough that she had a clear view through the scope of the man she had to kill tonight. She watched him—or at least, his shape. The Secret Service had closed the curtains at the house, but the smallest gap remained, allowing her to see Clifford Lelberger, the Secretary of Agriculture—whatever that was. She had memorized his face, his hair, and the way he walked from the materials provided to her.

He was in the living room, on the couch, holding one of his grandchildren—exactly as predicted by her superiors. She wouldn't purposefully target the child, but if it was still in the man's lap when it came time for her to take the shot, so be it. Given the distance and the window she had to punch through, she would aim for the man's center mass and not worry. The bullet would easily go through the child and still kill the target.

As long as the man stayed planted on the couch watching the upcoming presidential speech—as she'd been assured he would—he would die in less than an hour when she took her shot.

Cyra was picked because of her abilities and what some would call a cold heart. She merely considered herself a professional. If her superiors wanted a person killed, they chose her. Failure was not an option—hence her perfect record.

There were three guiding principles for the mission. The first: Clifford Lelberger had to die no earlier than 9:30 pm local time.

Second, she could not be captured—dead or alive.

Third, the man would be hard to kill at 9:30, but the difficulty would increase after 9:40. That was her window.

Almost two miles away, the small gap in the living room curtains disappeared as they were closed tight.

All the lights in the house went out.

Cyra swung the rifle to the side, checking the house next door. The dim front porch light was on.

Could be solar or battery operated.

The other nearby houses had lights on and the glow of television sets from many of their front rooms. The streetlights nearby were also still lit.

She examined the target's house one last time. Dark.

They know.

Somehow, the Americans had learned the man was in imminent danger and were increasing their protection accordingly.

In a flash, she was off the air handler and onto the gym's roof. From there, the roof of the rest of the school, then down the same drain spout she had used to access the roof after watching the Secret Service inspect it. She'd guessed they thought it was too far away, an extremely difficult shot, which is why they hadn't left a man stationed there.

The long rifle was slung on her back, and she jogged casually to the beat-up old car she and Jafar had stolen that afternoon, parked along the road in front of a house.

No one noticed her. It was 9 p.m. on a cold, dark Tuesday in February. Aside from a few die-hard runners and dog walkers, no one would be around to question her.

The rifle went into the trunk of the car, followed by her warm down jacket and snow pants which had kept her almost comfortable on the roof.

She kept the stupid black stocking cap with the pom-pom on top she had found in the stolen car. It made her look harmless, which might come in handy now.

With a quiet click, she closed the trunk and jogged toward the house, staying several feet from the curb, facing traffic, as was the custom here.

In her running shoes and spandex tights, she looked like any other young suburban woman working hard to stay in shape. No one would see the horizontal-carry fixed-blade combat knife at the small of her back or the 9mm pistol at her side, all covered by her black thermal top.

After a few dozen steps, she picked up the pace and checked her watch. She had time to decide how to handle the approach—whether to jog along the road like a fitness junkie, detouring straight to the front door or windows when she reached the house. Or to hurry the run and make the final approach stealthily. The target by now had been taken to the house's furnished basement, she guessed. Would the Secret Service be guarding the second floor of the house, or could she scale the small tree near the garage, access the upstairs bedroom window, and assault downward?

She had time to decide, but either way, Clifford Lelberger would die tonight.

106

UNSANCTIONED

Off the Coast of Caracas, Venezuela

Axe hit the water hard. His entire being screamed in agony, but he welcomed the feeling of the ocean's embrace.

As he plunged into the depths, his rattled mind, overcome with pain, was reminded of... something.

The dark water... I've been here before.

A part of him knew he would eventually have to breathe. The rest didn't really care. For the moment, he was safe. Free.

Then it hit him.

Kelton. Mexico.

In the lake by the blown-up hotel, a drugged, enraged Kelton had tried to kill him.

The memory faded again, along with his consciousness. He felt so light in the water. Like he was home. But a thought intruded, keeping him awake.

Kelton has been part of this since the beginning.

Axe remembered his first mission for Admiral Nalen when he had nearly drowned off the coast of Long Island while struggling to get to Kelton's superyacht.

Kelton...

Axe kept sinking. His entire body was on fire with pain, but the effects of the blast on his brain were wearing off. So was his air supply. His head cleared at the same time his lungs demanded air.

Kelton is out there. Waiting to pick me up.

Axe hurt all over. His strength was long gone. Right before the explosion, he'd known it was over.

Somehow he'd survived the blast and the guards, but now, in the arms of the ocean, he couldn't muster the will to return from the earlier decision to accept his death.

Sorry, Kelton, I'm not going to make the rendezvous. You're on your own this time.

Mariana would keep him safe and out of trouble.

Haley and Mariana are the future. I'm the past.

And the future can't come until the past is gone.

But... he didn't want to die underwater. Better to see the stars as he went, then slip beneath the surface as the sea claimed him.

Axe feebly kicked for the surface, regretting it instantly. His legs were in agony.

He pulled with his arms instead, but they hurt too.

Shrapnel. The big guy took most of it, but I must have gotten my share.

Maybe this was how he died after all.

Yes. In the deep.

No. He wanted to see the stars.

He focused on getting to the surface. His body's frantic demand for air overrode his willingness to slip away peacefully. He swam upward despite himself, ignoring the pain, the buoyancy of the wetsuit helping.

Each second felt like an hour. His mind was at war with itself. One side demanded he get to the surface and breathe. It didn't care about the big picture—living—only about the precious air his body needed.

The other part begged to let go, to finally find peace.

His head broke the surface, and he sucked in air over and over like he would never get another chance to breathe again.

The oxygen revitalized him, which was both good and bad.

He was badly injured. Bleeding. His brain scrambled. Exhausted—not in the sense an average person is, where they believe they can't go on. In training and after years of combat operations, he'd discovered how much farther the body can go when it is tired and supposedly at its limit. With the right mindset, there is so much more in the tank.

But he was way past that bullshit "can't go on" point. He'd left it on the helipad. After all these years, all the missions, ambushes, and close calls, he had finally reached his body's true limit.

Feebly treading water, with his gear weighing him down, the current carried him from the brightly lit oil platform in the distance. No one shot at him though he could hear guards yelling on the platform, looking for him in the maze of places to hide. A few would guess he'd gone into the water, but he was hard to see. And the platform didn't have any boats to chase him—unless they wanted to launch a life raft, which wasn't likely. For the moment, unless someone got lucky and spotted him before he drifted too far away to shoot, he was safe.

It was time to realistically consider his options.

He couldn't make it back to the platform—not that it would provide any safety if he could.

He had no fins or propulsion device.

His body and mind were in trouble. He hurt everywhere and it was all he could do to stay focused on his options.

Land was much too far away. Assuming he went with the current, he still wouldn't near shore until long after he lost the meager scrap of strength keeping him on the surface.

The rendezvous point for Kelton was miles—and hours—away.

Too far in all directions, and no way to—

Wait. The comm unit. He'd studied it on the flight to Curaçao, figuring out how to turn the silent mode on—and the tracking feature off. The last thing he needed was proof he'd been on an unsanctioned operation in a foreign country. But now he was in the open water, farther from the oil platform every minute. There was such a slight chance of discovery anyway, and now he could claim he'd fallen off the yacht at night and needed to be rescued.

The hope provided a surge of adrenaline. He unslung the dry bag from his back, then stopped.

Is saving my life worth the risk of exposure?

On one hand, the operators of the oil platform had tried to fire cruise missiles with what might have been nuclear, biological, or chemical warheads.

And I took them out.

He'd left a trail of bodies. Obviously, someone like him had been there. Was it so hard to guess who, in general, it was? And wasn't attempting to launch cruise missiles justification for his actions, anyway?

Who cared if a clever intel nerd somewhere discovered a yacht had swooped in and rescued him?

Still, he hesitated. The remaining guards on the oil platform would report the attack. A quick reaction force of either helicopters or ships would be on the way to search for more threats... and capture the people behind the assault.

Isn't this why Nalen and the president created our program? To be able to write off an unsanctioned operator instead of being discovered?

Axe wasn't thinking as clearly as he normally would. His mind bounced back and forth between the choices.

Was he far enough away to call for help?

He had to be realistic. He was in very bad shape physically and mentally.

I'm probably going to die in a few minutes, anyway.

He couldn't put Kelton, Mariana, and the entire clandestine organization at risk.

The dry bag with the comm unit went onto his back, unopened.

107

ADDRESS

The House of Representatives Chamber
The United States Capitol
Washington, DC

"Madam Speaker, Mr. Vice President, members of Congress and the Cabinet, Justices of the Supreme Court, and my fellow Americans," President of the United States of America James Heringten began. He had the entire speech memorized—the teleprompters would serve only as a backup in case he ad-libbed or got lost for a second over the next hour.

Standing at the podium in the grand chamber, he surveyed the assembled lawmakers and leaders of the country. There were no boycotts, no rumors of planned bad behavior from any of them. He had his detractors, and many would surely find ways to clobber him when interviewed by the media after his speech. But he worked hard to build and maintain relationships that were good with many, and still professional and civil with the few who disliked him.

Tonight's address would be at times inspiring, at times a frank and honest assessment of the true state of the union. It was largely uncontroversial. America is an amazing country that does most—but not everything—right. There was always room for improvement. Both sides generally agreed on the outcomes they wanted—peace, prosperity, freedom, and the pursuit of happiness by all citizens—but differed in how to achieve those aims.

James would touch on immigration, the economy, taxes, and the country's enemies, who were always waiting for an opportunity to gain the upper hand, pull ahead, or cause harm.

The speech would be a big-picture overview, acknowledging that the country and its people were doing pretty damn well under his watch, despite the recent terrorist attacks over the previous year.

If they knew how much worse those events could have been without Haley and the others at the CAG...

Plus the schemes which went nowhere, prevented by the defenses of the CIA, NSA, FBI, and other three-letter groups, along with local law enforcement across the country.

James faltered for an instant, thinking of Gregory's warning about the possibility of an attack during his speech.

Am I doing the right thing?

He hoped so. He'd made the best decision he could, which was the president's job, after all.

Senator Barbara Woodran had excused herself and left the building thirty minutes ago, he'd been informed.

The entire area was ringed by brave men and women who dedicated their lives to protecting this room tonight. Billions of dollars in military hardware guarded the building.

The Secretary of Agriculture watched the speech from the comfort and safety of his daughter's house in suburban Maryland.

And America couldn't allow suspected danger to stand in the way of its normal business.

James smiled, cleared his throat, and continued. He spoke the words of the first minute as planned, nailing the presidential tone. He had a sixty-minute speech planned and rehearsed, culminating in the one big idea of the night—his change in the war on drugs.

By design, that was the only topic juicy enough for his allies and enemies in the room to sink their teeth into. It's what everyone would be talking about in an hour.

Assuming we're all still alive.

108

FEELINGS

Prince George's County, Maryland
Southeast of Washington, DC

William followed behind Haley's SUV, struggling to keep up. They were in a hurry, sure, but the woman drove like a maniac.

As he weaved around the other cars on the road, he couldn't shake the feeling they were missing something.

It nagged at him for miles until he decided to listen to his intuition. He called Haley first.

"Blondie, I'm breaking away at the next exit. You're on your own. Be safe."

"Wait—where are you going?"

"There's a portable missile battery temporarily set up at Fort Washington Park. I have to check it out."

He waited for her argument or questions, but they didn't come. Probably because they were driving down the highway at over one hundred miles per hour and she had most of her concentration on the road.

"Be safe, Hammer," she said after a few seconds.

"You too. And happy hunting."

Next, he called Gregory. He would contact the right people and calm any ruffled feathers about a retired Navy admiral wanting to drop in for a snap inspection of an Army missile defense battery.

109

CONTINGENCIES II

The House of Representatives Chamber
The United States Capitol
Washington, DC

James paused after the first strong line of the State of the Union speech. The bipartisan applause gave him several seconds to consider the sensation he tried to ignore but couldn't shake.

The back of his neck tingled, a feeling he hadn't had in decades. The last time had been seconds before a sniper shot at him. When he felt the sensation, he'd ducked. A bullet had passed through the space occupied by his head an instant earlier.

He nodded as the applause slowed to a spatter.

I'm being targeted.

He had to glance at the teleprompter to find his place in the speech. As he resumed speaking, regaining his momentum, he looked around the chamber. Secret Service agents in suits stood discretely all around. At the back of the room near a door, he saw Chad—also a former SEAL—standing with his hands at his side. They had several pre-arranged signals planned for the evening. As long as Chad stood looking relaxed, all was well.

But James couldn't shake the feeling.

Always follow your instincts.

The saying sounded great, but could he really do it on the world stage with the eyes of millions on him?

If not now, when?

If he were targeting the speech, he'd plan the attack for either the first five minutes or the approximate middle of it—and likely the latter. One of the contingencies he had considered was cutting the speech short.

Chad liked it from a tactical standpoint but hated the idea from a political perspective. Now, with Haley's gut telling her something may be about to happen, along with his feeling of being in the crosshairs, it was time for bold action.

He paused again, shook his head with what he hoped was a disarming grin, and held up the printed pages of his speech on the podium in front of him, backup in case he both forgot the speech and the teleprompters broke.

"Ladies and gentlemen, I have this whole speech for you. But I'm tossing it aside. The press have a copy of it, and you're welcome to read it. Instead, I'm going to speak to you unprepared about what truly matters to me and, I believe, to every citizen of the country. I'll keep it short and sweet. So—straight up, let's talk."

110

HIDE

Cyra played the role of the dutiful jogger, keeping her eyes on the road in front of her as the black SUV rolled by.

That's an enemy.

There were few vehicles on the streets at this hour. People were mostly home from work and other activities by now. And the truck went a little too fast until it saw her. Then it slowed by a fraction as it passed.

This complicates matters.

Cyra wanted to use the stealth approach. Picking off the Secret Service agents one by one would be the safer play—and more fun for her. She liked using the knife. The pistol, even with the attached silencer, would alert the rest of the guards immediately. They would go into full lockdown, blockade the target in a closet or a small basement room, and she'd have to fight through a hail of gunfire to get him.

Or she could wait and set an ambush, killing them all when they eventually moved him to a safer location.

By which time there will be more people.

It had to be stealth. She'd made good time on the run. If the SUV contained backup guards, they would form a perimeter, and some might go into the house. That would be her chance.

An improvised plan formed that would only work if one of the arriving backup forces searched the exterior—or she gave away her position and allowed him to find her.

Slowing as she ran past the target house, she dropped to the ground at the row of trees where the target's yard ended and their neighbor's lawn began. It was such an obvious hiding place, she hesitated for a moment, but her instincts said her plan was sound. She needed a way to get into the house without getting shot. The best way was to use whatever warm body showed up as backup, either by claiming their identity or using them as a human shield.

She crawled until she found a perfect hiding place... then moved to a mediocre spot for the average person, but one she could make work.

If they're good, they will inspect the first location—then I will knife them in the back and proceed.

She had no worries. The mission had only been made easier by the addition of the new guards, not harder.

111

HUNT

Haley had planned to drive past the high school, park on a side street in front of a house, then slip a sweatshirt over her armor and go for a slow jog. Nancy had reconned the area via satellite maps and together they had worked out the best sniper spots in the area. The high school was the most obvious location. It would have been checked by the Secret Service. But given the one-off nature of the evening's protection and the extreme difficulty of a sniper shot through a window from that location, she bet there wouldn't be an agent stationed there.

And if there is, one agent against a trained killer might not be enough.

The plan changed as soon as she drove past the woman in the stocking cap jogging down the street a few blocks from the Secretary of Agriculture's daughter's house. Haley could sense the woman's faked nonchalance.

That's her—or at least, one of them.

Haley kept her eyes on the road and didn't give any indication of her suspicion.

This would be a lot better with Nalen or Axe along—or even Mad Dog.

She could slow and one of them would jump out to track the first terrorist while she backed them up or hunted for others.

This is what Axe must feel like working alone instead of with a whole team.

When she gone further, Haley shut off the lights, pulled to the curb, and parked.

The Secret Service will have Secretary Lelberger in a safe spot by now —a basement, if one's available.

Another body might be helpful to them, but she could do more good outside the house. In a moment, she'd have to decide whether she would search for the jogger—and any other tangos in the area—or find a good spot to observe the house and provide an early warning for the agents inside. But first, she had a call to make.

"It's me," she said to Nancy. "Possible ID of an enemy in the area. She was pretending to be a jogger, running straight down the road toward the house, but she looked... off."

"Are you sure?" Nancy asked.

Am I?

"No, but it feels right. Alert the Secret Service and get more people over here. Local police, whoever. Call it a possible threat, but this isn't a hypothetical anymore." She hung up and let Nancy get to work.

Backup would take some time to arrive but would come in force when it did.

What was the best use of her skills?

Park the SUV in front of the house and stand behind it with the M4 up and ready?

Get on the roof of the truck and watch the house from here?

'Opportunities multiply as they are seized.'

A Sun Tzu quote. One of Axe's favorites.

For a second, she felt guilty. She hadn't worried about Axe in hours.

I'm sure he's fine. He's hardcore and can take care of himself.

Ensuring the dome light wouldn't come on when she opened the door, she grabbed the M4 from the seat next to her, slid out of the car, and started toward the house at a brisk trot.

Time to hunt.

112

NASAMS

Fort Washington Park
Fort Washington, Maryland

William pulled slowly into the parking lot across from the Fort Washington Visitor Center. The National Advanced Surface-to-Air Missile System unit's commander would have received word by now of his arrival, and he'd already been vetted at a security checkpoint near the entrance to the park. But the president's speech was starting, the whole military was on high alert, and the last thing the men and women in charge of this mobile missile battery needed was some retired admiral coming to annoy them.

What the hell am I doing here?

Shouldn't he be with Blondie as she continued her hunt for the terrorists and protect the Secretary of Agriculture, only a few miles away?

Two people hunting?

It wouldn't work. He might be more skilled than Blondie in some ways, but his active days were mostly behind him. Haley was more than forty years younger and had more recent field experience than he did. She would handle the hunt.

Besides, twenty minutes ago, when the Secret Service changed their profile, hardening their defenses even more, the terrorists would have noticed. Their mission would go from a long-range shot with the rifle to either a full-on attack or an abort.

The Secret Service could handle an attack. Haley would be on the perimeter helping out, giving an early warning, or eliminating the threat before it reached them. He didn't need to be there.

But as he shut off the car and turned on the overhead light, waiting for permission from the armed soldier standing nearby to exit the car, his intuition continued to scream at him. He was needed here—for whatever reason.

Always follow your gut.

"Get out of the vehicle slowly, sir," the voice called.

He moved at half speed, opening the door and getting out of the car. A flashlight shone in his face, then lowered. "Welcome, Admiral Nalen. How can we help you tonight?" the man said, looking impossibly young to guard anything, let alone a multi-million-dollar system protecting the nation's capital on one of the most important nights of the year.

"I'd love my weapon if you don't mind. It's on the seat."

The soldier didn't like it, but he nodded his permission. William grabbed the M4 and closed the door.

How honest should I be with this kid?

"Son," he began, "I'm going to lay it on the line for you. I don't know why I'm here, but my intuition told me to come." He paused. "Have you seen combat, soldier?"

"Yes, sir," he said, but added nothing more.

"You ever have a feeling over there? A hunch?"

"Yes, sir. About thirty seconds before we got hit, I knew it was coming. Always trust your gut, sir."

He gets it.

"Absolutely. So give me a quick tour."

"Lots of tree line," Admiral Nalen noted, looking at the dark woods surrounding them.

The NASAMS launcher next to them on the slight hill—the National Advanced Surface to Air Missile System—was the typical dark camo green. It consisted of a flat base unit anchored low to the ground with four thick legs that could level the platform and adjust it up or down.

Six missile tubes sat on the base, pointed skyward, each more than twelve feet long.

The park also contained, for the evening, a second launcher with six more missiles, radars, a fire control center, and several other support vehicles.

"If you were deployed in or near a combat zone, how many guards would you have out compared to what you have tonight?" he asked his tour guide, who had lightened up slightly as they quickly toured the area.

"A lot more than we have now, sir. We're in Maryland. Sir."

He couldn't fault the man's logic. They were in the United States, not an active combat zone.

But if the terrorists that Axe eliminated had friends, this site and the others like it are sitting ducks.

But how many locations were there? Could so many tangos have infiltrated the country, either over the Mexico border like the ones a few nights before or legally, on tourist visas?

What would they use for weapons?

Access to weapons wasn't difficult in America, but getting quality, high-powered rifles quickly wouldn't be a walk in the park. It would take planning, money, and time.

Entirely possible if our enemy is Russia, Iran, and or Venezuela.

But for so many sites to be attacked at the same time? The precision would be demanding. That many men would have come to someone's attention.

"How would you take out this site if you were ordered to?" he asked the young man. "Where are its vulnerabilities?"

The kid thought about it for a second. "RPGs from the tree line, sir. Directed at the launchers. Without them, all this other equipment is pointless."

William agreed.

"What if you didn't have RPGs? If you had to stealth it? Would a hand grenade put it out of commission?"

The man shook his head doubtfully. "Maybe, but this thing is pretty sturdy. It has to contain the missile launch. No," he said, "it would take C-4 to be sure."

C-4? Oh hell.

William pulled a small flashlight from his cargo pants pocket as he turned to the young soldier. "Take the other side. Get down on the ground and look for an explosive charge."

"Sir?"

He thinks I've lost my mind.

"You heard me!" he said, the command voice coming naturally.

Instantly, the man obeyed, pulling his own flashlight and dropping to the frozen ground.

A second later, he spoke. "Oh, shit. Um, Admiral? I found something."

"Get me your CO on the radio this instant," William said calmly to the young soldier as he lay on the ground next to him, watching the timer on the block of C-4.

He pulled out his cell phone and speed-dialed Gregory, fearing the worst but knowing he had to try to get the alert out in every way possible.

There won't be enough time to stop them all.

113

SPEECH

The House of Representatives Chamber
The United States Capitol
Washington, DC

James looked at the audience of jaded lawmakers, judges, friends, family, and guests. A few wiped tears from their eyes at his heartfelt words about the country.

Time to wrap it up.

He'd spoken for fourteen minutes instead of the sixty he'd planned.

James glanced at Chad to see his reaction. The poor guy was probably having a heart attack at the President of the United States of America speaking so plainly and honestly.

Chad scratched the back of his neck—the signal for an increased concern of an attack, but still without solid evidence or intel.

"So that, my fellow Americans, is less the State of the Union and more how I and, I hope, you feel about this great country. Let us stand together, whether we agree on every nuance or not. We are, after all, united states. Right there, it says we have our differences, but we come together in a union. Let us disagree when necessary but commit to sticking together and resolving those differences to continue to preserve and protect this remarkable country. May God bless and guide us all, and the United States of America."

The entire audience stood and applauded, though a few were slower to their feet than others.

I can't cut this part short—can I?

114

C-4

Jafar's time was running out and the damn soldier wouldn't leave. The guard stamped his feet in the cold and hummed songs at the rear of the vehicle, right next to where Jafar hid underneath it.

Despite being only a few feet from his head, Jafar couldn't see the countdown timer's numbers in the dark. But he knew there wasn't much time left.

He faced a dilemma—start crawling away slowly, using the cover of the truck to avoid the eyes of the soldiers for several yards, then get up and run?

They won't shoot me in the back. Not in the middle of Washington during peacetime.

But would seeing him put the mission at risk?

Not with so little time left.

Was it breaking the second mission parameter—to not get caught?

His superiors had told him not to be captured or killed but hadn't mentioned being seen.

In a few minutes, when the charges I set blow up missile launchers all around the area, they'll know anyway.

He slowly moved his body, turning back toward the street and bridge over the Potomac. He'd make a run for it, get back to Cyra in time to pick her up after she completed her mission, and together they would drive to Miami where they would be extracted by boat.

The truck door opened, and a voice yelled out. "Search the underside of the launcher!"

Out of time.

He looked over his shoulder and met the surprised eyes of a young American soldier.

"Hey!" the man yelled.

They'll shoot me if I run, and I can no longer sneak away.

Jafar drew his pistol, but laying on the ground made him slower than usual. The man moved behind the rear tire before he could get off a shot.

"There's a guy under the launcher!" the American yelled.

Jafar swung his aim to the front. The guard who had been sitting in the warm truck dropped to the ground to see and got two bullets to the chest before he moved to cover behind a tire.

All I have to do is kill them all.

He felt bullets rip into his side from the first guard's weapon.

Rolling to avoid the next burst, he fired back, forcing the man to hide behind the large wheel again. H rolled from under the vehicle and stopped when he had an angle on the guard who had shot him.

Jafar fired twice, barely aiming. The man's gasp told him at least one of his bullets hit home.

Bullets kicked up dirt near his head. He was under fire from further away—he didn't see from where. He log rolled again, back underneath the vehicle to temporary safety, letting out an involuntary gasp of pain every time his side came in contact with the ground.

He was injured. Running away was no longer an option.

The other guard fired at him again, missing by a few inches.

Jafar shot back but didn't think he connected.

More guards will be coming. In a few seconds, their fire will be more accurate, and I'll be dead.

He instinctively knew what he had to do.

With fading strength, he dropped his pistol and reached for the timer. In the dark, he felt for the minute and second buttons. Smiling at the memory of his short but very enjoyable time with Cyra, he held both down at the same time and detonated the C-4.

115

LAUNCH

"We found explosives on the other launcher!" Nalen heard over the soldier's radio.

"First, tell him to calm down," Nalen said.

William pulled the blasting cap and timer from his hunk of C-4 and used his knife to cut the wires between them. The soldier with him spoke on the radio to his brother-in-arms on the other side of the park.

There's no way I'm explaining how to disarm it over the radio.

It would have been simpler to tell them to yank out the blasting cap, but over the radio with unknown troops, best to be safe. "Check the timer —make sure there's enough time. Then run it toward the woods. Toss it, come back, and take cover."

There was no need to take cover, but they'd do it anyway, so why not let them feel like they were following orders?

He and the soldier had found only one block of C-4 at their launcher, and the word had gone out to all the defenses in the area to immediately check radars, missile launchers, command vehicles, and ammo storage— anything necessary for the successful protection of Washington, D.C.

Sixty seconds later, the C-4 on the far side of the park exploded with a loud thud.

Did we catch this in time?

"Admiral Nalen," an officer's commanding voice called over the radio. "We're getting reports from other units. Some found explosives and disarmed them. But others... we've lost some missile launchers, sir."

The man stopped talking but left his mic open, allowing Nalen to hear the calls in the background of the command truck. "Incoming missiles. This is not a drill. Engage targets."

"Clear the launchers! Move, move, move!" the officer yelled into the radio.

Nalen and the soldier ran from the back of the missile launcher where they'd been standing. Seconds later, missile after missile launched with a trail of fire and smoke.

Nalen watched the sky and prayed they took out whatever was coming toward the city.

He ran toward the command vehicle. There was probably nothing he could do, but he needed an overview of the situation.

If any missiles get through, there's going to be chaos.

He needed to be ready to lend a hand in whatever capacity he could, whether as a former admiral or a member of the semi-clandestine World Intelligence Agency.

As he sprinted, he thought about Haley.

Damn, she was right again.

And if she was right about the missiles, Gregory was likely correct in predicting the Secretary of Agriculture was under attack a few miles away.

Be careful hunting, Blondie.

116

KNIVES

Fort Washington Estates
Fort Washington, Maryland

Haley slowed, crouching behind a car parked in the driveway of a neighbor's house, preparing herself. In front of her, at the T intersection, was the dark home of Secretary Lelberger's daughter.

I can do this. I've trained for it.

But training, no matter how intense, could never match the real world. One on one, she was at a tremendous disadvantage against a professional.

I'm good, but not world-class.

Could she apply her analytical abilities to this situation?

She considered where Axe would go if he had to assault the house on his own. And what he would do if an enemy were trying to stop him.

He'd set a trap and wait for them to walk into it.

But didn't she have the upper hand? The terrorist would be on a deadline of some sort, needing to kill Lelberger before or soon after the president's death.

Too early and it gives someone a chance to get another cabinet member out of the Capitol.

Too late—after the cruise missile strike—and a swarm of Secret Service agents and police would descend on the area to protect the new president.

All I have to do is wait. More agents will be here, either from my warning call to Nancy or from the missiles hitting home.

But even as she thought it, she realized it wouldn't be her plan. There could be more than one assassin, but her gut told her that with one sniper rifle missing, there would be one shooter. There were likely others doing something with the backpack of explosives—if that's what it was.

I can't hang back and wait—I have to do everything I can. Right now.

She would do exactly what Axe would: seize the moment.

After thinking a second, she did the only thing she could. She started toward the house, using herself as bait to draw out the terrorist.

She has to get into the house unless she has enough C-4 to blow it.

Even then, the enemy would want to be sure.

She's close.

There were several likely hiding places to prepare for assaulting the house, from the tree near the garage, a long row of trees to the east, which was the property line between houses, bushes in the backyard, and the woods behind it.

Could she be on the roof by now, ready to shoot me?

Haley spun and pointed the M4 upward but saw no one.

I'm too jumpy.

Breathing in for a count of four, holding, then exhaling, she focused her mind as she moved closer to the yard.

Hugging the tree line on the eastern edge of the lot, she edged forward, short barrel M4 up and ready.

Slow is smooth and smooth is fast.

Her senses were on high alert.

She was one with the night.

All her focus was on the search.

Haley hunted.

Cyra waited patiently, her side pressed to a thick tree. She had no tension, worries, or fears—no emotions a trained hunter could sense.

The man moved toward her, trying to be quiet but not succeeding.

He has training but not experience.

Merely a gifted amateur.

This will be fun.

Cyra hid behind the tree, easily tracking the man's progress toward her from the noises made. Her opponent had a grasp of the basics but lacked mastery.

Under other circumstances, Cyra would have waited him out. The man would pass her by without noticing. She was certain of that. Men and women better than this American had hunted her and failed.

But the window of opportunity to complete her mission was rapidly closing. And the man—or rather, his lifeless body—would be useful to gain entry into the house. He had to be dealt with.

But I can have a few seconds of fun first.

Haley was out of her depth and had second thoughts about her decision, but she pushed ahead.

While the patch of trees to her left would make an excellent hiding place, she knew Axe and the men of his former Team would often skip the best location for an ambush, sniper shot, or place to hole up. Their enemies could also read maps, note terrain, and see the advantages of specific locations. That's when the mental game began, and she wasn't sure how to play.

Is she in there, behind those trees? Closer to the backyard?

Or on the other side of the house, setting a charge to blow a hole in the wall and assault her way in?

One foot in front of the other. Stick with the plan.

Though at the moment, the plan of being the sacrificial lamb, drawing out the predator, then relying on her senses, speed, and training to survive didn't feel as smart as it had moments before.

Cyra left her spot and moved through the thin woods like a shadow. Her hunter had passed the best hiding place, his faltering steps showing he had recognized it for what it was. He would likely note the second-best location ahead in a moment.

The risk of exposure was small, given Cyra's vast experience. She made no noise, emitted little emotional vibe—though she had to consciously tamp down the thrill of the hunt and reclaim the cold, emotionless focus necessary to successfully sneak up behind the man without being sensed.

Haley didn't pause despite the warning signs from her senses. She kept her feelings locked down and completed the next slow step forward.

She's here!

But where? Ahead on the left at the second-best place to hide? Behind her, ready to attack? Aiming a silenced weapon from the roof or back yard?

She won't risk the noise of a gunshot, even a silenced one.

Without giving away her awareness of the enemy, Haley made her decision.

One more step, then I spin and start firing.

Cyra lunged forward as her enemy lifted a foot for what would be his last living step. Avoiding the armor plate the man wore, she slammed the knife blade into his back to the hilt. The lung would be pierced, the aorta cut, and the man dead within eight seconds. It was a slower death than the more standard method of slicing the throat from behind but could be accomplished from slightly further away. She'd used it successfully many times in her career against larger, stronger opponents.

Whether she'd heard or felt movement, Haley didn't finish her step forward. Instead, she wrenched her body, swinging around a half second earlier than planned.

She felt the woman's sharp punch to her back, near her scapula, just outside the protection offered by the ceramic armor in her plate carrier. It took her breath away and she stumbled, struggling to get the rifle around to shoot at the ghost that had materialized behind her.

Her foot caught on something, and she fell on her right side. Before she found anything to shoot at, the rifle was kicked from her hands. Then the terrorist fell on her. Haley's head rocked back, stunned by the pain and force of a blow.

Cyra delivered the strike to the enemy's head with expert precision, then hesitated. Her opponent was a woman.

She is beautiful.

Cyra's training kicked back in. The sex of her enemy didn't matter. But the combat knife was lodged in the woman's back, ripped from her hand by the woman's sudden turn before she could twist the blade and ensure the aorta was cut.

Smiling, she accepted the gift of the long knife hanging from the American's plate carrier.

"Thank you," she said in her own language as she slid it from its sheath and stabbed the woman in the stomach, again avoiding the armored plate, angling for the heart.

Whether by instinct or training, Haley had pulled her legs back when the blow to the head rocked her. She hadn't regained her senses completely but felt both the knife to her stomach and saw the woman crouching over her. She lashed out with her heel, driving it as hard and fast as she could into the only opening she saw—the woman's groin.

Cyra fell back out of range of a second kick, doubled over. She ignored most of the pain to her privates but couldn't hold back a moment of rage. Of course, the below-the-belt blow was legal—this was a fight to the death. There were no rules. But in all her sparring and combat, no one had ever kicked her down there.

As the enemy scrambled frantically backward on the ground, they locked eyes. Cyra made a decision. She could spare thirty more seconds to make the woman regret that kick.

The fight had only lasted a few seconds, and Haley was in trouble.

I'm outclassed.

But her reflexive kick had an effect. She sensed the change in the woman.

She's angry.

Getting emotional in a fight was bad news. Axe had drilled that into her head over and over as she sparred at the dojo the last several months.

I have a tiny edge.

Now, how could she capitalize on it?

"Please," she cried, her butt scraping the ground as she pushed herself backward with her heels and pulled with her arms behind her. "I'm sorry. Don't kill me!"

Cyra smiled again. She liked it when they begged. And while her English wasn't the best, she could get her point across.

"Kill you slower now. So pretty," she said in English, getting a better look at the woman in the glow from a distant streetlight. She wasn't just beautiful—she was stunning. Blond hair coming loose from a ponytail. An incredible figure the clothing and gear couldn't completely hide. Even in the dim light, the full lips, perfect nose, jawline, and chin were all incredible. She could be a supermodel.

"Your face," she said, still smiling. She knew the effect her smile had on people, both friends and foes. Some had called it inhuman. "Too bad." She held up the enemy's knife, pointed it at her cheek, and launched herself forward.

Haley cowered in fear, shaking her head urgently, eyes wide, playing her role to perfection.

The woman's speed surprised her, and while she was convinced the threat of cutting her face was a feint, it didn't matter. The enemy came for her, bloody combat knife in hand, the pompom on top of her stocking cap bouncing.

Haley drew the backup knife from its sheath behind her back and did the unexpected. She lunged forward, closing the distance between them as she stabbed upward with her second knife.

The American moved suddenly toward her, surprisingly quickly, no longer backing away in fear. Cyra adjusted the thrust of the knife, already transitioning from the fake face slash to another upward thrust through the stomach and into the heart. But her enemy changed the angle of her body too quickly. The knife slammed harmlessly into the woman's plate carrier and armor with a thud.

At the same moment, Cyra felt the sharp pain in her stomach. It took only an instant for her mind to fight through the surprise to tell her she'd been stabbed. But in that time, the knife traveled upward, missing the rib cage, and pierced her heart.

The assassin's eyes widened and her face grimaced in a mixture of rage, shock, and horror. Haley pushed the knife farther into the woman and twisted. The terrorist collapsed onto her, dying.

Haley fell onto her back and screamed. Her left shoulder blade area was in agony from the punch or whatever the woman had done back there.

Using the last of her strength, she shoved the dead woman off her.

Her phone was in her cargo pants pocket, but she suddenly had no energy. She could only lay on her side to avoid the pain in her back. But she was in less agony by the second as she went into shock. She felt a sense of peace as she looked up at the stars.

It's a beautiful night to die.

Twenty-one years didn't seem like enough time to have lived. But while it might be the end, she at least had gotten into the field and stopped the assassin.

She felt blood oozing out of her and drifted away.

117

CONTINGENCIES III

The House of Representatives Chamber
The United States Capitol
Washington, DC

James nodded and smiled as the applause slowed. Members of the other party stopped clapping. A few scrambled for the exits to be interviewed on TV.

No matter how much they agree with what I said, they'll find a way to stick it to me.

James scratched his right ear with one finger, giving Chad a sign to get the Secret Service to quietly clear the room.

He shook hands with the vice president, speaker of the house, and others. As planned, an aide came forward to hand him a slip of paper—blank—and whispered nonsense in his ear, giving him an excuse to finish his meet and greet earlier than was standard and exit the room.

The plan was for people to be told there was a security drill. Some would be whisked away. Others would be directed to secure areas below the building. If there was no threat, no one would lose face, and the country's enemies wouldn't be able to gloat about bluffing the country into running scared. But if an attack was imminent, the leadership of the United States of America would be saved.

Contingencies.

118

INBOUND

"We just detected cruise missiles inbound, Admiral," the officer said as Nalen burst through the door of the small command vehicle. A soldier sat at each of the two radar stations.

"How many?"

"Looks like ten, sir."

"Will we get them all?" Nalen asked.

The officer hesitated. "Probably."

Nalen turned to him.

"Your warning saved some launchers, Admiral, but we lost at least five of them. To destroy each cruise missile, we have to launch a bunch of ours —just to be sure. We should have plenty of missiles in the—"

"Sir," the young woman at the left station interrupted. "Four more missiles coming in on a different vector."

"A second wave?" Nalen asked.

No one answered him.

"Shit," the technician muttered.

"What is it, Stallmer?" the officer asked her.

"The second wave is coming in on the sector that lost the most launchers, sir."

119

CURSED

Villanueva raged. The china serving tray a snack had been on lay smashed to pieces next to his desk where he had flung it. The papers on his table were strewn around the room, and his heavy desk was tipped forward.

"Get out!" he yelled at the guards who rushed in to investigate the commotion.

With a moment's hesitation as they took in the scene, they retreated and closed the door behind them.

The President of the United States, going against tradition, had spoken for only fifteen minutes.

Villanueva checked his watch. The missiles were due to slam into the building soon—but Heringten wouldn't be there.

This whole operation has been cursed from the start.

The eight men sent to America—supposedly Iran's best special forces warriors—had vanished. No pipelines had blown up.

The liquid natural gas tanker hadn't exploded either, and the terminal was still functional. It was as if that team had disappeared as well.

Had the other Iranian commandos sent to Washington, D.C. done their jobs?

It doesn't matter.

Whether the radars and missile launchers were destroyed or not made little difference if the intended target wasn't there to die as planned.

And who cared about the designated survivor if the rest of the government was still alive?

Villanueva stood in front of the TV, seething at the images of President Heringten leaving the chamber where he'd given his brief address.

With superhuman effort, he turned his thoughts to what might happen next.

If the Americans discover it was me behind this...

He had to get more chemical and biological weapons immediately, whether from Iran or his scientists. And secure more cruise missiles from Russia, Iran, or buy them on the arms market.

The only way to protect the country was with weapons of mass destruction.

He had a rare moment of self-doubt.

Did I make the right choice?

Villanueva had decided not to travel the long road of negotiations with the United States of America and other countries of the world. The idea of begging and changing how he ran his country to appease others, just so they would ease their disgusting sanctions, filled him with white-hot anger.

Choosing to stick with the smaller, meaner dogs—Russia and Iran— made the most sense. Their three countries acting together were a formidable foe.

He'd jumped at the chance to destroy America and get his revenge on President Heringten, following Orlov's plan to the letter. It had seemed perfect. The small units would slip through the gaps in America's security. The early distractions of the pipelines, LNG ship, and natural gas terminal blowing up would keep all eyes on the west, not Washington, D.C.

This is all Orlov's fault. He's to blame, not me.

What would happen now?

How long before Orlov and the zealots in Iran turn on me?

If the missiles didn't do their job, the United States of America wouldn't rest until he was dead. If it took ruining his whole country to do it, they would.

President Heringten would be proven right; Venezuela could do better.

Never.

But first, either his allies had to give him up—implicating themselves —or his enemy had to connect the hard-to-find dots leading to him. No, he was safe.

He would start again and plan another attack—without Orlov this time. *I am not afraid. I will have my revenge.*

120

STARS

Off the Coast of Caracas, Venezuela

As he moved as little as possible to keep his head above water, Axe's frustration level grew. He was ready to die. With his injuries, he had little chance of surviving the night. And it made sense to not put the organization, Kelton, and Mariana at risk and request a rescue.

But his mind refused to allow him to let go. One of the first SEAL sayings that resonated with him, straight from BUD/S training, kept crashing into his mind.

'Never, ever ring the bell!'

To quit the training, recruits had to physically ring a large brass bell that was always placed conveniently nearby. The SEALs wanted only the strongest, most physically fit candidates to continue the training. Since the body was weaker than the mind and would lie to protect itself from overexertion and damage, mental strength was the real key. The SEALs valued it even more than physical strength.

From day one, the instructors yelled at the candidates, begging, cajoling, and demanding that faltering men give up and ring the bell.

They offered hot coffee, fresh donuts, and a warm ride in the truck for any quitters.

Axe was one of the few who toughed it out.

And now, thanks to those instructors who had worked tirelessly to kill him—at least, that's how it had seemed at the time—he couldn't allow himself to surrender his life.

The wetsuit made him naturally buoyant. He barely had to work at staying afloat. But he'd kept the M4 slung across his body, the pistol at his waist, and the lightweight armor, along with all his remaining ammo. It would eventually help his body sink and not be recovered.

But as he continued to not die despite himself, he had to reassess the situation.

If I might survive, I should put in the effort to live.

He unslung the M4 and let it sink.

The dry bag came off and bobbed gently next to him as he carefully removed the plate carrier and let it join the M4 descending to the ocean floor.

The pistol and knife don't weigh much… and you never know.

They stayed.

He was about to slip the dry bag back on when he reassessed again. It was still hours from the rendezvous with Kelton at dawn, but the current was doing much of the work for him, albeit slower than he could swim.

Through the mental fog and pain, he realized he was falling back on another old saying drilled into him years before. "Under pressure, we don't rise to the level of our expectations, we sink to the level of our training."

In the BUD/S program, he had learned "drown-proofing." More mental strength had been instilled in him and the rest of the candidates as they practiced not drowning.

Now that he was lighter, he put the experience to use. With the gear sunk, he switched from expending a little energy to stay on the surface to easily floating on his back. The wetsuit helped immensely.

The stars were beautiful. He resolved to stay alive and enjoy them for at least the next few minutes.

I'll do this for a while, then see how things look. One minute at a time.

121

ONE

Fort Washington Park
Fort Washington, Maryland

At this point, there was nothing William could do except wait, watch the radar screens in the command vehicle with the soldiers, and pray. He'd done all he could. Finding the explosives and getting the word out about them had helped, but would it be enough?

Or would his best friend, the President of the United States, soon be lying under a pile of rubble while he choked on mustard gas, his lungs burning as he died in agony?

"Hell yes!" Stallmer, the technician at the radar console, yelled, followed immediately by, "Sorry, sirs. They got one."

Three left.

"A second one is down," she continued, excited but under control as she nodded at her screen. It showed two more blips moving rapidly.

"They got number three! One more. Come on, come on…"

Seconds ticked by.

"Well?" Nalen asked.

"It looks like one is getting through our screen, Admiral," the soldier said.

122

FOX-3

For Esmerelda "Ese" Lopez, being a drone pilot had been her dream since she was a little girl playing video games with her five brothers.

Tonight, in the darkened, climate-controlled trailer on the desert airbase, the screens arrayed in front of her didn't show the Middle Eastern desert. Instead, she circled high over Washington, D.C.—a welcome change that had come a few months before. She'd had her share of successes in the desert, racking up kills while protecting her troops on the ground. But as the missions wound down there, an opportunity had come up. Having seniority, a steady hand with the drone, and a good head on her shoulders, she'd been rewarded with the boring yet necessary job of combat air patrol for presidential travel.

Now, she helped protect the President of the United States, though she couldn't tell her friends, family, or even her little boy who didn't understand why mommy had to work strange hours some days.

Ese banked the Reaper hard, fighting to get on the right vector quickly enough to make a difference.

She was the only asset in the right place to take a shot at the last inbound cruise missile.

Never mind that the Sidewinder missiles on her drone had only been used to shoot down a cruise missile twice before while testing an upgrade to the system—and those two "missiles" had been target drones instead of the real thing.

Or that this actual cruise missile flew faster—and lower—than the drones in the successful tests.

"Almost there," Andrew "Woody" Kollchester, her aircrew responsible for guiding weapons and operating the drone's sensors, whispered. "You've got this."

Ese leveled out the drone. The targeting and vectoring would be handled by the missile working with the radar from the Airborne Warning and Control System—AWACS—plane orbiting the city.

"Fox-3," she called over the radio, then repeated it as she fired a second missile, praying they would get the job done.

123

DETACHMENT

"Come on, come on…" one of the soldiers at the radar console in the command vehicle mumbled.

William wasn't sure what the radar showed, but it didn't sound good.

"What's happening?" he asked. He'd never been afraid of looking stupid in front of the troops. Better to find out what he didn't know than try to fake it and put lives at risk.

"The cruise missile is coming in fast. In a few seconds, it will close in on the Capitol building, which is what the AWACS thinks it's aimed at."

"And it may be designed to go faster the closer it gets to its target," the officer next to him said in a low tone.

"A Reaper has launched two sidewinders…" Stallmer said, one hand pressed to the headphones covering her ears.

"It's going to be close, sirs," Stallmer added.

William tried to find the sense of professional detachment required by leaders. While every individual in his command had mattered to him, he couldn't think in terms of the risk each man faced. He had to look at the big picture.

But in the cramped command vehicle, smelling the fear sweat of the crew, the feelings threatened to spill out of the box he instinctively shoved them into during a mission.

Axe hadn't responded to comms for hours.

Haley was somewhere nearby, going up against an unknown number of terrorists trying to kill Secretary Lelberger, the designated survivor.

And there was still a missile headed toward the Capitol building with the entire government of the United States inside.

He stuffed his fears and concerns back down, steeling himself for the worst while hoping for the best as the seconds ticked by.

"They got it!" Stallmer said and high-fived the operator next to her. "The missile is down, sirs, but oh my God, it was close. I hope it's too cold for protests or exercise because there are probably pieces of missile scattered across the Washington Mall right now."

"Well done," he said to the soldiers in the vehicle, pausing for a moment to shake the hand of the officer before going out. Their night was done, but his wasn't.

First, Haley. Then we figure out who was behind this attack... and deal with them accordingly.

124

REPORTS

Foreign Intelligence Service Building
Moscow, Russia

Dmitry knocked on the door to Orlov's old, pathetic office and immediately let himself in.

Someday, when I'm in charge, the first thing I'll do is find a better office.

He'd been down the hall in the cramped room he shared with two other high-level aides, watching the international news carrying the live broadcast of the American president's annual speech.

He wasn't looking forward to this next part. While Orlov never physically threatened anyone, and "killing the messenger" wasn't his style, it nonetheless would be excruciating.

I'm going to have to sit in that stupid room with him for hours, not speaking, while he thinks.

Dmitry would have to think as well, long and hard, about his future with the man. He dreamed of more action, more responsibility. Orlov rarely assigned him tasks.

Instead, he had to puzzle out Orlov's plans and intentions, doing little more than pondering moves and countermoves in the game of international espionage.

He opened the door to find Orlov in his usual pose, staring at the blank wall in front of the desk, hands on his lap, breathing through his partly opened mouth.

How did a mind like his end up in a body like that?

Dmitry quietly closed the door behind him and summarized the evening in America.

"President Heringten threw out his scripted speech and instead spoke extemporaneously—for fifteen minutes instead of the planned sixty. From the coverage on the television, no missiles impacted the building. There was no panic or evacuation, either. However, we have reports of extensive surface-to-air operations from in and around Washington." He paused, licked his lips, and continued. "We will have more from our agents in a few hours."

Orlov continued to stare at the wall, though Dmitry had caught the tiniest flicker of annoyance on the man's face during the report—the same look he'd seen when he learned that the Iranian special forces men had disappeared in the state of Texas and the liquid natural gas tanker had not exploded as expected.

Dmitry walked slowly to the chair next to the desk and sat down facing the wall on the other side of the small room. He stared at the old, faded map showing the former USSR in all its glory, placed his hands carefully on his lap, and waited. It could be a few minutes, or likely, several hours until Orlov spoke. In the meantime, Dmitry was expected to sit patiently and plan the next moves as if it were his operation. And there was always the chance he would be quizzed, so he couldn't just fake it.

This is the part I hate.

Working this way was boring but, he had to concede, educational. Too few people sat, plotted, and schemed. So he would do it, considering what moves the Americans might make. How Iran would react to the news. What the idiot Villanueva would do, say, and demand next.

And how Russia—or rather, Orlov—could turn the events of the past week from a disaster into a success.

An hour later, Orlov stirred slightly, the ancient metal chair creaking as he shifted his weight. "So hard to find good help these days," was all he said.

He means President Villanueva and the Iranians, not me, right? Dmitry wondered.

125

KNIVES II

Fort Washington Estates
Fort Washington, Maryland

All Haley wanted to do was sleep, but the bright white light and the noise made it impossible. The man yelling at her didn't help, either.

"Hey, wake up! Wake up! I need you to focus on my voice and stay with me," someone said.

Where am I?

She tried to open her eyes but they didn't budge.

"Go away," she mumbled, trying to use her warrior voice, the growl that made grown men tremble. Well, except for Axe and Nalen.

Axe. Nalen. What...

She was forgetting something important.

I have to...

She couldn't remember.

With a force of will, she got her eyes open but quickly closed them against the light.

"That's it. Tell me your name. What's your name?"

She opened her mouth to answer, but a warning light flashed in her mind.

I shouldn't tell him my name.

Why not? It was such a simple request.

Wait—what is my name?

It took a second, much longer than she knew it should, but it finally came.

Haley. I'm Haley Addison. I work at—

Adrenaline surged, giving her the boost she needed. Her eyes snapped open, fought the brightness, and turned on the man holding her left wrist and looking at his watch. She yanked her arm away from him and tried to punch him, aiming for his head but missing as he pulled away.

I'm too slow.

Struggling to get up, she couldn't. A strap held her down, pinning her on her right side.

I've been captured. I have to—

The puzzle pieces came together. The bright white light. The noise. The masked man above her.

I'm in an ambulance.

The man—an EMT, she now realized—had moved out of reach.

She fumbled for her cargo pants pocket, retrieved her phone, unlocked it, and hit the icon to dial work. Clumsily, she transferred it to her left hand so she could hold it to her ear.

"Where are you?" Gregory said a moment later.

"Ambulance," was all she could choke out. The rush of energy faded, and she let herself relax onto her side, her stomach and back screaming in pain.

The EMT gasped. "God, be careful!"

She looked at him blankly.

"You have a knife sticking out of your back!" he said, pointing.

Haley held the phone away from her ear and turned her head. Sure enough, the black handle of a combat knife stuck out of her left shoulder blade area.

"If you move," the EMT said, "the knife could nick your aorta and you'll die in seconds."

Well, shit.

"Did you get that?" she asked Gregory.

"Give the phone to the EMT and relax. We've got you. But don't say anything." He paused, then added. "And don't die!"

She faded as she held the phone out to the man attempting to save her life. He warily took it as she relaxed onto the stretcher. Once again, the tiredness took her, and she drifted out of consciousness.

PART 5

WEDNESDAY

126

RING THE BELL

Off the Coast of Caracas, Venezuela

Hours later, Axe was still alive. He wasn't sure how—or why. He floated on his back in the empty ocean, mentally, physically, and emotionally done.

He was close to finally allowing himself to slip away. If he had a good excuse, he might be able to give up and ring the bell.

His body had gone numb, which was a blessing.

There had been periods of sleep—or maybe he'd passed out. But many times he had come to choking after breathing in water as a wave splashed across his head.

The sky had the faintest lightness to it and the stars were harder to see.

I made it to dawn.

He felt a sense of accomplishment. Maybe he could leave this life with a success.

Dawn means Kelton will be nearing the rendezvous point.

Axe idly wondered how far he had drifted and how close he was to the yacht.

Not close enough.

The GPS in the satellite communicator would tell him.

Why the hell not?

It would be amusing to see how truly screwed he was before he let go and died.

He slung the dry bag around and opened it.

After nearly dropping the device in the water, he navigated the menus with barely functioning fingers.

He was too exhausted to laugh when he saw the location, but it brought the tiniest smile to his face.

Much too far to swim.

This was exactly the excuse he needed. Letting go finally made sense. Hours before, he couldn't do it. His training wouldn't let him. But now…

Yes. I think I can.

The map showed his location and the distance to the extraction point where the yacht would be soon.

I can't get there by then.

Kelton would wait a short time but had clear orders to not loiter in the area. He'd push it as far as he could, but Axe wasn't going to get there for hours given the speed of the current. And he couldn't swim. He could barely move.

I'm forgetting something.

He frowned and tried to work out the problem. There was a missing component to his final decision, but he couldn't put his finger on it.

During Hell Week, the final training of BUD/S, he stayed awake five days and nights… and had felt so much better than he did now. He'd been exhausted back then; now he was exhausted and injured.

But he and the other candidates had been forced for hours on end to use their minds despite their tiredness. He tapped into that training now.

Work the problem. One last time, then I can give up and ring the bell.

His focus slipped. He stared off at the sky for a while, then tried to recall what he'd been doing.

The GPS.

It took several more seconds, but he eventually worked it out.

I don't have to make it to the rendezvous point. The boat can come to me!

He marveled at his stupidity, and how long it had taken him to make the connection.

My mind isn't working right. Maybe a bad concussion?

He was far enough away now. The risk of discovery and capture was smaller than earlier. It was a calculated risk—one he was willing, finally, to take.

I want to live. I will not give up. I won't ring the bell.

He moved to the communication screen and composed a short text to Kelton, giving his location and need for rescue. After hitting send, he waited for only a minute before getting a reply.

On our way. Hold fast!

The device went into the dry bag. He eased onto his back to float and watch the sunrise. Now that he had hope and a renewed desire to live, his fears came crashing in.

Please don't let me die before they get here.

127

A NEW DAY

The sun rose over the airport as the small jet landed smoothly. Arturo felt only the slightest bump as the hired pilot expertly handled the plane.

It's going to be a beautiful day, he thought.

The previous hours had been some of the most trying of Arturo's life. It had been decades since he'd been in direct physical danger.

But I'm alive, free, and ready for the next chapter in my life.

The plane slowed and taxied off the runway to an executive area that had seen more use over the past few years as the cartel leaders had visited, along with wealthy Russian tourists.

A car would be waiting, ready to take him in comfort to a secure building he owned on the outskirts of the capital city.

The previous late afternoon, he and Hugo had run from the airplane hangar and escaped the area by getting into a taxi in front of the Uruapan International Airport.

Between Hugo's pistol and Arturo's wallet filled with cash, the driver had been "persuaded" to drive them the nearly four hours and 400 kilometers to Guadalajara after a brief stop at a store where Hugo had bought a cheap burner cell phone.

Hugo had placed calls and arranged for a charter flight from

Guadalajara to Caracas, where they elected to land at the smaller airport on the outskirts of the city.

The body of the taxi driver had been left locked in the trunk of his cab. They'd taken a risk by letting the pilot and co-pilot of the jet live. Pilots were harder to disappear than cab drivers.

But at last, Arturo was safe in his new country, ready to start over.

First, he had to learn what had happened to the other cartel leaders and manage the chaos resulting from either their capture or escape.

"Which would you prefer, *Jefe*?" Hugo had whispered earlier. "For them to be dead, in custody, or free?"

Arturo wasn't sure.

No matter what, there will be hell to pay all around.

"If the others are alive and free, I will look like a coward for running," he told Hugo. "Or a traitor, more likely. They will believe I set up an ambush and tried to kill them."

"If they are all dead? Or captured?"

"Then we will have a war on our hands as their people fight for leadership positions," he said. "And whoever emerges will wonder if I had a hand in it." He added, mostly to himself, "But where there is chaos, there is also opportunity."

He had a real passport in a fake name, cash in his pocket, and a base of operations in the country already up and running. It would be a simple matter to go to work here instead of in eastern Mexico. His family was already on the way and his captains had their orders.

A little coffee and the day will begin.

It would be busy, but he'd find at least some time to plot his revenge against whoever had nearly abducted him.

128

THE GAMBLE

"Axe! Axe!"

He heard his name being called and, with his scrambled brain and fading consciousness, assumed it was the voice of God.

Then the blackness came at last.

Mariana grabbed Axe under his arms and let herself fall backward, effectively using herself as a counterweight to heave Axe's limp body onto the yacht's swim platform.

"Grab his legs," she told Kelton. "Ready? Lift."

Together they managed to carry him up the steps to the main deck, setting him on the long dining table where she already had the first aid kit spread out.

She grabbed the safety shears and started cutting off his gear and wetsuit.

Kelton looked white as a sheet.

"Kelton. Kelton!"

He looked at her, startled.

"Get us the hell out of here," she said as she returned to her work.

But where? Returning to Curaçao would be fastest, but whatever Axe had been up to the previous evening would surely have brought planes and ships to the area. They'd already been boarded by the Venezuelan navy once the day before. With an injured man, they couldn't afford to let it happen again now.

However, anywhere further meant more time before they could get Axe proper medical care. She made up her mind. "North, as fast as you can while still looking somewhat normal if anyone spots us. We don't want to look like we're fleeing the area."

"Got it," Kelton said, looking better by the second. The boat was his kingdom—and his comfort zone. He fled to the bridge. A moment later, they turned north, on their way.

Mariana willed her hands not to shake as she cut Axe's wetsuit to shreds. As she peeled it off his arms and legs, dozens of wounds opened up and bled. Horrific bruises covered his chest, stomach, and sides, already transitioning from red to blackish blue.

She felt the back of his head and her hand came away bloody.

Her training kicked in. Coming from a small, out-of-the-way town, her police chief had all the officers cross-trained in basic firefighting and, more importantly for today, paramedic duties.

"Bleeding from a gash on the back of the head," she mumbled. "Probable concussion. Multiple lacerations on arms and legs. Bullet wounds to leg and hips. Extreme bruising across the torso. Likely cracked or broken ribs."

No one can have that much bruising and be okay underneath it.

She swabbed Axe's arm and steadied herself before inserting an IV needle. She hated needles, but she had made it through the training and could put it to good use now. She found the vein and nailed it on the first try.

"Question: does the patient have internal bleeding?"

She didn't have an answer and couldn't do anything about it if she had. The multi-day basic EMT course hadn't covered how to handle it.

But she could stop the external bleeding, bandage the wounds, get fluids in him, and make sure he was warm and comfortable.

Then they'd make the tough decision about diverting to a hospital and risking capture, or gambling with Axe's life in a straight run north to Puerto Rico.

129

THE CONSCIENCE

Outside San Luis Potosí
Central Mexico

Captain Hernandez stretched his legs, walking around the entire idling semi on the side of the road. Few cars drove by this early; the sky had light in it, but dawn was still coming.

He had a decision to make. After driving all night, first south, then east, then west, to throw off anyone looking for him, he'd finally turned north. Making occasional stops for coffee and once to fill up with diesel, he was four hours from the National Guard of Mexico Regional Command Center in Monterey—his office. Beneath the modern building was a parking garage, loading dock, and secure prisoner transfer area.

He could picture driving the semi down the long ramp beneath the building, parking, and announcing the contents of the shipping container turned into a secure, portable building on the truck's flatbed trailer. He'd be a national hero.

With a bigger bounty on his head than he had now, courtesy of the drug cartels.

And then, how long would it be before they bribed the right people, allowing the cartel leaders to escape prison?

If they didn't break free, they would go on trial, only to have witnesses, judges, and jurors threatened, bribed, or both, resulting in acquittals and freedom for the men.

A car zipped by, not slowing to check on the semi with its hazard lights on, which was fine with Hernandez.

He finished his latest coffee, welcoming the caffeine surge. He'd need it to stay awake the rest of the drive no matter what he decided.

Is there any place I could take them that is safe from corruption?

He was four hours away from the command center, but eight hours would get him to Brownsville, Texas.

No one would be looking for me or the cartel leaders there.

He removed a small phone case from his pocket. It blocked all signals, making him impossible to track. Taking the phone out and using it was a risk, but a manageable one.

Besides, anyone tracking me will assume I'm going straight toward Monterrey.

He hesitated to make the call. If anyone found out, it would be the end of his career as a police officer in Mexico.

But it's the only way... Isn't it?

He toyed with his other option, one he'd been trying unsuccessfully to embrace for the entire drive. Thirty minutes ahead was a national park and, near it, a reservoir. He had visited once with his family as a child. A dirt road circled the man-made lake.

I back the trailer up to the edge, unhook it, then give it a nudge with the truck. The whole thing slides into the water and sinks. Problem solved.

He'd have to wait until dark, but he could find a truck stop to hide until then.

The choice came down to whether he was willing to betray his country or his principles.

He walked to the metal container and pounded on the wall.

There was no response.

A full minute passed as he wrestled with his conscience. Another car drove by.

Every second I delay means more people see the truck.

The word would be out. Hundreds—thousands—of unofficial informants would be on the lookout for the distinctive vehicle.

The sure way is to drive straight to the reservoir right now, dump the container, and be done with it.

He shook his head, half annoyed with himself, half proud, and dialed the number in Washington, D.C.

I'll try the other route, but if they give me the runaround, I have a good backup plan.

There were plenty of rivers and lakes between here and the border with the United States of America.

130

THE PROMISE

Inside the Sensitive Compartmented Information Facility
Location Unknown

Salazar, the eldest of the drug cartel leaders, readied his weapon.

They will never take me alive.

The truck had stopped once again, bumping onto what felt like the shoulder of a highway.

The four men readied themselves, their weapons trained on the door at the far end. It was locked from the inside, of course, but that wouldn't stop their abductors from blowing it open. They'd have at least a few seconds of warning, though—the outer door to the shipping container had been closed and was locked from the outside. They were stuck until that door opened and their interior door was blown off its hinges.

A smart opponent might cut or blow a hole elsewhere in the container. But the drug cartel leaders would direct a wall of bullets at whatever opening appeared and at least shoot a few of the bastards before they were killed or taken into custody.

"If I ever get my hands on Ruiz," Duarte, the hothead youngest member of the group, muttered for approximately the hundredth time.

Not this again. He never shuts up.

Salazar looked at the younger man with his dead eyes. "If you speak again, I will shoot you." It was a simple statement. A promise. For a second, he saw the rage in Duarte's eyes and a childlike urge to push the limits and speak. He also caught the second impulse of self-preservation as rational thought kicked in.

Duarte nodded once and said nothing.

Guzman and Cortez glanced at him—they were happy with what he'd said.

They were all on edge from the bumpy roads, frequent changes in direction, and occasional stops where they prepared for the attack that didn't come.

Also, the small chemical toilet, included for a situation such as this, was proving inadequate for the four of them after so many hours.

But they had attained their positions through force of will, ruthlessness, and the ability to manage adversity.

Except for Duarte, who had taken over when his father went to prison in America.

A minute before, someone outside had pounded on the wall, but they hadn't answered.

After another few minutes, the truck pulled onto the highway. Sitting on the floor—the chairs had proven unstable—Salazar and the others—especially Duarte—rode in silence, waiting. They had food, water, weapons, and powerful organizations with massive resources looking for them.

But Salazar had been around. He knew the odds.

If our people don't find us soon... I know what I have to do.

131

THE DISGUISE

U.S. Customs and Border Protection Port of Entry
Brownsville, Texas

Mad Dog waited in the administrative building at the border, breathing deeply and refusing to check his watch again. He felt naked without his M4 and plate carrier. The 9mm on his hip, hidden by a jacket, wouldn't get him far in a firefight. But the lack of his primary weapon was the least of his problems.

The bigger issue: Captain Hernandez was late.

"He'll be here," Johnboy said.

"Easy for you to say. You have the patience of a saint."

The taller man chuckled and didn't disagree.

They watched the trucks creep forward. Many were directed to one side or another, where two huge drive-through machines scanned the contents, looking for drugs.

A Border Patrol agent with a dog also meandered up and down the long row of semis.

"There it is," Johnboy said, without pointing. In the right lane, exactly as instructed, was the semi and trailer containing the SCIF they'd left in Captain's hands twenty-four hours before.

They made their way over to the toll booth type building for lane one, beating the truck by a few minutes, but Mad Dog was happy to wait now that he knew Captain—and the contents of the container—were safe.

"Wouldn't it have been easier for us to ride along?" Johnboy asked.

"Yep."

That was all that needed to be said. They were both long past the point of digging too deeply into why the powers that be didn't choose the most logical option from the start.

The truck braked at the booth. A moment later, a truck driver opened the door and climbed down, carrying a duffel bag. It took Mad Dog a second to realize the trucker in the blue jeans, t-shirt, jacket, and cowboy hat was Captain Hernandez himself.

He stopped to buy a disguise. Smart man.

Captain walked toward Mad Dog, on his way to an unofficial car ride back to the Mexico side of the border. They didn't make eye contact or outwardly recognize each other, but Captain muttered, *"Gracias, amigos,"* as he passed.

Mad Dog stepped into the truck while Johnboy went to the passenger side to ride shotgun. Then he put it in gear and drove forward slowly.

They had a date at a nearby military base where the truck would be opened—eventually, after letting those inside go stir crazy for a few days —and the drug cartel leaders arrested.

Feeling ridiculous wearing his brand-new clothes and a cowboy hat as a disguise, Hernandez slipped into the waiting car without acknowledging the driver. They made a loop of the facility and headed south, over the bridge, back into Mexico.

They were waved through at the border crossing—someone had pulled strings exactly as he had requested.

A few minutes later, the driver pulled up to a hospital and dropped him off without a word. From here, Hernandez would take a taxi to a hotel, rest, and catch a bus to Monterey in the morning.

He would tell his boss the secret assignment had been a bust. Unfortunately, the cartel leaders had never arrived.

By tomorrow afternoon, there would be plenty of rumors—the cartel leaders were dead, had fled the country, or the Americans had somehow taken them into custody.

Hernandez would go back to work, chasing down whoever tried to take control of each of the crime syndicates.

The Americans would handle the drug lords. They would make the men pay for their crimes.

PART 6

THURSDAY

132

THE HOSPITAL

Alexandria Hospital
Alexandria, Virginia

Haley came to slowly, drifting lazily back to the world. She opened her eyes, took in the immediate area, and closed them again.

The ceiling was white and the walls were beige. Several machines stood near her bed and she felt the IV in her arm.

I'm in a hospital.

The quiet voice of a woman spoke from nearby. "Haley, how are you feeling? Everything's okay. Just rest."

She didn't recognize the voice, but through the tiredness and the drugs, she wasn't particularly worried.

"Who're you?"

There was a pause, and Haley wondered if she'd spoken the words clearly or just mumbled.

"I'm Mariana. Your parents will be back in a while—it's early in the morning."

Mariana? Oh.

"My replacement."

"I doubt it," the voice muttered.

Haley faded.

A while later, Haley came to again, feeling stronger and more focused, but in pain.

The meds have worn off.

Someone had been here earlier...

She looked around and found the face of a woman sitting next to her bed.

"Welcome back," Mariana said. "You're looking better. Your mom was here for a while, but she went to the cafeteria. She'll be back soon."

"Okay."

Haley wasn't sure she had the strength—or diplomacy—to get to the bottom of why Mariana was here in the room with her instead of back in... Mardale? Whatever the name of her town was. But instead, she skipped to her primary concern. Or one of them.

"Where's Axe? Is he okay?"

For a second, Haley saw... what?

Did she blush?

"Don't worry, he's fine—in a room a few doors down."

There was a brief knock on the door and Axe hobbled in, barely able to move on his own but making the effort. Relief flooded through her—along with concern. His hair had been cut short by what looked like a butcher. When he turned slowly to close the door, she saw a line of sutures across the back of his head, which was shaved. He wore a hospital gown that matched hers, along with a thin robe over it and cheap hospital slippers that made noise as he shuffled across the floor. Mariana took his arm and helped him to the chair she'd been sitting in, between the bed and the window, where he collapsed heavily.

He looks like hell.

"I should see the other guy?" she asked, offering a weak smile.

Axe's eyes got the thousand-yard stare she knew all too well.

He's seen some shit this time.

"No, you really shouldn't," he said. "You look like I feel," he added. "But we're both going to make it."

They regarded each other, then spoke at the same time.

"I should have been with you," they said together.

"Next time," Haley said. Then she had a thought. "Oh, hell! The president! What—"

"Don't worry, we did it," a voice said from the door, startling her.

Admiral Nalen leaned against the wall in jeans and a tight white t-shirt under his unzipped black parka as the door swung shut behind him.

"How did he do that?" Mariana muttered.

"The president is fine. There was a missile strike—you were right all along, Haley," Nalen said. "Our defenses got them—barely."

She closed her eyes and relaxed.

We did it again.

She felt much older than twenty-one.

Another knock on the door. Someone else came in.

She opened her eyes, looking forward to seeing her mother.

Mad Dog stood in front of her bed, smiling. "I heard D.C. is lovely this time of year. Cherry blossoms and all."

What the hell is he doing here?

"That's like six weeks away," Haley told him. "Maybe come back then."

"Aw, damn it! Guess I'll just have to hang around and do double duty as bodyguard and nurse to a couple of injured warriors."

"What?" Haley asked. "No. Come on. Hammer, I'm fine, really." She tried briefly to sit up before falling back, exhausted.

"Just a precaution, Blondie, until we figure out what's going on," Nalen said. "He'll take turns with Mariana watching over you two once you're discharged. Axe's cabin is secure and comfortable. Besides, we owe him one."

"You got them?" Haley asked.

Did he and Hernandez really pull it off?

"What? Of course we got them! You send the best, you get whatever your heart desires!"

"Oh Lord, have mercy," she whispered under her breath.

"Never fear, Blondie, Mad Dog's here!" He struck a superhero pose with his hands on his hips and barrel chest sticking out proudly.

Yet another knock on the door and it opened immediately. Mad Dog whispered an automatic, "Tennhut!" and came to attention.

Haley smiled, guessing what was coming. Axe struggled to his feet, Admiral Nalen straightened, and Mariana stood looking at them all like they had lost their minds... until the President of the United States walked into the room. Then Mariana's mouth dropped open and she stood up straighter.

"As you were, everyone," President Heringten said in a combination of his smooth political voice and rougher SEAL command tone, as a Secret

Service agent guarded the door. "And to be clear, I'm not here. I'm still in a room down the hall with one of the brave soldiers who was injured at a missile launch site Tuesday night. But I wanted to stop by and thank you all personally."

He turned to Haley and frowned. "You, young lady, have a lot of explaining to do. I believe you were given a direct order to not get hurt."

She smiled up at her Uncle Jimmy.

"No, sir… I was told not to die. And here I am."

He chuckled and nodded. "My mistake."

Yeah, right. I bet he knows exactly what Gregory told me because he's already chewed him out for sending me into the field without being surrounded by a platoon of SEALs.

"Anyway, glad you're alive. And thanks for the heads up—your hunch helped save the day."

The president turned to Axe. "Nice to meet you in person, Frogman. I understand you single-handedly took out four cruise missiles that we suspect might have had WMD warheads. Well done. You uphold our finest SEAL traditions."

"Thank you, Mr. President," Axe said. He stood a little taller—like his pain had been forgotten for a moment.

"And," he turned to Mariana. "Miss Rodriguez, correct?"

It took her an instant to respond, but she finally got it out. "Yes, Mr. President."

"I hear you saved this one's life," he said, nodding to Axe.

"No, sir," she said after a second of hesitation. "I patched him up, but he's a tough son of a bitch. Sir."

Haley was impressed. The policewoman from a tiny town in the back of the beyond Texas was holding her own in a surprise conversation with the President of the United States.

She's going to fit in just fine.

"And you're thinking about joining this team?"

"Yes, Mr. President."

President Heringten pointedly looked at Haley lying in bed. His eyes met hers and she saw the concern from her uncle briefly replace his presidential facade. He then turned to Axe, standing upright but looking pale and flat-out hurt. Finally, he turned back to Mariana and said seriously, "Choose wisely." A second went by as they locked eyes, then he moved to Mad Dog.

"And Douglas Frederick 'Mad Dog' McBellin."

Frederick?

"The man who brought us closer to winning the war on drugs."

Haley made a mental note to debrief Mad Dog fully when she got the chance.

There's a story I have to hear.

"I had a good team and excellent intel, Mr. President," Mad Dog said. For once, he seemed serious and not his normal jocular, pain-in-the-ass self.

"Well done to you, and them—and be sure they know I said so."

"Copy that, sir."

The president turned to address them all. "I have to run, but from myself and a grateful nation, thank you." He met the eyes of each of them individually, clapped Nalen on the shoulder, and was gone.

For a moment, after the door swung closed behind him, there was a silence in the room.

Then, from the foot of her bed, Mad Dog broke it. "Hot damn, I met the Commander in Chief!"

Next to her, Mariana muttered, "That was the coolest moment of my life."

Haley relaxed and closed her eyes, feeling herself falling asleep again.

That's my Uncle Jimmy.

133

THE GUESS

Nancy stared at the computer monitor, not at all liking what she saw.

The pieces are all here, but it's so thin.

Haley was in no shape to help—she'd be in the hospital several more days, then recuperating and unable to come into the office for a week or more after that.

Nancy and Dave had made remarkable progress in the last forty-eight hours. But as comfortable as she'd gotten swimming in data, falling into the zone, she didn't have the creativity, guts, or fearlessness Haley did when it came to making leaps of logic and tying it all together.

"It's there," she said quietly to Dave. They sat side by side in their shared, double-wide cubicle, conference room C abandoned for the time being.

The woman Haley had killed outside the Secretary of Agriculture's daughter's house was a ghost. There were no records of her, but her DNA showed her to be Middle Eastern.

What little remained of the person who had shot two soldiers at a mobile air defense site within a mile of the Capitol building hadn't allowed for much of an analysis, but the DNA was similar to the woman's: likely Middle Eastern.

The debrief they'd conducted with Axe via videoconference didn't give them much. A huge guy had attacked him, and Axe thought he was Russian.

Just like Haley suspected—Russians and Iranians working with Venezuela.

By the time they'd gotten a satellite repositioned, there was no evidence of an explosion on the oil platform off the coast of Venezuela. Gregory was fighting for a Navy mission to dive below the facility, hoping the remains of the shipping container Axe described had been simply pushed over the side to sink to the bottom of the ocean.

Nancy looked through her spreadsheet again.

Really, what I'm looking for is a smoking gun... and it's not there.

Others were backtracing the paths of the cruise missiles, but they weren't having much success. They flew too fast and too close to the ground to track easily. While it might work out in the end, it didn't seem likely and wouldn't happen fast enough.

They had some success recovering pieces of cruise missiles, but they were standard Russian export versions, available in several countries, the black market, and from legitimate arms dealers—none of whom were forthcoming about their clientele.

The Russians, Iranians, and Venezuelans could very well be working together and to blame. Who else would permit the cruise missile launch from the oil platform?

Haley would make the leaps and figure this out.

The downside—Haley would offer no proof, only her intuition.

But her intuition has proven correct over and over.

As if reading her mind, David sighed. "I wish Haley could look at this. Do you think we could do a videoconference?"

"She's still pretty weak. The knife in her back..." Nancy shuddered thinking about it. The long blade had nearly poked through the front of her body and only missed her aorta by an eighth of an inch.

"If it had gone in at a slightly different angle," Dave said, "she would have died."

And if she hadn't fought back, the other woman could have pulled the knife out. Haley would have bled to death.

"What does your gut tell you?" Dave asked.

Their phone rang, sparing her from answering. Dave picked it up. "Yes, sir. Be right there." He hung up. "Gregory wants an update."

They grabbed their laptops and joined Gregory in the conference room. Instead of their two usual chairs at the table, others were pushed back. Gregory nodded at those two seats.

"I need you to summarize what we have so far. Speak freely," he said as he pushed a button on the remote control for the large monitor on the wall. It came on, showing President Heringten sitting at the end of a long table Nancy realized was in the White House Situation Room. To his right sat his chief of staff. The rest of the room was deserted.

"Nancy, Dave, I hope you don't mind if I sit in," the president said.

It was the first time either of them had spoken directly to the man and Nancy found herself tongue-tied.

She glanced at Gregory sitting to the side, who nodded encouragingly. "Of course not, Mr. President," she got out.

"Before we get to the report, I want to thank you for your excellent work. Not only in this recent crisis, but for the past years as well. But specifically, thank you for helping save my life, and the lives of so many others Tuesday night."

"You're welcome, Mr. President," Dave said next to her.

"You're welcome, sir. Our pleasure," she said.

"Keep up the great work. Now, what do you have for me?"

Nancy started, gaining comfort after a few seconds.

Just another update. Never mind the powerful man on the other end of the video chat.

Dave took over when she finished, highlighting the efforts he had managed and how they were leaving no stone unturned. When he got to the part about the designated survivor and the assassin killed outside the house, Gregory jumped in.

"I've briefed him on that aspect of the situation."

Smart. Even over this secure line, we're not talking about the Russian sleeper spies.

"You're saying we're in the dark?" President Heringten summarized.

"If you're looking for concrete proof, then yes, sir, I'm sorry to report that's exactly where we're at," Nancy said.

"If you had to guess, who was behind it?" he asked her.

"Mr. President, we don't really—"

"Bullshit, Nancy," he interrupted. "Tell me what you think. Don't worry, I'm not going to nuke anybody over it. But I expect honest answers from the CAG or WIA, whatever you're calling yourselves tonight. You're both veteran analysts. What do you have?"

Dave tapped her leg three times with a finger. Their secret signal to be careful.

She took his hand, squeezed it reassuringly, and spoke. "You want me to speak freely? I will. My hunch is that Haley had it right before your speech on Tuesday night. We have little hard evidence, but what makes the most sense is Russia, Iran, and Venezuela are working together. The assault at Admiral Nalen's house coordinated with the attack on what we originally thought was Haley, but now believe to be on her mother—so your best friend and the First Lady's best friend. It points to a personal attack. It's logical the next attack Tuesday night wasn't about decapitating the country so much as it was about killing you."

"I'm not the most popular guy on the planet," the president said with a slight smile. "Why President Villanueva?"

"You said some things that hit pretty close to home right after you were elected four years ago, sir," Dave chimed in. "We think he took them to heart."

The president nodded. "Continue."

"He has likely gotten money from the Mexican drug cartels. In the last forty-eight hours, we've found more evidence that suggests they may be transitioning their main drug facilities from Mexico to Venezuela, paying for the country's protection and access to its small navy and air force."

"As you're aware," Dave added, "Venezuela has received an influx of money the last several years, enough to help jumpstart their economy and repair both their submarines."

"With the subs," Nancy continued, "the cartels could bring an enormous volume of drugs into any country with an ocean, virtually without detection."

"And Russia? Iran?"

"The rest of the logic follows. Venezuela can't do it on its own. Russia wants to beat us down but doesn't want to risk a direct confrontation. Iran and Venezuela are willing proxies for them. All benefit from our oil and natural gas pipeline infrastructure blowing up, which the terrorist cells tried to do." Nancy sighed. "As we said, sir, we have no proof, but it makes the most sense. Could it be North Korea and China working together? Yes, but why would they? This is logical."

"So why didn't it work?" the president asked.

Great question.

"I have an excellent team, Mr. President," Gregory said softly from the side of the table.

"What about the Mexican drug cartels? They helped smuggle the original men into the country. Are they in on it?"

"Unknown, sir," Gregory said after a moment.

They sat for several seconds in silence. Finally, the president spoke. "The new Russian president—Nikitin—is a moderate. I can't see him approving this plan."

Nancy shifted uncomfortably, recalling her hushed discussion with Haley a few days before.

This is getting into dangerous territory. Does he know what I suspect—that Haley and Axe somehow got Russian President Zimalev killed?

Neither she nor Dave spoke.

"Joseph Orlov," Gregory finally said. "The chief of their Foreign Intelligence Agency. He has been around for years and fits the description of what we're looking for—a hard-core Russian with the mind and will to think years ahead... and get his presidents to go along with his well-planned missions."

He could be behind the sleeper spy program—and the sleeper spy who learned about the designated survivor would have ultimately reported to him.

Nancy knew it was what they were all thinking. "I'm still working this angle," she chimed in, "but one of the men who attacked Admiral Nalen's house wasn't as careful as he should have been. There is a small paper trail. I have more work to do, but it may lead back to an account the NSA already suspects is linked to Orlov. Again, this is unconfirmed as yet. Call it an educated guess."

"Could Orlov have gone rogue?" the president asked. "Decided he didn't want to deal with yet another new president and just... 'forgot' to mention it to Nikitin? Or should I be preparing for war with Russia?"

Thankfully, it sounded more like the president was thinking out loud and not asking them a direct question.

Dave spoke up. "Remember, Mr. President, that we have only circumstantial evidence. It's slightly better than guesswork and supposition."

President Heringten fought to hold back a smile. "You don't have to cover your ass with me, Dave, but I get what you're saying." He nodded at them and continued. "Thanks for the update. Get to the bottom of it. I have faith in you. And thanks again for saving my life."

They said their goodbyes, and the president was gone.

"Well done, both of you," Gregory told them. "Now, go home and get some rest. We all need it. Come back in the morning refreshed."

The White House Situation Room
Washington, DC.

Once the videoconference connection was terminated, James turned to Chad.

"It feels right, but what are your thoughts?" he asked.

Chad took a few seconds to ponder the information. "It makes sense, but I don't think you can make a move without a whole lot more."

James frowned. "I agree. But..."

"'Hope for the best, prepare for the worst'?"

"You read my mind. Put me in a room with the new Russian president. A casual, unofficial meeting on the sidelines. A G-20 Summit or something in the next month—wherever he's going to be."

"He doesn't speak much English, and do you really want to trust whatever conversation you have in mind to interpreters?" Chad asked.

"If I have to, but I had something else planned." Chad looked at him questioningly. "I'm going to learn Russian."

134

THE SCIF

The eight men guarding the SCIF inside the airplane hangar already had a love-hate relationship with the assignment.

On one hand, they could sit on the provided folding chairs and chat through their shift.

On the other hand, time dragged by, hour after hour.

The captives inside the shipping container-turned-secure meeting room couldn't escape. And if somehow the base was attacked in an attempt to set them free, the guards in the hangar wouldn't see any action until every other defender on the base was dead—an unlikely scenario.

So at the shift change, a mere twenty-four hours after the truck had arrived, the eight soldiers of the day shift rose from the chairs, welcoming the night shift crew.

Seconds later, muffled gunshots from inside the SCIF made them call their officer, who called his officer, up the chain until someone made a decision. They wouldn't wait two more days until the drug lords were good and ready to come out peacefully. They'd go in immediately.

They unlocked and opened the large swinging door at the end of the container, ready to shoot if the men inside opened the inner door and started firing.

The smaller door was closed and locked from the inside—they checked.

Breaching charges were placed. While they weren't SEALs, the men knew what they were doing.

The door blew. One man yanked it open while another threw in two flash-bang grenades. They both ducked back and waited for the boom.

The instant after they detonated, two other men flooded the room, guns raised.

"Clear," one called.

"Clear," the other confirmed.

Four dead men, all shot at close range, slumped in chairs around a small table. Pistols dangled from hands and blood flowed from multiple wounds on each.

"Circular firing squad?" the first soldier into the room asked. "Or they decided not to be taken alive?"

"Nah. I bet they just got tired of listening to each other bitch and moan."

PART 7

TWO WEEKS LATER - THURSDAY

135

CONFRONTATION

The Climate and Economic Possibilities Summit
Stockholm, Sweden

A jetlagged President James Heringten drained the last of his coffee and passed the cup off to a nearby aide. He stood in a wide hallway, ready for his mission. It felt great being on an operation again, though he had no weapons other than his mind.

The two weeks of preparation had been like the old days—filled with planning, practice, and training. And while he was by no means a master of the Russian language, he'd focused on it with the same dedication he had learning any new skill during his time as a SEAL.

Gregory Addison's team at the CAG, backed up by a still-healing Haley for one day before it proved too much for her, had made progress. Nancy had traced the money paid to one member of the men who attacked Admiral Nalen's house. A mistake had been made. Someone wasn't careful enough. It was no smoking gun, but confidence was high that Joseph Orlov had hired the men—and the Russian gangsters who attacked the restaurant where Haley and her parents were dining.

One of the captured kitchen crew from the liquid natural gas ship had confessed. They were Iranian army soldiers. James and his advisors hadn't yet decided how to retaliate against Iran, but he was leaning toward a cyber-attack of some sort.

Gregory's team was no closer to having proof of who had been behind the attacks in Texas or the attempted cruise missile strike on the Capitol building during the State of the Union address. But in the intelligence business, concrete proof was hard to come by.

Given the Orlov piece of the puzzle and the kitchen crew confession though, it was enough. All agreed their original assessment made the most sense. Russia, Iran, and Venezuela were likely to blame.

I can't do much about the other two yet, but today we make our move against Russia.

"Here he comes," Chad whispered to James. The Russian president had agreed to stage an "accidental" meeting on the sidelines of the summit so the two could meet informally in person.

Showtime.

The entire event had been carefully planned. Each man had aides around him who would clear out shortly after the men met. The translators would stay. The two presidents would speak for a minute or two, smile, shake hands, and part. A few pictures would be taken showing the leaders engaged in world diplomacy. All in a day's work.

"Mr. President," James said first as Nikitin neared. As he was the one to suggest the supposed chance encounter, it was up to the United States to make the first move. He extended his hand, smiled, and stepped forward.

"Mr. President," Nikitin answered back with his own, less warm smile. The man wasn't a natural politician and had seemingly been happy further in the background as Russia's Prime Minister—their version of a Vice President—until thrust into the spotlight when President Zimalev had his "helicopter accident" several weeks earlier. His dark gray suit and perfectly pressed white shirt fit him well, but he seemed ill at ease in them. He was as tall as James—a bit over six feet—but slim, unlike James' more muscular physique. His dark hair was short and thinning.

He'll be bald within a year with the stress of running a country. Those thick, bushy eyebrows will last forever, though.

Nikitin seemed more like a bookish college history professor instead of a politician or leader of a nation.

"So happy to finally meet you in person," James continued as they shook hands. The Russian translator, a half step behind Nikitin's right shoulder, mumbled the translation into the man's ear.

Flash pictures were taken of the historic moment. Russia and America's cold war had ended decades before, but James knew Russia's continued intent: to weaken the United States through any means possible, from cyber-attacks to the sleeper spy program, which they still didn't know he knew about.

"It is my pleasure to meet you," Nikitin said. James heard the US translator's whispered translation in his ear but was relieved he hadn't needed it; he understood the Russian words.

"My hope is for our countries to work together to build a more sustainable world," James said, sticking with the script and the theme of the summit. He had to wait a few seconds while the translator finished.

"I'm sure we will have many opportunities to better the planet," Nikitin replied. James caught a few of the words but was grateful he had the translation an instant later.

The Russian president smiled again, the emotion not reaching his eyes, and stuck out his hand. The agreed-upon meeting was over.

This is going to be interesting.

The interpreters stepped away. James took the man's hand and they turned to the photographers, one from each country, exactly where they were expected to be.

Smile and shake…

The flashes went off, the moment was captured, and the photographers lowered their cameras.

…And strike.

Not letting go of the man's hand, James spoke. "Mr. President, please give me another moment of your time," he said quietly in English, then repeated the sentence in memorized Russian.

A cloud crossed Nikitin's face and he frowned, but James smiled as he let the man's hand go. "Please. It's important," he said in English and Russian.

Looking doubtful, the Russian president nodded slowly and turned for his interpreter.

The US Russian-speaking aide also stepped forward, uncertainty on his face because he wasn't in on the change of plans, either.

"No, we're okay," James said, waving the man away. The American interpreter stopped, looked at James in confusion, then turned to Chad, who nodded. The man reluctantly stepped back into the huddle of American support staff.

"I learn Russian," James whispered in Russian. "Learned," he corrected, belatedly getting the tense correct. "You. Me. Alone talk."

Damn it, I'm butchering this. I sound like a three-year-old child.

Nikitin's eyes narrowed in confusion but held his hand up. The

Russian translator, a shorter man in his thirties, stopped, then also backed away.

"Thank you, Mr. President," James said in English. "Please," he added, taking a few steps toward the wall, and gesturing with his hand for the other man to walk further away from their people for privacy.

"My English," Nikitin said as he joined him. "No good. Little only."

James smiled. "My Russian is bad. But we work together," he said in Russian. It came out well and he felt a little more confident. It was hard enough to speak the language but doing it while also angling to make his point and not create an international incident had kept him up late every night for the past two weeks.

This better work.

He had no time or words for diplomatic niceties, so he dove right in, hoping to get the Russian words correct. "Two weeks ago—Tuesday. Washington. My speech. Attempted attack. Bad."

"Yes," Nikitin said, then rattled off a long sentence.

Damn. He lost me.

The confusion must have shown on his face. "Sorry," the Russian said. "Slower? Understand?"

James nodded. "Slow, simple words, please."

"Very bad. Scary. Terrorists," he said a few words James didn't exactly catch.

'They grow stronger every year' or something like that.

James took a breath and shook his head with a frown. "No. Not terrorists." He watched the man as closely as he'd watched anyone in all the negotiations he'd had, searching for a tell… and he got one. The man seemed genuinely confused.

How much of that is exceptional acting? Or could I be messing up the Russian pronunciation?

He had to push ahead. "Iran," James said.

A furrowing of the eyebrows from the Russian.

More confusion. Interesting.

"Venezuela."

Now he looks surprised.

"Russia."

The word got an instant reaction. Nikitin's face tightened. He frowned and his brows furrowed.

Whoa. Anger.

"No. You are wrong." The words came fast, but James caught them.

James held the man's eye, willing him to see his belief in the message.

"Serious…" the Russian said in English, then searched for the next word and couldn't get there. "Accusation," he finished in Russian. James had made sure to learn that one.

"Yes, I am sorry. But," James said, feeling comfortable with this part because he'd memorized the specific sentences. "We think you, personally, are blameless." He paused and watched his opponent's face. The anger was gone. The man had rediscovered his poker face as the conversation went on.

James caught movement out of the corner of his eye. The Russian translator had taken a step in their direction. Nikitin held his hand up sharply, and the man stepped back.

"Russia is not to blame," Nikitin said in his language. "Terrorists attacked your country."

"We have solid leads. A trail, but no proof…" James set his face in stone but knew his eyes blazed. "Yet." He let the word hang for a full second. "If we find proof…" he didn't finish. He shouldn't have to.

If we find a shred of proof it was more than Orlov on his own, it's war. Pure and simple.

"However, maybe not Russia. Not President Nikitin. Maybe rogue operator," James said, carefully speaking the all-important last two words.

Nikitin was done with the conversation and shook his head. "No. Good day, Mr. President."

He's either extremely good or in the dark.

James had already learned a lot, but he had one final card to play.

"Joseph Orlov," James said as the president turned to walk away.

For an instant, James thought he saw concern cross the man's face, but he'd only seen the man's profile and wasn't sure.

The Russian walked to his group and continued down the hallway.

The meeting had gone better than James had hoped.

Now we wait and watch what happens.

136

DEMONSTRATIONS

The Vice President's Office
Caracas, Venezuela

Arturo Ruiz was escorted into the spacious, ornate office of the Vice President of Venezuela. The short, chubby man stood behind his desk and welcomed him with a smile, gesturing for Arturo to sit in one of the plush gold chairs before him.

For millions of dollars in 'political contributions,' the man could at least shake my hand.

Then again, Arturo was in the room as one of five cartel leaders during their ongoing power struggle. The other four, who had been in the secure shipping container at the airplane hangar, had disappeared without a trace. Their captains battled it out for the right to lead their organizations. The President of Venezuela was waiting to see who emerged as the leader of the five and would keep him at arm's length until his position as first among equals was clear.

"The president and I appreciate your ongoing generous support, Mr. Ruiz," Vice President Brancho said. His round face was flushed, as if the act of standing then sitting again had winded him.

Of course, they do. They need it now more than ever.

America would eventually figure out what Arturo had known the second he heard about the cruise missile attack on America's capital—it had to be Venezuela.

Arturo had been livid when he learned about it. He and the other leaders—wherever they were, and whoever emerged to take their places— were paying for safety and protection, not to be partnered with a country that had a giant target on it.

"My pleasure. I believe it's quite possible that someday you will be the president," Arturo told the man, "and I will be happy to offer my support then, as well."

"One day, perhaps," he said with fake humility, "if the people will it. And I will once again welcome your generosity."

"I'm sure I could also be of use in ways other than financial," Arturo said with a pleasant smile. "I have both a tactical and strategic mind. You may find calling on me helpful going forward."

The man nodded pleasantly, a smile fixed on his face, patronizing him. *This is going to be delightful.*

"Perhaps a demonstration of my usefulness is in order?" Arturo asked.

"A demonstration?" If Arturo read the man correctly, Brancho was growing annoyed at having to deal with his high-dollar donor. He glanced at his watch. "I'm afraid I don't have much time—" he started, but Arturo cut him off.

"I assure you it will only take a moment and will be well worth your trouble."

With a barely tolerant expression, the man nodded once for him to go ahead.

137

PEASANTS

The protestors were back again, chanting and carrying on, sounding closer than ever. After a few days of blissful silence, the sound grated on President Villanueva's nerves, but he dealt with it. He was in an exceptionally good mood. The Americans hadn't retaliated or given any indication they suspected him and his country of the attacks in Texas or Washington, D.C.

Rich Russian tourists continued to arrive and bring money to his country.

A shakeup was occurring in the Mexican drug cartels, and none of them had bothered him for two weeks. But he had their money, he knew exactly where their state-of-the-art drug labs were because his troops guarded them, and whoever won the fight to lead would end up at his door, eager to pay the final installment and ongoing monthly tax. His protection and submarine transportation for their drugs didn't come cheap.

And while the American president was still alive, he had to know how close he'd come to dying in the Capitol building.

The thought that President Heringten lived with a twinge of fear was satisfaction enough for Villanueva—for now.

The chanting from the crowd grew louder. Hundreds of people roared in approval a moment later.

Maybe after the cartel's next payment, I will give some of it to the people. Ease their suffering.

He would throw the ungrateful peasants another bone.

To his right, the ornate glass double doors leading to the small second-story balcony crashed open. Men with bandanas covering their faces rushed in while more climbed over the railing.

How did these idiots get in?

He was more outraged than afraid.

"Get out!" he said, standing from his desk.

Two moved toward him, carrying baseball bats.

"Guards," he yelled. "Get these—"

They were on him in seconds.

Villanueva laid out the first man with a punch to the face, but the second peasant's bat hit his arm. He felt the bone break and turned to the door. He couldn't fight with only one arm. He had to escape.

Where are my stupid guards?

A blow to his back caused him to fall to his knees halfway between the desk and the door.

"Guards!" he yelled—or tried to. A man's boot connected with his face as he opened his mouth.

Dazed, lying on the ground, the peasants descended on him. They kicked him and hit his body with their bats.

"Not the head!" one called out.

They're killing me—slowly.

"Make it last," he heard another say. "Make him suffer."

After what seemed like an eternity of pain and humiliation, his consciousness faded, and he welcomed death.

138

JEFE

The Vice President's Office
Caracas, Venezuela

Arturo checked his watch. It would be happening now.

He sat with a small, patient smile on his lips, staring at the Vice President of Venezuela—the third-most powerful man in the country.

After the soon-to-be-deceased president and myself, of course.

The vice president was not a patient man. Within ten seconds, he broke the silence. "Mr. Ruiz?"

Arturo raised a finger in a gesture asking for the man's indulgence.

Fifteen more seconds passed. The man across from him fidgeted and made a show of checking his watch again.

"Mr. Ruiz, I really must—"

Arturo interrupted him, dropping his pleasant smile and letting his voice grow cold. "Your president is dead."

"What are you talking about?" The man was more annoyed than outraged. He brought his bulk to his feet. "Thank you again, Mr. Ruiz, but it is time for you—"

Arturo didn't budge. "In a moment, your security team will enter and escort you to safety. I will be shown the door. You will be quite busy for a day or two. Then you will call and invite me to dinner. My wife and I will join you and your lovely wife for a quiet, private meal." The vice president stood behind his desk, his belly straining against a suit that needed to be loosened by a tailor, looking at him like he was crazy. "You will suggest that I become an informal advisor to you, visiting the palace a few times per week. I will be a trusted sounding board and offer my insights."

"Mr. Ruiz, I am sorry, and I wish you no offense, but you are living in a dream world. First, I am the vice president and will be for the foreseeable future. Second, while we are happy to accept your contributions, you will never be an advisor to—"

The thick, ornate double doors to the office flew open. Four large, muscular men in suits rushed into the room. One stood immediately in front of Arturo's chair, placing his bulk between Arturo and his protectee. "Mr. Vice President, please come with us immediately," another said.

The other three guards hustled the stunned man away, but not before he locked eyes with Arturo.

When the country's new leader was gone, the guard in front of him spoke. "You must leave now," he said in a firm, commanding tone.

Then, more quietly, he added the honorific. "*Jefe.*"

PART 8

FRIDAY

139

TEA

Moscow, Russia

The hood was removed from Dmitry's head. The bright light blinded him for a moment.

After squinting and blinking for a few seconds, he wished they'd left the hood on. The room was empty aside from a man who stood behind him, the chair he was tied to, and the white towel folded neatly next to the large jug of water like the kind at the water cooler dispenser in the office. He shuddered.

Please, not waterboarding.

He'd read the reports and seen the interrogations. The most hardened terrorists, criminals, and warriors begged, cried, and confessed to whatever they were told to, just to make it stop.

His bladder let go, wetting the dress slacks he'd worn to his standing Friday night date. He and another government worker had an arrangement. Neither had time to date; they were dedicating their lives to Russia. So once a week, either she came to his apartment or he went to hers for a quiet dinner, followed by sex.

The rest of the time, there were no phone calls, flowers, chocolates, love notes, or dinners with each other's parents. It worked for them.

He turned his head to catch a better glimpse of the man behind him, but he wore a black balaclava over his face. Seeing this gave him a moment of hope.

The man wouldn't hide his face if he meant to kill me. But who would torture me, and why?

He was—or had been—in the middle of Moscow. No foreign intelligence unit had the bravery, stupidity, or resources to take him as he'd been snatched.

This must be one of Orlov's tests.

Perhaps he was about to graduate at last to running his own operations.

This is just a scare tactic.

The door opened and President Nikitin entered. The tall, thin man with the bushy eyebrows looked pensive. "Dmitry," he said. "It is a pleasure to meet you."

"Mr. President?"

Orlov didn't have enough clout to involve the President of Russia in a game to test his protegee's level of commitment.

I am being thrown to the wolves. Orlov is blaming me for the failed Venezuela operation.

"You are rightly confused," the president continued. "This is not a test. We merely need truthful information from you." The man, who looked like one of the professors from Dmitry's college days, looked at the large water jug on the floor, then back at him. "As the President of Russia, I hereby order you to tell me all you know about the cruise missiles that flew at Washington, D.C. during the American president's speech."

Dmitry had received a direct order from his president. It dawned on him that this might not be a test after all. That he could get out of this alive —and without being tortured—if he told the truth.

Long accustomed to watching Orlov and piecing together the puzzle of his intentions, the realization clicked into place.

"Orlov didn't tell you about the plan," he said, half to himself.

The new president wasn't great at keeping emotions off his face. Dmitry saw the tell. He'd hit home.

"Mr. President, I'm happy to tell you all I know."

Tverskoy District
Moscow, Russia

Dmitry wasn't allowed to return to his apartment for a fresh pair of pants. While his slacks had dried during the time he'd told all to President Nikitin, they stank of urine.

He'd have to act fast.

Orlov will notice the smell immediately.

While Dmitry believed he could overpower the older man if he had to, he wasn't sure if Orlov had ever killed a man. And since this would be Dmitry's first, he would prefer not to get involved in a fight.

The syringe in his hand was supposed to make the murder easy. He'd asked for a pistol but had been denied. "Too noisy, too much blood," his would-be torturer had told him after President Nikitin had left the room. "Inject it anywhere, then leave. Bring the syringe and cap back with you," he'd warned. "If you manage that, the cause of death will be a heart attack."

Orlov's apartment was on the fifth floor of a luxury building in Moscow—with a doorman and security, of course. The element of surprise was gone when they called up to ask if Orlov would see him.

By the time he stepped off the elevator and walked down the plushly carpeted hallway, Dmitry's hands were shaking.

I'll be lucky if the man doesn't shoot me the moment I step inside.

The door was half-open.

The interrogation wasn't the test of my dedication and resolve. This will be.

"Come inside, Dmitry," Orlov called. "I have tea ready."

No matter what, Dmitry vowed as he removed the cover from the needle, he would not drink the tea.

140

MARRIAGE

Orlov sat waiting for his protegee at his small, simple kitchen table wearing plaid pajamas and a worn, fraying white flannel robe tied at his ample waist. Nearby, the luxurious dining room held a long table that sat twelve for dinner, but he'd never used it. He didn't entertain.

"Good evening, Dmitry," he said as his young aide stopped at the far end of the large, modern kitchen. The man looked terrified.

Orlov wrinkled his nose.

Barbarians. They could have let him change his pants, at least.

"Put the cap back on the syringe before you hurt yourself," he said in his slow, methodical way.

Dmitry stood frozen on the other side of the granite island.

How easy to break his neck and slip away.

Orlov had four escape routes from the building, including one he doubted the men waiting outside for him to run knew about. First, he would get to the secret garage with a car and a fake passport. A long drive to Estonia next. From there, a ferry to Helsinki, a plane to Germany, and then to Brazil. He could be happy there and the money he'd put away over the years would go far.

And do what?

Sit on the beach and gaze at women he could never have?

He was married to Russia.

And if she says it's over, it's over.

He picked up the pill from the table in front of him, showed it to Dmitry, who still hadn't moved, and put it in his mouth. He swallowed it with two gulps of tea.

"It will take a few minutes. There is time for your final lesson. Tell me, what have you learned?" he asked in his slow, methodical way. Even in death, he would not be rushed.

PART 9

SATURDAY

141

RUSSIA

Dmitry sat in the tired old office, trying to get comfortable in the metal chair with the worn green leather cushion.

It was the first time he'd been in the room without Orlov.

He tried not to think about his mentor and the way the man had taken the cyanide capsule, willingly going to his death. But he couldn't keep the scene from his mind.

The man's final words had been spoken in the same slow, methodical way as all his others. "Politicians come and go. Enemies become friends, then back again. Russia endures. Always do right by her, even if it means breaking the rules," Orlov had said.

Left unspoken but easily apparent by his body as it slumped in the kitchen chair—be prepared to suffer the consequences of your actions.

Would President Nikitin have gone along with Orlov's plan to destroy America if told about it ahead of time?

Dmitry regretted not asking the president while he'd had the chance. But in his urine-soaked pants, tied to the chair with the instruments of his torture next to him, he'd had more pressing issues on his mind.

In Dmitry's dream of assuming Orlov's position, it hadn't looked like this. There was no fancy office, no staff—though he'd been promised an aide soon.

Instead, he'd come into the windowless room on a rare sunny Saturday. The desk had screeched and complained as he turned it to face the opposite wall in a pathetic effort to make the office his own. It left behind a clear outline—where the desk had been pressed against the wall was cleaner than the surrounding area.

He sat staring at the decades-old map—barely held up by its peeling clear tape—elbows on the desk, chin resting on his clenched fists, and planned.

The new president wants the west put in its place, taken down a few notches, but with zero risk of blowback to Russia.

It was now his job to figure out how to accomplish this impossible task… and to keep the president informed every step of the way.

142

PROFESSIONALS

The wood in the fireplace popped and sparked as it warmed the cabin. They had a nice fire going against the late February cold as the sun set.

Axe kept his face still as he shifted his weight, not giving away his pain. His body was nearly healed, though the cracked ribs were still tender. It would take several more weeks before he'd be one hundred percent.

He relaxed at the kitchen table. They were a big, happy family. Mad Dog had toned down his schtick and proved himself to be the thoughtful, intelligent man Axe knew he was. Haley had tolerated him at first, grew to like him, and lately, they quietly played cards, board games, and chess together for hours at a time.

Mad Dog switched off guard duty with Mariana, who hadn't quite fit in at first. But over the past two weeks, she'd come around. She was on a sabbatical from her police officer duties in Texas while she helped care for and protect Axe and Haley.

They were all going a little stir crazy. Tonight's visitors would help.

Nalen showed up early so they could talk through the situation. He and Haley joined Axe around the kitchen table over beers while Mariana and Mad Dog played chess by the fire, mostly ignoring the conversation.

"I feel fine," Axe said, knowing how defensive he sounded. "At least well enough to protect myself."

"Me too," Haley said. She still moved gingerly. The deep stab wound to her stomach and pierced lung took time to heal. "Besides," she added, "no one is after us. And I need to get back to work."

Axe heard it in her voice.

She means it. She has a deep-seated need to be in the office, looking for the next threat facing the country.

Nalen pondered the decision for a second, but Axe could tell he was faking it. His mind was made up. "Fine. Mad Dog, Rodriguez," he called, "you're cut loose. Thanks for your time—expect a nice lump sum from your Uncle Sam to hit your accounts next week."

"Hot damn! California here I come," Mad Dog whooped.

"The quiet Mad Dog was nice while it lasted," Haley muttered.

Rodriguez nodded, then moved her rook.

"Checkmate," she announced with a smile to Mad Dog.

"Damn it, you're better than Haley!"

They grabbed beers and joined Axe and the other two at the table as the crunch of tires on the gravel driveway signaled the rest of the visitors had arrived.

"Sorry we're late," Gregory said as he entered with Nancy and Dave following. The smell of pizza from the stack of boxes in their hands accompanied them. "But I have news."

Inviting the intel people for dinner had been Nalen's idea of forging a more cohesive team. Haley had been all for it. Axe had his doubts. He wasn't sure the two very different groups would fit well together. But the admiral wanted the assets to know how the analysts worked—and vice versa.

I hope getting together like this works.

Over pizza and beers, Gregory provided an update—a final debrief of the past three weeks. "Nancy found a tenuous thread linking the men who attacked Haley's family and Admiral Nalen's house to Russian spymaster Joseph Orlov. Tonight, we have unconfirmed reports that Orlov had a heart attack in his apartment. We'll know more in a day or two." The announcement hung over the room. Mariana looked lost, but Axe didn't fill in the blanks for her.

Need to know—which goes for me, too, because I'd love to hear whether the USA had anything to do with it.

He shared a look with Haley. They'd discussed the matter quietly the previous week. They hadn't killed the wrong man when they assassinated President Zimalev. They just hadn't gone far enough.

We should have found Orlov back then and killed him, too.

"Also," Gregory said, "Venezuelan President Villanueva was attacked by his own countrymen and beaten to death. His vice president has assumed the role."

Axe kept his mouth shut and didn't ask the question he wanted to.

Did we have a hand in that?

After a pause, Gregory continued. "This is top secret—it all is," he said, glancing at Mariana. "But four of the five Mexico drug cartel leaders are dead." He nodded slightly at Mad Dog. "Few drugs are entering the country. Addicts are lining up for help to beat their addiction. President Heringten's plan is working—for now."

The president hadn't mentioned it in his shortened address, but the press had published his original State of the Union speech the next day. His experimental war on drugs plan had taken a beating from both sides of the political spectrum, but it looked like his ideas were paying off.

"What about Iran?" Axe asked.

"Nothing yet," Gregory admitted.

"I'm sure the president will take appropriate action in due time," Nalen reassured them.

"Any fallout over the missile attack during the State of the Union address?" Haley asked.

"Our troops are being praised as the extremely competent, fast-acting heroes they are," Gregory said. "And the intelligence agencies are taking the blame for not catching it in time," he added with a rueful smile and a tired shrug.

"If they only knew," Axe said, thinking of all the team had done. Stopping the drug shipment at the Texas border, saving the pipelines, preventing the LNG ship from blowing up, destroying the cruise missiles on the oil platform, providing the early warning to the president about the situation, Haley eliminating the sniper, Nalen's discovery of the C-4 that saved missile batteries from destruction, and finding the trail leading to Orlov.

We may not all be SEALs, but everyone at this table is truly a 'Silent Professional.'

Haley raised her beer. "To saving the country—whether people know about us or not."

Everyone raised their glasses. "To saving the country," they said, proudly toasting their secret accomplishments.

After dinner, they gathered by the fire.

Haley surveyed the room. Gregory, Nancy, and Dave sat on the couch. Haley sat on a chair next to them, nearest the fire. Across from her, Nalen, Axe, and Mad Dog lounged in comfortable chairs.

The two teams of three—with me as the fourth member of each of them.

And Rodriguez, a possible fifth team member, sitting nearest the kitchen.

Ready to take my place if I decide I should be in the office as an analyst and not in the field with Axe.

Haley took a deep breath, preparing herself. Axe's words from several weeks before rang in her ear. "At some point soon, it'll be your turn to tell a tale."

Rodriguez needed to know what she was possibly getting into. This wasn't the police department. They weren't after the average criminal.

And the intelligence analysts would benefit from a first-hand report of what happened outside the confines of the office.

She shifted in her chair, got an encouraging nod from Axe, cleared her throat... then paused. She felt more nervous now than when she walked past the assassin hiding in the woods.

Nalen, Axe, and Mad Dog stared at her expectantly. They knew how these evenings of camaraderie worked. It was time to tell stories of their adventures.

She took a deep breath. "So no shit, there I was," she started in the traditional way. "I can't tell you where, of course," she continued, though they all knew. "I didn't have much to go on—the number of tangos, their location, or anything."

Haley paused for a moment, remembering.

Then she began the story of the night she lay dying on the cold ground, staring up at the stars, a knife sticking out of her back.

Author's Note

Thank you so much for reading! Continue with *A Team of Five*, the next book in the series:

Danger lurks in the shadows.

From the outside, America looks safe and secure. But those on the inside know the truth. Friends can be enemies... and enemies friends. Uncovering threats is only half the battle. Knowing who to trust is the rest.

On a mission far from home, Axe and the team face an enemy they never dreamed of.

While at the Central Analysis Group headquarters, physical scars heal more easily than damage to the soul.

Working together, the team is stronger than ever. But America's hidden enemies have more money, more power, and a growing desperation.

The warriors and analysts face a world filled with surprises, feints, and deceit.

Where facts are hard to come by.

And one wrong move means exposure... or death.

The stakes couldn't be higher for Axe, Haley, Mad Dog, Johnboy, and the newest member of the team.

Join them as they risk it all in a fight for what they believe in. Enter this link into your browser to get your copy:

https://geni.us/a-team-of-five

- If you haven't signed up yet, get a free Axe/Haley story each month in my newsletter. Go to: www.authorbradlee.com/shortstoryclub
- If you enjoyed the book, please leave a five-star or written review. It helps new readers discover the book and makes it possible for me to continue bringing you stories.
- I'm active on social media, sharing photos (like Axe would take) and writing progress updates. I also occasionally ask for input on character names, plot points, or reader preferences as I'm writing, so follow me and help out. Find me here:
- Facebook: https://www.facebook.com/AuthorBradLee
- Instagram: https://www.instagram.com/bradleeauthor/
- Also, I use the names of real places but fictionalize some details. I also take inspiration from areas but change names and some features to improve the story. My apologies if you live in

or are acquainted with one of the areas and think, "Wait, that's not right." You're correct. License was taken in describing places as well as technology, equipment, weapons, tactics, and military capabilities. Where location details, distances, or technical issues conflicted with the story, I made the story paramount.

Finally, please join me in thanking Beth, David, and Mac for their help. The book is far better because of them.

Made in the USA
Middletown, DE
30 January 2024

48843312R00274